S0-AYR-030

Allison Lane's novels and novellas have won many awards. Her novella *Heart's Desire* was a RITA finalist. Details of her books and awards can be found at www.eclectics.com/allisonlane.

Edith Layton, critically acclaimed for her short stories, also writes historicals for Avon Books and has won numerous awards. She loves to hear from readers and can be reached at www.edithlayton.com.

Lynn Kerstan's Regency and historical romances have won a score of awards, including the Golden Quill, the Award of Excellence, and the coveted RITA. For more information about Lynn and her books, visit www.lynnkerstan.com.

Barbara Metzger, one of the stars of the genre, has won numerous awards, including two Career Achievement Awards and a RITA for Best Regency. She can be reached at www.barbarametzger.com.

Carla Kelly has written more than a dozen novels and won several awards, including two RITAs for Best Regency. She lives in Valley City, North Dakota.

SIGNET

REGENCY ROMANCE
COMING IN JUNE 2004

Viscount Vagabond and *The Devil's Delilah*
by Loretta Chase
Now, for the first time, these two wonderful classics
are bound together in one volume!
0-451-21223-1

The Barkin Emeralds
by Nancy Bulter
On behalf of her mistress, Miss Maggie Bonner is
returning a rejected betrothal gift to Lord Barkin in
Scotland. But when she is mistaken for his intended,
she is kidnapped by a dashing pirate.
0-451-21175-8

A Worthy Opponent
by Louise Bergin
Miss Judith Shelton is happy to admit that she's a
fortune hunter, but she has her orphaned sibling's best
interests at heart. Judith has no romantic notions of
love—until she meets the cunning friend of the man
whose fortune she's hunting.
0-451-21013-1

Available wherever books are sold, or
to order call: 1-800-788-6262

Wedding Belles

Five Stories by

Allison Lane
Edith Layton
Lynn Kerstan
Barbara Metzger
Carla Kelly

A SIGNET BOOK

SIGNET
Published by New American Library, a division of
Penguin Group (USA) Inc., 375 Hudson Street,
New York, New York 10014, U.S.A.
Penguin Books Ltd, 80 Strand,
London WC2R 0RL, England
Penguin Books Australia Ltd, 250 Camberwell Road,
Camberwell, Victoria 3124, Australia
Penguin Books Canada Ltd, 10 Alcorn Avenue,
Toronto, Ontario, Canada M4V 3B2
Penguin Books (N.Z.) Ltd, Cnr Rosedale and Airborne Roads,
Albany, Auckland 1310, New Zealand

Penguin Books Ltd, Registered Offices:
80 Strand, London WC2R 0RL, England

First published by Signet, an imprint of New American Library,
a division of Penguin Group (USA) Inc.

First Printing, May 2004
10 9 8 7 6 5 4 3 2 1

Copyright © New American Library, a division of Penguin Group (USA) Inc., 2004
"For Richer or Poorer" copyright © Susan Ann Pace, 2004
"A Marriage of True Minds" copyright © Edith Felber, 2004
"The Marriage Scheme" copyright © Lynn Kerstan, 2004
"A Match Made in Heaven—Or Hell" copyright © Barbara Metzger, 2004
"A Hasty Marriage" copyright © Carla Kelly, 2004
All rights reserved

 REGISTERED TRADEMARK—MARCA REGISTRADA

Printed in the United States of America

Without limiting the rights under copyright reserved above, no part of this
publication may be reproduced, stored in or introduced into a retrieval system,
or transmitted, in any form, or by any means (electronic, mechanical, photo-
copying, recording, or otherwise), without the prior written permission of both
the copyright owner and the above publisher of this book.

PUBLISHER'S NOTE
These are works of fiction. Names, characters, places, and incidents either are
the product of the authors' imagination or are used fictitiously, and any resem-
blance to actual persons, living or dead, business establishments, events, or
locales is entirely coincidental.

BOOKS ARE AVAILABLE AT QUANTITY DISCOUNTS WHEN USED TO PROMOTE PROD-
UCTS OR SERVICES. FOR INFORMATION PLEASE WRITE TO PREMIUM MARKETING DI-
VISION, PENGUIN GROUP (USA) INC., 375 HUDSON STREET, NEW YORK, NEW YORK
10014.

If you purchased this book without a cover you should be aware that this book
is stolen property. It was reported as "unsold and destroyed" to the publisher
and neither the author nor the publisher has received any payment for this
"stripped book."

The scanning, uploading and distribution of this book via the Internet or via any
other means without the permission of the publisher is illegal and punishable by
law. Please purchase only authorized electronic editions, and do not participate
in or encourage electronic piracy of copyrighted materials. Your support of the
authors' rights is appreciated.

Contents

For Richer or Poorer

by
Allison Lane

1

"Dearly beloved . . ." The bishop's voice filled the nave.

Richard Hughes finally relaxed. There was nothing more he could do. The bride and groom glowed with a happiness no one could mistake, and the witnesses validated the match.

He stood to one side of the altar, where he could see both the wedding party and the guests. Every gossip in town was in attendance, so the scandal should finally dissipate, leaving only envy that his sister had snared one of society's prizes.

The phrase annoyed him, though he didn't let it show. Emily was lucky. Because she was female, attaching a wealthy suitor increased her credit. Even if she'd deliberately sought such a prize, no one would condemn her—not that Jacob's fortune mattered; the pair were wildly in love.

But he was not so lucky. His modest means meant many considered him a fortune hunter. Gossips watched his every move, waiting for him to pounce on an heiress. He need only dance with a girl who had a good dowry to ignite whispers. Fathers looked at him askance. That his closest friends were wealthy enough to rival Midas increased people's suspicions.

He forced himself to calm down lest the guests mistake the cause.

Damn the gossips and their constant buzzing. He might have to watch his purse, but he was not in debt. Never would he stoop to wedding money. When he took a wife, she would be sweet, frugal, and have no more than a modest dowry.

He nearly cursed as he recalled the most recent rumors. All he'd done was speak to Miss Downes at a rout—a conversation *she* had initiated with a question about Emily. They hadn't exchanged a dozen words, yet half of London expected him to seduce her so he could claim her ten-thousand-pound dowry. Lord Downes was furious.

Herriard had to have started the tale. If the scoundrel had discovered Richard's investigation, he might think that discrediting him would prevent people from listening to his accusations. No one else would blow the incident so badly out of proportion. Herriard was a cheat, a liar, a vicious—

"Do you take this man . . ." The words recalled his attention to the service.

He unclenched his fists, hoping no one had noticed. His sister's wedding was no place to think about Herriard. Renewed speculation about why Emily had switched grooms only five days ago[1] would undo all his efforts.

He searched the crowd for Lady Beatrice, London's most powerful gossip. With luck, she was watching Emily, not him. Only her support would rid this union of scandal.

Georgiana Whittaker scrambled to her feet, suppressing a shudder when she noted the gutter's filth. She had no time to fret about horse droppings.

Ignoring the pain slicing her left ankle, she hobbled up George Street. Derrick had been gaining on her even before her fall. Now it would be worse. She had to reach Hanover Square before he spotted her. It was her only chance. The square had a dozen exits. Derrick would never guess which one she chose.

But Hanover Square was two blocks away, and every step was agony. Her pace slowed, then slowed again. Even terror couldn't prod her ankle faster. She was doomed.

A sob escaped as reality crashed over her.

Horses and carriages crowded George Street and jammed Hanover Square. Pedestrians thronged the

[1]See *Emily's Beau*, Signet Regency, October 2003.

walkways. Vendors accosted every passerby. With so many eyes peering about, someone would remember her. Many someones. They would tell Derrick.

Desperate, she ducked behind the broad columns of St. George's Church, rushed up the steps, and stumbled inside. Maybe the rector would offer her refuge. Maybe—

As the door closed, a woman's voice replaced the cacophony from the street. ". . . for richer or poorer, in sickness and in health . . ."

A wedding. She nearly groaned. She should have known that the crowded street meant the church was full.

Curses nearly tumbled from her lips. A hundred people had gathered here. A hundred aristocrats, judging from their finery.

So far no one had noticed her. All eyes were fixed on five people standing before the altar. Four faced the bishop, who was prompting the bride. But the fifth was half turned toward the crowd.

She frowned.

His presence so near the altar was odd enough, but he seemed too aloof to be part of the proceedings. The bride and groom glowed with happiness, even when seen from behind. The redheaded witnesses radiated joy. But the lone blond was tense, almost poised for battle, with his gloved hands clenched and his weight balanced on his toes. It was an odd posture for a wedding. Who did he think would attack?

She shook away the thought, her own problems more urgent than a puzzle of no import. The rector stood behind the bishop, so she could not approach him. Nor could she afford to be seen. Yet leaving was impossible. Derrick would have reached George Stre—

Angry voices outside sent her heart into her throat. He was closer than she'd thought.

Trapped but not yet ready to surrender, she limped quickly along the wall and ducked into a chapel.

He doesn't know I fell, she prayed as she crouched behind the chapel's altar. *Let him believe I at least reached Maddox Street. Send him around the church, not into it. Please!*

But she knew her luck had run out.

*   *   *

Richard studied Lady Beatrice. Did she recognize the love that bound Emily and Jacob, or was she too devoted to rules to excuse so juicy a scandal? He couldn't tell, for the gossip's face showed nothing. Unlike him, she was in complete control.

In the days since Emily had jilted Charles, Richard had done what he could to minimize the scandal. Charles stood beside Jacob at the altar. Charles's sister stood beside Emily. Charles's cousin, the bishop, presided. Charles's mother was overseeing the wedding breakfast. But one never knew what Lady Beatrice would do. And without her support . . .

A disheveled maid slipped into the church and paused in dismay—as well she might. She was caked with mud and intruding on her betters. Yet his gaze was caught by an enchanting face whose big eyes, tilted nose, and blond curls belonged to an angel. The contrast with her tattered cloak was striking.

Her eyes suddenly widened. Glancing wildly around, she ducked into the chapel.

At least she wouldn't interrupt. Relaxing, he concentrated on the service. Or tried to. Her face teased his mind, igniting a familiar heat that distracted him from Emily's vows. He wondered where the girl worked. Maids often enjoyed a lighthearted romp in bed. Would she—

The door banged open, fracturing his fantasy.

Everyone turned to stare as two men stormed inside— Herriard and his maggoty friend Stagleigh, their faces black with fury. Both were undoubtedly drunk.

Richard nearly snarled.

As Jacob raised his voice for the ring ceremony, reclaiming the crowd's attention, Richard hurried toward the door. It would be just like Herriard to stage an embarrassing scene.

"Is there a problem?" he murmured, blocking access to the nave.

"Nothing I can't handle." Herriard glared.

"Hawthorne's wedding is no concern of yours."

"But the wench who stole my purse is. She ducked in here."

Richard raised his brows. "When?"

"Just now. Two minutes ago. Maybe three."

"I've had the door in sight since the service started,"
he lied. "Only Hawthorne's guests came in." The girl
must be fleeing Herriard. No wonder she was terrified.
He dismissed the theft charge, for Herriard was a liar.
And even if it were true, Richard could not in good
conscience help Herriard catch her. Whether making
love or war, the man had a reputation for brutality that
turned Richard's stomach. And Stagleigh was worse.

Herriard clenched his fists. "You must have seen
her—blond hair, brown cloak, height about here." He
extended his hand level with his shoulder. "A coachman
saw her enter."

"The only brown cloak was his." He nodded toward
Leonard Waters, who was standing at the back of the
crowd. "He arrived about five minutes ago—late, as
usual."

Herriard glared at the diminutive dandy. Golden hair
glistened above brown velvet.

"You are certain?" demanded Stagleigh.

"Absolutely. The wench probably slipped around the
corner." He looked pointedly at the door.

"She didn't have time to reach the corner," insisted
Herriard. "She's here somewhere, and I'm going to
find her."

"If you want to find her, check Maddox Street. No
one came this way. The longer you delay, the more likely
she is to escape."

"But—"

"Shall we ask the bishop who came in? He was also
facing the door. As was the rector."

To his relief, Herriard shook his head and left, dragging Stagleigh with him.

Richard returned to the altar, but his mind remained
on the girl. Herriard had to be lying—all else aside, he
had nothing to steal. So she must be fleeing his advances.

He shook his head, wondering how she'd been unfortunate enough to catch Herriard's eye.

As the brief ceremony drew to a close, he nodded.
Misdirecting Herriard wouldn't protect the girl for
long—Herriard had to know where she worked. The

man would press her again in the future. So the only way to help her was to find her a new position.

While the bishop led the wedding party to the rector's office to sign the register, Richard sped the guests toward Hawthorne House for the wedding breakfast, keeping one eye on the chapel lest the girl slip away before he could address her problem. She wouldn't be the first he'd helped, though Lady Beatrice would likely expire of shock to learn of it. Such activities stood at odds with his reputation.

Georgiana scrubbed the tears from her cheeks, berating herself for falling into despair. No matter what happened, she could not give up. And perhaps her prayers had been answered. Had Derrick really left? She'd heard the front door open and close.

But it was likely only a brief reprieve.

Voices rose as the wedding guests departed. She considered mingling with the crowd, but her fall had turned her cloak from shabby to disgusting. Someone was bound to object.

And Derrick would be watching. He might have hesitated to interrupt a society wedding, but he knew she was here—had probably seen her enter. So he would also know that she was limping. The moment the church was empty, he would search every nook and cranny. He was only waiting because he wanted no witnesses when he found her.

She was trapped.

Questions without answers battered her mind. How many exits did the church have? Which ones would Derrick watch? How many men were helping him? Would the rector stand up to a lord?

Her task seemed hopeless. If she hadn't caught him by surprise, she would never have escaped the first time. That wouldn't happen again, and not just because of Derrick's vigilance. Her swelling ankle was already twice its usual size. The very thought of standing made it throb. And where would she go?

But she had to try. Remaining here was impossible.

The last of the voices died away. The doors closed,

again muffling the street noise. She was rising when footsteps approached the chapel.

Derrick! She shrank against the back of the altar.

"You can come out now," said an unfamiliar voice. "Everyone is gone."

She paused, suspecting a trick.

"Are you a thief, as Lord Herriard claims?" asked the man.

"Thief!" she choked. "How dare he?"

"Come out. I can't advise you until I know what he wants."

With no real alternative, she shakily stood, grasping the corner of the altar when her leg tried to buckle. Her eyes widened as she turned toward the door. The blond man from the wedding party blocked her escape.

"You're hurt." His voice gentled.

"Ankle."

Before she realized his intent, he swept her into his arms and carried her to a bench.

He was strong.

Also tall. And handsome. His hair brushed the collar of his blue superfine jacket. Brown eyes beamed from a face that reminded her of a Greek god—a rather wicked Eros, actually. Something about him demanded her touch.

Her heart lodged in her throat as she clasped her hands to keep them still.

He joined her on the bench. "Richard, at your service. And you are . . . ?"

"Georgiana." She hesitantly offered her hand. Heat tingled up her arm when he raised it to his lips.

"If you aren't a thief, why does Herriard claim you stole his purse?" His tone seemed curious rather than accusatory. That in itself set her at ease. Most men accepted a lord's word as gospel, no matter how ridiculous his charges.

"He is my cousin and guardian."

His eyes widened. "Guardian? I've not heard that he has a ward."

"Hardly a surprise. He keeps me hidden. Despising my mother's marriage, he refused to bring me out. But his debts are now so great that he's selling me to Lord Stagleigh."

"Not good. Stagleigh is venal."

"I'm glad you agree. My skin crawls whenever he is in the house. I try to avoid him."

"Wise."

"But no longer possible. Stagleigh agreed to pay Derrick's debts in exchange for my hand. Neither of them cares a whit for me. But Derrick needs money so badly that he swore to beat me into compliance. Stagleigh doesn't care. He considers my hatred a challenge."

Richard nodded. "He would. So how did you escape?"

"They didn't realize I overheard them negotiating terms. I slipped out before they could give me the good news. Unfortunately, they discovered my absence almost immediately and chased me here."

"I sent them away."

She shook her head. "They won't go far. Derrick may have declined to make a scene in front of society's *crème de la crème*, but he knows I'm here. He was too close behind not to have seen me enter."

"Where were you going?"

She sighed. "I had no time to think." She hesitated to say more, but Richard was her best hope of escape. Unless he believed her, he would turn her over to her guardian. So she must reveal the full story—or most of it. "I have no other close relatives, and I have no money—my quarterly allowance is only two pounds."

"That's less than a maid makes."

"I know." She patted the large reticule hanging from her arm. "I grabbed Mama's pearls and a few other things before fleeing. Selling them will pay my keep for a time." She shrugged.

"Do you think he will change his mind?"

"No. But I turn twenty-one in six days. My dowry will then come to me. It will let me set up my own household."

"Not if you hope to retain your reputation."

Again she shrugged. "Society doesn't know I exist and would reject me if it did. My mother may have been a baron's daughter, but my father was a merchant. The business went to his partner, of course, but my inheritance will do. One can live on very little in the country."

"But what about marriage?"

She laughed bitterly. "Why should I put myself at the mercy of yet another man? Five years with Derrick has cured me of any romantical notions." She had yet to meet a man she could trust when her needs opposed his desires. Even Grandfather had ignored her preferences.

"This isn't the time to argue your future. We must leave. How bad is your ankle?"

"I fell rounding the corner from Conduit to George Street." She lifted her skirts to reveal the ankle, which had swollen even larger. "It can't be broken, for I continued running on it, but it hurts like blazes."

Richard knelt, gently bending the ankle as his fingers prodded the bones. She nearly screamed.

He shook his head. "It's the worst sprain I've seen in some time. I'll have to carry you."

"Where?"

"To my horse. It's waiting on Mill Street, just outside the rector's office."

She tried to protest, but he cut her off.

"I can't remain here. My sister will already be wondering where I am—she just married my best friend, so I'm expected at the breakfast. We'll stash you out of sight until I have time to think about your problem."

"I won't return to Derrick."

"Of course not. What the devil was your father about to leave Herriard in charge of you in the first place? He must have known the man is a scoundrel."

"He named Grandfather. But Grandfather and Derrick's father died in a carriage accident a week after my father died, so Derrick inherited my guardianship along with the title." She still shuddered to recall those days. Her grandfather had wanted her to make the society match her mother had refused, though he'd long since come to terms with his daughter's elopement. Derrick abhorred his grandfather's acceptance of so base a union, but he'd been careful not to admit it while the old man controlled his allowance. Only after the accident had he shown his true colors, relegating his low-class ward to the attics and refusing to recognize their blood ties.

"We will discuss alternatives later. Come along." He lifted her easily, then peeked out the chapel door to make sure the nave was empty before heading for the office and his horse.

2

Richard was shaking with fury by the time he reached Hawthorne House. Their departure from St. George's had not gone as smoothly as he'd expected. He had set Georgiana across his horse, then mounted behind her. But he'd hardly settled into the saddle before Herriard had attacked. If the man had been mounted, they would never have escaped. As it was, Herriard had caught Georgiana's foot and nearly pulled her off. Only a sharp kick had freed her.

Herriard was a menace and a disgrace to his breeding. He should never have been put in charge of an innocent maiden. But no one who might have objected had known about her. Once her mother had eloped with a merchant, she'd ceased to exist in society.

It wasn't the first time he'd questioned the dictates of his class. Young ladies ought to be more than breeding stock or assets to stave off financial disaster. Guardians should not have total control of their wards. Nor should parents. Society should protect girls from the Herriards of the world—or so he'd argued with Charles more than once.

Georgiana was a prime example. Imagining her under Herriard's roof made his blood boil. And Stagleigh would be worse. So lovely a girl was no match for a lecher. He had to protect her—and not just because it would let him pursue Herriard openly. She deserved more than a life of abuse.

The question was how to proceed.

Keeping her at Hughes House until he dealt with Herriard would expose his mother to Herriard's spite. Not a price he was willing to pay; her health was too fragile. Yet there was nowhere else he could take her. He had no rooms of his own and lacked the means to lease something. Even an inexpensive hotel would cost too much just now—his pockets were empty until next quarter day, still two weeks away.

His only option was to swallow his pride and beg help from his friends.

"Stay here," he ordered, laying Georgiana on the couch in Jacob's study. "I must attend the wedding breakfast, but I will lock the door so no one can bother you. As soon as I can get away, we will discuss the next step."

"But—"

"Relax. I won't return you to Herriard. The man is a cad. But this is my sister's wedding day. I cannot abandon her."

"Of course not."

"I'd rather keep your presence quiet for now, even from the staff, so I'll bring refreshments when I return."

She nodded.

He didn't like to leave her alone, but he had no choice. Slipping the key into his pocket, he hurried toward the drawing room. Locking the door protected her, but it also protected him if he'd misjudged her—as occasionally happened. She could not rob Jacob and flee before he returned.

"Where have you been?" hissed Emily as he joined the receiving line.

"Finishing up at the church."

Jacob raised an aristocratic brow, but said nothing as he turned to greet Lady Debenham, another of London's most ferocious gossips.

An hour passed before arrivals dwindled to a trickle. As usual, many more people attended the wedding breakfast than had witnessed the actual wedding.

When Emily finally headed for the drawing room, Richard held Jacob back. "I need your help. Let me know when you can get free."

"Can't Charles—"

"Not this time." Though the three had been friends

for twenty years, Charles supported the rights of guardians, even when doing so was not in the ward's best interests. Jacob had no such reservations.

"Very well, but why now?"

"I didn't choose the time. The problem arose without warning."

"Is this why you were late?" Jacob asked as they entered the drawing room.

Richard nodded, then flashed a practiced smile at Lady Beatrice as Jacob moved to his wife's side.

Lady Beatrice glared at Jacob's retreating back and snorted. "I know the Beaux share everything, but passing around a fiancée is beyond enough." She transferred her scowl to Emily.

"My sister would object to that charge," he said lightly, though this was exactly what he'd feared. Jilting a gentleman always raised brows, but the Beaux' reputations made it worse.

He, Jacob, and Charles had acquired the sobriquet The Three Beaux ten years earlier, in part because of their closeness, but mostly because all three were rakes—though not as incorrigible as rumor claimed; he knew of only one female who'd actually lain with all three of them, and he knew about her only because she'd thrown a public fit when Jacob turned down a second encounter. The incident had tarred them with an unwarranted reputation for sharing conquests, adding to the scandal when Emily jilted Charles to wed Jacob.

Richard met Lady Beatrice's stare. "Emily and Lord Charles mistook friendship for something deeper. I find it commendable that they addressed the problem as soon as they recognized it. Their marriage would have made all three of them miserable. Since the decision occurred only a few days ago, it was easier to change grooms than to cancel the wedding arrangements."

"Perhaps." She raised a lorgnette to study the new Countess of Hawthorne. "I must admit I've rarely seen two people so pleased with each other."

"Exactly. This was meant to be." He stifled a spurt of envy as he watched the pair move through the room. Even as they spoke with guests, they were enclosed in a bubble of mutual awareness that excluded those around them. Their joy shone brightly enough to cast all others in the shade.

"She has done very well for herself," Lady Beatrice continued. "Impoverished girls have sought Hawthorne's eye for years. No one else has his combination of title, wealth, and good looks. The connection will serve you well, too. Better than the other would have done."

Richard nearly ground his teeth. Why did she insist that Emily was a fortune hunter? Not only had the pair been close since childhood, but Em had a decent dowry. And why did she think Em's marriage could help him? Jacob was his closest friend. They didn't need weddings to further that bond.

But he refused to vent his frustration aloud and even managed several more exchanges before moving on, though his mood remained black. He was tired of her relentless suspicion and very tired of how she pounced on every sign that he might need money.

This wedding breakfast was yet another thorn in his side, for it was far more elaborate than they had originally planned—thanks to Lady Inslip's handling the arrangements and tapping Jacob's bottomless coffers. His own marriage would not be celebrated in such style. His family couldn't afford it, and he was determined that his wife would never overshadow him, financially or otherwise.

Long practice stifled any resentment, for thinking of money always strained his friendship with the very wealthy Beaux. It had nearly fractured the group when they'd pressed him too hard to join an expensive outing one summer. Jacob had finally healed the rift and no longer argued when Richard refused. But memories continued to hover, casting shadows on his soul.

The next hour passed in a blur as he dampened further hints at scandal and toasted the bride and groom. The gossips grumbled, but followed Charles's lead. Lady Beatrice's toast finally eliminated his fears for Emily's future, allowing him to fully relax.

Now he could concentrate on Georgiana.

The thought ignited anticipation—because helping her would irritate Herriard, he assured himself. It was the battle, not the girl, that stirred his senses. He could hardly wait to learn her full story. She might even have information that could help his investigation.

Jacob found Richard in the refreshment room half an hour later. "What happened?" he demanded softly, helping himself to a lobster patty.

"Herriard and Stagleigh." Richard handed him a plate.

Jacob tensed, noting the fury that changed Richard's warm brown eyes to a feral ocher. To keep his hands busy, he piled delicacies on the plate. "Is that who barged in during the service?"

Richard nodded. "I maneuvered them outside, but they accosted me afterward."

"What do they want this time?" The pair had long been a wart on society's backside and were no longer included in even the most inclusive invitations. But their feud with the Beaux was personal. Herriard had cheated Richard some years earlier. If the Beaux had not recovered the funds, Richard would have been forced to leave London. It was unlikely that he could have returned.

Herriard had hated the Beaux ever since, especially Richard, who wasn't satisfied with recouping his losses. Determined to protect other young men from Herriard's predations, he kept a close eye on Herriard's gaming, seeking evidence of cheating that would expel him from the clubs.

"Did you know that Herriard has a ward? A female ward?" Richard added cream cakes and a lemon biscuit to his own plate.

"My God!" Jacob lowered his voice when heads turned his way. "Who would trust him within a hundred miles of an innocent? How old is she?"

"Twenty—until Friday, when she gains control of her dowry and hopes to move out."

"Herriard won't stand for that. He's always deep in the River Tick, so he'll demand the money as payment for keeping her. Especially now." Herriard had lost badly the night before. It was doubtful that he could cover his vowels.

"Her small inheritance won't begin to pay his debts,"

said Richard, pat on the thought. "So he's selling her to Stagleigh."

Jacob cursed. His butler took one look at his face, then herded nearby guests toward the drawing room. "Why didn't you say something earlier?" Jacob asked when he had his temper under control.

"I told you, I just found out about it. She escaped this morning and is currently in your study."

"Devil take it. Can't you keep your lame ducks away from my wedding?"

Richard glared.

Jacob waved a hand in apology. "That was uncalled-for. But why the devil don't you let people know about your crusades? At least then you could ask someone besides us to help you."

"It isn't even *us* this time. I can't involve Charles."

"I know." He grimaced. "He can be a real prig when it comes to the letter of the law. What do you need?"

"A place where she can stay."

Jacob frowned.

"Not here," Richard added. "Herriard nearly grabbed her as we left St. George's. Since everyone in town knows where I was headed, he must already be watching the house. I hoped she could use Oakhaven for a week."

"Possibly. But first I need to meet her." He had to decide for himself if she was telling the truth. Richard had fallen prey to false pleas for help before. He had no sense when his compassion stirred. Herriard's involvement would skew his logic even further. "What is her name?"

"Georgiana. Her mother and Herriard's father were siblings. The mother married beneath her, drawing Herriard's contempt, but I haven't had time to learn more."

Jacob shook his head as he led the way to his study, the plate still in his hand. Richard regularly leaped to the rescue without learning anything relevant. But Jacob wasn't so gullible.

The library door refused to open.

"It's locked," said Richard, proffering the key. "I didn't want her to be disturbed."

"Ah." And maybe Richard wasn't as oblivious as he seemed.

His papers seemed undisturbed, allowing him to relax—his parliamentary work meant he often kept sensitive documents at home. The girl was asleep on the couch, a filthy cloak jumbled on the floor beside it. While her face was fair enough in a vapid blond way, her body could best be described as plump. And her gown was frankly hideous.

He could see why she'd caught Richard's eye, though. The lost-waif expression would appeal to his soft heart. And her connection to Herriard made her irresistible.

"Georgiana?" Having set his plate on the desk, Richard gently shook her shoulder. "Wake up."

Startled, she shot upright, then groaned.

"Be careful of that ankle," he added.

"What happened?" asked Jacob.

"Bad sprain." He helped her settle, his hand lingering overlong on her shoulder, then joined her on the couch. "This is the Earl of Hawthorne, Georgiana. He will help you."

"Georgiana what?" Jacob sat behind the desk. A surreptitious glance into the top drawer confirmed that his cash box remained intact.

"Whittaker."

"And your father?"

She paused. "Humphrey Whittaker, my lord."

"Ah." Jacob nearly laughed at the puzzlement in Richard's eyes. Richard rarely heeded financial opportunities because he didn't have any money. Thus he didn't recognize the name. But Humphrey Whittaker had founded one of the more profitable independent import companies. Jacob had reaped several fortunes by investing in it. *Small inheritance*, indeed. Miss Whittaker was a considerable heiress—which explained Herriard's interest. And Stagleigh's.

Despite his frequent protests to the contrary, Richard needed an heiress. Jacob had sworn only last week to see that his friends found suitable wives. It was time that Richard swallowed his pride and stopped pretending he liked living frugally.

He could summon the bishop from the drawing room and demand an immediate hearing on replacing Miss Whittaker's guardian, but this was not the time to exercise his in-

fluence. Far better to make Richard stay with her while the
matter crept through the legal process. Already he could see
sparks flying between them. All he had to do was shut them
up somewhere safe and let nature take its course.

But first he must verify his impressions.

He soon set her at ease and elicited the full tale of
her life with Herriard. It wasn't pretty.

Richard's fists clenched as Georgiana revealed Herriard's refusal to bring her out, the petty cruelties he'd
inflicted, and her duties as an unofficial—and thus
unpaid—governess for Herriard's three hellions. She'd
been a virtual slave. Never mind that Herriard's wife
was nearly as abused. The thought of Georgiana endur-
ing such hardships fanned his fury.

When she finished describing her flight, Jacob nodded.
"You are right," he told Richard. "She must stay out of
sight until her birthday. Take her to Oakhaven. My solicitor will file a petition on Monday to end Herriard's
guardianship."

"So I will be free?" Hope lit her face.

"Not completely." Richard patted her hand. "You still
need a guardian. The court will not dismiss Herriard
unless there is another willing to assume responsibility
for you. Who would you prefer?"

"But—"

"That is the law, Miss Whittaker," said Jacob firmly.
"All unmarried females must be under the care of a
parent or guardian. Consider it a form of protection.
Many businesses won't deal with females. Others will
cheat you beyond charging you higher prices. You need
someone who can see after your interests and prevent
scoundrels from taking advantage of you."

Georgiana wanted to scream. At the world. At Hawthorne. But mostly at herself. This wasn't something
she'd learned in childhood, nor had the subject come up
under Derrick's roof. All her plans had focused on escape. She'd not considered how she would go on afterward. How many other problems would prove
troublesome? It was a question she must answer.

"Finding another guardian will be difficult," she ad-

mitted. "I know very few people. Father's partner now
owns the business, but he criticized Father's marriage
and accused him of giving me airs above my station, so
he would not make a comfortable guardian. I know no
other relatives. And I was not allowed to meet callers
while living with Lord Herriard."

Richard shook his head. "We can discuss possible
guardians after the guests leave. For now, Hawthorne
and I must return to the drawing room." He stood.

But she had more questions. "Where is Oakhaven?"

Hawthorne smiled. "Four hours south of London. It's
one of my smaller estates. My staff will make you comfortable." He picked up a pen.

"You know we can't stay here," added Richard as
Hawthorne pulled out a sheet of paper and began to
write. "It's the first place Herriard will look. And moving you to another town house—or even a hotel—would
start rumors that would attract his attention. My friend
Charles can't help either. So going to Oakhaven will
keep you out of sight."

She nodded, then froze as his friend's name suddenly
connected the other two. Richard. Charles. The Earl of
Hawthorne.

The Three Beaux.

Dear Lord, she'd fallen into a nest of degenerate
rakehells.

Even living as an unpaid servant didn't insulate her
from gossip. Everyone knew of the Beaux, for the tales
titillated all classes. Their escapades were legion. So
were their conquests.

The Earl of Hawthorne was renowned for the swath
he'd cut through the demimonde. Tales claimed he bedded someone every night, but never the same person
twice. His wealth was legendary, his exploits larger than
life. Even seducing his best friend's fiancée did not tar-
nish his social standing, though he'd had to wed the girl.
Richard's sister.

She shuddered.

Lord Charles Beaumont always had the most desirable
courtesan in London under his protection, yet he flirted
with everyone he met and wasn't averse to seducing matrons. Rumors claimed he'd bedded most of society's

hostesses. Like Hawthorne, he was wealthy, with an inviolable social position. Even being jilted in favor of Hawthorne hadn't hurt him.

Richard Hughes was different. Not in breeding—he was heir to a viscountcy. But the family coffers were dry, so he couldn't afford courtesans. Thus he limited his attentions to widows and matrons, who expected nothing beyond a sample of his amazing prowess. Such conquests had led to threats, fisticuffs, and at least one duel, all of which diminished his credit. Only the support of the other Beaux kept him acceptable. He was also known as a hellion, with many pranks and scrapes to his credit. Derrick hated Hughes. She didn't know why, but they were bitter enemies—which raised the question of why Richard was helping her.

She could understand his reputation as a rake. His potent masculinity demanded attention, saturating the air until it was hard to breathe. His gentleness made him all the more attractive. But if she had any sense, she would decline further assistance.

"Before we leave, she needs to have her ankle wrapped," Richard was saying. "It's the worst sprain I've ever seen."

"That bad?" Hawthorne shook his head. "My housekeeper can see after it. And you will need to change clothes. You can hardly travel unnoticed in formal attire. Help yourself to my wardrobe."

"What?" asked Georgiana, realizing she'd missed something.

Richard smiled. "Once the guests are gone, you will borrow a cloak and bonnet from Emily, then leave, accompanied by Hawthorne. If Herriard is watching, he will think you are Lady Hawthorne leaving on your wedding journey."

"But—"

"Don't fret. The Hawthornes aren't actually leaving until tomorrow. I will slip out the back, then follow. Once I'm certain Herriard isn't behind you, Hawthorne and I will change places. He can return to his bride, while you and I go to Oakhaven."

"You needn't accompany me. I appreciate the use of his estate, but I cannot trouble you further."

"Nonsense. Herriard will remain a threat until the court severs his guardianship. If this ruse does not work—and it might not, for he knows you are here, and he might know when Hawthorne plans to leave—then he will follow. Even if we escape him now, he might check Oakhaven when he discovers that Hawthorne remains in town. I must be there to protect you."

He was right. The very thought of Derrick finding her alone in the earl's carriage made her stomach clench. Even Oakhaven would not be completely safe, for how could she trust the earl's staff to turn away a lord who had a legal claim on her person?

She reluctantly nodded.

"Good. The housekeeper will bind your ankle and help you change. I will return when it is time to leave— we've been away from the guests too long already. In the meantime, eat. You've had nothing in hours and won't have another chance for some time."

He slipped out. Hawthorne studied her a moment longer, then followed. But before the door latched, she heard him murmur, "At least this lame duck is better than the last one."

Lame duck? She shook her irritation away and turned to the plates on the desk. How could she have missed them? They were loaded with a vast array of delicacies the like of which she'd never seen before. Delectable aromas filled the room.

But even fabulous food could not keep her mind from the Beaux. The future had never seemed so uncertain. Would Richard seduce her? And would it matter if he did? Even losing her virtue to a rake was better than staying with Derrick.

Not that it would happen, she assured herself stoutly. The Beaux might have larger-than-life reputations, but no one had ever accused them of forcing a reluctant female. So as long as she remained reluctant, she would be safe.

Her only fight would be against her own base nature, which wondered why every voice that mentioned his prowess held awe. She must not let this unexpected attraction grow. He had no reason to push her.

Unless . . .

But he did not know how large her inheritance was. She'd already made light of it. Since the business had gone to her father's partner, he wouldn't expect her to have anything beyond a reasonable dowry. If he ever found out otherwise . . .

One more reason to remain aloof. She could not cope with another fortune hunter.

3

Richard peered out the window as the carriage drew away from the tollgate and moved briskly south. So far their escape had gone smoothly. He'd given the carriage a ten-minute head start before following, then examined every rider and vehicle he passed as he caught up. There was no sign of Herriard, who must still be watching Hawthorne House. Their ruse had worked.

He hoped.

Unfortunately, his machinations couldn't guarantee safety. Herriard would play least in sight where there were witnesses. And he might suspect their destination. The man would have studied the Beaux during their years of animosity. Everyone in town knew about Oakhaven, for Jacob stayed there often, as did Richard. Scrutiny of their every move was the price the Beaux paid for notoriety.

He bit back a sigh. There was no point in mentioning the possibility to Georgiana. She had enough problems as it was. Her ankle had to hurt like the very devil. Binding it had let her walk from door to carriage without limping, aided by Jacob's arm around her shoulders. But she had been white-faced with pain by the time he and Jacob had traded places at the second tollgate. Now she sat on the facing seat, alternately biting her lip and staring out the window.

Richard wished he'd kept his horse instead of turning it over to Jacob. Riding inside the carriage was torturing him. Georgiana was too attractive. He'd chosen the opposite seat because he'd feared that rubbing her with every jolt would severely test his control. What he hadn't counted on was the effect of looking at her for four hours.

The housekeeper had arranged her hair into soft curls that did interesting things to his libido. As did her current gown—a different one than she'd worn earlier. It might be unfashionable, but it stretched tightly across a stunning bosom, leaving him awash in sensation as his body recalled how perfectly she fit against him.

"Have you given further thought to a new guardian?" he asked to avoid hauling her into his lap so he could ravish those luscious lips.

She shook her head. "The court will have to appoint someone. I have no suggestions."

"None?"

"Think," she snapped. "Few people know I exist. Even before Papa died, I spent most of my time with my governess. I'd barely recovered from his burial before Grandfather and my uncle died. Derrick kept me confined to the house, less visible even than his wife."

He nodded. "Now that I think on it, she never accepts invitations."

"Of course not. She must even deny callers."

"Why?"

"Derrick's orders. The house has not been redecorated in sixty years, so most of the furnishings are shabby. He refuses to waste money on it. Then there is the matter of fashion. Despite being a baroness, Margaret has a wardrobe no better than mine—simple gowns more suited to the working classes. Which proved fortunate in the end. Before I fled, I was able to don all of my gowns. Carrying a valise would have drawn attention."

He nodded, irritated that his investigations had revealed none of this information. Her words also explained why her bosom seemed more prominent than before. The borrowed valise under her seat must contain the rest of her wardrobe. "I will consider possible guardians. I know several men who might do."

"I doubt it. Aristocrats don't soil their hands with merchants' daughters."

"Wrong!" His temper snapped at yet another cut of a class she knew little about. "Hawthorne had a ward until recently. Her father was a soldier of no particular breeding, and her mother the bastard daughter of a whore. Yet he took her in and found her a decent husband. The only reason I won't ask him to take charge of you is his marriage. He deserves privacy for a time. Nor can I ask my father. Not because of your background," he added over her protest. "My mother's health is failing. I doubt she'll see Christmas. New responsibilities will hasten her demise."

"Oh." She had the grace to look abashed.

"Herriard's behavior is not typical of the aristocracy," he continued sternly. "Nor is Stagleigh's. Most of us can't stand either of them. Instead, remember your grandfather. I did not know him well, but he struck me as a reasonable and kindly gentleman."

"True." She sighed. "But you must know that most of your peers consider themselves superior to merchants. Perhaps we should find my guardian outside the aristocracy. Even Grandfather admitted that my breeding would reduce my credit."

"Not necessarily. While there are a few sticklers who will frown, the fact remains that many ladies are in your position. Consider Lady Jersey, whose mother was a banker's daughter. Yet she is an Almack's patroness with the power to ostracize the highest in the land. As long as your manners conform, you should be fine. You mentioned a governess. Who was she?"

"Miss Elizabeth Coburn, Sir Reginald Coburn's youngest daughter."

Richard raised his brows.

"Did you know him?"

"Not personally, though I've heard the stories. He lost everything at cards, including his estate. Drunk, of course, though that is no excuse for ignoring his duty. The shock drove him to his death."

"You are putting too nice a face on the incident. He wasn't a greenling gaming away his allowance. He was a forty-year-old man responsible for his own extensive family, four tenant families, and a hundred employees. Family and friends had often urged him to protect his estate by entailing it, but he refused. Just as he refused to learn anything from earlier losses—except cowardice. His wife had been furious after the previous disaster lost all of her jewelry, so rather than tell her that they must leave their home, he shot himself. Miss Elizabeth found his body the next morning.''

''Poor girl.''

''She rarely spoke of it. And she was never openly bitter. She did her best to mold me into a lady.'' She sighed. ''Derrick turned her off the day Grandfather died. I'd always suspected he was cold, but that confirmed it. She would have starved if I hadn't written a glowing reference and convinced Grandfather's secretary to sign his name to it. It let her find a position with a squire in Hampshire. When Derrick discovered that we were corresponding, he burned her letters and forbade further contact. Never again was the post left where anyone else could see it.''

''I'm liking Herriard less and less.''

''He deserves it. But returning to your question, Miss Elizabeth came to us when I was five, so I had her for ten years. And Mother was quick to correct any mistakes. She died when I was fourteen.''

''Good. Your training settles the matter. I will speak to Lady Inslip—my friend Charles's mother,'' he added when she frowned. ''Once she agrees to present you, we can ask Inslip to stand as your guardian. A marquess will carry the day in court no matter what protest Herriard raises.''

''You don't know Derrick.''

''I know Herriard very well. He'll lose—not that it matters, for he won't be able to bother you much longer anyway.''

''Why?''

''He is a cheat. I've been trying to catch him for years.''

''Why? Cheating at cards isn't illegal.''

''True, but he would be banned from the clubs and dunned by his victims for recompense. The unpleasantness would probably drive him to the Continent. Not a satisfactory solution, but the only one available, at least until recently.''

''What happened?''

''He switched to fraud. I'll be presenting evidence to Lords next week. In the meantime, the bishop will readily sever his guardianship. Fraud aside, the bishop is Inslip's cousin."

She frowned. "That should work in my favor," she agreed. "But I have no intention of letting Lady Inslip push me into society. I fully intend to set up my own establishment."

"We will discuss that later. For now, relax. In another hour we will stop for dinner. I can't ask the Oakhaven staff to feed us without warning."

Georgiana laid down her fork and smiled. The food at the Yellow Oak was surprisingly tasty. Only the refreshments at Hawthorne House had been better—but they had been made for a wedding.

"Delicious," she said, wishing she had room for more. "Do all inns serve food like this?"

Richard looked surprised. "Delicious? I would describe it as average myself. You *have* had a rough time of it, haven't you?"

"It is over."

He was opening his mouth to respond when a voice boomed outside the door. "Herriard! What are you doing so far from town?"

Georgiana gasped as all the blood drained from her head. "How—"

"Shhh!" Richard covered her mouth. He'd removed his gloves to dine, so his hand felt shockingly warm.

"Looking for my cousin." Herriard made his disgust clear.

"I didn't know you had a cousin."

"We don't talk about it much. My aunt married a tradesman."

"Who?"

"It doesn't matter. The girl's a thief. I've tracked her this far, but . . ." The voices faded as the men moved across the hall to the taproom.

"Damn!" cursed Richard softly, dropping his hand.

"Who was that?" she hissed.

"Sir William Trent. He and Herriard are friends, though not close." He pressed his ear to the door, then frowned. "Herriard must have spotted Jacob returning to Hawthorne House. And he will have noted the carriage outside."

"I have to leave." She could barely choke out the words as her eyes searched frantically for another exit. Her thinking had been muddled in the church, but that was no longer true. Derrick was more devious than she'd thought. Branding her a thief gave him a huge advantage, for his oath alone would convince any court of her guilt. No one would accept a female's word over a lord's. Even worse, Richard would be prosecuted for helping her. Was that part of the plot? Derrick hated Richard. If he knew Richard meant to lay charges . . .

Hopelessness nearly overwhelmed her.

"Sit down and let me think." Richard paced to the window and back.

She sat, but her mind continued circling. She should have known that flight was useless. Unless she wed Stagleigh, Derrick would transport her for thef—

Dear God, but she was stupid. Transportation wouldn't help him. But convicting her of grand theft would see her hung. As next of kin, he could then claim her inheritance. She might have to throw herself at Stagleigh to escape death.

She should have refused Richard's help the moment she'd realized his identity. He might be heir to a title, but for now he was a commoner. Even *his* word would be suspect when set against a lord's.

"I've got it." Richard's voice startled her. "Stay here while I speak to the coachman."

"I can't let you risk your reputation, or worse," she said, shaking her head. "This changes everything. He will see me hanged."

"No." He pulled her tightly against him, forcing her to meet his gaze.

Frissons of electricity rampaged along her nerves, making her dizzy. Rake, indeed. One touch could melt lead.

"You've done nothing wrong, Georgiana," he swore. "I will not let him abuse you. And Fate is clearly on your side. Witness Sir William's providential arrival. Gather your courage, my dear. I'll be back in a moment." He dropped a light kiss on her mouth and released her.

Before she could respond, he was gone.

Her lips tingled, muddling her thoughts. She could still feel his muscular form pressed against her. Was there really an alternative to Stagleigh or death?

She couldn't risk it. Nor could she believe anyone would risk his reputation—let alone his life—for a stranger. No man was that magnanimous. Richard must have an ulterior motive.

The most obvious one was her inheritance. Many aristocrats had invested in her father's ventures, to their benefit. And Richard admitted that he'd studied Derrick's family. It was possible that he'd not recognized her in the church—she rarely left the house. But he would certainly have known her father's name.

That she didn't want to believe he was driven by greed proved how dangerous he was. His charm was already affecting her. His every touch made her crave more. But succumbing to seduction played into his hands. Remaining with him also played into Derrick's. So she must leave. Maybe she could escape, or maybe Derrick would win. But either way, she must go now.

She limped to the door. As she reached for the latch, it opened.

Richard shut the door behind him and glared. "Where are you going?"

"I have to do this alone, Richard. Anyone who helps me risks prosecution. I couldn't bear to harm you."

"You don't trust me."

"It isn't a matter of trust," she insisted, cursing her delay. "I know Derrick. He won't back down. Charging me with theft will supersede my petition to the bishop. Charging you with abetting a thief will prevent your presentation to Lords and might well see you transported."

"And what will he claim was stolen?" Arms akimbo, he glared—and blocked the door.

"God knows. But his claims will convince any court that I'm guilty. He's a lord."

"I can produce a hundred lords who will testify that he is a liar and a cheat. I can also produce witnesses who will swear that he had nothing left to steal after last night's losses, and that you took nothing but the clothes on your back when you escaped his house."

"You don't know him."

Richard's face hardened. "I know him. Too well. Now, enough of this. He and Sir William are sharing a tankard of ale. We must be gone before they finish. Give me your cloak."

"Why?"

"It is leaving now. The bonnet, too." He handed her a black cloak and a man's hat.

"What are you doing?" she demanded even as she passed him her borrowed garments.

"One of Hawthorne's grooms is about your height. He will climb into the carriage and leave." A patterned tap sounded. Richard opened it to a man wearing the Hawthorne livery. "Here," said Richard, draping the cloak around the man's shoulders. He handed over the bonnet. "You know what to do."

The man tied the ribbons and left.

"I don't understand," said Georgiana. Her head was swimming.

"He now looks like you—that bonnet shields the face, which is why we chose it for you to begin with. The coachman will assist him inside, then address him by your name as he closes the door. They will continue to Oakhaven. The stable staff is too busy to watch closely, so they will remember only that a lady drove off alone in the Hawthorne carriage."

"But what about us? The landlord knows we are here. If we do not disappear along with the carriage, Derrick will find out."

He ignored her. "How is your ankle?"

"It hurts."

"Can you walk a hundred yards without drawing attention?"

"If I must."

"Good. You will slip out the back and follow the stream to the spinney around the hill. It is out of sight of the inn. I will hire a horse and return to London, having seen you safely on your way to Oakhaven. I'll pick you up by the spinney."

"And return to town? I thought—"

"We will discuss that later. For the moment, we need distance between us and Herriard." He tucked her hair under the hat, sorry to lose sight of those soft curls even for a few minutes. "Keep your head down and your skirts tucked in. No one should think twice about a gentleman slipping down to the stream to stretch his legs and take care of business. Just be grateful that Hawthorne's footmen wear long cloaks."

4

Richard waited until Georgiana reached the stream before heading for the stable. He could only pray she would be all right. Her face was several shades whiter than it had been earlier. He wasn't sure if it was from pain or fear, but his only choice had been to watch her walk away. Alone. If they left together, someone would spot them.

He hired a horse and joked with the grooms, letting them know that his escort was no longer necessary. The lady could finish her journey alone while he returned to town for his usual evening activities—a wink hinted at what tonight's activity would be. Then he rode back up the road. He'd known Herriard was in desperate straits. If Georgiana were not involved, he would let events play out on their own, for it was only fitting that Herriard's own vices had been turned against him.

Last night had been the climax of a monthlong debauch during which Herriard had lost all the money he'd taken in that fraud scheme, and then some. So he'd returned to what he knew best—cardsharping.

The game had not gone according to plan, though. Herriard had been desperate and too drunk to think clearly. Watson was a known cheat who took his own brand of revenge against anyone who reneged on a debt. Smart men avoided him. Stupid men paid dearly.

Herriard might have thought he was the better cheat, but he hadn't even noticed when Watson replaced Herriard's deck with his own. Thus when Herriard made his move, Watson laid down a better hand. Herriard had signed vowels for ten thousand pounds. He had until Wednesday to pay.

Stagleigh was flush from recent wins, so he was the obvious choice to purchase Herriard's last remaining asset. And since Stagleigh enjoyed defiling innocence, he would pay a pretty penny for her. The situation made both men very dangerous.

Richard couldn't allow it, but he had no delusions about the lengths to which Herriard would go to regain possession of Georgiana. The only true protection he could offer her was his name.

Heat pooled in his groin.

He must wed soon if he wanted his mother to attend the ceremony. Assuring the succession would ease her mind at a time when fretting worsened her condition. With Emily now wed, marriage became even more urgent, for Emily had run the household for years. So he'd intended to use the remainder of the Season to find a wife.

Fate seemed to be helping him. Georgiana was much like his ideal wife. Marginal breeding. No fortune to speak of—merchants' dowries would hardly impress society. Excellent training. And after five years as Herriard's slave, even his modest circumstances would seem like heaven. As a bonus, her antipathy to society meant they could remain in the country much of the year, reducing his expenses.

He'd stayed in London after coming down from school because he'd needed freedom from his parents' scrutiny. And because liaisons were more difficult to arrange in Gloucestershire. But marriage negated both reasons. The Beaux had long since taken vows of marital fidelity.

This was no time to broach the subject, though. Despite that riding off alone technically compromised her, he felt no obligation, for she was unharmed and would remain so. He had time to learn more about her, for they could not wed before her birthday. But soon . . .

He nodded as the spinney appeared around the corner. His immediate goal was to slip back into London without Herriard's knowledge. Once she was safely hidden, he could consider the future.

*   *   *

Georgiana bit back a whimper as pain slashed up her leg, buckling her knee. Only grabbing a branch kept her upright. Walking a hundred yards had seemed easy when Richard had suggested it, but she'd barely made it.

She leaned weakly against a tree, praying that he could slip away without drawing Derrick's attention. She couldn't move another step. But at least Richard had revived her determination to escape. Giving up had never been her way. Even if Derrick won, she had to thank Richard for renewing her hope and her courage. She would not face her fate as a coward.

He'll win, whispered a voice in her mind. *Derrick always does. No one can keep you safe.*

Her newfound courage wavered, then collapsed entirely when hoofbeats approached along the road.

Derrick!

She tried to dodge behind the tree, but her legs wouldn't move. A sob escaped. When Richard appeared, she nearly swooned in relief.

"Are you all right?" he asked softly, sliding to the ground. The horse stood dully behind him, showing no sign of spirit. A sluggard.

"Of course," she answered.

His eyes turned skeptical. "How bad is the pain?"

She sighed. "I can't walk another step."

He cut off a curse. "I shouldn't have—"

"There was no other choice."

"I know, but . . ." He shook his head, then lifted her across the horse, mounting behind her. Before she realized his intent, she was tight against his chest with his cloak encasing both of them. She had to work to keep from melting against him. His heat was too enticing, especially when his hand caressed her arm before taking up the reins. He was a rake to the bone.

"Relax, Georgiana," he murmured, letting the horse pick its way through the spinney. "I will take care of you. Herriard won't threaten you again." His mouth nearly touched her ear.

"He won't give up."

"He will have no choice. So set aside your fear." His arms pulled her closer against him. Her heartbeat quickened to match his.

She fought the warmth that spread from his touch. This sudden seductiveness—for how else could she describe his current behavior?—was suspicious, to say the least. Her fortune would tempt a saint, and God knew the Beaux weren't saints, especially Richard. Now that they were alone, he might claim compromise, forcing her into marriage.

It wouldn't be force.

Of course it would, she snapped at Temptation. She had no use for aristocrats and less for fortune hunters. Tying herself to Richard would destroy her.

They emerged from the trees and turned down a footpath between two fields, heading straight into the setting sun.

She stiffened. "I thought we were returning to London."

"We are, but not by the Brighton Road. Herriard's carriage cannot follow us if we circle out to Richmond before turning back to town."

"We'll never make it before dark," she protested. It would have been difficult anyway, but now they wouldn't reach London for many hours.

"It can't be helped. The ostler knows I am returning to town, which means that Herriard will also know. I hope he believes we parted company, but we can't count on it, so remaining on the road is foolish."

She had to admit the logic of his argument. Riders could go anywhere, while drivers were restricted to roads. And even if Derrick left his carriage behind and hired a horse—which was unlikely, given his finances— he would have no trail to follow.

She relaxed, letting her head fall against Richard's shoulder. She knew she shouldn't, but she was tired and in too much pain to care. She needed to absorb his strength. There would be time later to plan the next step.

Richard smiled when Georgiana fell asleep. She felt good curled against him. And maybe she finally trusted him.

But his smile soon slipped. The horse was a slug that refused to move faster than a walk. He'd known the moment the groom led it out that it would be a problem, but raising a fuss would have drawn unwanted attention. And a better horse would have cost more than he had. His pride had turned down a loan from Jacob, which in retrospect had been stupid. He should have foreseen that plans could change, separating them from the carriage and Oakhaven.

Feeling far too exposed, he picked a path between fields and along rutted lanes, keeping hedgerows and stands of trees behind him. He also bypassed villages, for the fewer people who saw them, the more likely they would reach London undetected.

An hour passed before his fears waned. There was no sign of pursuit and no interest in their passage.

A second hour slid by. The sun dipped lower, playing peekaboo with the treetops and dazzling his eyes whenever it pierced the foliage.

Georgiana stirred in his arms.

"Feeling better?" he asked.

"Mmm." She stiffened as her eyes blinked open.

"Relax." He shifted her to a more comfortable position, ignoring what the motion did to his groin. "Are you thirsty?"

"Not quite."

"We should stop, though. London is still hours away. Most travelers halt at dusk, so seeking refreshments now will draw less notice than it would later."

"Are we at Richmond yet?"

"No. It's about five miles north of us."

"We could stop there."

An objection hovered on his lips, for he hadn't intended to go through Richmond itself, where he would likely encounter acquaintances—and not only his peers. Most of the innkeepers knew him, for he'd often eaten there with friends or liaisons.

Running into friends would settle the question of marriage, though. Georgiana would have to accept him, saving him from an argument. He could already imagine her objections.

But she had no idea how hard it would be to set up her own establishment. Nor did she understand how isolated she would become if she tried. It would sever any ties to society, of course. But her father's peers would also condemn her. Where would she find friends? Marriage was clearly her best course. Even if a few brows lifted now, she would be ennobled when he inherited the viscountcy. That would terminate any doubts. The easiest way to assure that course was to be caught traveling together.

"Very well," he agreed. "Richmond it is. The Crown and Anchor has excellent ale and a meat pie that melts in your mouth." It was also the inn most likely to be jammed with acquaintances.

He turned north, following another footpath between two fields.

Georgiana was appalled that she'd fallen asleep in Richard's arms. How had she relaxed so thoroughly? Her ankle should have kept her awake, if nothing else.

But this proved how dangerous he could be. One heated look from those brown eyes could seduce a statue, and those talented hands . . .

He'd carried her, held her, embraced her, caressed her. It was the first time she'd been touched since her father's death. She had never considered herself susceptible to male charm, so it was unnerving to realize how vulnerable she really was. A little kindness, a little warmth, and she melted into a pool of need.

It had to stop.

To divert her mind, she concentrated on her naïveté. Only an idiot would have thought Derrick would give up the income from her trust. He'd been living on it for five years. Losing it would force him to sell the town house and retire to his derelict country estate. He hated the country. And now that she understood his character, she had to admit that Margaret had saved her from an even worse fate. If Derrick had not already been saddled with a wife five years ago, he would have forced her to the altar much earlier. With him.

An intelligent ward would have run away long ago, slipping out when everyone was asleep. London was big enough so that he would never have found her. And proper planning would have turned up someone to help her. Someone besides a notorious rake.

Instead she had grown complaisant, thinking that car-

ing for the boys made her indispensable. So while she'd
dreamed of breaking free once she controlled her inheritance, she had done nothing to further that goal, not
even consider the obstacles she would face. Learning
that unwed ladies required guardians had shocked her.
It wasn't true of gentlemen, who were free when they
came of age. But Derrick's guardianship would not have
ended. Nor would he have stopped dipping into her
funds. He would have found a way to confiscate everything.

What else had her ignorance overlooked?

Richard's arm shifted along her back, sending excitement rippling along her skin. Even his inadvertent
touches burned her to the core. They felt nothing like
her grandfather's pats as she'd cried on his shoulder
after the funeral. Nor did they resemble her father's protective hugs—or even his congratulatory ones when he'd
shared her excitement over a new accomplishment.

She banished the memories. Richard was not for her.
No one was, least of all a fortune hunter.

To distract herself from his touch, she studied the sun
as it dipped below the horizon, turning previously unnoticed cloudlets a brilliant orange. Lingering rays pierced
the gathering night. "Pretty."

"Very. Are you warm enough?" He tugged his cloak
tighter—forcing her closer against his chest.

"Quite."

"How is your ankle?"

"Much better. It no longer throbs."

"I wouldn't risk walking on it, though. The Crown and
Anchor has a private parlor just inside the door, so I'll
carry you."

"I can walk that far," she protested, not wanting to
appear in public in his arms.

"We'll see." His tone made it clear that she would not
walk, but she didn't argue. Time enough for that later.

He forded a stream, then turned down a narrow road.
"We'll have to follow lanes from now on," he said.
"Darkness makes it hard to see the footpaths. I don't
want to ruin someone's crops."

His concern surprised her even more than his courtesy
in stopping at the Yellow Oak so Hawthorne's staff

needn't provide an unexpected meal. The aristocrats she knew cared only for themselves. Few would notice if they trampled a tenant's fields or disrupted a household. Fewer would care. Especially Derrick, who delighted in exerting his authority over underlings.

Richard's consideration was even odder, for it did not mesh with the Beaux' reputations as conscienceless rake-hells. Which raised questions about Richard's character. Did gossip malign him?

"Why did you let your sister wed a rake like Hawthorne?" The question was out before she realized how rude it sounded.

"Jacob?" He sounded surprised. "He is one of the best men I know."

"But his reputation—"

"If you judge people solely on gossip, what are you doing with me?"

"I'm not quite sure," she admitted with a sigh. "I've had no time to think since fleeing this morning. It gave me a jolt to realize you were one of the Beaux."

"I suppose it was too much to hope you hadn't heard of us."

"Quite." She grinned. "People more isolated than I am know of your exploits."

"Not true. Oh, they've doubtless heard tales, but most rumors are exaggerated, and many are downright false."

"Really?" She twisted to look him in the eye.

"Really. Gossip loves scandal, so it twists anything out of the ordinary to make it more shocking. Events that contradict a scandalous image get swept under the rug. Virtues are ignored unless their owners are saints. Too boring."

"Are you saying that you didn't loose a bear in Lord Cardway's drawing room, where his prospective bride's father would find it?"

He laughed. "That one is true, I must admit. But a great many details disappeared in the retelling."

"Such as?"

"The girl had already refused Cardway's suit, but her father insisted she accept him—Cardway had offered a fortune for her. Very like Stagleigh's offer for you."

She gasped.

"Exactly. Cardway was obsessed with her—she is quite lovely. Convinced that she was just being coy, he ignored her refusal. Only after her father encountered the bear did the man reconsider the proposed alliance. By the time he learned that Cardway was not responsible for his scare, his daughter had accepted another suitor. Someone she loved."

"How did you become involved?"

"The man she loved is a friend."

"So why not tell people the truth?"

"Sometimes truth can do more harm than good. Cardway is a wealthy viscount, which makes him a marital prize. Her father was admired for negotiating such a good match. Had people known about her refusal, they would have ridiculed her, reducing her credit. Had they learned why the bear was there, I would have been roundly condemned for interfering. So I let people believe that a joke on Cardway had gone awry. Better for all concerned."

"Except Cardway."

"Actually, Cardway formed a new obsession within months. And the girl's father did not need the fortune Cardway offered. Neither of them was harmed by the incident. Both gained sympathy from society."

She fell silent, reflecting that the one who had been hurt was Richard, whose reputation had suffered from his presumed irresponsibility. Yet it didn't seem to bother him.

Perhaps he didn't know about her inheritance after all. She was obviously not the first lady he'd helped to escape an unwanted match, which explained Hawthorne's *lame duck* comment. Richard must make a habit of helping others. But such a virtue stood at odds with his reputation as a rake and prankster, so society ignored it.

Her heart warmed. There was more substance to him than she'd expected. He wasn't the malicious prankster rumor supposed. Was his reputation as a rake likewise exaggerated?

Before she could ask, he pulled the horse to a halt and backed up.

She glanced around, surprised that they were approaching an inn. Or had been. Richard whisked them around a corner, out of sight of the stable yard. His reason became clear when Stagleigh's voice cut through the night.

". . . crested carriage with yellow wheels. A man and a woman. Both blond."

A coarser murmur was too soft to understand.

"My betrothed, damn him. Hughes abducted her. I must catch them before he ruins her."

Georgiana gasped.

Richard's hand slid up to cover her mouth. "Quiet," he whispered in her ear. "I underestimated Herriard. He is checking all the likely routes from London. This is another way to Oakhaven. And it's also the route to Gloucestershire."

"I cain't believe that, milord," drawled the ostler. Georgiana could almost see him shaking his head. "Master Hughes is a real gentleman, he is. Always 'as a kind word for us."

Stagleigh cursed. "The man's a villain. Have you seen him?"

"Not lately. Must be all of a month since he last drove this way. Part of a party, he was. Ten, maybe twelve others."

"Today, man! Have you seen him today?"

"No, not today. Now Mr. Montgomery, he's in the taproom with a party of bucks. And—"

"Peter!" exclaimed another voice. "What are you doing out here? Thought you hated Richmond."

"I could say the same for you, Francis."

Francis laughed. "Sister's wedding next week. Dragged my feet so I could stop on the road—Mother is terrifying when she readies the castle for guests, and I've no use for my cousins. But you?"

"Chasing Hughes. He abducted my betrothed."

"Betrothed! I hadn't heard."

"I hadn't made an announcement. And if I don't catch the bastard—"

"That doesn't sound like Hughes," said Francis slowly. "Granted, he's a prankster, but he's never hurt anyone."

"But this is different." Stagleigh's voice grew fainter as he turned toward the inn. "Share a pint with me. My horse threw a shoe and won't be ready for a quarter hour."

"What is different about it?" Francis ignored the change of subject.

"The girl's an heiress. Hughes started sniffing around when he discovered her inheritance. Pounced whenever she poked her nose out the door. She complained, of course, to him and to me—we've been promised for years. But he must be in the briers again, for he snatched her this afternoon."

"Who is she?"

"Herriard's cousin. Father made a fortune in trade. All hers now—" A door slapped shut, cutting off their voices.

Richard's hand dug into her chin as he twisted her head to face him. "Heiress?"

"He exaggerates. The business went to Father's partner," she reminded him.

"He would hardly leave his only daughter penniless. I need facts, Miss Whittaker. How desperate is Herriard to find you?" Fury threaded his whisper. The combination seemed more ferocious than any of Derrick's rants.

But she refused to collapse. "Derrick demanded fifty thousand pounds. Stagleigh signed a contract to pay it."

5

Fifty thou—Richard nearly fell off the horse. "How much would that leave Stagleigh?"

"Nothing."

"You can't expect me to believe that. Stagleigh isn't stupid."

"But Derrick lied. He swore I was worth two hundred, but I can't be."

"Why?"

She sighed. "Papa left me thirty. There is no way the trustees could have increased the principle that much."

"It's possible."

"Not without investing returns. I've not seen a statement from the trust in five years, but Derrick has been living on the quarterly income. I would be shocked if anything was reinvested."

Richard gritted his teeth. He believed her, not that it mattered. Ten thousand made a girl an heiress. If Georgiana had thirty . . .

Dear Lord. He was squiring a damned heiress, not a waif. Why didn't she simply hire guards to keep Herriard away until her birthday? He had to get free of her before someone spotted them.

Stifling the attraction that had been growing all day, he kicked himself for not asking questions earlier. But at least he hadn't offered for her. Marriage was now out of the question.

Paying his own way was the only way he could live with himself and was how he'd retained his friendship with Jacob and Charles. He would never accept money from others. Nor could he keep Georgiana in the style she'd enjoyed before Herriard. No one with her background would be satisfied with what he could offer.

Cold to the bone, he guided the horse around Richmond and headed for London.

"What's wrong?" she asked, sounding surprised.

"You should have mentioned your inheritance earlier. If I'd known how desperate Herriard was . . ." The man must be even more desperate than Richard had thought. Why else would he stoop to cheating his closest friend?

He kicked the horse into a reluctant trot. "At least the road to London will be clear. But we can't stop until we have you safely hidden."

"Where? Hawthorne House?"

"No. There is no way to hide you in Mayfair. Servants talk." How else did Lady Beatrice learn everything that happened? "But Charles owns a cottage that is currently empty. On Monday we'll speak to the solicitor. Inslip can expedite your petition to the bishop. With luck, it will be decided this week."

He would have to stay with her, though, he admitted grimly. If Herriard was this desperate, he might find her.

Damnation! The last thing he needed was to live in a cottage with a damned heiress. But he would never forgive himself if Herriard found her before she was free.

At least Stagleigh would be easy to handle. Once he learned the truth, he would wash his hands of the affair.

But his earlier conclusion was truer than ever. Georgiana would never be safe without a husband. He must find her one. Immediately. Not him, of course. But only marriage would protect her.

By the time they reached London, Richard was mad at the world and everything in it. Fate had played him a prank worse than any he'd ever pulled. Lust was driving him insane. Holding Georgiana in his lap for six hours had stretched his control to the limit. How the devil was he to remain aloof under the same roof with her for a week or more?

But he had to. Even if Herriard had dipped into her principle—which wasn't likely under most trust rules— she was far beyond his reach. He should have realized it earlier. She might be uninformed about some things, but her merchant father would have taught her enough about finances that she would never try to live on the few hundred pounds he'd expected her to have.

He'd been unbelievably stupid. Even after he'd realized that her clothes did not match her breeding, he had not questioned his other impressions. He was too accustomed to people who hid empty purses behind the latest fashion to think an heiress would dress in rags. Now he was trapped.

He'd wracked his brains for a solution that would keep her safe without risking scandal or involving others. But there wasn't one. Until she was no longer Herriard's ward, he could not approach her trustees or anyone else who cared more for legalities than people.

So he was on his own. And the prospects were no better than they'd been earlier. He couldn't afford an inn—which would be dangerously compromising anyway. None of his many friends could house her. Which returned him to Charles's love nest.

Charles had dismissed his most recent mistress after proposing to Emily and hadn't yet replaced her. So the cottage remained vacant. Its staff was accustomed to ignoring whatever occurred under its roof. And it was far enough from Mayfair that gossip would spread slowly.

He would use false names, though, and wouldn't mention Georgiana to Charles.

"Where is this cottage?" asked Georgiana once they passed Hyde Park.

"A couple miles back. But I have to get permission to use it—which means finding Charles."

"Do you know where he is?"

"Probably White's. Pull that hat down to shade your face," he murmured into her ear. "You will have to hold the horse while I'm inside. Pretend to be a groom."

He turned up St. James's Street, his eyes searching the shadows for anyone he knew. So far they were in luck. It was after midnight, but the balls had not yet ended, and the farce was still under way at the theaters. In another hour the street would be mobbed as gentlemen converged on the clubs, but for now it was quiet. Only two carriages moved toward him, with another parked in front of Brooks's. The bow window at White's was empty, and the street denizens were not yet out in force. Most waited until they had their pick of inebriated targets.

He ducked into a narrow passage between buildings and dismounted.

"Steady," he murmured, setting Georgiana on her feet. She was so stiff she nearly fell.

"What do I do?"

"Stay against the wall so the horse shields you from view. Don't talk to anyone."

She nodded, accepting the reins.

"I will be back as soon as possible." He strode away, praying that Charles was inside. The last thing he needed was to make a round of the brothels. Charles patronized several. Or he might have changed his mind and accepted one of the invitations that still arrived by the dozen every day. It would be another month before the Season wound down.

But his luck held. Charles was leaning over the hazard table—just as Richard had found him a week earlier. At least this time he wasn't drunk.

He waited until Charles lost the throw, then tapped him on the shoulder. "I need a moment," he murmured.

Charles raised his brows, but followed without a word.

"What?" he asked once they reached an empty corner of the reading room.

"Is your Kensington cottage still vacant?"

Charles nodded.

"May I use it for a few days?"

"Of course." But his eyes widened. Richard never begged favors.

"Thank you. When you write to the butler, please omit my name."

"Curious." Charles moved to a writing table and pulled out a piece of paper. "You've been odd all day."

"I'm avoiding Herriard."

"Ah. I thought I recognized that bellow in church this morning. What the devil does he want?"

Richard hesitated, but Charles was too stiff-rumped to risk the truth. "He may have learned about my meeting at Lords next week."

"So you found the evidence."

"And an unimpeachable witness. I've an appointment on Monday."

"If you live that long."

"Exactly. Herriard enlisted Stagleigh's help to find me. I don't want them bothering Mother. She was ready to collapse by the time she headed home this afternoon."

"True. Should I mention that you've moved out of Hughes House?"

Richard nodded. "Casually. I've left town now that Emily is settled."

"Let me know if you need anything else."

"Of course." Not that he could involve Charles any further. He would demand marriage if he learned of to-day's escapade with Georgiana.

He couldn't wed her. Period.

But he couldn't help fretting over her, he admitted as he hurried toward the walkway. Not until he found her unscathed did he recognize the fear that had been knotting his shoulders.

Swearing under his breath, he shoved the letter into his pocket. In moments they were back on the horse and heading for Kensington.

6

On Monday morning Georgiana sharpened a pen, hoping she could complete a letter to her trustees. But, as had happened all three times she'd tried on Sunday, her brain refused to cooperate. Richard dominated her thoughts, confusing her more with each passing hour.

When they'd fled the Yellow Oak, he'd been warm. Almost seductive. By the time they'd reached this cottage, he'd turned curt, barely controlling fury. At breakfast yesterday he'd been pleasant but aloof. At lunch he'd sent her into gales of laughter by describing mishaps he'd witnessed and pranks he'd played. His eyes had flashed with humor and camaraderie. Yet an hour later she'd heard him pacing and muttering in the next room, so irritated that his tension had seeped through the closed door to stifle her. And last night he'd blown hot and cold throughout dinner, then retired without even bidding her good night. So she shouldn't have been surprised that he'd been gone when she'd come down for breakfast.

Another oddity was that he'd stationed the maid outside her door both nights, as if he expected her to bolt at any moment. She didn't like the implication. It couldn't be for protection against Derrick—the maid was all of sixty and quite dull-witted. So he must be keeping her fortune within reach.

She tried to force her mind back to the letter. It was time to remind her trustees that she was to take charge of her inheritance on her birthday. She must also warn them of Derrick's greed. Giving the money to Derrick to handle for her would not only break faith with her

father but guarantee she never saw a groat of the funds.
It shouldn't happen, of course, but she was rapidly learning that men too often twisted the law for their own
benefit. And few believed females could be trusted with
more than a few shillings.

She penned a salutation, then paused, mind blank.

Perhaps her problem was this sitting room instead of
Richard. It was not designed to facilitate thought, being
sumptuously furnished in red and gold, its satins and
velvets blatantly sensual. A painting of naked nymphs
cavorting in a garden hung above the fireplace. Several
well-thumbed books sat atop a table, but she'd not dared
examine them closely after one fell open to a shocking
illustration. The memory had produced some very odd
dreams last night.

Richard had seemed oblivious to the décor, proving
his familiarity with such rooms—why this surprised her
was a question she ignored. He *had* taken the main bed-
chamber for himself, though. Her one glimpse through
the door had revealed some provocatively placed mirrors, so he did have some concern for her sensibilities.

Concentrate on the letter.

Yes, the letter. No purpose was served by imagining
that illustration brought to life in front of a mirror, with
Richard's hand on her—

She wrenched her mind back to business. How could
she convince her trustees to ignore Derrick's claims?
Derrick was a lord. She was an unknown who had met
them only once, when she'd been fifteen. Why would
he—

Richard pushed open the door. He was frowning.

"Is there a problem?" she asked.

"Nothing you need to fret over." He smoothed his
expression. "I met with Hawthorne's solicitor. He will
present your petition to the bishop this afternoon. Inslip's support should gain you a hearing tomorrow. A
notice to that effect is on its way to Herriard."

"So fast."

"There are times when influence is useful. I also spoke
with Inslip. He will call on you this afternoon and will
accept your guardianship, if you approve. We can still
find someone else if need be, but I believe you will suit."

She wasn't so sure, but he was in no mood to argue. So she must prepare to meet a marquess.

A glance at her gown made her cringe. Brushing had helped, but it remained unfashionable and shabby. It was also her only gown at the moment. She'd left her other ones in Hawthorne's carriage.

Shaking her head, she returned to her letter. Now that she had a willing guardian and a definite hearing with the bishop, her words flowed easily.

Richard stood when Tester showed Inslip into the sitting room. Once the butler left, Richard performed introductions.

Arranging this meeting had been tricky. The staff did not know his name or Georgiana's. He hoped to survive Inslip's call with that situation intact. And inviting Charles's father into Charles's love nest was not done, so he'd not mentioned whose cottage he was using. If he wasn't careful, the half-truths would soon strangle him.

"Miss Whittaker," Inslip said, pressing her hand before taking the seat she indicated. He turned his gaze on Richard. "This tangle is worse than you implied, Hughes."

"What happened?"

"Stagleigh and Herriard returned to town this morning."

"Then Stagleigh should now be at Herriard's throat."

"Why?" asked Georgiana.

"I sent him proof that Herriard was cheating him."

"He hasn't received it," said Inslip. "They went directly to Herriard House. Half an hour later, Stagleigh rode north."

"Why?" This time Richard asked the question.

"Herriard claims you abducted his ward and are headed for Scotland."

"Absurd!" Georgiana snapped.

"So they've adopted Stagleigh's explanation," murmured Richard. "I'm surprised Herriard gave in on that point. Or perhaps not. He must know he can't prove theft."

"What theft?" asked Inslip.

"Yesterday Herriard claimed Miss Whittaker had robbed him. It was Stagleigh who swore I'd abducted his betrothed."

"Which is ridiculous," insisted Georgiana. "Even the groom at that inn didn't believe him, so why would they expect society to?"

"But it fits his reputation very well," said Inslip. "Many will accept the claim."

Richard's face heated as Inslip's gaze clashed with his own. "Not those who know me," he swore. "I have no use for heiresses."

"I know that. The Beaux know that. But most of society believes otherwise. This escapade has placed Miss Whittaker in an untenable position and destroyed what was left of your reputation."

Richard shrugged. He cared nothing for what society thought of him. Only his friends' opinions mattered.

"I won't be responsible for hurting you," said Georgiana. "Surely there is a way to counter these lies."

"They will die the moment Stagleigh realizes that Herriard tricked him into handing over your entire trust and then some," swore Richard. When Inslip raised his brows, he let Georgiana explain her cousin's perfidy, then added, "So there is no problem. Stagleigh will recant his claims. Herriard's credibility is already suspect and will disappear entirely once I present my evidence to Lords."

"Wasn't your meeting today?"

"I rescheduled for Wednesday. By then the bishop will have ruled on Miss Whittaker's petition."

"Maybe, but she should immediately move to Inslip House. That will—"

"No." Richard glared.

Inslip raised his brows.

"That would play into Herriard's hands. Moving her now would raise the question of where she has been for two days. Once you are officially her guardian, bringing her to Inslip House will seem natural. Few will wonder where she was previously."

"I don't see—"

"If anyone who deserves a response wants details, you

are keeping her at another property until your status is official. You don't wish to burden Lady Inslip and your daughter with Herriard's temper."

"But I have no other property near town."

Richard gave in to the inevitable. "Charles does."

Inslip's gaze took in the décor. "I see."

Richard pressed his advantage. "Knowing that Herriard is greedy and vicious, you had to hide her until her legal status was settled."

"Your reputation will still suffer."

"I doubt it. Herriard must already regret mentioning her. People will demand to know who she is and what she's been doing these past five years. The barrage must fluster him."

"What are you planning?" Inslip's eyes gleamed.

"I will make the usual social rounds tonight, disproving his claim that I am headed for Scotland." It might make Charles seem curiously uninformed, but there was no help for it. "A few words to Lady Beatrice will raise the awkward questions that Herriard doesn't want to face—like why society knows nothing of his ward's existence though she's lived with him for years, what his arrangement was with Stagleigh, and how that arrangement relates to Friday's losses. Once he is exposed as a scoundrel, society will welcome Miss Whittaker with open arms. She will be feted for surviving his plots. If anyone asks where you met her, you were introduced at Emily's wedding breakfast. Upon hearing her story, you immediately offered your support."

"Perhaps that will work," he grudgingly agreed. "But don't wait to call on Lady Beatrice. Go now. Herriard's lies are already on every tongue. You want the truth out before evening. I will remain here and become acquainted with Miss Whittaker."

Richard nodded. The errand should take only an hour. Inslip would watch her until then.

His growing need to protect her nearly suffocated him. He beat it back, reminding himself that she was not for him. Never would it be said that he had feathered his nest with a lady's fortune.

7

Richard inhaled deeply as he followed the butler to the drawing room. Lady Beatrice was not a woman he enjoyed confronting, especially when he was the subject of gossip.

She gestured him to a seat, her face the grimmest he'd ever seen it. Even Emily's announcement that she had jilted Charles to wed Jacob hadn't made her this disapproving.

"Thank you for seeing me," he said, feigning calm.

"I trust you have an explanation."

He nodded. "The very fact that I am in London should tell you that Herriard is lying."

"Why?"

"To confiscate his ward's trust so he can cover Friday's gaming debts. To discredit me before I can present evidence to Lords accusing him of fraud. To—"

His tongue froze as her eyes widened in shock. He'd done a better job of hiding his investigation than he'd thought. Few people could surprise Lady Beatrice. No one surpassed her knowledge of society. She knew everything that happened almost before the participants did.

She stroked her chin. "Let's start with his ward. Who is she?"

"Miss Georgiana Whittaker. Her mother was Herriard's paternal aunt. Her father was a merchant—Whittaker and Metcalf Imports." Again her eyes widened. "Herriard has had the care of her since his grandfather's death."

"Five years?" Her face relaxed, thawing the air. She

handed him a glass of wine, then poured tea for herself.

"Five years. Miss Whittaker's father died a week before the old baron's accident. His will named the baron as her guardian. Herriard inherited that duty along with the title."

"How old was she?"

"Fifteen. Her grandfather had planned to bring her out, but Herriard refused. He has used her as an unpaid governess while squandering her income on his gaming."

Lady Beatrice made a sound that in a less exalted person might be called a growl. "How long have you known?"

This was where he must be careful, Richard reminded himself. "Not long," he said calmly. "Herriard kept her well hidden, so even though I've been keeping an eye on him for some time—"

"Since he cheated you."

He nodded, not surprised she knew about it, though he'd kept the matter quiet. "Exactly. The Beaux dealt with that incident and warned him what would happen if he fleeced anyone else. For a time he was careful to live within his income—at least, I thought it was his until recently."

"How recently?"

"Last week. But Herriard is incapable of watching his purse. The next time he ran short, he fleeced Rothmore."

"Precipitating his suicide."

"Exactly. It was a private game that I learned about too late." A mistake he still rued. "I dug deeper into Herriard's affairs afterward, forcing him to abandon cardsharping. The next time he needed money, he set up a railroad scheme that fleeced Jameson, among others."

"Ahh." Her eyes gleamed.

"It was out-and-out fraud—no rail company existed. So he'll finally pay. I'll present the evidence to Lords on Wednesday."

"You've hidden your activities well."

"I would not have succeeded if I'd talked about it."

She nodded. "So how does abducting Miss Whittaker fit your plans?"

"I didn't abduct her. She has long sought to escape Herriard's abuse. When she heard him blustering about my investigation, she decided to seek my help once she came of age. Herriard's losses last Friday forced her to act early. She heard him selling her to Stagleigh the next morning, so she fled. It was easy to find me. Everyone in town knew I'd be at St. George's for Emily's wedding."

"True. So you helped her."

He nodded. "I introduced her to Inslip, who will take over as her guardian, but she must remain hidden until the bishop rules on her petition tomorrow."

"Herriard swears he tracked you to Oakhaven."

"He did. I had to distract him while Inslip spirited Miss Whittaker away. One of Hawthorne's grooms accompanied me, dressed in a cloak and bonnet."

She shook her head. "Another of your pranks."

"I wouldn't call it that." He kept his hands relaxed, but it wasn't easy.

She ignored his protest. "This one went too far, Hughes."

His eyes snapped together. "Should I have returned her to Herriard when she begged for help? No one deserves that fate, especially Georg—Miss Whittaker. Her breeding is every bit as good as Lady Jersey's. And despite years of mistreatment at Herriard's hands, she remains sweet."

"You know her well."

Richard cursed himself for losing his temper. "My studies of Herriard made it easy to investigate her claims once I learned of her existence."

"Hmm." She pursed her lips for a long moment. "It's true about her breeding, and it's true that her grandfather accepted her parents' marriage. I remember the incident well."

She would.

"I can quash most of the stories, Hughes," she continued. "And I will, for I agree that Herriard is lying. But your little charade with the groom succeeded too well. People saw you, and now that Herriard claims abduction, they no longer think that jaunt was one of your affairs. Her reputation will suffer unless you wed her."

"No." He continued over her protest. "She has come

to no harm, as you know full well. She is under Inslip's care and attended by servants." He almost offered to produce the groom, but didn't know if the man would back his half-truths. Or if Inslip would, for that matter. Any hint that Georgiana had accompanied him in truth would doom her. "I will not condemn Miss Whittaker to another situation not of her choosing. Nor will I be branded a fortune hunter."

"You would rather be branded a cad?"

"That is not an issue. If necessary, I will retire to the country. London is rapidly losing its charm anyway."

"Flight would imply guilt, raising new suspicions about her." She held his eyes. "You will wed the girl. If pride won't let you use her fortune, then put it in trust for your children."

"No. Do you want to lend credence to Herriard's lie?"

"I'll see that it won't."

"Even your power has bounds, my lady. You cannot force me, nor will your conscience let you malign her when you know full well that she is blameless. As for marriage, Inslip will bring her out next Season, though she may surprise him by refusing. She has a low opinion of men and a lower one of the aristocracy—not that I can blame her, given her experiences."

"You did not think poorly of my power when you came here."

"I don't. Your word can expose Herriard's lies in a trice. But I draw the line at accepting a marriage I do not want. Miss Whittaker is in good hands and will remain so."

"Oh, you want her. I can see it in your eyes."

"Balderdash!"

She smiled. "You haven't changed a bit, Hughes. Just as prideful and touchy as when you came down from school. I won't condemn you in public, and I'll refute Herriard's claims. But I urge you to reconsider. There is a spark in your eye whenever you mention her that tells me you are not indifferent. I suspect you know her better than you care to admit. Don't let pride stand in the way of the best marriage you could find."

Richard cursed himself, but relief was stronger than irritation. Lady Beatrice would expose Herriard, and she would let Georgiana prove herself worthy. One meeting would convince her of Georgiana's character.

He needed to return to the cottage posthaste but kept himself in check for another quarter hour while Lady Beatrice related the news of the day. Then he excused himself and headed back to Kensington.

Georgiana nearly followed Richard out of the sitting room. She knew nothing about entertaining lords—not even barons like Derrick. What was she supposed to do with a marquess?

The question was answered when Tester silently deposited a tea tray at her elbow and departed. It had been years since she'd presided over one, but she hadn't forgotten how.

Inslip set her at ease with tales of her grandfather, who had been one of his closer friends. They were alike in many ways. While she suspected that Inslip could be ruthless when necessary, today he had chosen kindness and the same bluff camaraderie she had found with her grandfather. Perhaps she could be comfortable with his family after all.

"It would be best if you accepted invitations immediately," he said once he'd explained how the guardianship would work. "All else aside, your appearance will go far to lay Herriard's lies to rest."

"You do understand that my governess left when I was fifteen."

"It doesn't show. And my wife will review manners with you. Your most pressing concern will be learning the names and stations of those you will meet. And clothing, of course, though her dressmaker can remedy that soon enough."

Her reply died when Tester returned, a round silver tray resting on one palm. "A message for you, my lord. Urgent, he said."

Inslip accepted the missive and broke the seal. His forehead creased into a frown.

"Problem?" asked Georgiana as Tester departed.

"A small one, but it needs immediate attention. If you will excuse me, my dear? We will expect you by dinner tomorrow. Tell Hughes to arrange for a decent gown. Mademoiselle Jeanette dresses my wife. Let her know

that Lady Inslip will return with you on Wednesday to
order a complete wardrobe.''

"Thank you, my lord.''

He pressed her hand, then left.

Georgiana paced the sitting room, turning the meeting
over in her mind. Richard was right. Not all nobles were
venal. Her grandfather had been a loving man who had
tried always to do the right thing. Inslip seemed the
same—as did Richard, she admitted. He was kind and
caring and nothing like his reputation. He might be a
prankster, but he wasn't callous or cruel. Even the bear
had served a purpose and done no real harm.

She was guilty of judging without facts. Worse, her
complaint that Richard blew hot and cold and held himself aloof applied a higher standard to him than to herself. She was doing the same thing—pushing him away
for fear that he wanted her trust.

I have no use for heiresses.

It was true. He'd not turned cold until Stagleigh mentioned her inheritance. Then his eyes had flashed in fury—
not because she'd withheld information, as he'd claimed,
but because he wanted none of her money. If anyone had
seen them together and cried compromise . . .

She reviewed everything that had happened since
she'd entered St. George's. He'd put himself out to help
her, even during his sister's wedding. He'd protected her
from Derrick, made arrangements for an honorable future, and kept servants close at hand to guard her reputation even as Derrick was blackening his. Not once had
he taken advantage of her. She wished he had.

You are so blind!

She needed his arms around her. And not just because
she felt safe in his embrace. He stirred her as no other
man could, making her long for his touch, his lips, his—

It was only gratitude, she insisted, refusing to believe
that she could fall in love so quickly—and with a rake,
of all people. She'd been desperate to escape Derrick.
Richard had stepped in to help. Of course she would
feel grateful.

But her heart didn't believe it. Inslip's plan to bring
her out did not interest her. She did not want to parade
about London's marriage mart seeking a husband. The

only man she wanted would walk through that door any minute.

So how could she overcome his antipathy to her fortune?

Pacing produced no ideas. Nor did leafing through those books. They merely raised peculiar sensations she didn't know what to do with. She was wondering if throwing herself into his arms might work when a commotion in the hall announced his return.

She sank onto the couch and raised the cup of now-cold tea to her lips.

Derrick strode through the door.

Tea splashed across the carpet.

"What are you doing here?" she demanded coldly. But her heart was already hammering in her chest. She'd seen that look before, though never directed at her. The last time, he'd beaten his heir badly enough to confine the boy to bed for a week.

"Returning you to the bosom of your family." His smile belied his cold eyes.

"No."

"I am your guardian, Georgie. You will do as I say."

"The bishop disagrees. Now leave. You are not welcome here."

He laughed, a dangerous sound. "The bishop won't rule until tomorrow. Today I'm your guardian and master of your fate. Did you really think to escape me?"

"How did you find me?"

"Followed Inslip. The minute I got that notice, I knew he would lead me to you."

"So you lured him away."

"Enough. It's time you learned your place, Georgie."

"Never!"

"You have no choice. My word is all that matters. The arrangements are made. You will be Stagleigh's wife by dinner."

"Not when he learns how badly you are cheating him."

"I have a signed contract. There is nothing he can do now." He jerked her to her feet.

She screamed, dragging her nails down his face before he could pin her arms.

"You'll pay for that," he grunted as she kicked him. His slap snapped her head sideways. Twisting her against him with an arm like a steel band, he dragged her toward the door.

Tester was sprawled in the hall, unconscious.

8

Richard spurred his horse toward Kensington, a growing fear that something was wrong urging him faster. It made no sense, but he had to make sure that Georgiana was safe.

He dodged through a narrow gap between two wagons and cut down an alley, grateful to have his own horse beneath him instead of Saturday's slug. It willingly broke into a canter.

Tension mounted as he considered the disasters that might befall her. He shouldn't have left her behind, even with Inslip. The man didn't understand how beastly Herriard could be.

Logic stepped in to point out that Herriard didn't know where she was. There was no need to ride *ventre à terre* to her rescue. But he didn't slow. Nor could he outrun Lady Beatrice's voice, which still hammered at his head.

She could not seriously believe that Herriard's lies could harm Georgiana. Not with both she and Inslip denying them. So she must mean to manipulate him into marriage. She smiled indulgently on young men sowing oats, as long as they played by the rules. But her indulgence ended at age thirty, by which time she demanded responsibility and an eye to the future. Since he was rapidly approaching that age, she would expect him to set up his nursery. Jacob's marriage had cracked the carefree image of the Beaux, encouraging her.

He admitted that he needed a wife. Just not Georgiana. No matter how much he liked her—and two days in her company had made him like her a lot—she remained ineligible. His allowance let him live comfortably. Once he acceded to the title, he would have even more, though he hoped that day would not arrive for many years. He did not need to fill his coffers with someone else's fortune.

He turned a corner and nearly ran down a carriage headed toward Mayfair. Not until it passed did he identify the crest.

Inslip.

He kicked his horse to a gallop. There was no reason that Inslip's departure should portend disaster, but he knew Georgiana was in trouble. His dread increased when he spotted a strange carriage in front of the cottage.

Herriard. It had to be.

He tossed the reins over a bush, then charged through the door. Tester lay bleeding on the floor. Herriard was dragging Georgiana from the sitting room. His bloody face stirred Richard's pride that Georgiana had put up a good fight.

"Let her go," he snapped, leaping forward. His fist caught Herriard's shoulder.

Georgiana twisted free.

"You've annoyed me for the last time, Hughes." Herriard shoved Richard off balance.

Richard ducked a would-be facer, then landed a blow to the chest.

Herriard yelled for his coachman.

Georgiana gasped as Derrick's coachman jumped down from the carriage, clearly visible through the open front door. She bolted across the hall to lock it.

"Bitch!" snapped Derrick even as his fist slammed into Richard's jaw.

The housekeeper rushed in and screamed when she spotted her husband.

Derrick sidestepped a punch, tripped on Tester's leg, and staggered.

Georgiana pulled the butler out of the way as Richard took advantage of Derrick's distraction to aim a kick at his groin.

"Foul!" cursed Derrick, twisting so the blow landed on his thigh.

"Gentlemen's rules apply only to gentlemen," snapped Richard.

"Then counter this." Derrick pulled a long-bladed knife from his boot and charged.

"No!" Georgiana grabbed Tester's tray and spun it toward Derrick. It struck his wrist, deflecting the blow. She jumped on his back, ripping at his hair as Richard grasped the man's knife hand.

"I'll kill you!" choked Derrick.

"Never!" Richard's free fist plowed into his jaw. A second blow struck his temple.

Derrick crumbled, unconscious.

Richard kicked the knife aside, then pulled her into his arms. "Are you all right?"

"Yes."

"Are you sure? He hit you." His hand gently traced her cheek.

Sparks raced down her spine, weakening her knees. She hooked her arms around his neck to keep from falling. "It was only one slap, but thank God you arrived when you did." The memory set her whole body trembling.

"Steady, sweetheart," he murmured, pulling her head against his shoulder. "You acquitted yourself well. Don't fall apart now."

"I c-can't stop."

"Reaction. I should have realized . . ." He sat on the stairs, pulling her into his lap. "Put your head down. You'll feel better in a minute."

Rushing blood muffled all sound. Spots danced before her eyes, but closing them but made the world seem even vaguer. From a great distance, she heard Richard send the housekeeper for cord.

By the time the woman returned, Georgiana had pulled herself together, so Richard set her down and trussed Derrick, then bent over Tester.

"Is he all right?" she asked, irritated that weakness kept her from helping. But the thought of rising turned her stomach over.

"He's coming around. Can you get him to bed?" he added to Mrs. Tester as the butler shakily sat up.

The housekeeper nodded.

"Good. Send for a constable when you have him settled."

Richard helped Georgiana into the sitting room, berating himself for leaving her. He should have postponed his visit to Lady Beatrice. Salvaging his reputation meant nothing compared to Georgiana's safety.

Seeing her in Herriard's grasp had put his pride in perspective. He loved her. Even the thought of her wed to someone else made his blood boil. No one would cherish her as he could—and would. The devil with what others might think of his choice. And the devil with whatever names they called him.

Instead of settling her on the couch, as he'd intended, he pulled her against him, needing her warmth to convince himself that she was truly all right.

"Forgive me, sweetheart," he murmured in her ear. "I should have protected you better."

"You did everything you could."

"Obviously not. Herriard found you."

She pulled back to meet his gaze. "Richard, you have done more than anyone could expect. If not for you, Derrick would have caught me at St. George's. Or at Hawthorne House. Or the Yellow Oak. Or any other place we've been." Her hand cupped his cheek.

He turned to place a kiss on her palm. "I should have done more."

"Why?"

"Because I love you." When her eyes widened, he kicked himself for making the declaration sound like a curse. "I love you," he repeated, softening the tone. "I should have realized it earlier, but my pride refused to accept that Fate had offered me the perfect wife when I least expected it."

"Pride can be a problem," she agreed, sliding her hands into his hair. "I've enough of it myself. When I realized who you were, I thought you were helping me so you could take over my inheritance."

"I ignored my attraction because I didn't want your inheritance."

She nodded. "I finally realized that. Only then could I admit that I love you."

His heart swelled at the words. Bending, he kissed her softly, then with increasing urgency. Her taste exploded in his mouth, branding itself on his soul. Her hands explored his shoulders as she pressed closer against him. Love burned away the last fear, opening the doors to a future he had never dared consider.

"I love you," he repeated, laying her on the couch. "You're mine. Forever."

Epilogue

Four weeks later Richard stood before the altar at St. George's of Hanover Square and watched Georgiana approach. She was breathtakingly beautiful in a gown that showed off her glorious bosom and clung to her sleek legs. Her smile made him wish the service was over so they could be alone.

Totally alone. The past month had been too frustrating.

Herriard had escaped from the constable and fled the country. But he was no longer a problem. If he ever returned, he would be hanged, thanks to Stagleigh.

Stagleigh's fury when he discovered Herriard's deceit had forged an alliance with Richard. His revelations had not only supported Richard's charges but added new, more serious ones, sealing Herriard's fate.

Richard was content to give Stagleigh the credit. All he wanted was Georgiana. She had taken society by storm, becoming so popular that they could rarely steal a moment alone. But their betrothal was finally over. Tonight . . .

She reached his side, radiant in the light streaming through the stained-glass window beyond the choir. Thunderous organ music lifted his spirits higher than ever. As he raised her hand for a lingering kiss, the heat in her eyes nearly buckled his knees. Tonight . . .

The bishop stepped forward. "Dearly beloved . . ."

Richard kept his eyes fixed on Georgiana's. Only a month had passed since he'd last heard those words. Who would have guessed how much could change?

When it was time for his vows, his voice filled the

nave. "I, Richard . . . take thee, Georgiana . . . for richer or poorer . . ."

Love was worth more than any fortune. Love and Georgiana.

A Marriage of
True Minds

by
Edith Layton

They came out of the shadows, and he was surprised to see they were smiling.

"Wotcher," the bigger one said conversationally, greeting him.

The gentleman paused. It might only be that they'd ask for money, he thought. But he doubted it.

The night was advanced, at least so far as he could calculate after all the brandy and wine he'd drunk. It was definitely nearer dawn than midnight. That was why he'd lowered his guard, walking the empty, darkened streets without looking to see who else was there, strolling along unconcerned as though it were noon. That, and the fact that he was on the street where he lived. So far as he knew, there was never any crime here. He suspected that was about to change.

They stood under one of the new flickering gaslights, and so he could see they were both big men with rock-hard faces. What surprised him apart from their affability was that they were dressed like gentlemen in fashionable evening dress, with clean white linen and impeccably tied neck cloths, and they both wore greatcoats and high beaver hats. But he didn't recognize them, and he thought he knew all the gentlemen in London.

"Good evening," he answered calmly. He wasn't afraid as much as he was curious. That wasn't wine- and brandy-born courage; he knew he could handle himself. It remained to be seen if he could handle two men.

"Evening, m'lord," the first one said pleasantly enough. "Do we have the pleasure of addressing Lord Powell, then?"

"I'm no lord, but yes, I am Powell," the gentleman said.

The smaller of the two—which was like saying the cliffs of Dover were smaller than the Alps, the gentleman thought, spoke up. "Well, then," he said, "we'd like a word or three with you, your lordship."

"I'm not a lordship," the gentleman repeated. "But I'm listening."

"Leave our sister alone," the bigger man said.

The gentleman frowned and cocked his head to the side. "And she is . . . ?" he asked, trying to think which of his flirts at the opera, theater, flower market, dressmaker's shops, or any of his favorite brothels she might be. But none of those females seemed likely to have protective friends or relatives. If anything, they'd have relatives or friends trying to promote them. And these well-dressed but rough-spoken fellows obviously couldn't be related to any of his highborn paramours.

"See?" the smaller man asked the larger one. "She means so little to him he don't even know who she is. This'll be easy. Look, your lordship," he said, turning his attention back to the gentleman. "Thing is, she means a lot to us. She's young and impressionable. We got nothing against a gent sowing his oats. Only natural. But we got a lot against one trying it on with our sister. She ain't no fancy mort, and we're here to dissuade you from paying her your attentions." He looked at the larger man again, seemingly proud of the large words he'd used.

"And she is?" the gentleman asked again. "Forgive me, gentlemen, but it's late, I've drunk deep, and this isn't making any sense to me."

"We're not gentlemen," the bigger man said, "but we'll tell you. She's Joanna Littleton."

The gentleman's expression of mild inquiry didn't change. He shook his head. "Again, please? Or at least, if you'd tell me where she and I met?"

Now both men's expressions hardened. "You having us on?" The bigger man growled. "It won't wash. You know who she is, and we're telling you it would be healthier if you forgot. We don't want you to see her no more, period."

The gentleman's head began to ache. Brandy and wine did not mix, at least not in his stomach or his brain. He rubbed his temples. "Forget her? Gladly," he said. "Because I don't remember having seen her in the first place."

A sound came from the bigger man, very much like a growl. The gentleman looked up—just in time to see a fist coming his way. He ducked reflexively. When he bobbed up he swung his own fist, deliberately. He had the pleasure of feeling it connect with the big man's jaw. And then the pain of his knuckles felt as though they had hit a wall.

The smaller man tried to grab his arms and clip them behind his back. The gentleman snarled, twisted, turned, and hit him square in the nose.

"Nay, leave off, Jules," the big man told the smaller one, as he shook his head. "This is betwixt me and him. One on one, the gent's way."

"But I owes him one!" Jules protested somewhat thickly, as he held his bleeding nose. "He drew my cork!"

The bigger man didn't listen; he was too busy circling the gentleman, looking for a way to get through his guard. He did, spectacularly, throwing a punch that made the gentleman reel back, seeing stars, wondering if his head would fly off the way his hat had done. Then he plunged back with a right fist that spun the man around as it hit his shoulder, because he'd ducked and avoided a certain hit to his chin.

They bobbed and weaved and punched, the gentleman flying back and lunging forward, the big man landing a blow and then receiving one. They kept at it, no one man winning or losing, until a window in a house above them was thrown open with a loud snap.

"You ruffians!" a furious female voice screeched. "A fine thing, roistering in the streets when decent people are sleeping. I've sent my footman for the watch!"

The fighting stopped abruptly.

The large man looked at his opponent, who had taken the pause as an opportunity to bend and gulp in great gasps of air. "Aye, we're leaving," he said, panting and glowering at the gentleman. "But I'm telling you, Viscount, leave our sister alone. Next time I won't play by Queensbury rules. And next time I'll let my brother join in too!"

"We got to go, Malcolm," Jules told him anxiously, glancing up and down the dark street. "We stay on till the watch comes and Dad'll skin us, he will!"

"Aye," Malcolm said. Giving the gentleman one last threatening look, he added, "Remember!" before he bent, scooped up his hat, and lumbered off back into the shadows with his brother.

The gentleman stayed, bent double, one hand on the rib he was sure was now cracked, the other on his knee as he hung his head and caught his breath. "Viscount, eh?" he muttered low. "By God, I do not believe it. But I'd best go see, anyway."

And then, seeing figures appearing at the top of the street, he straightened and strode away as fast as his aching body permitted.

Leslie, Lord Powell, the Viscount Powell, turned his eyes from the papers on his desk in his study, rose, and greeted his brother warmly.

"Terence! What brings you here at this early hour . . . and what happened to your eye?" he asked as he got a better look at his brother. "I thought you reigned over everyone at Gentleman Jackson's boxing salon. Who clipped you one?"

"Nothing gentlemanly about it," his brother said wryly, tentatively touching the black-and-blue swelling even his valet's application of a leech this morning hadn't reduced much. "I got it in the street last night, or rather, early this morning, as I was toddling home. I was attacked by some villains who thought I was you."

His brother checked. He cocked his head. "Surely not," he said. "No one's angry at me. Except for old Baron Witticombe, of course, because I snatched that excellent book on the history of the Barbary apes right out from under his nose, so to speak. But he's hardly a villain. Though he is a fool, because he left the bidding at the auction up to his man of business, and that fellow didn't know that Witticombe would have paid twice over what I got the book for. If he does take revenge, it will be at the next rare-book auction and not in the streets. I doubt I've offended anyone else, and know no one who would resort to bodily harm if I had."

It didn't look as though anyone would be angry with the Viscount Powell enough to so much as snub him. He was a slight young man who usually wore a pleasant expression, and looked as gentle as he was soft-spoken. He had light brown hair, his teeth were white and in excellent condition, and he often showed them in a peaceful smile. But he looked older than his years because of his mild expression and manner. His face was as thin and craggy as his brother's, and his blue eyes were as keen, but he wore spectacles over those eyes when he was reading, and that was most of the time. Overall, the impression he gave was that of a sober, sensible, and much older man.

His younger brother, Terence, looked very like him, but had darker hair and eyes, and more musculature, because he was a bruising rider and an avid sportsman. But Terence had the same noble nose and high cheekbones. On him they looked rakish and dangerous.

Terence frowned. He knew Leslie's life was as mild as his manner. "Thing is," he said, looking at his brother's walls of books instead of directly at him, "they got angry when I said I didn't know what they were talking about. They were commoners rigged out like gentlemen, but they spoke like barrowmongers. They said you were to leave their sister alone."

Terence expected laughter or an exclamation of incredulity. The absolute silence that greeted his statement made him look at his brother, who was frowning and looking uneasy. Then his was an expression of absolute incredulity. "You *have* been messing about with a cit?" he asked in astonishment.

His brother's thin cheeks grew ruddy. "I shouldn't call her that, because it's insulting. Though I suppose the slang term means only that her parents are not of the nobility, though they now have the funds to live like such. But I'd rather you didn't use the term, Terence; I really would rather you did not."

"No!" his brother breathed, sinking slowly to a chair. "After all these years of living like a monk in a book cellar, when you finally do feel some sap rising, you take up with a commoner? And a mushroom at that? Lud, Leslie! It isn't just because she's beneath our class. You could cozy up with any bit of muslin you care to, and no one would say a word—but a bourgeois? A respectable burgher's daughter? It isn't done. They expect marriage. You can't deliver that!"

"Can I not?" Leslie asked softly.

His brother stared.

"I first saw her at a booksellers'," the viscount explained quietly. "And though we'd not been introduced, we began speaking, because we'd both reached for the same book at the same time and our fingers met. In no time I realized that our minds met and matched as well. Of course, I couldn't help but notice how lovely she was. In short, I returned to the same shop the following day, at the same hour. And so did she. We spoke again. Then I knew we had to meet again. I introduced myself and asked if I might call on her. And she quietly refused."

"Refused?" Terence asked in surprise.

His brother nodded. "She said it would not do, because we were not of the same class and station."

"Well, the chit's got sense, then," his brother said with relief.

"But I could see that she wanted to say yes," the viscount went on. "It was in her eyes. She has remarkable eyes," he added dreamily. "So I kept going back to the shop. So did she. And soon she agreed to meet me in the park so we could walk and talk together. We did; we do. And now the thing is that I wish to marry her." He ignored his brother's gasp. "I know her emotions match mine and that she wants to accept my offer. However, there are obstacles."

"I should say!"

"Her family would not welcome me."

His brother rose from his chair as though he were being pulled upright by invisible hands. "What?" he cried. "What family wouldn't want you as a son-in-law? Why, if you'd ever get your nose out of books long enough to go to some *ton* parties you'd see you're prime goods on the marriage mart. You'd be like a spring lamb offered to the wolves—I mean the mamas and their unwed daughters. You're young; you're titled and rich as you can stare! And a nest of cits—they'd be on their knees thanking God if you just looked at one of their daughters." He began to pace. "Mark my words," he said darkly, "this must be some deep scheme, a fine rig they're running. Lucky I'm here to see you don't fall into it."

"You, Terence?" his brother said softly. "But now here I thought I was the one who extricated you from that difficulty with the opera dancer your first year at university. Speaking of which, wasn't I the one who met with that professor of English studies a few years later, and proved that you deserved to be graduated, and with honors, no matter what you'd said to him? Proved with a little help from my friends on the faculty, that is."

Now his brother's face grew ruddy. "That was years ago. I've grown up since then."

"So you have. But I also remind you that though I may be only a year older than you, my dear Terence, I was made head of the family at an early age, and never disappointed anyone in the performance of my duties."

"That's exactly it!" his brother said. "If you'd sown a few wild oats, you wouldn't be so vulnerable now."

"But I did, though admittedly more quietly than you did."

"Oh, certainly," his brother said dismissively. "That's why I've never seen you on the town or heard a word about a mistress or a flirt of yours."

The viscount smiled. "Yes, that's exactly why. I haven't been celibate, brother, only selective. Because I discovered early on that making love without having love be part of it was unsatisfactory. At least, so it is for me. I know it's unusual, but I can't enjoy the act of sex unless I enjoy the person I'm indulging in it with." He shrugged. "An abnormality, to be sure. But if I don't at least like the woman, it's not very much fun, and is actually uncomfortable for me. The face and form may be there, and may entice, but I don't like to make love to a creature with no mind or heart. Mannequins don't tempt me much, or if they do, they never satisfy me."

His brother looked acutely uncomfortable.

The viscount's smile was apologetic as he gazed at his

brother. "So you see, since few women who sell themselves are to my liking, and fewer still those who simply
look for sport without emotions involved, my indul-
gences are infrequent and seldom result in long-lasting
relationships. But what else is there for men of our class,
apart from marriage?" He sighed. "Now I've met a
woman who suits me heart and soul, and who I know
would suit my body. But she won't marry me."

Terence sighed too. "All right, then, just for the sake
of argument. Why won't she marry you?"

"Her family has utter disdain for the upper classes;
they want her to marry among her own kind. The problem is, they don't understand there are few her equal
and fewer still of her kind. She was brilliant to begin
with, and they've educated her far beyond their class,
and ours. Not many women even in our set are half so
learned or in love with knowledge. She is a swan among
geese, you see, and would be in any class. She's exceptional. She's beautiful and gentle, and wise, and—"

His brother flung up a hand. "Enough! She's Athena
and Aphrodite and Aristotle all in one. I understand."

"I hope not Aristotle," the viscount said, smiling. "I
should hate for her to grow a beard."

"And her family wouldn't want her to marry an eligible young nobleman?" Terence added, raising an eyebrow at the nonsense of the idea.

"No. You see, their experience of our breed is not a
happy one. Her family is part of a huge clan here in
London. They are artisans, or merchants: greengrocers,
haberdashers, and the like. Her father made his fortune
by the work of his hands. He was a wheelwright who
invented a most ingenious device, a simple pin for carriage wheels, ensuring their stability. It's now used on
every carriage in England. He invested his money to
make even more. They live well, and have educated their
children, but they tend to stay with their own kind, as
we do. And the point is that her family does not care
for our sort. Well, and who can blame them?" he asked,
and answered himself by adding, "Being merchants and
the like, they came to know the nobility as people who
live on credit, paying their bills only under duress. They
see members of our society as unfeeling, self-involved,

ignorant, and either abusive or unaware of any people they consider of a lower class—which is most of humanity."

The viscount's thin face grew sad. "They want her to marry well, but not above her class. They're afraid that if she does she'd be snubbed by her husband's family and friends, and eventually disdained by him as well."

"Well, that's so. I mean the rest, not that you'd disdain her, ever," Terence said quickly, as he saw a rare gleam of anger flare in his brother's mild eyes. He knew what most people did not: Leslie, Viscount Powell, possessed a wicked temper, though it was rarely seen and even more seldom acted upon. "Society would not accept her easily, if at all."

"The world is changing, Terence," his brother said. "We are in a new century."

"But with the same people who were in the old one. And so I'd think if you want her to be happy, you'd let her alone."

"Ah, but I *am* an arrogant, selfish nobleman," the viscount said with a slight smile. "I want *me* to be happy. And I earnestly and honestly think I'm the best one to make her happy too. As for acceptance, you know I'll never be comfortable in high society, as you are. I'll be very glad to settle with her at the Hall, far from London and its styles and fancies, where we can raise our children and read our books in peace." A faraway look appeared in his eyes. "Maybe we'll take an occasional tour of some interesting archeological site. I think she'd like that too."

He straightened and looked straight into his brother's appalled eyes. "So I intend to keep seeing her, and courting her. If you fear her relatives' wrath, take a footman with you when you go out raking of a night. You don't look *that* much like me, after all, except in the dark."

"But what about your safety?" Terence asked.

"Oh, I can take care of myself," his brother said airily. "Thank you for the warning, though. With any luck we'll be wed before much more harm is done. Once we are, there'll be no more trouble. Then you'll see for yourself what a joy she is, and as much as I love you, brother, I so believe that to be true that I don't dare let you meet her until she's promised to be mine. You haven't that reputation of a rake for no reason."

"And her family?" Terence asked, so aghast at the extent of his brother's infatuation that he let the slur on his honor slide.

"They will come 'round, in time. I'm not such a bad fellow after all, and they do love their daughter dearly enough to accept whomever she marries. They've let her choose her own way until now, after all. There's been many a suitor she's rejected that they approved. In time, I hope they will more than approve of me."

"And her brothers?"

"I imagine their idea was to keep me away from her. Her brothers may not be happy when we marry, but I'm convinced they'll accept it. As will our family, or so I hope and expect. They've been urging me to wed since I came of age, you know. We're a small family, after all."

"About to get smaller," his brother said glumly. "This will kill Mama."

The viscount lived in the family town house in a select part of London. Terence's bachelor quarters were only a street away. He left his brother's study and went down the hall to the door, deep in thought. This was a marriage he had to prevent.

Leslie's attitude toward sex gave him more food for thought. Terence knew his own reputation; that didn't mean he liked having it. He didn't precisely *enjoy* purchasing his pleasures. It wasn't his preference. It was just that he'd found no other way to have them. So instead of buying a female for a night, he'd always taken some willing and lovely young woman under his protection for a month or two . . . seldom longer, he realized now. Because what his brother had said about making love to a mannequin rang true. He, too, found physical attraction and spiritual repletion seldom came in the same pretty package. It was just that he tried not to think about it and seldom acted on it . . . or rather, he corrected himself with a cynical smile, he seldom didn't *not* act on it.

But then, Leslie was the deep thinker, after all. He

himself, as second son, was the man of action, the joke-ster and roisterer. Always had been, so they'd said. Odd, he thought now, how willingly he'd accepted his parents' assignment of his expectations. He had to admire his brother's willingness to strike out for himself, even as he deplored the way in which he wanted to do it.

Their father had died when he and Leslie had been boys. Their mother had looked for a man to lead her, although she didn't want to marry again. And so Leslie, always studious, had grown right into the role. Terence had accepted him as head of the family too. He'd never doubted Leslie's role as the elder and wiser. Until now.

But this! Marriage to a commoner? Doubtless the girl was lovely; Leslie wasn't entirely ruled by his mind. A tasty young tidbit would be just the thing to make him act like a boy for the first time. And if she were shrewd as she could hold together, she might well have him thinking like a prospective husband for the first time too.

Terence pictured a lively buxom lovely with a dazzling smile and flashing eyes, tempting as Salome, and what-ever Leslie had said, common as the dirt in Hyde Park. She'd be hard to displace, especially if she was wise enough to withhold her body until his brother gave her his hand.

Terence took his hat from a footman and left the house, still preoccupied with thoughts about his brother's paramour. Would she be redheaded or blond or Gypsy dark? He wondered about it as he went out the door. His brother might live for his mind, but he had eyes and other working glands. He couldn't see Leslie being so seduced by a mouse. Or a dunce. No, he envisioned the temptress as bright and wanton, a captivating piece with curls and smiles, and breasts like buttresses. . . .

He stopped in his tracks when he saw the very image of the girl he was picturing standing waiting for him as he came down the short stair to the street.

She was dressed like a lady, but her looks were so bright and vivid she might have been an actress—and one he'd pay to see more of. She wore a fashionably correct high-necked blue gown, but there was nothing correct about the high breasts and slender but amazingly shapely form it covered. She wore no paint, but didn't need any to emphasize her startling good looks. Her eyes were wide and green-gold, her skin clear and white, and her hair . . . what he could see of it under her dashing bonnet shone smooth as a banner of silk, and was the color of sunset.

"There you are!" she said in a well-bred, modulated voice. "I must have a word with you."

He inclined his head. "Gladly," he said. "And the person I am going to have a word with is . . . ?"

"Oh," she said wrathfully, "I think you know that!"

"I'm afraid I do," he said. "It is Miss Littleton I am speaking to? And your brothers I had the pleasure of meeting last night? How is Jules's nose, by the way?"

"A deal better than your eye," she said spitefully.

"Doubtless," he said mildly.

She cocked her head to the side. "But wait. You're not Viscount Powell. You fought like a fury, they said, and had a left like Molyneaux himself. I wondered about that, because I'd heard that the viscount was a scholar, more at home in a library than a court of fives. . . . Aha! I have it. You must be his brother, the rake. Of course! I told them they'd got the wrong man. Never mind," she told Terence, dismissing him and looking up at the door, as she gathered the hem of her skirt in her hand, preparing to mount the stair. "It's your brother I have to talk with."

"And you're not the Miss Littleton your brothers were warning my brother against, are you?" he asked, assessing her openly.

"No," she said, holding up her head. "I should say not! Joanna wouldn't visit him at his house, and I'm here to see she never does."

"So am I," he said.

She paused and looked at him searchingly.

"I think, Miss Littleton, that we have much in common," he said. "Speaking of which, it is rather common to discuss it here in the street. Would you like to come back to my rooms?"

Color flew to her cheeks at the word *common*. It flared to flame when he suggested she go with him. Her eyes widened. "I should not like to go back to your rooms," she said through clenched teeth. "I don't like even speaking with you in the open." Then her magnificent eyes narrowed. "If you think that is common, let me tell you it is most uncommon for me to accost a man in the street, even one who styles himself a gentleman. One, because I see no such thing before me. And two, because only the most dire need would move me to speak to you at all, sir!"

She stopped and stood breathing heavily, looking as though there were much more she could say, but had thought better of it.

He eyed her with interest. "I always thought the phrase 'bosom swelling with indignation' was merely literary license," he commented. "Now I know better."

She clenched little gloved fists, as well as her teeth. "If I didn't have manners, I promise you you'd soon find out what else can swell—you do have another eye, you know," she said wrathfully. "You, sir," she said, lifting her chin, "are no gentleman, and no better than your brother, I expect."

"Now, wait just one minute," he said, taken aback. "I'm all sorts of a rogue, and don't deny it. But my brother is innocence himself."

"Indeed?" she asked triumphantly. "You think luring a decent young woman into his clutches is innocent? Well, I can see we do indeed come from different worlds."

"He is not the one being lured," Terence said. "He is not a lurer. I mean, he is the one being primed for the trap."

"Oh? And striking up a conversation with my poor innocent sister, and then scraping up an acquaintance, and *then* arranging to meet her on the sly is not luring?" she asked angrily. "An interesting interpretation you put on words, I see."

"This is getting us nowhere," he said. "Except for one thing. I begin to see you don't seem to want this match any more than I do."

"Much less than you do!" she cried.

"I doubt that," he answered with as much of a superior smile as he could manage, considering that one side of his face didn't respond as well as it usually did. "But if that's how you really feel, we might work together to both our benefits, and for the betterment of our siblings. Allow me to introduce myself. I am Terence Powell, the viscount Powell's younger brother," he said, giving her a curt bow. "And I have the dubious pleasure of addressing . . . ?"

"Miss Valerie Littleton," she said, head high.

His difficult but definite attempt at a superior smile grew wider.

"I daresay you don't know any Valeries," she added haughtily. "My parents were very taken with the name, although it is not common in your circles, I believe. In fact, it's likely that all the young women you know, or at least all the young *ladies* you know," she corrected herself with a smirk of her own, "are named either Mary, Elizabeth, or Charlotte."

He looked stung. Because in that moment he couldn't think of any other names of any proper young females that he did know. It took him a moment to reply. "Harriet, too," he finally said. "And I have a distant cousin named Jane."

She bit back a smile.

He didn't. "Come," he said with a more natural grin. "We agree at least on one thing: This is a match neither of us wants. Not because of your class," he added quickly.

"Indeed?" she asked, arching one thin russet eyebrow. "Then it is something about my sister you don't care for?"

"I don't know her," he admitted.

"Aha," she said. "So I thought. Well, at least I will tell you straight-out that I don't want my sister marrying into your family or your class. She's tender, softhearted, and sensitive. Even if your brother's intentions are honorable—especially if they are, in fact—you and your kind would run right over her and squash her flat. I won't have that."

"I agree," he said. "Not that I would, but I do know my world. But just as devil's advocate, I wonder why you think that. Your parents' dealings with their customers must have been very bitter, indeed."

"Perhaps they were," she said. "I can't say. They haven't been actively in trade—at least, not in a shop—for a generation. I speak for myself in this, sir. You see, I went to the same fine academy for well-brought-up young ladies that my sister did. The same kind of one that your sisters went to as well, I daresay."

"I have no sisters," he said.

"Nevertheless," she said, tossing her head, "I meant sisters of those of your kind. I know plenty of their sort, and too intimately, I promise you. I learned my letters and figures at school with them, and also learned that young women of high birth are closed-minded, snobbish, and cruel to anyone they consider beneath them. Never mind that only garden snails are beneath them in intellect. They judge everyone by blood."

"I'll wager you let out enough of theirs if they dared judge you, at least if they did so aloud," he murmured.

"You'd win," she said with a pleased nod. "Now, as to what we are to do. I have a few ideas."

"Good," he said. "But we can't keep standing discussing it here. If you won't come to my rooms, at least let us walk."

She nodded.

They strolled off down the street, close enough to talk. And yet, for both of them, not nearly far enough away for comfort. They walked in silence for a while.

"Are you alone?" he finally asked.

"I should think not," she said, holding her head high.

He couldn't help approving the sight of that proud head. She was really remarkably attractive, he thought. However, he couldn't approve of the fact that she didn't have a maidservant following them.

She saw his expression. "Your reputation's very well known," she commented, "and believe it or not, I have a care for my own. But my class of person doesn't require that I have some easily bribed maidservant creeping along behind me, pretending to keep my virtue. The fact that I have a footman and a brother or two in the carriage that is slowly following us down the street is good enough for us. We're merchants, we Littletons, you see, and so we're literal-minded. We prefer results to window dressing, reality to illusion, truth to—"

"I see," he said, cutting her off, "that you also prefer to gild the lily in your analogies. I understand: You're well protected. And that I am an evil, good-for-nothing rake. The point is taken."

"I don't know how evil you are," she said fairly. "Nor do I care. What I do care about is making sure my sister doesn't fall into your brother's clutches."

"My brother doesn't have a clutch to fall into," he said testily. "He's a scholar, pious as a church mouse, in fact."

"Oh," she said thoughtfully. "Then we must have been misinformed. He never had Lily Orton, that dancer from the opera, in his keeping? Or financed La Starr, the famous courtesan, for at least a month of Sundays last year, when I suppose he ought to have been delivering his mousy sermons—at least, to hear you speak."

She smiled, turned her head to see his reaction, and had the pleasure of seeing the rim of a nicely shaped, closely set ear turn red under his high beaver hat. He was furious at her, but managed to keep his temper reined in. But then, his manners were very fine. His looks, of course, were devilishly good. She could easily see how the fellow had gotten his reputation. *Poor Joanna,* she thought sadly, *if his brother is a patch on him, this will be even harder. than I thought.*

"We did some research, you see," she said sweetly, when he didn't answer.

"I do see," he said angrily. "But if you wanted to bring those sorts of liaisons up, you should have sent your brothers to talk to me again. I remind you that a well-bred young woman should never even mention such things!"

"There," she said with satisfaction. "See? More pretense. We're supposed to know these things and never say them? Absurd. Perhaps it would do for females from your set. We're used to plain pound dealing. So, now that I've established how far we are from each other, though we share the same city, shall we at last get down to brass tacks? Can you keep your brother away from my sister?"

He glared at her. "Can you keep your sister from him?"

"I'll try. But it would be simpler if he stopped tempting her."

"The shoe," he said carefully, "is on the other foot."

She stopped in her tracks. "My sister is not the one who started this."

He admired the way her eyes lit with anger.

"My brother is a healthy male, to be sure," he said reasonably, "as you so carefully pointed out. But he's not in the habit of enticing anyone. He wouldn't know how. All he's ever has done, I think, is open his wallet and he finds females clustered around him. Opening his mouth would bore most of his paramours to death."

She gritted her fine, even white teeth. "But my sister neither needs or understands money," she said through them. "Books are the only things that excite her. Books, and small furry animals," she added fastidiously, "and evidently also vicious, lying, deceiving noblemen."

"Well, that's rather too bad," he said mildly. "And I don't know why you came to me, then. I know some men like that, but I'm happy to say I'm not related to any of them."

"So you won't help me!" she said furiously, wheeling around to confront him.

"I never said that. I just don't know what you want of me."

They faced off opposite each other.

"I want you to keep your brother away from my sister!"

"And I want you to keep your sister away from my brother."

The carriage that had been following them stopped. It took both of her brothers to argue the livid Miss Littleton into leaving the street, and then bodily remove her from the area.

"Nicely done, lads," Terence said, as they gently but firmly maneuvered her into the carriage.

They glared at him. But not so furiously as their sister did as the coach drove off.

Too bad, Terence thought, when she'd left. That had been exhilarating. And worrisome. If Valerie Littleton's sister had half her verve and life, not to mention charm and address, he was going to have a formidable job ahead of him.

The town house that the coach stopped at was a fine, high, brick-faced building on a street of similar elegant houses not far from the park, and not so very far from the Viscount Powell's town house, either. It was, however, Valerie Littleton knew, worlds apart from his. This was a different section of town, however fine; it was one where no person in society would live.

Two houses, like in money but unalike in dignity, she thought sadly, deliberately misquoting her favorite poet, as she went into her house.

The agitated woman who confronted Valerie as she stepped into her front parlor was plump and middle-aged, with a sweet face that looked unfamiliar with the lines of distress it showed now. "Well, did you see him?" she asked Valerie. "What did he say? Lord, you look knackered! Mind, I said he'd be surprised, and mad as fire. Your going to talk with him must have put the cork in it. So did it work?"

"Oh, yes," Valerie said wearily, taking off her hat and putting it on a side table. "He was taken aback, and mad as fire, and he hates the idea of a match with Joanna as much as we do."

"Well, there you are," her mother said in relief, smiling again.

"But I didn't speak with the viscount, Mama," Valerie said, "only his brother. And I don't know if he can do any better with his brother than we can with Joanna. He as much as said the viscount is fixed on her. And as his brother is the elder and the one with the title, I don't think he has that much say in the matter. We can, of course, try to speak to the viscount himself. But now I don't have high hopes of that doing any good, not if he's as stubborn and proud as his brother. In fact, it might make matters worse. Tell a man like that, one accustomed to having his high-handed way, that he can't have something, and he'll want it all the more."

"So what do we do?" her mother asked anxiously.

"Well, you know what I say," Valerie's brother Malcolm said as he and his brother trailed her into the room.

"And I know that's impossible, Malcolm, so do forget it," Valerie said with annoyance. "You and Jules may be big as dray horses and fancy the idea of being wicked young bloods, talking rough and acting tough as all the young blades do, but you're not criminals. In fact, you've never mixed it up with more than your friends, have you?"

They looked as sheepish as big men could.

"You, Malcolm," his sister persisted, "are studying law. And Jules, what of your plans to buy your colors and go for the cavalry? Neither of you needs a prison term—and I promise you, laying hands on a nobleman would net you that; even Father's money wouldn't buy you out of it. It's only blind luck that you attacked the fellow's brother by mistake."

"We could hire one—a criminal, I mean," Jules said petulantly.

"Aye, so I said," a voice said from the doorway. A thin old man with wispy hair stood there. "I could find us a few regular bone crushers!" he added.

"I'm sure you could, Grandpa," Valerie said kindly. "But we won't be using them."

"Oh, aye," he said petulantly. "What was good enough for your grandpa ain't good enough for you no more."

"It was never good—or bad—enough for you, Papa," Valerie's mother said in appalled shock. "Whatever are you going on about? You may have known them from the old neighborhood, but you never used bullyboys to sell your goods, never once, not ever. Right, Mama?"

The tiny old woman ensconced in a deep chair by the window nodded her silver-white head. "Right and tight, lass. Never once did he. Never had to neither, not even when bad lads tried to give us trouble and get him to move his barrow to another street, or pay them off for staying on. There was enough of them other lads—good ones, even if they had the name of bad ones, you ken—to stand up to 'em. Because we had respect in the old place. Respect is better than two fists in the eye, says I. So stop spouting nonsense and belt up, Nigel, do," she told her husband before she turned her attention back to her granddaughter. "Now, what's to do, lass? Let some flash nob ruin our Joanna?"

"Never," Valerie said. "But there's no talking to their sort, as you said, Granny. We have to solve it ourselves. And it's best we keep Father out of this too."

"Not 'ard," her grandfather said. "Your da's got 'is nose so deep in 'is workshop, 'e wouldn't know if the 'ouse burned down over 'is 'ead."

His granddaughter nodded. "So it's up to us. We can'
kill the fellow, no matter what the boys say. And we
can't cripple him either," she said, shooting a look to
Malcolm, "if only because I don't think it would stop
him. The nobility have fixed ideas that force can't shake.
They love the idea of a challenge because they're so
unused to it. That's why they're always the first to ride
off to war. They refuse to take no for an answer." She
frowned as she remembered how the wellborn girls from
her school used to keep at her until she agreed to help
them with their studies, and the more she protested, the
harder they'd try.

"No," she said, shaking her head. "We have to end
the matter at its source: with Joanna. He can't lure what
isn't interested in being caught."

"Aye," her grandmother said. "That's it. Can't catch
a fish that won't take the bait, like I said!"

They all looked at Valerie. She sighed. "All right,"
she said wearily, "I'll try again."

"Right," her grandmother said comfortably. "There's
a good girl. Go have a nice long coze with her, dearie.
Try to make her see common sense. And then we'll lock
her in her room."

The carriage slowed, then stopped, but no one got
out immediately. Whoever was sitting in it was gathering
courage, no doubt, Terence thought with a surge of satisfaction. He let the edge of the curtain in his brother's
front salon drop back into place, and felt his pulse race.
His instincts were right: She was back—she or her sister.
Though he wanted to see what the girl who'd gotten her
hooks in his brother looked like, he hoped it was her
sister come to see him again. *Come to see Leslie again,*
he corrected himself.

"What are you looking at?" his brother asked.

"You're about to have a visitor," Terence said.

"Ah!" Leslie said, "which explains why you've been
visiting me every day since Joanna's sister met you. I
knew there had to be a reason for such sudden fraternal
devotion. Not that I don't like your company, Terence,
you know I do. But I mistrust it."

"I'm simply watching out for you."

"Indeed? Why? What do you think would be the worst consequence of my relationship with my Joanna?" his brother asked mildly.

Terence felt a knot in his stomach at the words. Leslie was saying "his" Joanna? And this after he'd gone out again last afternoon, and then disappeared, at least from his surveillance, just as he'd done the day before.

"The worst?" Terence asked, trying to sound casual. He reached for a seedcake on the tea tray for something to do while he composed himself. "I suppose hearing that you're being ostracized, as well as talked and laughed about all over town. After that? I imagine seeing you suffer the slow realization that a misalliance of the first water had been made. After the first blush of infatuation even the soundest marriages are held up to scrutiny, or so I hear from disgruntled husbands as soon as they are no longer newly wed." He took a bite of cake he didn't want and added, "And then later, the knowledge that your children are bearing the brunt of it as well. That's all."

"Indeed?" the viscount asked, glancing at his brother. "You know, I'd throw you out on your ear right now if I didn't think you'd come back in again." There was steel in his voice and a glitter in his eyes behind his spectacles as he added, "You've said your piece, and that's the last of it I want to hear. You speak of what you know nothing about."

"He jests at scars that never felt a wound? No," Terence said. "I agree I've never thought I was in love. I worry because I have heard the way those who flount convention are talked about. I'd like to see you spared that indignity."

"It's only an indignity if I care about it, which I don't."

"And as for Mama and the rest of the family?" Terence asked.

His brother shrugged. "I try to be a good son and I have a care for the family name. But I won't sacrifice my future happiness on society's altar, because I believe it to be that of a false god. And so, I thought, did you." He eyed his brother. "You're not entirely the rascal you pretend to be, Terence. You read and write as well as you drive and ride, and I know it. You attend the theater for more than meeting actresses in the greenroom, and you go to the opera for more than selecting dancers from the corps de ballet. You can quote the Bard as well as I can, and you're not insensitive . . . or so, at least, I'd thought. Ah," he said with relief, looking up as the butler appeared in the doorway. "We have company?"

"Yes, milord," the butler said. "A Miss Littleton wishes to speak with you."

The viscount straightened, his eyes suddenly aglow. "Bring her in at once," he said.

Terence rose from his chair. He looked to the doorway, and his polite smile slowly grew into a genuine, if smugly satisfied one. It was Valerie Littleton who stood there. She wore a green walking dress, and a pert straw bonnet sat atop her shining hair. Green suited her to perfection; she looked like a breath of spring in the countryside, Terence thought. His thoughts immediately turned to other country things she'd look good on or in, like on a bed of grass, or in a sweet-smelling haystack. . . .

She looked at Terence, raised her pretty little nose in the air, and turned to his brother. Those keen golden-green eyes studied the viscount for a moment before she spoke.

"My lord," she said, "I am Joanna's older sister, Valerie. I come here today only to return some of your property." She handed him a book whose spine proclaimed it was a study of early Roman waterworks in rural England. "This is yours. Or so my sister said. As she's not going to meet you again, neither in public or private, I am delivering it to you."

"I see," Leslie said softly, turning the book in his hands. "And she agreed to this of her own free will?"

"Eventually," Valerie said. "I know she had an appointment with you yesterday that she didn't keep, as she won't keep the one she had today, or any in future. It's true that at first she didn't see reason, but in time she did. When she did she asked me to return the book to you. I'm here to tell you that your revels now are ended." She looked enormously pleased with the way his eyebrows went up at her quote. "It was an ill-advised friendship, my lord, and in time I hope she will come to see the absolute truth of that."

"My intentions were honorable," Leslie said softly, looking down at the book.

Terence grew rigid.

"As were hers," Valerie said. "But though you mightn't think it, as I know your brother doesn't, our family doesn't wish to see such an alliance. If," she added, "such was, indeed, really the case." She raised a gloved hand. "I'm not here to argue that, my lord. That's as may be. One thing I do want to make sure you understand: Many in our position *would* wish to advance themselves by cutting a dash in society. Our family doesn't, thank you very much."

She met his eyes steadily. "We have attained wealth to equal yours, my lord. You claim to know my sister, so you'll surely agree that we've achieved as much scholarship as well. We always had wisdom. So then why should we court rejection by trying to foist ourselves on a society that clearly disdains us? If our class tries to join yours in any fashion, whether in housing or clothing, or even by going to the same plays or parties, we're sneered at, denigrated, and snubbed. We're called mushrooms, I suppose for the way we seem to have pushed ourselves up through the dirt."

She raised her head high. "We did come from the dirt, the good earth we tended. And we may have been serfs when your ancestors ruled us. But our ancestors were here before yours came, and we are fully as proud as you are. You may breath a sigh of relief, Mr. Powell," she said, turning to Terence, "as we did, when my sister came to her senses." She nodded a curt excuse for a bow. "Good day, then."

Leslie looked at her thoughtfully. "Good day," he said, sketching a bow. "See Miss Littleton out, Terence, would you?" he asked his brother.

Valerie frowned.

Terence shot his brother a troubled look before he joined Valerie. He walked out of the salon at her side. He didn't speak until the footman had opened the front door and she was on her way down the steps.

"It is really over, then?" he asked.

She paused and looked up at him. "Yes, of course; otherwise I wouldn't have said it. But is your brother always so . . . tepid? I mean wishy-washy? It was rather like being afraid to beard a lion and finding only a lamb instead."

He scowled. "Yes and no. I expected more bombast too. At least a good argument."

"Me too," she said, looking puzzled. "And if you knew Joanna, you'd know it wasn't like her to give up so easily. I mean, we were going to keep her in the house. Not by tying her up, I assure you," she said quickly, "or even locking her in her room, as my grandmother suggested. But we were going to keep her under close watch. There didn't seem to be any need, though. She's been perfectly complacent, only asking to go to the lending library, and when she did she never minded my going along with her. Apart from an initial argument, she's absolutely accepted the ban on her seeing your brother. . . ." Her remarkable eyes met his dark knowing ones.

They stared at each other.

"She's up to something!" she exclaimed just as he said, "He's up to something!"

They smiled, both looking happier than they ought to have been.

"I suggest we discuss this," he said.

She nodded. "But not here."

"Of course not. Over lunch, then? You don't have to like me, Miss Littleton, but surely you don't want to starve me. I *am* hungry. So would you accompany me to Thatchers? It's a very respectable restaurant not far from here." He glanced at the coach waiting at the curb. "We can sit in the window so your brothers can see us dine. Of course, if you'd rather not be seen with me, we can sit in a dark corner. But I refuse to take lunch with either Malcolm or Jules."

"You remembered their names," she said, sounding curiously pleased.

He touched the almost vanished splotch of a yellowish green bruise around his eye. "Not likely to forget. So how about it? We can walk or I can call a hackney, but

I'd rather not ride with them. And I think your brothers will have a fit if we get into a different carriage alone."

"You're right," she agreed. "We'll walk. Let me just tell them where I'm going . . . and why," she added with a slight frown, as though she anticipated trouble with that. "And then we can eat if you like, but I know we must talk."

Terence frowned as he glanced around the restaurant. "This might not have been such a good idea," he said.

"Why?" Valerie asked.

"I hadn't realized, but we're being looked at by more than your brothers. A gentleman doesn't take a young woman to luncheon alone."

She shrugged. "Much I care. Or at least, I don't care if you don't. But if the thought bothers you . . ." She started to rise.

"No," he said quickly, "please sit. It was for your sake that I mentioned it."

"I don't travel in your circles, sir, and have no intention of doing so."

He looked puzzled. "Don't the men in your set care about such things as reputations?"

"Of course!" she said with a smile. "Even more than in your set, I think. But everyone knows our predicament now. If word of this luncheon got out I think I'd be seen as a heroine for trying to protect my sister, and daring to beard you in this den."

He smiled at her play on words.

"And then there's Jules and Malcolm, of course," she added. "It's easy to be courageous when you have two absurdly big brothers. Admittedly it was rude of them to threaten all the other carriage drivers away from that spot in front of the restaurant. But I confess, Malcolm's getting out of the coach and loitering there at the curb would be enough to spoil anyone's appetite, much less any rake's intentions. So my reputation, at least, is secure, at least where it counts."

"You really don't care what people will say?" he asked curiously.

"*Your* people, no," she said. "What can they say, anyway?"

"You're young and lovely, and an unknown, and dining with me? They'll put the worst construction on this meeting, you know."

"Oh, *that*." She laughed. "They'll hardly put that sort of construction on it. My hair might be an unfortunate shade, but I'm dressed as conservatively as any proper miss. I don't look like any of your bits of muslin!"

He gazed at her a moment before he spoke. He looked so serious she thought he was going to scold her again for mentioning things a lady shouldn't. His face was even more handsome when set in serious lines, she thought sadly. A somber expression allowed his classic features to be seen clearly, without the overlay of his charming smile to distract from them. It was just too bad that he was what he was, she thought, and surprised herself by feeling a tiny bit rueful because she wasn't the sort of female he'd thought she was.

"I do have the reputation of a rake," he said, "although, believe it or not, it's exaggerated. But since I do have the name, I admit I have some experience of the women you mean. And so I have to agree. You don't look like any of them. You're far lovelier."

Her cheeks grew pink. But she didn't look away from him. "Just exactly what you should say," she said, nodding. "You've confirmed every one of my preconceived notions. You see, I've never met a rake before."

He raised an eyebrow.

"Not a bonafide high-society rake," she explained. "Although of course we have many a fellow who's known to be in the petticoat line. But in my set, rakes are called 'ladies men.' Though that's too mealymouthed for most of my relatives. They'd call you a John-among-the maids, a man of the town, a muttonmonger . . . a buttock merch—" She stopped before she finished the phrase she realized was much too rude to utter. Her color rose higher as she looked down and concluded quickly, "And worse."

He started. Then he threw back his head and roared with laughter. If they hadn't been noticed before, they certainly were now. Even Malcolm, pacing outside where he couldn't have heard, saw Terence's obvious merriment and scowled.

"I can imagine," Terence said as he subsided to grins. "Don't blush. I asked for it."

"Yes, but you see," she said sadly, "I'm not joking. That *is* how they speak. You've heard those expressions before because it's how the young bucks of your set speak—until they decide to grow up and stop slumming." She leaned forward and spoke softly, her words measured. "Mr. Powell, that's only one way in which your family deals with mine. For generations my family provided services for your family, and still would, if my father weren't so amazingly inventive. Your father didn't have to do anything to improve your lot in life, I daresay. Mine improved ours out of mind, exactly by the use of his fertile mind."

She took a deep breath. "My family likely served yours on farms and in stables," she said bluntly, "or in haberdashers' and at dressmakers' shops, and at fruit barrows and yes, even fish markets. But come what may, we are determined that my sister will not serve your brother as his mistress. And," she added forcefully, "we won't have her shamed and shunned, even if he has decided to ask her to be his wife. For so she would be. Not only by your family, you see, but by ours. We don't like people who try to reach above their stations either."

"But your father did," he said.

She shook her head. He thought her smile grew as soft and sad as that of a medieval painting of a sorrowing Madonna. "No," she said. "My father reached above his economic station. We cheer him for that. He did not, could not, and would not try to reach above his social station. Nor would your family and those like them permit it. You see? It is a crucial difference."

She saw a waiter approach and took another deep breath. "So," she said, starting to rise from her chair again, "perhaps it would be best if we ended this meeting now, and simply promised to keep watch on our siblings, for both our sakes."

"Please sit," he said, "and stay for lunch. We are agreed. So we can meet here, at least, as equals, to try to save our families, can't we?"

She hesitated, and then sat again.

"But first," he said, "We have to order. The oyster pie here is a real treat."

She grinned. "Well, so, of course a rake would want that, wouldn't he? I think the shepherds' pie for me, though." As soon as the words were out, her eyes widened and her hand flew to her mouth. "I didn't mean to be crude," she said. "I spoke lightly, without thinking. We are not so straitlaced at home, you see, and I—"

He held up a hand. "Please," he said, "don't apologize. It's refreshing to meet a young woman who isn't mealymouthed." But she still looked distressed, so he added, "I don't know about most young misses, but I assure you that once a lady is married she can say much warmer things and still be considered a lady. My own mother is particularly fond of racy jests. Don't let it bother you."

She smiled with effort, and tried to believe him. It was one thing to not want his brother to marry her sister, another to think she'd given him good reason to feel that way too.

"Now let's have something to eat," he said, "and not worry about anything else just yet."

He ordered their luncheon, and then started to ask her questions, and in no time she forgot to be ill at ease. In fact, they talked and talked, and time flew by. They both regretted the moment when their plates were cleared from the table, because they had so much more to say.

"But we haven't decided how to tell each other about the surveillance we must keep," Terence told her when she rose from the table.

She bit her lip, realizing that they hadn't spoken much about Joanne or the viscount at all. They'd started with discussing menus, and then gone on to their favorite foods, and then they'd talked about what they'd liked as children, and how they'd started to talk about the theater she couldn't say, but they'd been discussing Lord Byron's latest effort when the waiter presented Terence with the bill.

"I'll send a footman to you with the news," she said quickly, "if I so much as see Joanna stirring from her room."

"I'll do the same with Leslie," he said. "It won't be as easy, but I live only a street from him, and I'm on excellent terms with his butler."

"Good," she said with relief. She extended a hand. "Good day then, Mr. Powell, and thank you for a lovely lunch." She hesitated. "You made what might have been an onerous task into an enjoyable one."

He took her hand. "You understand," he said bleakly, "my wishing to prevent this marriage has absolutely nothing to do with you."

"Oh, yes," she said in an equally hollow voice. "As you must, of course, understand is the case with me. I do this entirely for my sister's future happiness."

He nodded. "I do understand."

They were still standing staring at each other, holding hands, when Jules stormed into the restaurant and took his sister's other hand, shot Terence an ugly look, and marched her away.

"It's not a very original place for us to meet," Terence apologized when he saw Valerie approach him. "But it was all I could think of."

"Oh, it will do," she said, looking around. "Originality doesn't matter. My brothers wouldn't think to ever find you in a library. Oh!" she added when she saw his expression, "I'm sorry. I didn't mean to be offensive." She smiled. "Believe me, when I mean to be, there'd be no mistaking it."

He grinned. "Yes, I can see that." He ran a hand over the back of his neck. "It's just that I hadn't realized I had such a dark reputation."

"It's not dark, exactly," she said. "But you are known as a . . ."

"A rake as well as a care-for-nothing?" he asked. "I'm not. It's just that by contrast to my brother I seem to be worse than I am. All I am is aimless, I suppose." His eyes searched hers. "I have sufficient money and insufficient inspiration, although that's no excuse. For what it's worth, since I realized that, I find myself dissatisfied with my reputation, as well as with my life."

She frowned, and pretended it was because of something she saw in the book she held. They stood side by side before a bookshelf, and spoke in whispers so as not to disturb the other patrons of the lending library. It was a vast place, filled with books and fashionable patrons. There were more scholarly libraries in London, but Valerie knew her family would become suspicious if she suddenly went to one. And so she told him, because she wanted to say anything that might ease his troubled look.

"Well, I'm no scholar," she explained, "at least not like Joanna is. I like a good book. But I don't do any studying now that I'm out of school, except of clouds in the sky and the fire in the hearth, when I'm daydreaming."

"What else do you like?" he asked suddenly.

She smiled. "Oh, music. And dancing—I do love to dance. I suppose I get that from my grandmother; she wanted to go on the stage. But of course the family wouldn't allow it."

"Interesting," he said. "My grandmother loved to sing. I remember her always singing as she arranged flowers or did little things about the house."

She wasn't surprised. He himself had a lovely voice, rich and soft. She could listen to him speak for hours.

"She always sang in the garden too," he went on. "She loved to garden."

He saw his companion raise one perfectly arched brow.

"She actually worked in a garden?" Valerie asked.

"Of course. Why shouldn't she?"

"I mean, got her hands dirty?" Valerie asked with a small smile.

He laughed softly. "My dear Miss Littleton, let me tell you that true ladies are usually up to their elbows in muck or manure, since most of them adore either horses or gardening, or both."

She ducked her head. "Maybe that comes with age," she murmured. "I only knew young ladies. I assure you the girls I went to school with left all the messes for the lower orders to clean up."

He felt terrible. "Do you like to garden?" he asked, and then could have bitten his tongue. She'd said her ancestors came from the dirt, and he hoped she wouldn't think he was referring to that.

"Actually, I do," she said thoughtfully. "I love the

countryside, especially if there's somewhere to swim."
She lowered her voice. "It's not done by ladies, I know.
The girls I knew didn't swim. I love to. When my father
made his fortune he bought a country house, a lovely
place by a river, and there's also a lake on the property.
My brothers taught me to swim because they were afraid
of what might happen if my sister or I fell in and they
weren't there. What happened is that I love to swim!"

He smiled, and at the last moment was able to refrain
from telling her how much he'd like to see it.

"And I like sweets too much," she added. "And
sketching. But I suppose that sounds very tame to you."

"No. I like more than the ladies, you know," he said.
"In fact, as I said, my reputation in that respect is exaggerated. I mean to say that knowing women . . . that
having a . . . that enjoying the company of . . ." He ran
a hand through his hair. "Lord! Do you know there's
practically no decent way I can tell you why I'm not
really as indecent as you think?"

He looked endearingly confused. Valerie found she
didn't know whether to laugh or to pat his shoulder and
commiserate with him. She did neither. His was a very
broad shoulder indeed, and she remembered that reputation he was denying. She pulled herself up and said a
little too abruptly, "Well! This is all very interesting, but
time is marching on. Why did you ask me to meet you
today? Did you find that your brother is still seeing my
sister, or if he has plans to?"

"No," he said. "Actually, I wanted to meet with you
to find out what you knew. So far as I can see—and
I've been looking hard, believe me—he's accepting the
family's objections. He seems to have simply stopped
seeing your sister. That's not like him. He's mild-
mannered and polite. But also fiendishly determined.
And though he's not a bully or an autocrat, he *is* used
to getting his way."

She nodded slowly. "Like Joanna. A sweeter girl
never lived. But neither did a more stubborn one." She
raised her eyes to his. "What can we do?"

He stared down into her eyes and didn't say anything
for a moment.

Neither of them seemed to notice.

"We must keep watching, and meeting," he finally said.

She nodded, and swallowed hard.

He watched her mouth as she spoke.

"Oh, yes," she agreed.

They met in the dark, near the park, both of them having escaped the constant notice of those who had reason to watch them.

Terence took her hands, looked around, and frowned. "I didn't see your carriage. Your brothers aren't near? That wasn't wise. London after dark isn't safe for a young woman alone."

"I know," Valerie said. "I'm not alone. My maid is waiting in that hackney cab. We only have a moment. I had to tell you, and I didn't want them to know, because if I'm wrong they'll give Joanna a hard time. But now I'm very suspicious. She's much too complacent. She even hums when she reads. That isn't like her. You could blast a cannon by her ear when she's reading and she wouldn't know it. Humming means she isn't paying attention to what she's reading. Oh, you know what I mean. What has your blasted brother done?"

It was twilight, too dark to see well, but light enough for Terence to see the entreaty in her eyes. Her bright, lovely eyes. He wished he could see their color now. He'd been wondering if they were greener than gold, or more gold than green. The thought had preoccupied him since they'd last met. He hadn't been able to concentrate on the play the other night for thinking of it, and certainly hadn't a moment to spare a glance at any of the actresses in the greenroom. The mere name of the room had reminded him of her. He'd lost disastrously at Hazard too—the table had been covered with green felt. That was why he'd stayed in last night, and the night before, waiting for Valerie's summons. No sense gambling or hunting up other females when there was only one game in town, and one woman he waited to see.

"My brother is up to nothing, which is what alarms me," he said.

She nodded as though he'd made sense. "Exactly," she said. "So what do we do?"

"We keep watching," he said, watching her mouth.

"And waiting," she said, staring at him and licking her lips.

So, of course, he kissed her.

She gasped. He did too. But neither stopped. She leaned into his kiss; he gathered her closer. They sighed as one, and clung.

And then, finally, she remembered where she was, and who he was, and she found the strength to pull back. He let her go at once. She looked up at him and breathed a soft sigh of protest. And so did he. So he kissed her again.

She didn't have a thing to tell him, Valerie thought unhappily. Well, nothing apart from all the "how could yous?" and "how dare yous" she'd finally thought of saying a dozen times since the night they'd met. Because, of course, she hadn't said one of them then. Then all she'd done was to try to catch her breath and stand staring at him. After she'd finally brought herself to step away from him and his electric, startling, and utterly intoxicating kisses, of course. And then she'd turned and run back to her waiting hackney carriage.

Three days and nights had gone by since she'd met Terence Powell in the twilight, and there wasn't a reason to send him a note. Because apart from the fact that it would be not only unsatisfying but incriminating to berate him for behaving like a rake with her, at least on paper, she knew that she'd cooperated too well to have cause for such a complaint. And there wasn't a scrap of evidence of his brother's perfidy to provide him.

So Valerie hadn't been able to find one real reason to try on him that superior look she was perfecting. Nor one excuse to show him how easily she had forgotten those burning kisses, those disastrously sweet kisses, those devilishly unforgettable kisses.

He'd known just how long to hold those kisses too, she thought darkly. And just exactly how close to hold her. It had been like nothing she'd ever known. Well, but of course, she told herself again, he'd had practice. He was a rake. It was just that she hadn't known how very well rakes could kiss. And she wasn't likely ever to get another chance to find out, either.

Valerie sighed. But there it was. There was no reason to write to him to tell him anything. It seemed over. Joanna was smiling and happy, going about her everyday schedule with perfect calm, being so good, in fact, that her sister just knew she was up to something. Or was it, she thought with a twinge of guilt, only that she so earnestly wished she had something to tell Terence Powell? To tell him, while showing him how absolutely untouched she was by his kisses, of course, she corrected herself quickly, and slumped down in the window seat again. She stared off into space, and felt the phantom touch of those lips again.

It wasn't just the kisses, of course. Or the fact that he was so handsome, and smelled like soap and fresh-mown hay, and felt so right in her arms. She'd loved the way he laughed at her jests and had made her laugh too. He was clever and witty, and learned besides, shockingly so for a fellow with such a reputation. Even so, she'd felt she'd known him forever, and at the same time she'd felt there was so much she didn't know and yearned to learn. She supposed all rakes were like that, though. It was just too bad that was a thing she'd never get to know.

"Is it young McNulty, or that Cooper fellow you're dreaming on?" her grandmother asked.

Valerie's head whipped around. Her grandmother had come into the room and was watching her closely.

"Neither," Valerie said. "I'm just thinking."

"Oh, aye. Thinking about country matters, 'less I miss my guess. Now who could it be?" her grandmother wondered aloud. "Young Cooper's got blue eyes, but he's got a weasel's nose, and no gal of mine ever went for a face like that."

"Oh, I dunno," her husband said as he wandered into the room. "Fella's got a good foundry, coins money, I 'ears."

"Huh," his wife commented. "Hot iron ain't appealin' to any female, 'less'n it's his flesh that feels like that, o' course."

Valerie looked pained, but her grandfather and grandmother grinned at each other.

"Now, that McNulty fellow has shoulders," her grandmother added thoughtfully. "But a weak chin. Though I got to admit he rakes it in with that farm produce trade of his. But no female never looked so moony-eyed over a fellow's rutabagas," she said, and added with a low chuckle. "'Less'n they're calling somethin' else that these days, of course."

"I don't know how you can make everything sound so salacious, Granny," Valerie complained, shaking her head.

"Aye, ain't she somethin'!" her grandfather chortled.

It was only true, Valerie thought. Granny had been a wild young thing, or so everyone said. She'd wanted to go on the stage in her youth, because she could sing a treat and dance like a Gypsy girl. Her family had had conniptions at the very idea. It was one thing for a female to turn her mind and her hand at a trade. There was no harm in honest toil. But everyone knew an actress worked at dishonest—or at least immoral—toil. Their family might be working and merchant class. But they were fanatically moral. Every female in their clan who ever gotten with child had married the fellow who had gotten them that way, as Granny herself always said.

Valerie tried for a faint smile, so she'd look faintly amused and not disturbed by what her grandmother said. Because her own shoulders had leaped at some of the words Granny had used, as she'd gone on about dark eyes, and mentioned a rake, and wide shoulders.

Valerie knew just how wide those shoulders had been. She'd clung to them to keep from falling as her knees had gone weak as water when he'd kissed her. Fire and water, she mused, because her stomach had felt on fire, and her—

"Oho," her grandmother said wisely, watching her. "Looks like lightning has struck twice around here. You and your sister."

Valerie sprang to attention. "What do you mean? What has Joanna done?"

"Nothing," her grandmother said with a wink as she put her forefinger to the side of her nose. "That's how I knows!"

"Oh," Valerie said in a little voice, as her shoulders slumped again. "Yes, *that* I know. So you don't think she's forgotten the viscount?"

"Oh, a gal never forgets," her grandmother said.

"So you think she's up to something?" Valerie asked, hope springing to her heart again. Because she could meet with him if she had something to tell him. Not that anything could ever come of it even if she did, except to ruin her sister's chance at happiness, she realized.

"A female is always up to somethin'," her grandfather said.

"Ain't that the truth?" his wife agreed.

"But you don't know of anything specific?" Valerie asked.

"Not a word," her grandmother said proudly. "If she's plotting, she's doing it good. My girls are always canny ones."

"Oh," Valerie said sadly.

"I understand that your brother is finally enthralled with a young female," Lady Powell said.

Her youngest son flinched. "That is as it may be," Terence said evasively.

"It may be disastrous," his great-aunt Elizabeth said. She was the matriarch of their family, a woman of great dignity and influence over them all. She sat straight in her chair, no part of her upper back touching it, the way she'd been taught to do since she could sit up at all. "As I understand, the young woman in question is of low birth. Don't try to deny it, Terence," she said. "Lady Bell had it from the Countess Foyle, and though they are dreadful gossips, they're seldom wrong."

His mother sighed. "I fear your great-aunt is right, Terry. After all, why ever else would you be spending all your time here at his house these days? You're fond of your brother, but you've never lived in his pocket before. I'm pleased that you're looking out for him, Terence, but it disturbs me precisely because you've never had to look out for him."

"Yes. He's the one who's forever taking care of you," his great-aunt said. "It was ever so, even when you and he were boys."

"Oh, yes," his mother agreed. "Remember the time when . . ."

Terence let her go on, because he knew no way to stop her. It hardly mattered; he wouldn't have to listen until he heard a question asked. He loved his mama, but she did like to talk. She loved to laugh and to be entertained too, and so she was lonely, even though she had two devoted sons, many lady friends, and a host of faithful servants. Tall, slender, with smooth skin and a sweet smile, she wasn't unattractive, even now. Still, after his father had died, she'd never encouraged any beaux.

Terence hardly remembered his father. He retained the impression of a tall, cool, dignified fellow he didn't see often, but who would always ask him if he'd been a good boy when he did. Since he could seldom say yes, there'd been little for them to talk about. After his father died he'd thought his mother hadn't formed another attachment because she couldn't find a man to equal his father. When he got older and saw the coldhearted arranged marriages common in the *ton* and remembered how reserved his father had been, he wondered if he hadn't been right all along, only in the wrong way. It occurred to him that his mother's extended widowhood might be precisely because she didn't want to find anyone remotely like his father.

Her family had been well connected, but were nevertheless enormously proud of the fact that she had married a nobleman. It was a matter of great pride. His father's family hadn't been mad for the match but had become reconciled. Leslie was now head of their clan, and Leslie's inherited wealth was as formidable as his intellect.

"But really, my dear, what do you have to say about all this?" he heard his mother ask. "A mushroom! No matter how much money he's amassed, her father was only a common laborer. It isn't as if she has any connections at all."

"Except in the fish market, or at the ironmongers'," his great-aunt added.

Terence scowled. But his mother didn't notice. She was too busy lamenting, "What could have possessed Leslie to think of aligning himself with such a female?"

Her son answered carefully: "No telling if he wanted to align himself with her, Mama. Except perhaps in a horizontal fashion."

"Wicked boy!" she said, very pleased, playfully tapping his shoulder. "You'd think you'd behave more properly with your mama."

"If I did, she might not talk to me as much," he said to earn another smile from her. "At any rate," he said glumly, "there's no evidence the thing was more than a passing fancy. My brother hasn't shown a hint of interest in anything but his books and his studies, at least not for the last few days that you say I've been loitering around here."

Or so it seemed to be, he thought on a concealed sigh. Because he'd been hanging around his brother like a sticking plaster since that glorious evening with Valerie, and those kisses he couldn't forget. Those kisses he'd woken in the morning thinking about, and gone to bed the previous night remembering. And he hadn't discovered a hint of a reason to send to Valerie since. Not so much as a rumor to tell her about so she could come meet him so they could discuss their siblings—and he could try for another kiss, or another hour of stimulating conversation. Because it was odd, but he found himself remembering the fun they'd had talking almost as much as he did those kisses. Though nothing could quite equal those kisses. He started to wonder again if the fact that he so liked talking to her was the reason that her kisses had moved him so much more than any other female's ever had done.

He wanted to see her again so he could know. But they weren't likely to meet anywhere by chance. They lived in the same city, but in entirely different worlds. They might brush shoulders at a public masquerade, or in a shop. Or walk in the park at the same time, sometime, or be at the same play or opera. But that was all, unless they arranged to meet.

And he couldn't just ask her to meet him. Then she'd have real reason to think him a rake. How could a gentleman of his class ask to see a woman from hers? Because though he now realized it didn't matter to him, he was sure that it would to her. She'd said so, after all.

And it would matter to Leslie, of course, he realized on an inward flinch, especially if Leslie had given up his interest in the sister because of objections to the match. He himself had made those objections perfectly clear, Terence thought, hadn't he, damn his hide?

Whatever the reason, his brother seemed entirely over his infatuation with "his" Joanna. And so what was he himself going to do with his very real interest in the fiery, charming, intelligent, and enthralling Valerie? And how could he find an excuse to see her so he could find out?

"But why then are you always here these days, Terry?" his mother asked slyly, cutting into his reveries. "I vow, I couldn't believe my ears when I heard about it. But I can't doubt my eyes. Here it is noon, we come to see Leslie, and here you are already camped out in his parlor, nice as you please, or jauntering about town, as is your wont to do."

"Jauntering?" he asked.

"Oh, well, you know. Going to Gentleman Jackson's to plant a facer, or some such. Or fencing at Angelo's salon, or riding, or sleeping off a night of gaming—the sort of nonsense you young bucks get up to. Most of you, that is. Not Leslie, of course." She sighed again. "So why is he vexing us in this way? Why couldn't he just sow his wild oats in the usual fashion, as you did, and do?"

Terence felt a twinge of annoyance. "I'm not exactly a worthless reprobate, Mama," he said. "I was perhaps a bit more of a rogue in my day than my brother, but—"

"But who couldn't be more of one than I was?" Leslie said as he strolled into the room. "At least, so far as you knew. Good afternoon, Mama, Aunt," he said, as he bent to kiss them both. "I expect you're here to see if I've kicked over the traces, given away my money, ruined the estate, and run off? Or even worse than I've heard the gossips are saying?"

"Why no," his mama said, looking guilty.

"Certainly not!" his great-aunt exclaimed, with outsize innocence.

"You're being a bit harsh," Terence said.

"Others will be more so," Leslie said calmly. "Be-

cause I do have an announcement, and I'm glad you're
here for it. It's about Miss Littleton, *my* Miss Littleton,"
he told his brother. "We've come to an understanding."

"But how?" Terence blurted. "How did you manage
it? I kept you under constant watch."

"Not quite," his brother said proudly. "You watched
me, but not the books I was reading and returning to
the lending library. We passed notes hidden in them,
like children at school. It's a true meeting of the minds,
you see. But I want more than that to meet. And so I
am delighted to tell you that she has agreed to be my
bride. I'm engaged to be married to Miss Joanna Littleton, and I've come to tell you that you will just have to
get used to it."

"Leslie!" His mother gasped.

"My word!" his great-aunt exclaimed.

"Oh, wonderful!" Terence said before he could stop
himself.

The family stood in a group at the front of the church,
and waited for the guests to pass by and congratulate
them.

"You can tell at a glance who's from which family, at
least the older ones," Valerie, who was standing next to
the groom's brother, said glumly. She gazed at the company that had crowded into St. George's to see the mis-
matched wedding of the year taking place after a
whirlwind courtship of only a few months.

Terence nodded.

One half of the older guests present were dressed to
their teeth, all rigged out in the highest stare of fashion.
The other half of elder relatives were dressed well, but
not in the height of the latest style. Not by a long shot.

He looked at his great-aunt, dressed in a rather rusty
green gown that might have been all the crack in the
last century. "Well"—he sighed—"but my family always
felt that a dollar spent has to serve the spender well—
and until their dying day," he added in a low voice.

Valerie looked at her grandmother, togged out in a
low-cut gown straight from the window of the finest
dressmaker in town. It was a pity, she thought, that the
fashion was to be barely clad. She was only glad that all

the jewelry her grandmother wore distracted the eye from all that bared wrinkled flesh. Distracted . . . or blinded, she thought, as she saw all her grandmother's diamonds winking and sparkling even in the low light. Her grandfather, at the other end of the room, was also dressed in the latest fashion. She thought he looked rather like an elderly organ grinder's monkey in its best penny-collecting suit.

She sighed too. "Yes, and my family believes that if it's not new, it's not worth putting on your back. Because if you have money, you must spend it so everyone can see you have it."

They sighed in unison and stood waiting, neither knowing what to say next, neither looking happy.

"Wotcher," the bride's grandmother said to the lady next to her as they stood together in the great vaulted vestry hall of the church. "That's a grand gown you got on, Lady Elizabeth, and that's a fact. Them styles are more the thing than this wipe . . . ahem, this hankie I'm wearing. It's got stays, don't it?" she asked, critically eyeing the antique gown the lady was wearing.

The lady nodded.

"Ah," the old women said wisely, "thought so. A woman knowed where she was when she put on one of them things; they kept everything in its place. Like pouring yourself into a mold, it was, not like this thing," she said, staring down at her high waisted gown with disgust, "with everything left free, to be jiggling higgledy-piggledy."

The groom's great-aunt, Lady Elizabeth, smiled with pride as she looked down at her own gown. "You're right. I never thought of it quite like that. Mind, this isn't what I wanted to wear today either. But my niece said I could not wear the full fashion, because she said she'd disown me if I wore a hoop."

"Young people today," the grandmother of the bride said, and shook her head as she glowered at the mother of the groom, who was deep in conversation with the bride's mama. "Still, your niece got a lot to say to my girl; I never seen two females take to each other so quick."

"They both complain about their children," Lady Elizabeth said. "Endlessly. It appears to make them very happy. No one else will listen to them do it, I imagine."

"Aye, and whilst your niece is a widow, and my daughter's married, she might as well not be, for all the attention her husband pays to anything that ain't on wheels."

"Is that the bride's father?" the lady asked, raising her quizzing glass to peer at a small, neatly dressed man standing deep in conversation with a gentleman. "Surely not."

"None other," the old woman said brightly. "Cleans up a treat, don't he? Hardly recognized him myself. Looks at least a shade lighter than when you seen him at the engagement ball, don't he? Well, but he's been soaking every day, on my daughter's command. Used cucumber mash on his face and hands too. See, he's always got grease and oil on hisself, 'cause he's always got his mitts in the gizzards of wheels and machines, inventing whatnot. Don't look like that gent he's chatting up cares what he looks like, though. Them two ain't stopped yammering since we got here."

"My nephew, Lord Chadwick," Lady Elizabeth said, clearly torn between pride and impatience as she looked at the dapper gentleman who was talking nonstop to the bride's father. "He's mad about carriages. He owns at least a score of them. Drives them too, when he's not pulling them apart and putting them back together, that is. They must be speaking about wheels and cogs."

The bride's grandmother nodded. "Likely."

They gazed around the great stone vestry and saw many of the relatives deep in conversation as well. If not everyone was as enthusiastically chatting, at least there was some intermingling of the families going on.

"Tell you the truth, Lady E," the bride's grandmother said, "I had me a bad time just thinking about today. But so far's I can see, it will all work out. You don't have to worry none. We won't live in your pocket no more than you'd want to live in ours."

"I cannot see where it would necessarily be a bad thing," Lady Elizabeth said. "It is a new century, after all. What cannot be changed must be endured, and I

believe we can do rather better than that. We all will
want to see the offspring that will doubtless result from
this day's work too. I also cannot see how we can avoid
it," she added, motioning with her chin to a couple
standing to the side of the vestry.

Valerie sighed again. "I suppose it was the right thing,
even though we tried to stop it. Just look at Joanna; I've
never seen her happier. Lord! She's radiant."

Terence glanced at the bride, who was holding hands
with her obviously besotted groom. Joanna was a pretty
enough little creature, he thought, but only a pale copy
of her vibrant sister. He glanced at Valerie again; he
couldn't stop doing that. She wore a peach-colored
gown, and she was the one who glowed, he thought.

"Speaking about radiant," he said, "look at Leslie.
He's incandescent with happiness. It suits him, lights him
from within. I haven't seen him look like that in years—
if ever."

Valerie thought the viscount was a perfectly fine fellow, but though he certainly looked happy, still she
thought he looked like a pale imitation of his vital, devastatingly handsome brother. Still, she could see that the
viscount made her sister happy. That was enough for
her. She could only hope it would always be so. After
all, she thought sadly, look at his brother, though she
herself could hardly bear to today. He had changed entirely in such a short time.

Terence had seemed smitten with her—until her sister
had become officially engaged to his brother. Since then
he'd been charming but distant, the very model of propriety. He never tried to kiss her again after that one
time. He didn't even stare at her lips anymore.

They'd seen each other often in the weeks since the
engagement, and talked to each other whenever they
did. She'd come to wait for those times eagerly, because
she found him even more entrancing than she'd first suspected. But he took no liberties, and didn't even look
as though he wanted to. She wondered if that was because of disdain for her class or dislike for her personally. The worst thing she could think was that it was
simply because even a rake wouldn't flirt with an in-law,

out of fear of having to become something even more intimately connected. She'd stayed awake too long on too many nights, wondering about that.

Now she dared ask him, in a roundabout way: "Do you think they can stand up to society and their families?" she asked him.

"They have no need to stand up to my family. My family's become reconciled to the idea. Your sister has obviously made Leslie happy, and we all want nothing but that. And too," he added with a tilted smile, "there's the fact that she's bright and charming. And there's the fact that your father is rich as Croesus, and an intelligent, well-spoken person. As are you and your mother. Malcolm and Jules aren't so bad either, once you get to know them. You should see some of the lads in the families Leslie might have married into."

Valerie didn't smile. "I see you didn't mention my grandmother and grandfather."

"You will note I didn't speak about Cousin Henry and Aunt Margaret, either," he said, tilting a shoulder toward that pair. "It's a matter of accents in both cases, I think. If you can understand one word in seven that Cousin Henry says, I'll award a prize. He's so highly educated no one can communicate with him. We *think* it's English he's speaking. And my aunt Margaret comes from Yorkshire. I'll say no more. Every family has its interesting relatives. It just requires getting accustomed to it."

She nodded. "Well, there will be sufficient testing of that theory today. But it's more than accents; it's the way we live. Wait until you see the feast my family has prepared," she said glumly. "It's not so much a wedding breakfast as a royal banquet. I suppose your family would have served only tea and toast?"

"With a smear of jam or two to liven things up," he agreed with a teasing grin. "You know, I believe that from this thesis and antithesis, we'll have a wonderful synthesis."

"Yes," she said. "At least for Joanna and your brother." She glanced at the couple with a wistful expression. "They are blissfully happy, as well as perfectly suited, aren't they?"

"I was talking about something even closer to my heart," he said.

She looked up at him.

"You must know," he told her seriously, taking her hand in his. "I've said it in every way I could, without speaking. I've tried so hard. I resisted touching you in order to show you I wasn't a rake anymore. I've not ogled you, not once, so you won't feel uncomfortable with me. I watched you out of the corner of my eye instead," he added. "You've no idea of how worried I was that my eyes would stick that way—just as my nurse always warned."

She smiled, and he took heart. "I talked to you for hours," he went on, "and never talked warm, not once. I don't know how I did it. Not that I'm a lecher," he added quickly, "but like to hear you laugh, and my best jests are a little warm."

His expression grew grave. "I haven't looked at another female either, nor do I want to, because not one of them is as good to look at as you are. By God, Valerie," he said desperately, taking her other hand as well, "by now I think I've proved my good intentions."

"What?" she asked, blinking.

"This is what," he said, and lowered his head. "I'm tired of being good," he whispered to her. "I don't think I can *stand* being good anymore. I'm tired of pretending. I don't want to see you at family affairs and try to think of reasons to see you again. I don't want to hang around Leslie's house in the hopes of seeing you, either. I don't want to be just your brother-in-law, Valerie. I want to be your own personal exclusive rake. Yours and no other's. I want to marry you, Miss Littleton."

"But our stations!" she exclaimed, her eyes searching his.

"Yes, I know. You are above me, far above my touch," he said desperately.

"Don't joke," she said in a frantic whisper. "You were ready to move heaven and earth to prevent your brother and my sister from being married. You can't have forgotten that!"

"Yes, I wish I could. I'm ashamed of myself. I've never seen him happier or more fulfilled. Your sister is perfect for him. And remember, had you not wanted them married we might never have met in the way we did, or been together scheming to keep them apart the way we did. You're responsible too. You *do* recall that you didn't want anything to do with my family either? I hope you've changed your mind. I tell you right now, I mean to make you change your mind. Unless I offend?" he asked quickly. "Unless you can't bear the sight of me? I won't force myself on you."

"You'd never have to," she whispered.

He smiled. "Miss Valerie Littleton," he said, drawing her close, "I don't care if you're connected to the king or to my dustman. I don't want to marry a family; I want to marry you."

She caught her breath.

That was answer enough for him. He kissed her.

"Well, there's a thing," the bride's grandmother said as she watched her granddaughter go into the best man's embrace. She frowned as she watched how enthusiastically her granddaughter was welcomed there. "I don't hold with carrying on, Lady E," she commented. "Leastways not in church. Nor nowhere if he's only trifling. I hope that lad's got intentions other than dishonorable, or he'll find his teeth on the floor, and I ain't sure I won't be the one to do it."

"Oh, his intentions are clear," the lady said. "And honorable. His mother and I remarked it days ago. And he confessed as much to us. We were pleased. She's handsome, bright, and good-natured, and it looks as though childbearing will be no problem for her."

"I had my five without breathing hard," the old woman bragged.

"As I thought," the lady said. "Excellent. His mother could have only the two. New blood will be good for the family. We have some cousins you will never meet, Mrs. Littleton. I need say no more. It occurs in the best of families, after all; only think of our poor king. But it does happen more often in those families that are not more . . . adventuresome in their unions, I believe. Terence pointed that out to us the other night, and one cannot help but think he is right. And not the least reason for his mother's and my satisfaction about the matter is that a wife will be the making of him, we think. He is not a wicked fellow, only aimless, with no good woman to keep him in line. How do you feel about the match?"

"Fine," the other woman said. "Well, mebbe not so fine. But there's no stopping a female in love. But what about you and your kin?"

"*I* think they suit. As for the others in my family? They'll just have to get used to it," the lady said, holding her chin high.

The old woman nodded. "Spoken like a true lady. Still, *two* of our gals moving in with the gentry?" she asked, shaking her head. "I ain't sure I like that."

"My dear woman," the lady said loftily, "I hardly see how that matters."

"Well, but you see, it ain't just my opinion that rankles. When our Joanna took up with a viscount, I thought his title would protect her from hurtful gossip and such. But now our Valerie and the younger son, rich and well positioned as he may be?" the old woman said doubtfully. "Truth is, I worries about gossip and slander. That would hurt her. And try as we might to toe the line, I can see where there might be cause. See, our side, y'know, they all doesn't speak so good. And not all of them is rich. And what they done in the past don't bear talking about, some of them, that is."

"The same," the lady said loftily, "may be said of our side. Only not within my hearing."

"S'truth," the old woman said with admiration, "I think we'll get on just fine."

"Naturally," the lady said. "And now? I hear you've prepared quite a wedding breakfast for us."

"The tables are groaning," the bride's grandmother said happily. "We hired a caterer that cost an arm and a leg."

"Good," the lady said. "I'm famished."

"We got musicians too," her companion said. "Some lad to play our new pianoforte—cost the earth, that piano did, for it's got paintings all over it, along with all the right keys. We also got three violinists, and a chap with a flute to join in. And a fellow with a squeeze box, 'cause I insisted. There ain't no good music without one. They'll be playing in the background whilst we eats. But I was hoping . . ." she said longingly, looking up at her companion, "if your side aint too stiff, we might just have us a knees-up later too?"

"Indeed? I was accounted quite light-footed in my day," the lady said, nodding.

"I *knowed* we'd get along! So now if we can just get our Valerie to leave off kissing your grand-nevvy, and him to let her go, and then get the bride and groom moving smartly, we can start the festivities."

"An excellent idea," the lady said as she offered the older woman her arm and began to move across the room like a ship under sail. "Shall we begin?"

The Marriage
Scheme

by
Lynn Kerstan

1

Pushing aside a screen of palm fronds, Julia Flyte crouched behind the ornate railing of the musicians' gallery and looked down on the Duke of Sarne's grand reception hall. Like fish in a clear pond, colorful and languid, the wedding guests glided across the marble floors, displaying themselves to acquaintances.

She doubted the bride had ever met any one of them.

Harriet the Bride, who had ordered her sister to keep her impertinent self out of the way, stood almost directly beneath the gallery, next to the ornate chair where the Duchess of Sarne was holding court. Harriet's repellent fiancé, Frederick the Many-fingered, had taken himself elsewhere, most likely in pursuit of a hapless parlormaid.

The reception hall was the size of a cricket pitch, or seemed that way to a girl who had spent nearly all her life in a rustic Staffordshire village. And yet, she had dreamy memories of assemblies in grand villas and palacios. Masquerades along the canals at Carnival time. Elegant ladies and flirtatious gentlemen dancing through life in silks and satins and jewels. She had watched them all from a distance, as she did now. But then she had been a child, huddled behind a balustrade or peering from out a window, imagining that one day she would swan into a glittering ballroom and capture the heart of a gallant prince, the way her mama had done.

"Come forward and identify yourself!"

Whirling, Julia unsettled one of the potted palms, grabbed for it, and found herself with arms wrapped around a rough tree trunk as she gazed toward the door at the rear of the gallery. Framed by the casement, a

sandy-haired young man was holding a folded umbrella
to his shoulder and fiercely sighting down it.

"Don't think this isn't loaded," he said, moving aside
to let a girl slip by him. "What think you, Ensign Eve?
A saboteur? A spy?"

The girl tugged at his sleeve. "Johnnie! You are frightening her."

Julia detached herself from the palm tree, made sure
it intended to remain upright, and brushed off her hands.
"Indeed he is not. I am never frightened. But I am, in
fact, something of a spy, because I am not supposed to
be in company before the wedding. I wished to see what
was occurring."

"Ah," said the man, grinning as he set down the umbrella. "Reconnaissance. Exactly what we are up to. I
think you must be Miss Flyte."

"Not yet. I am Miss Julia until Miss Flyte becomes
Mrs. Pildon."

"Two days until your promotion, then. Let me introduce you to Lady Eve Halliday, my adjutant, and I am
Johnnie Branden, or Lord John if you must. The youngest of the troublesome Branden brothers."

"He likes to be called General," Lady Eve said. She
looked to be about fourteen, all arms and legs and
angles, and was carrying a pair of toy soldiers. "He promoted himself."

"It's my army." He gave a little shrug. "I'm forced to
invent my own, you see. Ensign, you should take yourself off now. Go set up the Blenheim campaign while I
speak with Miss Julia."

Lady Eve looked mutinous. "We played with Marlborough's army last week. Besides, I already know what
you are going to tell her. I do reconnaissance, too."

Julia, a perpetual outsider, saw rejection darken the girl's
blue eyes. "If it matters, General, I should be glad of her
company. You appear to have come to me with bad news."

"Not necessarily. You might be delighted. But when
I glimpsed you skulking up here, I decided to make sure
you did not become the victim of a surprise attack."

"Now you really do frighten me."

He moved to the railing, Lady Eve following. Bookended by potted palms, the three of them gazed down on the reception hall, now more crowded than before. "This," he said with a sweep of his arm, "is a battlefield. It has been since before I was born, twenty-three years ago, and possibly since the day my parents were wed. Richard, Nicholas, and I are evidence of the occasional truce, and at times the war goes underground. Then the duke or duchess takes a decision or makes a demand, the other leaps to the opposite position, and the battle is on."

She looked up at him, at the serious expression on a face shaped for smiling, and felt her pulse begin to jump.

"Every year at this time," he said, "the Sarnes mark the anniversary of their marriage with a house party. The guests all know what to expect. Some accept the invitation because they enjoy the carnage, while others scrape up excuses to stay away. As you see, my parents enticed an exceptional number of witnesses this year by permitting Miss Flyte to be wed at Sarne Abbey."

"But how does this concern me?" Nothing *ever* concerned her. She and Harriet were wards of the duke, had been for nearly a decade, but she might not have existed for all the attention paid them by His Grace.

Color washed over Lord John's freckled cheeks. "Now's where it becomes a trifle awkward. I am not a disinterested party, you see. If the duke has his way, you are to become my wife."

Stunned, Julia saw the bleak amusement in his eyes—and the color leaching from Lady Eve's face. The girl hadn't known, after all, what he was going to say.

"S-surely not. I was presented to His Grace yesterday, when we arrived, but he said nothing of this. He didn't speak to me at all."

"At present, the duke and duchess are plotting tactics and recruiting allies. Most likely the guests are laying private wagers on the outcome. As soon as your sister and Freddy have set out on their wedding trip, the opening shots of the next campaign will be fired."

"I presume Her Grace has set herself to prevent the marriage?"

"The one to me, yes. She has targeted Richard, Lord Whitley, as your groom."

Lady Eve brightened. "If you choose Lord Whitley, you would one day be the Duchess of Sarne."

Julia went light-headed, thought she might swoon and tumble right over the balcony. From where she was standing, there was a good chance she'd land directly atop the current Duchess of Sarne.

"I am clearly at a disadvantage," said Lord John. "No money, not even enough to purchase a lieutenancy in a foot regiment. And as my wife, you'd become Lady John, hardly a title any self-respecting female would aspire to. There is my gazetted charm, to be sure, and my splendid good looks—"

"And your thick head," put in Lady Eve, regarding him with proprietary scorn.

He ruffled her hair. "No insulting the general, Ensign. Not while I am consulting with my fellow pawn. Giving her fair warning, at any rate."

"But what am I to do?" Julia said. "There is no sense to this. How have I become something to be quarreled over?"

"Oh, well, if you're looking for sense, you won't find it here. The Sarnes ran out of sensible things to quarrel about a long time ago. There are, certainly, good reasons for the duchess to provide Whitley a wife, who would be expected to quickly provide him with an heir. And Sarne imagines that a leg shackle would keep me anchored here, in safe harbor. But our wishes, you must understand, are irrelevant. Yours will not be considered at all."

"How will a decision be made? Will someone drag me to the altar?"

"No, indeed. We may be barbarians in spirit, Miss Julia, but on the surface we are quite civilized. I don't know what sort of pressure will be brought to bear on you, but if you are vulnerable on any count, they will suss it out and exploit it."

"You could refuse to marry me."

"Yes. And so could Richard. And you could refuse to marry either of us." He regarded her speculatively. "But if I were laying a bet, it would be that none of us will refuse. The only question is, which Branden brother will slip a ring onto your finger?"

A fire of anticipation kindled deep inside her. Could

it be? A young woman with no prospects suddenly furnished with a pair of potential grooms? From a ducal family, no less, and if the parents were a little odd, they were scarcely the only aristocrats in England with bats in their attics. Besides, a normal family would never consider inviting the likes of her into their company. She looked up into Lord John's hazel eyes. "Would you rather I chose you?"

"It would be ungallant to say otherwise, Miss Julia. Should you find yourself leaning in my direction, let us form an alliance and negotiate terms to our mutual benefit. I should like a property of my own, and you would not, I think, wish to live here at Sarne Abbey."

She thought, glancing again at the lavish marble reception hall, that she would like it very well indeed.

"Oh, Johnnie. Look there."

Lady Eve was pointing to the far end of the room, where the duke, surrounded on three sides by guests, was acknowledging a tall gentleman with dark hair. At this distance Julia could discern nothing more about the new arrival.

"By Jove," said Lord John, clearly astonished. "Hell must have frozen over. Lord Nick is paying us a call."

The middle brother. "Is anyone proposing *him* as my bridegroom?"

"Good God, no. Nicholas does precisely as he wishes, and he can get away with it because he has what we lesser mortals want above all things—independence. And the money to thumb his nose at an allowance from the parents, with all those sticky strings attached. He's heir to the Spanish grandmother, Doña Ysabella MacMinnus. After Grandfather died, she scandalized the family by marrying a rich Scot who owned a great parcel of land. Then he died, and she brought Nicholas up there to manage the estate. He could manage all of England, I suspect, if he put his mind to it. Don't let him intimidate you. He's a good fellow, when he unbends a little."

"I never saw him unbend," said Lady Eve.

Julia had returned her attention to the guests. "Which one is Lord Whitley?"

A short pause. "He lives elsewhere on the estate."

Lord John seemed to be picking out his words with care. "When she has primed you, Mother will take you there to meet him."

"Don't worry," said Lady Eve. "There are strict rules to obey, but I call on him all the time. You'll like Lord Whitley. Everyone does."

A biased opinion, from a girl who wanted her to marry anyone but Lord John. "Is there more I should know, sir, before the duke and duchess begin pulling at me like a wishbone?"

He laughed. "I'm sure there is, but if we are seen speaking privately, Mother will make things unpleasant for us both. In future Lady Eve shall act as our vedette, running messages back and forth while we adopt whatever pose best advances our strategy."

Before Julia could ask what strategy he meant, he had taken Lady Eve's arm and made his way to the door. There he picked up his umbrella, laid it over his shoulder like a musket, and in perfect unison, the general and his ensign saluted with clenched fists to their chests.

She responded with a curtsy, watched them go, and turned back to the reception hall just in time to see the tall man—Lord Nicholas—break from his father's circle and make his way the length of the room to where his mother was seated. People moved aside to let him pass, and a few smiled or nodded a greeting, but he paid them no heed.

As he drew nearer, Julia marked the straight posture, the severely cut dark hair, and an austere face that closely resembled the duke's. His bow to his mother was precise, the kiss he brushed on her wrist perfunctory.

Julia was suddenly very glad that Lord Nicholas would play no part in the Great Bridal Wars.

2

Nicholas turned from the sideboard in the duke's study, where he had just poured two glasses of sherry. "You cannot have expected me to approve this infernal scheme."

"In fact, I thought it would be settled before you learned of it." Sarne leaned back in his plush chair. "All the same, the matter is none of your concern. It is between me and the duchess."

"And Richard, and Johnnie."

"Only John. There is no question about the outcome, although the duchess will make sure my victory does not come easily."

Nicholas silently directed his temper to coil up in the dark corner where he stored his other emotions. "You are forgetting the young woman. Is the choice not to be hers?"

"I cannot compel her to marry, certainly. But then, what options does she have? No property or money, no family save for that harpy of a sister and, in two days, a foul brother-in-law. She may prefer to live with them, of course, and if she does, I shall provide a small sum for her support. But the chit is a dependant, no more than that. She has only to choose who will take her. And she'll choose John, mark my words. If nothing else, he is nearer her age, and almost as empty-headed."

Nicholas made a dismissive gesture. Johnnie might be single-minded, but he was also sharp-witted. "Is there any point to this, other than another dreary skirmish in the Thirty Years War?"

"Thirty-four, although it seems a hundred. You ought

to come more often to our anniversary celebrations."
The duke took a drink of sherry. "John's obsession with
getting himself shot on the Peninsula has grown tedious.
He requires a distraction. A new wife will keep him busy
long enough to forget all this military nonsense."

"A wife he scarcely knows and did not select."

"Despite my own experience, an arranged marriage
need not be a prelude to warfare. In this case, a young
and energetic bride will keep John off the battlefield and
in the bedroom, where he can expend his considerable
energy."

"And if he should not find her appealing?"

A crack of laughter from the duke, who rarely
laughed. "You haven't seen the girl, I take it. A stone
would rise up at the prospect of having her. Even you,
I suspect, might feel a human twinge or two. But she's
for John. Don't think of interfering with my plans."

"Why not me?" Nicholas asked, only because he was
making no headway with logic. Marriage was the second-
furthest thing from his mind, moving back to Sarne
Abbey being the first. "Unlike my brothers, I can support a wife."

"By all means, take a bride. I profoundly wish that
you would. But not this one. You must look higher than
a chit of dubious birth and no fortune."

"And yet you think her good enough for your heir?"

Color rose on the duke's knife-edged cheekbones.
"That's your mother's tack. Richard is content as he is,
and I am content to leave him that way. But his mother
does not know of his circumstances, nor would she toler-
ate them if she did. It is better I defeat her attempt to
arrange his marriage than to reveal why it should not
take place."

"What if the girl chooses Richard, and he decides to
have her?"

"Don't be absurd." The duke raised a mocking brow.
"He knows his duty. Do you imagine Richard would
defy me?"

Not on his own account, Nicholas had to concede, although he didn't say so. "You ought not to enmesh inno-
cents in your jousts. Find something else to quarrel
about."

"I'm more than willing, but it's the duchess's turn to set the game. Besides, if Julia Flyte is an innocent, she'll not remain so for long. Ungovernable, I can tell, and a wanton like her mother. Better to marry her off at once, before she can get herself into trouble."

Nicholas put down his glass, still nearly full, and bowed. "If you will excuse me, sir—"

"Oh, by all means," said the duke, waving a hand. "I count myself privileged that you stopped by for . . . what is it? Ten minutes?"

It had felt like a month. "The journey was long. And I wish to see Richard tonight."

"My mother has done me a disservice, Nicholas, stealing you away. You are wasted in that desolate place, with nothing but bad weather, cows, and a crotchety old woman for company. You belong here, managing the estate that will one day be yours. Don't scowl at me. You know that it will."

Nicholas felt a heaviness settle in his chest. "Richard's health has declined?"

"Not that I've noticed. He would not tell me, of course, if it had. But he cannot endure long enough to inherit."

"Probably none of us can. You will surely outlast your sons, if only because you'll refuse to die until you have brought us all under your thumb." At the door, Nicholas glanced back over his shoulder. "And that, Your Grace, will never happen."

"Not in your case," said the duke with a satisfied smile.

Early the next morning Nicholas rode out to inspect the estate, as he invariably did, and saw what he invariably saw. His father's steward, competent and dedicated, kept everything in good order. But where the steward preserved what had always been, Nicholas perceived land that should be drained, or planted with a different crop, or used for some other purpose.

Nothing would change, though. Not while the duke imagined his favored son could be lured home by the prospect of transforming Sarne Abbey.

On his way back to the house Nicholas passed the

walled garden that had been built centuries earlier by
the monks, and where he had devoted several years to
experimenting with plants. After returning his horse to
the stable and locating the key to the gate, he walked
back to the sheltered glen and strode around the garden
perimeter to inspect the high stone walls.

Like everything else on the estate, they were in excellent repair. At the far end, where the woodlands began,
he walked in shade part of the time, the grass soft and
springy under his feet. All was quiet, save for the whirr
of insect wings and the chatter of birds overhead. Now
and again he heard a light, musical sound that came and
went, carried on the breeze like thistledown. Once he
paused to listen, but it stopped before he could trace
its origin.

He made the last turn, moved past a large oak, and
saw just beyond it a small bundle nearly concealed by a
cluster of daffodils. Fabric of some sort, he decided, with
a fringe. Perhaps a shawl. The toe of a slipper peeked
out at one side. Bending closer, he detected part of a
stocking.

Leaving the bundle where it was, he proceeded to the
entrance, used his key, and the heavy wooden gate
swung open on well-oiled hinges.

Directly ahead he saw the familiar tiled paths laid out
in formal Elizabethan patterns, the ornamental hedge-
knots, the mosaics of flowers, all radiating from a fountain
at the center. Along the wall, the herbs and medicinal
plants he had imported and cared for seemed to be
flourishing. Frustration, always at a simmer beneath his
usual calm, began to roil. He had been so hopeful then.
But it had all come to nothing.

A movement at the opposite corner of the garden
caught his eye. He shaded his forehead with one hand
and squinted into the bright sunlight. A figure, perhaps
a child, dipping and swaying in a game. Or a dance. How
the devil . . . ?

He took the closest path, which led to the fountain.
Water streamed from four marble scallop shells held
aloft by four marble fish, and the breeze lifted a cloud
of droplets made golden by the late-morning sun. Partly

concealed by the fountain, he looked through the fish and water at the intruder.

Not a child. God, no. Blood rushed from his head to lower parts of his anatomy and remained there.

Young, though. Small-boned, finely shaped, graceful as a faerie. She was wearing—half wearing—a dress of some light, pale green material. There were short sleeves with little puffs at the shoulders. She'd hiked up the skirts above her knees—he couldn't see how—and was giving a performance to a line of sunflowers standing against the wall. To one of them she curtsied. To the next she raised a hand as if the flower were bending down to kiss it.

His gaze dropped to her lovely legs, and to their well-formed ankles, and to the small bare feet moving lightly across the tiles. She proceeded down the receiving line of sunflowers, her shapely back to him, her red-blond hair loose around her shoulders.

He felt like a voyeur. He *was* a voyeur. He raised his arm, swiped it across his damp forehead, held it over his eyes. Wilding male instincts clamored for him to leap the fountain, gallop to where she was, and sweep her away to a bed for a week.

Even you might feel a human twinge, his father had said, laughing.

A small sound, like that of a startled kitten, came from her direction. He lowered his arm.

She had turned, had frozen in the position she was in when she caught sight of him, her mouth open and her eyes wide. But she recovered quickly, drew herself up, tilted her head in acknowledgment, and reached for her skirts. She clearly meant to lift them and make a curtsy, but they weren't where she'd put her hands.

Her eyes went wider. Both hands swept to a clump of fabric near her left hip, which he now apprehended was a knot. Her fingers wrestled with it for a few moments, and then she made a *tsk*ing noise, gave a little shrug, and let her hands settle at her sides.

It occurred to the tiny portion of his brain still in working order that he ought to remove himself from behind the fountain. Summoning his lifelong gift for self-discipline, he made a mental inventory of his body, determined that it would function without causing notable embarrassment, squared his shoulders, and marched around the curve of the fountain.

As he came onto the path that led to where she was standing, he deliberately kept his gaze on her face. An entire drama was playing out there, expressions flitting by like swallows looking for a place to roost. The red of chagrin flagging her cheekbones. A rueful twitch of her lips, as if she'd been caught with her pretty fingers in the biscuit tin. A glint of devilry in her eyes, as if she was used to getting into trouble and didn't mind paying the price for it. And confidence, surprising in a girl so young, one with half her body exposed to a strange man, and the two of them alone in a place where no one could see them.

If she is an innocent, she won't be so for long.

The duke's words echoing in his ears, Nicholas stopped a careful distance away and gave a stiff bow. "Miss Julia Flyte, I apprehend."

"Apprehend indeed. You have caught me trespassing in a private garden. I do beg your pardon, Lord Nicholas, but I couldn't resist. I hope the penalty will not be too great."

She knew who he was. But then, he looked very like his father. "There is no harm in your being here. But how did you manage to get inside?"

Her gaze flitted toward a tall oak outside the wall to her left, the tree near where he'd seen the bundle. A thick branch overhung the garden, at least a dozen feet above the ground. More than that. She could not have safely jumped.

"I went up that tree, crawled out onto the largest branch, and swung down onto the wall. Then I hung from the wall by my hands and dropped onto the ground. It wasn't difficult."

"And how, exactly, did you plan to get out?"

"That, of course, is the problem." She flashed him a rueful smile. "I never think of planning ahead. But I would have managed something. Not very long ago I heard a horse go by. If I had been ready to leave, I would have called for help."

"Few people come here," he said. "Or anywhere near here."

"There's water," she pointed out, and had her mouth open to continue before she seemed to think better of debating the point. "I was wrong. I often am. But I had been told not to appear in public until the wedding, and truly, I could not bear being shut up in my bedchamber on such a beautiful day. So there it is. Besides, here you are, come to my rescue."

His gaze had ventured south to her legs, and to the foot she was rubbing against the opposite ankle. A streak of red followed. There were small scratches on both ankles, he saw, and on her feet, probably from the tree bark. "Come with me," he said in a tone sharper than he'd intended. "You have injured yourself."

When he reached the fountain, he pulled out his handkerchief, gave it to her, and turned his back. Heard her dip the handkerchief, squeeze out the excess water. . . . The rest was down to his imagination. And where that was leading him, he dared not go.

"Perhaps you will satisfy my curiosity," he said to distract himself. "I understand that you and your sister are wards of my father. Is there a blood connection I am unaware of, or is there some other reason you have fallen under his guardianship?"

"*Fallen* is an interesting way to put it. *Dragged* is probably more accurate. But you should ask His Grace, sir. I babble far too much. People are always telling me so."

"Would it help if we agreed to hold our conversation in strictest confidence?"

"All of it? Including the part where I ask questions of you?"

Neatly done. "That would be fair," he conceded. "What is your age?"

"I had my official seventeenth birthday in February. I look younger, so I'm told. But in most other ways I am a good deal older. And *your* age, my lord?"

"A decade older in years, three times that in experience. As for the family connection . . . ?"

"There is none. Only a slight acquaintance between my father and yours, until Father came into possession of something the duke wanted. An arrangement was struck between them."

From the sound of her voice she was crouching down, or perhaps sitting on the lip of the fountain. A small rustle of cloth made him think she was trying to untie her skirts. "Did the arrangement, by chance, include your marriage into the family?"

She laughed. "Not likely. I was seven at the time, with skinned knees and no front teeth. His Grace merely agreed to stand guardian to Harriet and me if it became necessary, which it did a few years later. The duke paid off the creditors, secured the house for my sister's inheritance, and provided living expenses and a governess. Otherwise, he paid us no mind. We were both surprised when two Sarne cousins came calling on Harriet, one sent by the duchess and one by the duke, to court her."

"And now you are to select one of their sons as your own bridegroom."

"Lord John said so. *Drat this knot!* If you say so as well, it must be true."

Nicholas wondered if he should offer to help. Knew the answer and clasped his hands tightly behind his back. "You will refuse, surely, to be a part of this."

Silence for a few moments, and then a release of breath. "That did it," she said. "You may turn around now, if you wish to."

He did, and saw her standing with her wrinkled skirts down where they should be. "You didn't answer my question, Miss Julia."

"I beg your pardon, my lord." Green-gold eyes, shining with challenge, met his. "I thought it was by way of an order."

Most everything he said sounded like an order, or so he had been told. "More in the way of advice," he said at length. "Neither marriage would suit you. Shall we fetch your shoes? I will escort you back to the house."

"Must you? I'll be required to hide away in my bed-chamber again, and it has the smallest window ever in existence. Can you not leave me here to explore the garden? And leave the gate open as well? I can lock it behind me when I go."

He could. But he didn't want to. Besides, as the only detached and clear-thinking member of the family, he'd a duty to protect his brothers. "As you wish. But you cannot be let to wander about alone."

"And you have not finished your inquisition." She began to stroll along one of the paths, leaving him to catch up. "I believe, though, that it is my turn to ask a question. Will you tell me, sir, why Lord Whitley lives apart? Is he . . . well, not altogether—"

"In his right mind?" She wasn't the first to place that interpretation on Richard's isolation. "Would you wed him if he were not, simply because he is heir to the title?"

She glanced over, a smile curving her lips. "I'll not lie to you, sir. I've a great fancy to be a duchess. If Lord Whitley is agreeable, I will happily marry him. But if he is not competent to enter such a contract, then I must consider accepting Lord John instead."

"By God, you *do* intend to exploit this rivalry." He swung in front of her so swiftly that she ran straight into him. For a moment her small body was fitted against his, her chin at the level of his chest, her upturned eyes both shocked and amused. He took a quick step back, but not before wrapping his hands around her arms, just above the elbows. "I cannot prevent you. And your ambition will probably trump your good sense, if you have any. But before you leap into the fire, I will lay out for you the truth of what you may expect. You'll not hear much of it from Sarne or the duchess."

"That will be helpful, my lord." Again she met his gaze directly. Shamelessly. "Their schemes are their concern, but the opportunity is mine to seize. And you cannot keep hold of me forever."

"Just long enough to make clear the destruction you will cause by leaping in where you do not belong." But he let her go, his hands burning, and took a distancing step away. "It will require me to divulge information private to the family. Have I your word that you will not disclose it to anyone else?"

"Oh, yes," she said promptly. "But do you believe me?"

Irrationally, he rather thought that he did. "I am compelled to hope you are an honorable woman. And if you prove otherwise, to make sure that you regret it."

"Fair enough. Now, about Lord Whitley . . ."

"We can save time if you are permitted to see for yourself. Shall I take you to meet him?"

"Oh, yes. I should like very much to . . ." Her gaze went to her crushed skirts, scratched ankles, bare feet. "Dear me."

"Whitley never stands on ceremony, and there may not be another opportunity. One thing only. Are you wearing scent?"

"You mean perfume? No."

"Very well. I believe I spotted your footwear under a tree. Let me know when you are shod, and I will take you to the dower house."

3

Arriving at the patch of daffodils where she'd left her bundle, Julia unwrapped the shawl and gathered up her stockings. *What a disconcerting gentleman!* Lord Nicholas managed to be more intimidating than the duke himself, and nearly as arrogant. He had entered the garden already disliking her—that was certain. *Ramshackle hoyden*, his expression had said.

That was, she had to admit, fairly accurate. But he had also decided that she, an entirely unsuitable bride for the son of a duke, was sharpening her claws to entrap one of his brothers.

And of course, he was right about that as well.

Propping her back against the wall, she drew on a stocking and secured it with a ribbon around her calf. That wasn't all he was thinking, though. She could not mistake the heated look in his dark eyes. Frederick the Many-fingered gazed at her in much the same way before finding an excuse to put his hands on her person. She could not walk up the stairs without him forcing his assistance on her.

Strangely, she had not minded Lord Nicholas's intense scrutiny. Her intuition told her he would never act on any primitive desires he might possess, and besides, men seemed to respond like automatons when in the vicinity of bare female limbs. Perhaps they couldn't help themselves.

The other stocking went on, and then she had to go looking for the ribbon, which she must have dropped. Green like her gown, it was invisible in the high grass.

No matter what Lord Nicholas thought of her, she

must not permit him to stand in her way. Marriage was
her only means of escaping a lifetime of unpaid servitude
in her sister's household, and she had already rejected
the only eligible man in Pawson Ribble.

Ah, there it was! She tied the ribbon, put on her
shoes, and examined the sad little bonnet with its faded
ribbons and shapeless straw brim. Setting it on her head,
she scrunched her hair inside it before tying the ribbons.
Then she shook out her fringed shawl, embroidered with
cherries because they were easier than flowers, and
sighed. As first impressions went, this one was going to
be a disaster.

She started back toward the gate and arrived there
just as Lord Nicholas was coming through it. He barely
glanced at her slightly more dignified appearance before
turning to relock the gate. "It is nearly a mile to the
dower house," he said. "Can you walk so far in those
flimsy slippers?"

He'd paid more notice than it had seemed. "They are
fairly sturdy, my lord. Where I live, we all do a great
deal of walking."

He led her along a path to a narrow stile with two
steps. Frederick would have seized hold of her to help,
but Lord Nicholas left her to navigate the crossing on
her own. The path continued on the other side, through
a meadow painted with wildflowers and musical with the
wings of honeybees.

"Perhaps I should explain," he said, "why Whitley
lives apart from the family and rarely goes into company.
The difficulties with his health are not apparent unless
he is experiencing an attack, which his living conditions
are designed to prevent."

An *attack*? Julia glanced over at Lord Nicholas, but
his gaze was focused on the ground.

"From childhood, my brother has been afflicted with
a breathing disorder that on many occasions has come
near to killing him. We cannot determine the cause, and
there is no sure remedy. But my studies disclosed several
ways to reduce the frequency of his attacks."

"You are a physician, my lord?"

"Hardly. But a physician who suffered from it, Lord
John Floyer, recorded in *A Treatise of the Asthma* his

own symptoms and the results of his experiments. I have read everything I can find on the subject and spoken with others who have experience with the malady. It is usually worse in childhood. Of those who survive, some eventually become free of it, or nearly so, while others continue to suffer."

"Oh, my. What have you discovered that is of help?"

"When an attack begins, it must simply run its course, although some books and pamphlets recommend potions, infusions, poultices, or teas made from various plants and herbs. The garden we just left was my laboratory for several years, but nothing helped my brother and, I am sorry to say, his cooperation with my experiments probably did him more harm than good. Only one blend of pungent spices and other ingredients, which he keeps in a vinaigrette, offers a little relief when his throat closes up."

"Must he live in isolation, then? Is the illness infectious?"

"It seems not. But like many other patients, he is affected by perfumes, dust, animals, and smoke. A simple cold could trigger a deadly attack. Whitley spends much of the year confined to the house, pursuing his interests and welcoming his many friends. But in late spring, he will remove to the seashore. He has a small house in Devonshire."

Until the last few minutes, she would never have guessed this man capable of such devotion. He invariably kept his voice level, but when speaking of his brother, the intensity of his feelings vibrated in every word.

"You will like Whitley," he said. "But even if you entice him to make an offer, don't imagine you shall be allowed to marry him."

"Because the duke is my guardian, and he will refuse permission. Yes, I have considered that."

"So has the duchess. I am unacquainted with the rules of their latest game, but some accommodation will have been made. An announcement of your betrothal, perhaps, and an engagement lasting until you come of age."

"But during that time, would His Grace permit me to live at Sarne Abbey?"

"More likely he will send you home, where you might draw the attention of a more appropriate gentleman."

Such as the vicar, fifty if he was a day, who had taken in a distant relative's orphaned children and gone casting about for a desperate female to marry. The entire village had thought it her duty to accept him. "Anyone who thinks eligible men are thick on the ground in Pawson Ribble has never been there," she said. "I could marry Lord John straightaway, don't you think?"

"Probably." Slowing, he cast her an assessing look, one that settled on her belly. "Is there some great hurry?"

"Not of the sort you are imagining," she said with a snap in her voice. "I am trying to understand my options, is all. Lord John said I am expected to come to a decision within the week."

"Ah. I hadn't heard that. But yes, I can imagine the victor will wish to flaunt his success, or hers, before the company departs. Guests have come to expect a grande finale at a Sarne house party."

He had picked up speed again, and she was having nearly to trot to keep alongside him. "This is becoming complicated," she said. "I'm not even supposed to know about the marriage scheme, and already I am conspiring with two of the duke's sons, and on my way to meet the third."

"A lifelong commitment ought to require a bit of time and consideration, don't you think? An impulsive decision can only lead to trouble for everyone concerned."

Yet another stern lecture from Lord Nicholas. He seemed to hold her responsible for what was happening, when she was only trying to beat a path for herself through the jungle. "I don't want to make trouble for anyone," she said. "Yes, I do have a care for my own interests. I must, because no one else in the world gives two feathers for what becomes of me. If there is a conclusion better than the other possibilities, I intend to find it. But first, I need to understand what everyone has at stake."

"Let us start with you, then. I already know you will grasp this chance to marry into the family, and that you hope to become the next Duchess of Sarne. But you are concerned about a long engagement, because Whitley's uncertain health may cause you to be stranded without a ring on your finger. So you might settle for John, who is a better prospect than can be found in Pawson Ribble. Am I correct?"

"For the most part," she acknowledged, "although you are putting the worst possible interpretation on everything. I suspect you always do that."

A short laugh, the first she'd heard from him. "Doña Ysabella, my grandmother, tells me the same thing. If I am misjudging you, Miss Julia, set me straight. What is it you most want for yourself?"

Somewhat breathless from matching his long stride, she debated whether to give him the truth or try to impress him. And wondered why she wanted to impress him. And decided it was too late for that, so she might as well reveal the vain, superficial creature she could sometimes be. He wouldn't believe there was more dimension to her than that, and so far, she had to admit, there wasn't. Those new dimensions were there, though. She felt them all the time, sleeping restlessly inside her, lying in wait for an opportunity to push up shoots and open to the sun.

Meantime, she had nothing of worth in herself but the dreams that enabled her to survive. And although they would cause him to despise her all the more, it would be a betrayal of herself to deny them.

"My wishes are neither laudable nor exemplary," she said, turning her gaze to the rolling meadows. "Merely the fantasies of a young girl. I wish to dance, and listen to music. Beauty enchants me. I want to wear lovely gowns and be surrounded by beautiful things, by paintings and sculptures and gardens. I have passions as well, that I shall not speak of, but they burn inside me. I desire to be welcome in good company, and to engage in good conversation. I want to learn and to grow wise, but not if it means growing too serious. Above all things, I want to laugh and be joyful. I am on fire with ambitions of every kind. I overflow with longings."

His pace had slowed while she spoke. The brim of his

hat shadowed his forehead, but she could tell he was frowning. "I suppose no more should be expected," he said at length, "from so young a female."

Insufferable man. What had he expected her to say? That she wished to manage a household? Watch over the upbringing of her children? Tend to her husband's needs and desires? She would do those things when the time came, and do them as best she could. But her secret fantasies did not run to counting silver, planning menus, or embroidering a fire screen while her husband went off with his cronies. Or to war, as Lord John seemed bent on doing. Which reminded her—

"I could not help noticing, sir, that Lord John has an interest in military matters. Is it not customary in a great family for one son to elect a career in the army or navy?"

"Usually the second son. Are you making a point of some kind?"

"Well, since you have not chosen to take up arms in the war, what is preventing Lord John from doing so? Clearly he wishes to go, and he is of age."

"Little escapes your attention, does it?" From his tone, Lord Nicholas seemed to welcome the change of subject. "If he could buy a commission in the army, John would be on the next ship to the Peninsula. He would *swim* there, if need be. But he is kept poor, with an allowance barely adequate for the needs of a young gentleman. While he has put away most of it these past several years, a decade will pass before he has saved enough to buy into the lowliest regiment."

"But cannot he just *go*? Recruiters are everywhere these days. They even came to our village, but all the young men who could escape Pawson Ribble had already done so."

"A duke's son, Miss Julia, cannot simply take the king's shilling. He would not be welcome in the ranks. Indeed, he would immediately become a disruption and a hazard. John is wise enough to know it. From boyhood, he has studied military history and strategy. After I removed to Scotland, I began bringing him north in the summers to be trained by one of my servants, who was a sergeant-major before being invalided out. John is an expert horseman, map reader, strategist, swordsman, and shot. A friend at Horseguards sends him copies of the dispatches, which he practically memorizes."

They had come to another stile, this one without steps, and Lord Nicholas held it open for her. Placid cows grazed in the pasture beyond. "John would make a superb officer, but Sarne has made sure he can't afford to buy in. By way of compensation, you are being served up as a diversion."

"Oh." She threaded that information into the tapestry she was weaving, hoping a picture would eventually appear. Or a map, to guide her in the right direction. "So the duke and duchess are not merely entertaining themselves with this duel. There are reasons for what they do."

"*Reasons* may be coming it too strong. Schemes within plots within strategems is more like."

"And you know what they are."

"I can guess," he said. "But whatever my parents' objectives, you are no more than a pawn in this game."

"And you an observer, like a picnicker at a cricket match. Except that the outcome of this particular match will determine the course of a brother's life. Does that not trouble you?"

"My troubles are my own, Miss Julia. And as you say, I am not in the game."

4

Not long after, the dower house came into sight and the girl ceased her prattle. Busy scheming how best to seduce her prey, Nicholas supposed, and make of herself a duchess-in-waiting.

For him, the silence felt . . . empty. Speaking with her had been difficult, to be sure, but challenging, and he had always relished a challenge. He liked her voice as well, light and clear, edged with intelligence and amusement.

Richard was bound to find her appealing, especially after a long winter of isolation. Spring marked the end of what he called the lonely season, and here was Julia Flyte to measure him for leg shackles. When she began working her wiles on him, he'd tumble like a cheese rolling downhill.

The land around the dower house had been cleared for a hundred yards in all directions, with gravel and fountains and tiled terraces replacing the trees and gardens that had once surrounded it. The inside of the seventeenth-century house had been gutted, leaving only the stone walls and oak floors. Windows, a great many of them, were added, and all the rooms configured so that they could be heated without smoke fires. For more than a year, Nicholas had worked with an architect to create a place where his brother could safely breathe.

"How lovely," the girl exclaimed when they came to the terraces. "I have never seen tiles like these. The colors are wonderful. It's almost like a garden of flowers."

"They were imported from Spain. My grandmother,

Doña Ysabella, recommended the artist and the tile makers." He sounded like a Cambridge don, the sort Johnnie had fled after his second term. "Much of the house is tiled as well."

As they drew near the front door, he began in earnest to regret this ill-conceived visit. The would-be duchess was looking about her with greedy interest, her eyes alight. Austere as it was, the residence was probably unmatched by the finest house in that village she came from—Parson Rubble, or something of the sort.

And when had he ever before forgotten a detail? *Your mind is a storage bin,* Richard had once told him. *Everything goes in, and nothing escapes.* But since about two hours ago, when he first set eyes on Julia Flyte, his mind had been more like overcooked porridge.

"Is there any chance," she said, looking sideways at him through a fringe of long eyelashes, "that I could refresh myself before meeting Lord Whitley?"

"I'll arrange it," he said, his pulse leaping like a trapped deer.

A few minutes later he turned her over to a neatly uniformed maid and took himself to a large, sunny room where his brother, bent over a worktable spread out with Roman coins, greeted him with a smile of pleased surprise.

"Two visits in as many days," said Richard. "Should I be alarmed?"

"You should beware. I come bearing gifts. It seems that Miss Julia likes the sound of 'Your Grace' and wishes to discover if the two of you would suit."

"And you brought her here?" Richard lifted a brow. "Are you trying to compromise us into marriage, or was this her idea?"

"Good God." Cold sweat gathered along Nicholas's spine. "I must have left my brain in Scotland. The whole situation is so grotesque that I never gave thought to the proprieties. For that matter, the girl and I have been alone together for the better part of an hour. If someone saw us—"

"You'll be the one in parson's mousetrap." Richard regarded him through the magnifying glass he'd been using to identify the coins. "Not a bad idea, really. If you marry the young woman, both parents will be thwarted. Just imagine their bewilderment."

"Almost worth it," Nicholas conceded. "But I am in thrall, financially and otherwise, to Doña Ysabella. And in any case, I've no wish to take a wife. Nor have you, or so I believed until our conversation last night. Tell me you have come to your senses."

"I rather expect Miss Julia will come to hers. But I'm glad you brought her, Nick, before Mother has set her talons into the girl. Now I can explain how quiet an existence she would lead as my wife, and how small are her chances of becoming Duchess of Sarne."

"But if she . . . Never mind. We have already plucked that crow. Just remember, Richard. You need not put aside your happiness to please anyone, especially those concerned only with their own satisfaction."

"And this pompous lecture from a man who spends every bit of his time serving others. Heed your own advice, Nick. For all your excellent health and prospects, I do believe I am living a richer and fuller life than you will permit yourself to enjoy."

Richard had never said so, but Nicholas understood that if his brother had not been the firstborn, he would have entered the church. And so were they all trapped by expectations not their own, by those who held the power and the money, by heritage and duty and guilt. "I had better go," he said. "Will you see the girl gets back to the Abbey?"

"In company with a chaperon," Richard affirmed. "And you needn't be concerned. What with all the daft theatricals staged by our parents and expected by their guests, no one pays the slightest heed to us."

"I hope you are right. And Richard, when Miss Julia is shown in, try not to let your mouth hang open."

The next morning, low clouds and a soft drizzle enveloped the estate. Nicholas, after a restless night spent wishing he'd followed through on his intention to pack up and return to Scotland, dutifully got himself to the parish church only a little late for Hester Flyte's marriage to his repellent second cousin. He slid into a pew box near the back, noting that few of the houseguests had troubled to make an appearance. The bride, garishly attired, spoke her vows too loudly, and the groom fumbled his way through the ceremony like a man who'd had too much to drink, which was likely the case.

Sarne was there, seated beside Johnnie in the ducal pew. And across the aisle the slender duchess, still lovely in her fifties, had secured Miss Julia's company. Score one for Her Grace.

Of the young lady, he could see only a finer bonnet than she had worn the day before, and a stray tendril of apricot-colored hair curling out the back of it. She had spent more than three hours with Richard yesterday afternoon. He knew because he had kept watch for her return.

Shortly before the final blessing, he made his escape from the church. He doubted anyone had noticed he'd bothered to come, and no one would expect him to attend the wedding breakfast.

But he did. To his regret, because he found himself near the head of the table and beside his mother, where he least wanted to be. The bride, determined to be the center of attention, brayed like a donkey whenever she spoke, which was far too often. He began to entertain fantasies of stuffing his napkin in her mouth. Across the table the duke, a smug smile on his face, celebrated his triumph. Frederick, a boil on the family buttocks, had been Sarne's choice to wed his elder ward, and Nicholas had to grant that the bride and groom richly deserved each other.

Near the end of the table, a long way down for the sister of the bride to be exiled, Miss Julia was ensconced between the nearly deaf Sir Warren Trype and an elderly lady Nicholas could not identify. Nor could he see who was seated across from them, on his side of the table, but all the lively conversation and laughter seemed to be coming from that location. However hard he tried to leash it, his gaze kept straying to her animated face. Her glossy hair, threaded with lavender ribbons that matched her gown, seemed to cast its own light.

He should have gone to Scotland.

Shortly before noon, Nicholas was back in his bed-chamber, looking down from his window on the depar-

ture—none too soon—of the bride and groom. As a
farewell gift to his elder ward, now blessedly off his
hands, Sarne had provided a carriage and the use of his
small estate in the Lake District for their honeymoon.
The guests huddled beneath the portico to keep dry
while they dutifully waved farewell. Then they scurried
back into the house . . . all except the duchess and Miss
Julia, whom she had taken by the arm. A servant
promptly appeared with their wraps, and another carriage drew up in front of the portico.

Nicholas didn't have to guess their destination. The
game was under way, and Her Grace was about to make
the opening move.

While Richard was introduced to his future bride for
the second time, Nicholas decided to ride over to Wych-
wood and see when Robin was expected back. The
neighboring estate was about two hours' ride on horse-
back and would keep him safely out of the way for the
entire afternoon.

Sir Gerard Branden, Sarne's scholarly brother, had
better sense than to attend a ducal anniversary party,
although his wife occasionally made an appearance.
Robin, their only son and everyone's favorite relative,
had run tame at Sarne Abbey since Nicholas could remember. He was about Johnnie's age and his lifelong
friend, although the death of his young wife in childbirth
two years ago had plunged him into mourning so deep
that he rarely left his rooms. Johnnie would ride over
nearly every day to distract him with card games or stra-
tegic battles with their collection of miniature armies.

Just lately, though, Robin's spirits had begun to improve, and at his mother's urging he had agreed to take
his son to visit the boy's maternal grandparents for a
fortnight. Nicholas had never seen John, named for Johnnie, and had no wish to. He knew little about young
children and expected he wouldn't get on well with
them. They could not, he had been told, be reasoned
with.

Johnnie had said that Robin was due back any day,
and in fact, he was there when Nicholas arrived at Wych-
wood. After a brief visit with his aunt, uncle, and the
female cousins, he was taken off by Robin to a room

filled with large tables, their surfaces covered with mock landscapes, miniature artillery, and lead soldiers.

"Did it go well, your call on the boy's grandparents?" Nicholas asked when the pleasantries were done with. The sooner Robin returned to his former good-natured, optimistic self, the better for Johnnie and all his other friends.

"Easier than expected. They want to raise the child, and I am thinking that might be wise. Elizabeth is to come out this year, and Madeleine the next, which will keep all the ladies too busy for nursery matters. And the earl has offered to buy me the commission that Father refuses to supply, any regiment I choose and all the equipment as well."

"In exchange for your son?"

"None of us are being so crass about it, but we're all dancing about, trying to get what we most want. In my case, I'm not sure what that is. For too long a time I senselessly blamed the infant for Anna's death, as if the poor sod had any choice about being born. I wouldn't go near to him. Later, when I began to see Anna in his face and his expressions, I realized that I owed it to her to devote myself to his care. Now I wonder if that is in his best interest. She was Penborough's only child, and while her son cannot inherit the title, I think the earl would leave to him any unentailed properties and much of the fortune. If, of course, his grandchild is placed into his keeping."

"While you scamper off to the Peninsula."

Robin grinned. "I've already chosen my regiment, found a supplier of good horses, determined the cost of a lieutenancy—I think I can aspire to that—and arranged for uniforms and equipment. If the Earl of Penborough will stand the expense, how can I refuse?"

As suddenly as it had appeared, the grin collapsed. "Then again, how could I accept? A tragedy has opened for me a door, but this opportunity should be Johnnie's. His desire, and his talents, are much greater than mine. Say nothing of this, Nick. Not until I've made up my mind what to do. And then, let me be the one to tell him."

"Gladly. I'll also let him tell you about the bride Sarne

is trying to foist on him. Or, you could come back with me and meet her for yourself."

Robin's soft brown eyes lit up at the prospect. "A foisted bride need not turn out badly. Mine did not. And yes, I'll ride over with you and stay a day or two. Go let m'sisters practice flirting with you while I make arrangements."

5

Her very first ball! Julia, pleased at what she saw in the mirror, hugged herself in delight. Then she hugged her startled maid, on loan from the Sarne staff, who had worked magic to transform her one plain party dress into a rather lovely, if still plain, gown. And done a miracle with her hair as well, catching it up in Grecian style with green and gold ribbons to match her eyes. She wouldn't be the belle of this or any other fashionable ball, but she needn't hide in a corner either.

Not that she would have done, even if rigged out like a Pawson Ribble bumpkin. She had learned all the traditional dances, and while she had only ever partnered her sister and the dyspeptic dance master, she fancied herself both competent and graceful. She wondered if anyone would claim her as a partner.

A knocking sent her maid to the door, where Miss Ann Crane, a distant relation of Lady Eve who served as her companion, stood wringing her hands. "L-Lord Nicholas wishes to speak with Miss J-Julia before the ball," she said. "I am to escort her when she is ready."

"I'm ready now," Julia said, picking up the fan Lady Eve had given her. The daunting, dashing lord probably intended to read her a salutary lecture before permitting her to be loosed in a society ballroom.

Let him have his say. One day she might well preside over a ball in that very ballroom. Not many hours earlier, when the duchess had left her meaningfully alone with Lord Whitley, he had made his intentions clear. She had nearly accepted on the spot, but decided it would

153

be unsophisticated to jump at an offer without pretending to think it over.

Miss Crane led her to a room she had never seen before. Long and narrow, it held groupings of chairs and small tables, and at the far end a faux wall of Chinese painted screens shielded whatever lay beyond them from view.

"Back there," said Miss Crane, pointing. "I am to wait here, as chaperon."

Drawing closer to the screens, Julia detected an opening and stepped through it. More chairs and tables, but her gaze went immediately to the tall man wearing formal dress, all of it black save for a blaze of white at cuffs and collar and the hint of a silver-and-black-striped waistcoat.

Without thinking, she snapped open her fan.

"Thank you for coming," he said, as though she'd had a choice. "I'll not keep you long. Will you take a seat, please? Perhaps on that chair."

She selected another, one not directly in front of where he was standing by the empty hearth, and sat with the grace taught her by her mother.

"I wished to speak to you without fear of being discovered by the guests. You have been careless, Miss Julia. To be seen gallivanting half-unclothed in gardens or walking in company with a gentleman, however innocent the circumstances, would irreparably ruin you."

"I shall endeavor to mend my ways," she said sweetly.

His eyes narrowed. "You had better, if you hope to enter society on the coattails of this family. Sarne and the duchess are famously intolerant of scandal, unless it is of their own making."

"I wonder that you give me this warning, sir. Wouldn't you rather I scandalize myself right back to Pawson Ribble?"

"I wish you no ill, Miss Julia. And as everyone will tell you, I am notoriously heavy-handed when pursuing an objective. Do not take personal offense at my rudeness."

"Shall I expect more of it? Right now, for example?"

"That depends. I should like to know the outcome, if any, of the call you paid on Whitley in company with the duchess. Did he explain his circumstances, the quiet and enclosed existence forced upon him by his health?"

She wanted to suggest that he ask his brother, but one unmannerly person in a confined space was more than enough. "He did that when first we met. It does not greatly matter."

"Of course it does. To you, anyway. Marry Whitley and there will be no society parties, no dancing, no travel, no company, no London Season."

"I don't expect to achieve everything I wish, my lord. He is kind, intelligent, and has many interests. He showed me his collections and read to me from his poetry. I will be a cheerful companion for him and learn to share his pastimes. With all of that, I can be more than content."

"You say that now, but when you find the confinement tedious, how will you conduct yourself?"

"For that I will answer to my husband, not to his relatives. We discussed how it would be if we married, and the possible risks. He told me the duke does not wish him to sire children for fear they will inherit his illness, but that he has reason to believe the danger is not great. And it only makes sense, for if the illness is passed from parent to child, how is it you and Lord John are not afflicted? We agreed to try to have children together."

"Then he has made an offer!" Lord Nicholas broke away from the hearth and began to pace the room, the part of it closed off by the screens. "And what is to become of Maria? What of their son?"

"I . . . Who? I don't know what you mean."

"He didn't tell you, then. I rather expected he would not. But you should know, Miss Julia, exactly what your intrusion into his life will destroy. Several years ago, when selecting a housekeeper for his summer residence, he insisted on hiring a woman who had a broken arm. I naturally objected, but his judgment of her fine character proved accurate. Within a few months they had fallen in love, and a son was born the following year."

"Sarne forbade them to marry?"

"He would do his best to prevent such a misalliance, I am sure. But in fact, Maria Fletcher is already married.

She had fled her brute of a husband, whose last beating left her with the broken arm, and was destitute when she sought employment with Whitley. She was also terrified that Fletcher would track her down, so to ease her mind I saw to it he was impressed into the navy."

"You can arrange such things?"

"It is simple enough." He waved a dismissive hand. "Pay attention, Miss Julia. Whitley has a strict conscience, but his devotion to Maria has carried him beyond its boundaries, at least to the point of taking her as his mistress. He does not think of her as such, but their child will always be a bastard, and neither of them are welcomed here. Sarne knows the situation, but Her Grace does not. Or perhaps she knows and refuses to acknowledge it. The point is, Whitley's circumstances are complex. He is not simply a ripe apple for you to pluck."

Is that how he saw her? Yes, there was a bit of opportunism in her nature, but how could she swim away from the lifeline that had been tossed in her direction? "In a marriage of convenience, sir, such arrangements are not unusual. If Lord Whitley wishes to continue his liaison and spend a portion of the year apart from me, I would have no objection."

"By God, but you are a mercenary little creature. Is there nothing you will not do, or accept, to become Lady Whitley?"

"A great deal, my lord. I can, however, endure a loveless marriage, so long as there is a degree of friendship and respect. Lord Whitley will provide both in abundance. And in return, I would never demand that he be separated from the woman he truly loves, or from his son. Such agreements are understood and accepted in many parts of the world."

"Is that so? You are remarkably cynical for one so young."

"I am also the child of just such a liaison." She took a steadying breath. "It seems that if any understanding is to be reached, Lord Nicholas, my family laundry must be hung up beside yours. Shall I put it there?"

He paused to cast her a dark look. "By all means, proceed. I will not promise to believe what you say."

"His Grace can confirm the important bits. Harriet as

well, and most of the village. But you are, I think, merely trying to insult me. I don't mind. Your intent is to protect your brother from an ambitious tart."

Another dark look as he paced by her again, but his lips were tightly sealed.

"When Harriet was three years old, my mother ran away with a young Italian nobleman who was making a Grand Tour. He settled her in a small town not far from Venice, where I was born. We all lived together for several years, but then it came time for him to marry the woman his family had chosen. After that, he visited us when he could. His wife and family knew of the liaison. They even sent presents for my birthday. And while my mother was unaccepted in the highest circles, she was respected as the mistress of an important man."

She had come to the difficult part of her story. "One summer, a fever swept through the area. Father sent me to stay at a convent in the mountains, but my mother refused to leave him, and along with most of his family, they both died. Father left instructions and funds to have me carried to England and put into the custody of my mother's husband, William Flyte. I had never met him, of course. Later I discovered that he had always been a wastrel, frequently abandoning his wife and daughter for months at a time. He did not improve when I was dropped into his life, but for reasons I can only guess at, he acknowledged me as his own child."

"And you were not?" Lord Nicholas frowned. "No Italian could have fathered a child of your coloring."

"Not all Italians have dark hair and eyes, my lord. Many are descended from Viking raiders, especially in the north, and my father had hair not unlike my own."

She closed her fan and settled her trembling hands on her lap. "Mr. Flyte gave me his name and a new birth date to allow him the opportunity to have sired me. I will always be grateful, for he might have repudiated me and thrown me on the parish or into a workhouse. But not unnaturally, my new family resented my very existence. Harriet, abandoned by her mother and left to the care of an indifferent father, was reminded of her unhappy fate every time she looked at me. It is no wonder we never got on together."

He had stopped directly in front of her, an arrested look on his face. "I see. And yet you have taken no lesson from the harm produced by such unconventional affairs. By casting yourself in the role of privileged, tolerant wife, you declare yourself free of moral responsibility."

"I have already played the beloved child of my parents, sir. That is what I would hope for your brother's child. I have experienced the kindness of my father's legitimate wife and family. That is what I would offer Maria Fletcher and her son. But I have also been the bastard child thrown onto the thorny mercy of those who despised me. Do not imagine I am naïve and fanciful about such matters. In this one thing, I am perhaps more experienced than you."

"To a point," he acknowledged with transparent effort. "But you do not know, or understand, my brother. He never speaks untruthfully and is incapable of taking vows he does not mean to keep. If he weds you, he will put aside his relationship with Maria."

Somewhere in her imagination, a door she had longed to go through began to close. She recognized the truth in his eyes, and her own assessment of Lord Whitley's character gave evidence as well. "But why, then, would he give me leave to choose him, and say he would be honored to make me his wife?"

Lord Nicholas looked down, his long lashes concealing his eyes. "That is difficult to explain. He did not mean to hurt you. I will say only this. Recently, he has come to understand the purpose behind so much of what Sarne does. Whatever it requires, the duke has set himself to ensure that I inherit his title."

"But that is barbaric!"

"I share your repugnance, and he knows it. Even so, he has selected me as the next duke, probably because I am, for my sins, very much like him. Now it appears that Whitley has decided to free me from Sarne's trap by producing a legitimate son."

"He would marry me to please *you*?"

"And to make a sacrifice, because he feels indebted to me. It is utter nonsense, to be sure, born of too much time spent helpless and alone."

"He should live all the time with Maria and his son. Then he would not have these delusions." Julia's feelings did not bear close inspection either, not at the moment. Rising, she brushed down her skirts and fixed Lord Nicholas with a wry smile. "Well, then. Later I shall tell Lord Whitley that on reflection, I have decided a quiet life would not suit me."

Lord Nicholas's brows shot up. "You are abandoning the field? Just like that?"

"Certainly. I'll not seek my happiness at the expense of Lord Whitley's. Besides, Lord John is still on offer. If you will excuse me, sir, I shall go try my luck with him."

For the ball, the marble floor of the reception hall had been covered with polished marquetry wood, and some of the portraits on the wall replaced with long mirrors in gilded frames. The minstrels' gallery where Julia had lurked two days earlier held an orchestra now. At the far end of the hall, French windows opened to a wide terrace lit with colorful lanterns and set with copper braziers against the chilly spring night.

Guests, many invited only for the ball, streamed through the doors and paused to be announced by the butler. Julia decided she must be the only commoner admitted to Sarne Abbey. She was standing with Lady Eve, who was permitted to remain for half an hour to practice her company manners, and with Miss Crane, who kept apologizing because she'd fallen asleep in her chair when she was supposed to be acting as chaperon. Just as well, given all the secrets shared behind the screens at the other end of that drawing room.

"Ah, there you are, my dear." The Duchess of Sarne, regal in a gown of shimmering gold, took Julia's arm and led her toward a clutch of women who were regarding her with avid curiosity. "You'll not wish to dance, if indeed you know how, since Lord Whitley cannot be here to partner you. Perhaps you should sit in company with—"

"Good evening, Eleanor." The Duke of Sarne stepped neatly into their path. "I had thought we would come downstairs together, but my valet had difficulty with my cravat. Perhaps later we can go into supper together. Meantime, let me take this young lady off your hands. John is to lead her out for the first dance."

And just like that, Julia was swept off in another direction, with Lord John at the end of it. He was standing beside a young gentleman not quite as tall as he, with brown hair and a pleasant face. The duke left them together—dropped her off like a parcel, in fact—and Lord John presented her to his cousin, Mr. Robert Branden.

"We all call him Robin, though. I've told him about Sarne's plot, and he thinks you'd be a fool to marry a havey-cavey fellow like me."

"I assure you, Miss Julia, that this havey-cavey fellow is misrepresenting my words entirely," Mr. Branden said. "But if you decide to have him, apply to me in advance for a catalog of his bad habits. You ought to be prepared."

The orchestra, which had been playing softly in the background, struck an attention-getting chord, and couples began to move to the center of the floor.

"The opening dance," said Lord John with a groan. "You are stuck with me, Miss Julia, and I am no dab hand at the minuet."

"Nor am I," she said, taking his arm. "We'll muddle along together."

To her surprise, Lord Nicholas was at the head of the center line of dancers, partnering his mother. Now and again he moved into her field of vision, solemn and athletically graceful, his near-black hair shining under the light of crystal chandeliers. At one point he glanced in her direction, and his jaw tightened when he saw her hand in hand with his brother. After that he seemed deliberately to keep his gaze averted.

"So, have you made up your mind yet?" Lord John kept up a run of chatter whenever the figures brought them together. "I know the duke carried you off this afternoon for a lesson in selecting the proper husband, meaning the one he has already chosen for you."

"Yes, indeed. After Her Grace had already carried me off to the dower house and presented me to her candidate. Lord Whitley is exceedingly charming and kind, but I do not believe we would suit." She smiled up at him. "Does that news frighten you, my lord?"

"N-not at all," he said, color washing over his cheeks. "You seem a jolly sort of girl, and you're prettier than a field of daisies. But I can't think what you'd want with a husband who longs to be elsewhere. Given the opportunity, or put in the way of sneaking it, I would be off to the Peninsula in a heartbeat."

"I know. And I would not impede you. Would our marriage provide funds that we could use to your advantage?"

He gave her a look of astonishment. "I've thought of that. And felt badly, knowing that if we were given money to set up a household, I would likely make off with the better part of it. Does that shock you?"

"No. But why is it Sarne will not buy you a commission? I understand it would pain him to risk a son—"

A harsh laugh, surprising from the good-natured Lord John. "In his way, Sarne is fond of us all. But his prime intent is to secure the ducal line, which he does not wish to see perpetuated by Rich . . . by Whitley. And since Nick doesn't show signs of marrying in the near future, if ever, it falls to the least worthy son to breed more sons."

He stumbled, made a swift recovery, and grinned an apology. "If you could produce a son—make that twin sons, because Sarne will demand a spare—he might relent and let me go to the army. But it takes time, I know. Months and months. And by then, the war could be over."

As all right-thinking people profoundly wished, she thought, making sure her feelings didn't show on her face. "I would do my best, of course."

The music slowed, and the dance brought them into closer contact. "You have never explained," he said, "why you would consider marrying a chap who can't wait to scarper. If the duke is bullying you—"

"Not exactly." She thought, because Lord John had been so honest with her, that she owed him frankness in return. "But he told me this afternoon that if I do not agree by the end of the week to wed you, he will send me to live in the household of my sister and her new husband. In truth, sir, I would find that insupportable."

"God, yes. So would anyone. I mean, I don't know your sister, but Frederick is a toad. If marrying me will keep you free of him, it's well worth the trouble. I mean, it's not really any trouble. I've nothing to lose. That is . . . Dash it! My words are coming out all twisted. A fellow can't dance and plan his future at the same time."

She had started laughing in the middle of his speech, and when he realized it, he broke out laughing as well.

"Shall I consider myself betrothed, Lord John, or must I wait until the dance has ended?"

"Yes. Betrothed, I mean. You do me great honor. And let's peel away when we reach that spot over there, near where Robin is holding up the wall. Who decided these dances had to last so blasted long?"

For the next two hours she kept watching Lord John's face for any sign of regret or sense of entrapment, but his spirits, probably elevated by the flask he and Mr. Branden sometimes passed back and forth, remained high. She danced with the polite Mr. Branden, and with a young man from a nearby estate who took one close look at her, flushed the color of a red Japanese lantern, and stayed that way the entire time. Then Johnnie—he insisted she call him that—led her out for a Scottish reel. It was her favorite dance, and when it was over, they found glasses of lemonade and took refuge on the terrace to cool down.

"Let's not tell anyone yet," he said. "Mother will sulk and spend all week nagging at Whitley to win you away from me. And Sarne's smug as a bulldog when he gets his own way. Shall we let them play out their war until the last minute?"

"If you like. Except I should like to let Lord Whitley know he is clear of the snare. And I doubt any secret can long be kept from Lord Nicholas."

"Just so. We'll hold it to the brothers then, and Robin as well. He can always sniff out what's in the wind."

"So will everyone else, if we are discovered alone together. I should like to remain here for a little time, so would you mind being the one to go?"

"Glad to oblige." Grinning, he exited smartly, and a

few minutes later she spotted him among a group of gentlemen his age, probably talking about the war.

She carried her lemonade to the farthest corner of the terrace, took the steps down to a sweep of lawn, and wandered a little way out. Overhead, stars blazed in a clear sky.

Her future was settled. Assured. She could not yet believe her good fortune. Only three days ago a bleak existence had awaited her. Or a dangerous gamble, if she had elected to try her luck as an opera dancer or a courtesan. She had met several courtesans in Italy—they were friends of her mother—and thought she might make a success of it. But instead, she was soon to marry into one of the great families of England and spend her life with an honorable, good-natured gentleman. Perhaps one day they would even come to love each other.

She thought her mother would be pleased for her, and wondered if, from the mysterious realms beyond death, she still kept watch over her daughter.

A ring of smoke, followed by two more, wafted past her. Startled, she turned to see Lord Nicholas leaning against a tree trunk about ten yards away, his arms folded, a thin cigar dangling from one hand. A lantern, swinging in the breeze, sent light and shadows flickering across his face. He looked positively demonic, especially when his teeth showed in a humorless smile.

"Are all the young men blind, that they are not queuing up for a dance?" he said. "Or do they know you are already spoken for?"

"You have been speaking with Joh— Lord John?"

"I didn't have to. He's wearing the harried look of a man about to become a tenant for life. Exceedingly fast work, Miss Julia. Only a short time ago you were scheming to wed someone else entirely. Or is one Branden brother as good as the next, so long as you manage to insinuate yourself into the family?"

"You are not all the same, my lord. For one thing, neither of your brothers has ever insulted me."

"But then, they don't know you so well as I do." He lifted himself away from the tree and ambled over, a dark, imposing figure bringing with him the scents of rich, aromatic smoke and, she could tell when he drew closer, brandy. "Poor Johnnie, bridegroom by default. I hope he finds some way to profit from this."

"For once we are in agreement."

"Not so. Nothing good will come of this marriage. I can see you might have shared Whitley's enclosed life, what with the prospect of becoming a duchess. And Whitley would have done everything in his power to secure your happiness in the interim. But Johnnie . . . ah, he will ignore you twenty-three hours out of twenty-four. Not from unkindness, but because in his world, only the army has his full attention. He'll want you to be happy, so long as it requires no effort on his part."

"It won't, you know." She looked up at his disapproving face. "Happiness cannot be subject to another person, or to anything that can be taken away. I refuse to pass my life in misery, regret, guilt, or longing for what I cannot have. My mother taught me that I must always carry my happiness within myself. So whatever my circumstances, I always find ways to create happiness, and I give as much of it to others as they will accept. No matter what occurs, Lord Nicholas, I *will* be happy."

After a time, he gave a small shrug. "I envy you your temperament. If you can be satisfied with very little, you may yet carve out a place in the Branden family."

"But why do you all settle for less than you want, when you have the means to change your lives? I know you have done much to help Lord Whitley, sir. Why has no one provided Lord John what he so desperately wants? Surely you could find a way."

"To send him to *war*? Possibly to his death?"

"Families all over England are sending their husbands and brothers and sons to war. If they do not, the war will come here to them. You said yourself that Lord John has prepared himself, that he has the skills to be a good officer. All he lacks is the money. I would give it him myself, but the only thing of value I ever possessed is now owned by the duke."

"He took it from you?"

"William Flyte did that, when he had spent or gambled away the money sent for my care. He knew the duke was a collector of beautiful artifacts, so he traded my legacy for the duke's promise to secure my future, and Harriet's. It was a fair deal. I've no idea what would have become of us otherwise. I am speaking of a necklace that once belonged to Catherine de' Medici. Perhaps you have seen it."

"Sarne generally keeps his acquisitions locked away. Are you suggesting I should steal it for you, and use it to buy John into the army?"

"Gracious, no. I was only making a point. Those who have must give to those who need. You have money. Why do you not give it to your brother?"

"I don't, actually. I have expectations based on the promise of a rich estate, but very little of the ready. Not enough to purchase a commission, let alone uniforms, horses, and the rest."

"What of Lord Whitley?"

"Again, expectations of a future inheritance. Sarne keeps us all in his pocket. We could borrow, of course, enough to supply John what he needs. But that would set us in open rebellion against the duke."

"Would that be so bad? Lord John is miserable. You rarely spend time at the Abbey. Lord Whitley is forced to live alone and made to believe he is of no value."

Anger flashed in his eyes. "I have always defied my father. And when Whitley agreed to marry you, he was prepared to do the same. If we banded together, I expect we could raise the money. But it's not so simple as that. If Sarne got wind of our plans, he would scotch them immediately. He has influence where it counts. John would be refused a commission."

"And if it were already purchased, and Lord John on his way to Portugal, what then? Would Sarne have him snatched back?"

Lord Nicholas rubbed his chin. "Probably not. That would be too public a meal for the gossips to chew on. I thought you intended to marry my brother, Miss Julia. Now you are urging me to send him away."

"Not before the wedding," she said immediately. "And I know you can succeed. You arranged for a man to be impressed into the navy. How much more difficult can it be to help a man voluntarily join the army?"

"I can't count that high." But there was a new light in his eyes, and she could all but hear the wheels turning in his head. "It will have to be done within the week. Once the betrothal is announced, you and John will be the focus of too much attention. So a run for the border and a quick marriage in Scotland, because that's the only place we can do it without Sarne's consent. Doña Ysabella might advance me funds. Then John goes south to London by ship. But first we must all escape the Abbey without arousing suspicion, and be well beyond reach before anyone learns where we've gone. Even then Sarne cannot be allowed to learn about the commission. It might be a fortnight before John is safely out of the country."

He was no longer speaking to her, she knew. This man thrived on having a goal, on working out a puzzle, on achieving an objective. She found it exciting to be even a small part of this, to have planted the seed in his mind.

And best of all, to have thought up a wedding gift for Johnnie.

"If you are not to ruin yourself before you can be wed," said Lord Nicholas, "mind your deportment the next few days. Pretend you cannot decide between John and Whitley, because I may need you to carry messages to the dower house. For now, return to the ball, but do not dance again with John. A third dance will confirm you have chosen him."

"Oh. I didn't know. Thank you."

A smile, the first real smile she had ever seen on his handsome face. Dear heavens, he had a beautiful smile. A dangerous smile. In its light, a foolish young female could easily lose her wits, her virtue, and her future.

Fortunately for her, she was betrothed. Not to mention that Lord Nicholas despised her. And that he was already gone, blending into the shadows before she realized he had moved away.

6

All was going well.
Too well.

Nicholas Branden, master of plots and schemes, knew that any plan could be overturned by the most insignificant random occurrence. And this particular plan, jury-rigged and subject to every vagary, was more fragile than most. His instincts buzzed like a housefly trapped in a small room. Disaster lay ahead.

But the weather was fine. No one had suspected their true intentions when they set out that morning for an all-day picnic at Rutland Water. He'd taken the precaution of bringing along a fourteen-year-old girl and her ineffectual chaperon as decoys.

They had headed southeast, but the party soon changed direction, with Johnnie quieting Lady Eve's objections by mentioning a Derbyshire cave exploration. Not long after, they were on the Great North Road.

Nicholas had ridden it often enough to know distances and times. In the early afternoon, as arranged, the lead carriage suffered a minor accident, requiring the right front wheel to be replaced.

He insisted that Lady Eve's coach turn back immediately, escorted by the two reliable footmen he'd brought along for just that purpose. No telling how much time it would take to locate a proper-size wheel and repair the damage, so why should they all wait around under a surprisingly warm sun? An unfortunate occurrence, everyone agreed. Perhaps they would attempt another outing the next day.

When Lady Eve's party was gone, the spare wheel

concealed by a tarp was hauled down from the top of the carriage and put into place. Within half an hour the runaways were heading north again at a swift pace.

Nicholas and Johnnie had chosen to ride, leaving Julia alone in the carriage with a maidservant and several picnic baskets. They intended to drive straight through, changing horses when necessary, hoping to cross the border by the following afternoon.

With the escape well under way, Nicholas reviewed the other elements of his plot. Word had been sent to Jordan Blair, Johnnie's friend at Horseguards, to quietly prepare for a fast commissioning of two young officers. Robin had been dispatched north two days earlier, his first assignment to deliver Nicholas's letter to Doña Ysabella and collect the money . . . if she agreed to advance it.

If not, the plan could still go forward. Richard had supplied five hundred pounds, all he could put his hands on at short notice. Should worse come to worst, Johnnie would buy into a foot regiment and, when enough blunt was raised and sent to him, move on to the hussars. It was not uncommon to transfer in the field, he said. Dead officers needed replacing.

With or without Doña Ysabella's money in hand, Robin would go next to Leith, the port near Edinburgh, and arrange passage for himself and Johnnie to London. Then, if he had the strength to stay in the saddle, he'd cut southeast and be waiting for them at Gretna Green.

And still the housefly buzzed a warning. Nicholas lifted his wide-brimmed hat and swiped his forearm over his damp brow. Could Sarne have got word of the plan? He'd several hundred pairs of ears at the Abbey. It would be just like him to let the miscreants think they had got away, only to pounce on them before they reached their destination.

It was about three o'clock when Johnnie, riding ahead for most of the day, dropped back to Nicholas's side. "I think we're being followed," he said. "A carriage, pacing us for a while, then disappearing for a while, and back again. Pretty sure it's the same one."

"There's a good deal of traffic, John. How can you distinguish one coach from the next?"

"I . . . just can. I've been watching. It's moving in a peculiar fashion. I want to investigate."

"Very well. But I'm the one to deal with this. You continue on with the girl. If Robin's done his job, I'm no longer necessary except to get your new wife to Strathwylde. And you can manage that, one way or another. I'll catch you up if I can."

Just after they crested the next hill, Nicholas guided his horse into the woodland, found a narrow path running parallel to the road, and set out after the mysterious carriage. How he was to recognize it, he had no idea.

A few minutes later, he spotted it straightaway.

Dusk was falling over the posthouse where they had stopped to change horses. "Can something have happened to Lord Nicholas?" Julia said. "He's been gone nearly four hours."

She had persuaded Johnnie to accompany her for a brisk walk to shake out her cramped legs, and they reentered the courtyard as their carriage, fifth in line for attention, was led out by an ostler.

"Nicholas can take care of himself," Johnnie said. "Since we're driving straight through, I'll have them tie the baskets on top of the coach to give you more room. You'll need blankets, and I'd better get my greatcoat out of the portmanteau."

They were waiting for the baskets to be secured when another coach drove into the yard, flanked by a rider.

"It's Nick!" Johnnie ran over to take the reins as his brother dismounted.

Julia had seen a great many disapproving expressions on Lord Nicholas's face, most of them directed at her. But this time his anger was focused on the occupants of the coach. Wordlessly he strode to the door, wrenched it open, and jerked down the stairs.

"Out!" he said offering a stiff arm.

Lady Eve grasped his forearm and let him assist her to the ground. But the moment her shoes touched dirt, she rushed over to Johnnie. "How *could* you?" she demanded, looking for a moment as if she might strike him. Then she planted her hands on her hips. "You weren't even going to *tell* me! Am I not your ensign?

We have fought wars together, side by side, since I was eight years old. Have I no right to know that you are taking your place in the real army?"

"Apparently you *do* know, sprout. How did you find out?"

"I told you before. I do reconnaissance too. And don't call me sprout. That's a baby name."

"Sorry. You did have a right to know, Ensign. But this was put together quickly, and Nicholas said to tell no one. I would have written to you."

"No one ever writes. Mama says she will, when she sends me to stay at the Abbey, but she's never written even one letter. The minute you leave England, you will forget all about me."

"That's enough from you, young lady," said Lord Nicholas. "The proprietor is arranging a private room where you can wash up, and then we'll all have a hot supper before traveling though the night. Go along with Miss Crane and behave yourself."

She gave him a look that would fry eggs before setting off after her chaperon. When his back was turned, Julia saw Lady Eve stick out her tongue at him.

"Obviously you were right," Lord Nicholas said to Johnnie. "She'd persuaded the driver, the devil knows how, to shadow us. And ordered the footmen to Sarne Abbey, but they had the sense to follow behind her, in case of trouble. We were just one long parade, weren't we?"

He pulled off his hat and slapped it against his thigh. "Lady Eve will have to come with us. I sent the footmen back with a letter for Richard, and he will tell the duke and duchess as much as we want them to know."

"Why didn't you just take the lot of them home yourself? It would have been less trouble than towing them around Scotland."

"I know. But Lady Eve said that if I didn't let her see you off, she'd tell Sarne about the commission."

"And you believed her? Good God, Nick. Fourteen years old, and she played you like a fiddle. Evie would never betray me. She only said that to get you to do . . . well, what you did."

Lord Nicholas swore softly, using words Julia wasn't

supposed to know. Then he cast her a withering look. "Are all females as self-willed and devious as the pair of you?"

"I hope so," she responded equably. "Females require cunning, because males have reserved the power for themselves. And if you are wondering, I did not tell Lady Eve about our plans."

"I didn't suppose you had, if only because she doesn't appear to know about the wedding. I expect she's an eavesdropper who picked up bits and pieces. In any case, let's agree that she will learn nothing more from us. She has always followed Johnnie around like a duckling, and given what I just witnessed, there's no telling how she'll react when she learns he's to be married. We can do without more of her public hysterics. They draw too much attention."

"But surely we're out of reach by now," Johnnie said.

"Sarne has pigeons, and friends in the north. Just . . . let's take care and keep our mouths shut."

About an hour before sunset, when someone—probably the servants—might grow concerned about the long-absent picnickers, Richard sent a message to the duke and duchess. His request that they attend him at the dower house was sufficiently unusual to arouse their curiosity, and he was unsurprised to receive affirmative replies from them both.

They arrived separately, but at the same time, and warily settled on plain wooden chairs in the spartan sitting room.

Richard, who had just scanned Nick's letter again to make sure he had the change of plans straight in his mind, took up a position by the window. "I have been asked to inform you," he said, "that John has proposed marriage to Miss Julia, and she has accepted."

"Ha!" from the duke.

"She can't have done," protested the duchess. "She would never prefer John to you."

"I can tell you only what has occurred. They have decided to marry privately in Scotland and by now are well on their way there."

"An elopement!" The duchess's usually refined tone

came out as a squeak. "Like some common fieldhand and his wench? I may disapprove the bride, but our son is obliged to live up to his rank. I wish to provide him a grand wedding."

"Too late." The duke, having won the wager, was enjoying himself. "You had your chance with Harriet and Frederick."

"I believe, Mother, that when the two of you made a public circus of your sons and Miss Julia, you forfeited considerations you might otherwise have expected."

"Nicholas arranged it all, I daresay." Sarne stretched out his long legs. "So that is the end of our game, Eleanor. I suppose there is time for another, if you have something in mind."

"If you will," said Richard, "plot your next war elsewhere. Yes, Nicholas has taken charge of events, and Doña Ysabella will likely invite them all to stay at Strathwylde for a week or two. There is one small difficulty. Lady Eve and her servants were supposed to enjoy traveling along for a bit, but turn around in time to arrive here before dark. Instead, I have just received word that she is continuing all the way to Scotland, and that Nicholas will escort her back within a fortnight."

"Oh, dear! What I am to tell her parents?" the duchess wailed, wringing drama from her disappointment.

Sarne chuckled. "When was the last time they made contact with you during one of Eve's spring visits? We meddle with our children. The Maldons ignore theirs."

"That is all I can tell you about John and Miss Julia," said Richard, determined to finish the speech he had been rehearsing for several days. "But before you go, I have one more thing to say. My life has always been measured from one day to the next, and yet I have only now begun to learn its most important lesson. Not a moment should be left to wither when there is so much happiness to be found, and to be given. As you are aware, Father, there is in Devon a young woman I love, and with whom I have a child."

The duchess threw up her hands. "How *can* you speak of this in our presence!"

"You needed to know about her, Mother."

"I do know. I've always known. But a gentleman

keeps such liaisons strictly apart from his family. He certainly does not discuss them with a lady."

"Then I shall never again do so in your presence. But I have decided that I cannot spend, as I have been doing, more than half the year apart from them. Next month I shall remove to Devon, as always. But when I return in the autumn, I should like to bring them here."

"Impossible." The duchess rose and began to pace off her anger. "This is a respectable house and a respectable family."

"Some would dispute that," put in the duke.

"You are not being asked to acknowledge her," Richard said, "or to open Sarne Abbey to her. She would not wish that in any case. And you so rarely come here that nothing of significance would change, except that I would have the company of Maria and Stephen. And I would be happy."

"The dower house does not belong to you," said the duke. "You live here because we permit it."

"I am, of course, grateful for your generosity, and for the work done by Nicholas to rebuild it. But since you forbid me to live as I choose, I shall either remain in Devon for the winter or attempt to find a more suitable residence. That is all I had to say to you. Thank you for coming here at my request."

"Well, I think we can agree that winter winds at the seashore would not be good for your health. Sit down, Eleanor. High dudgeon is so wearying to observe. I think it past time we all had a tot of brandy. Have you any, Richard? Is it drinkable?"

Things had turned around so quickly that Richard's hands were shaking while he poured the drinks and handed glasses to his mother and father. He hadn't thought they would even hear him out. He'd assumed the duke would be pleased to see the last of him. Might they be persuaded after all?

"A toast to John," said the duke, lifting his glass, "and to his bride. I chose well, don't you think?"

Glaring at him, the duchess took a delicate sip.

Richard drank deeply, something he rarely did, reflecting that John was a lucky fellow to have Miss Julia and most likely did not appreciate his good fortune.

The duke held out his glass for a refill. "How old is that boy of yours now?"

"Rising six, sir."

"He'll be needing a pony, then. When the bores infesting the Abbey have gone, I'll ride over to Clark Lorson's stud and see what he has to offer. Or perhaps I should import a Connemara pony, although one can never strike a really good deal with an Irishman. Are you inviting us to stay for supper, Richard? And remind me to send over a stock of decent brandy from the Abbey cellars."

"Don't forget to have a servant wash the bottles beforehand," said the duchess. "Nicholas says the dust can be harmful."

Richard, his heart thumping with joy, went to give instructions to the housekeeper. Over supper, perhaps he'd push his luck and make the case for Sarne's return to Parliament, with the duchess taking her place as a political hostess. Rarely had two intelligent, talented people been more in need of a useful occupation.

7

Around midnight the travelers were required to wait out a downpour that was turning the road to mush. Lord Nicholas guided them off the turnpike road and to a small inn, where he managed to secure two small bedchambers. With the women crowding into one and the men packed into the other, they slept for a few hours and set off again at dawn. Lord Nicholas, noting familiar landmarks, traffic, and the condition of the road, estimated they would cross the border around nine o'clock that night.

They did so, and no sooner were they inside Scotland than Julia's heart began thumping with . . . well, she didn't know. Anticipation, probably. Or satisfaction. Relief.

A degree of fear as well. And dread.

An hour from now, perhaps two, she would be married and her husband would be gone.

With two days spent mostly alone with her thoughts, she'd had plenty of time to measure her decision for flaws. There were a frightful number of them. But she found even more arguments against declining the marriage and setting out on her own. Because of her appearance, no household that included a male resident would accept her as a governess, or even as a lower servant. Her experiences with Frederick told her what she might expect if someone did take her in.

Her more fanciful notions, such as dancing with the opera, meant getting herself to London. She didn't think her savings, five shillings and tuppence, would carry her very far.

Johnnie still seemed content with their arrangement, probably because he was already imagining himself at the head of a cavalry charge. A man with a lifelong dream about to come true had no thoughts to spare for a wife of convenience.

Her convenience. So far as she could tell, he hadn't a thing to gain by saddling himself with a wife. They wouldn't even consummate the marriage, she presumed, until he returned from the war.

Her thoughts kept chasing themselves around in circles, but always she landed in the same spot. With her situation dire and her bridegroom willing, if indifferent, she could not bring herself to call off the wedding.

Within a short time she saw a large white building with a steep roof and tall chimneys, all its windows brightly lit. Gretna Hall, where she was to be wed. And then she heard the tolling of a bell, as if her arrival were being announced. Moments later the coach turned into the stableyard, where servants swarmed out to assist them.

Her knees, shaky after the long confinement, almost buckled when she tried to descend the steps. She smiled at a young man who rushed over to help and directed him to Lady Eve's carriage, just pulling in. Lord Nicholas was stalking around, giving orders. As usual.

Then a shout from Johnnie, and she looked over to see Mr. Branden running in their direction. They went to meet him, joining up on a torch-lined path that led to the front entrance.

"I've got it," he said. "All the money we need, and extra too. Doña Ysabella wasn't keen on the idea until I told her Sarne would disapprove. Then willy-nilly, we were on the way to her bank."

Lady Eve came up beside Julia. "The duke didn't want his mother to remarry," she said, always full of news. "Especially to a commoner. After the fuss he made about it, she likes to get her own back."

Johnnie, bouncing with excitement, pumped his cousin's hand. "Good work, cuz. Did you hear that, Nick? I'm in!"

"Not until you're boring everyone in the officers mess

with the story of how you got there. Robin, what about passage to London?"

"If we leave immediately and ride hard, we can make the first sailing I booked. The second goes out tomorrow night."

"I need to hire a fresh horse." said Johnnie, his excitement brighter than the torches. "Get your things and let's be off."

"Aren't you forgetting something?" Lord Nicholas said in a dry voice.

"Oh." Frowning, Johnnie looked over at Julia. "Yes. Sorry. Robin, did you make the arrangements?"

"The proprietor has set aside the room, but David Lang won't trundle over to do the business until the bride and groom have arrived."

A gasp from Lady Eve.

"He's the priest," Mr. Branden explained. "Used to be a smuggler, but now he's the chap who presides. When I heard the announcing bell and saw you pull in, I sent a servant to fetch him."

"Go on in," Lord Nicholas said, "and get it over with. I'll see about horses."

As he started back the way they'd come, Lady Eve, who had been shaking like a pot about to boil over, rushed forward. Shoving past Lord Nicholas, she advanced on Johnnie and began to pummel his chest. "You mean to marry *her*? But you cannot! You are promised to me!"

Gently he took hold of Lady Eve's wrists and held then apart. "I don't know what you mean, Ensign. You are my comrade and my ally, but I am betrothed to Miss Julia."

"She's Miss Flyte now. And what's the use of marrying her to please the duke if you're going to the army? The one won't cancel out the other. Besides, you don't even *know* her. She is nothing to you."

"I'm sorry to distress you, Evie. But she is to be my wife."

"No!" She kicked him on the shin. "You said you would wait for me. You gave your word. Don't you even *remember*?"

Johnnie, a helpless expression on his face, looked over

the girl's head at Julia. "I've been scatty with plans for the escape and the commission. Tell me how I have offended."

"You asked me what I wanted for my birthday. And I said you should promise not to marry anyone else until I was old enough to be your bride. So you promised. And gave me a puppy, but Mama wouldn't let me keep it."

"Confound it, Evie. You were turning ten years old. What did you know of marriage? I didn't think you meant it." He let her go and threaded his fingers through his hair. "And you never mentioned it since."

"Why would I? You had given your word. I knew you would keep it. Except you didn't. Or won't. I'm only three years younger than she is, Johnnie. You didn't have to wait very much longer. Just until you saw what kind of woman I was to be. Then if you didn't want me, I . . . oh, I don't know what I would do. How does one live a whole life with a broken heart? But I wouldn't have asked more of you than to give me a chance."

Julia's conscience stretched, yawned, and came fully awake. She saw Lady Eve drooped against Johnnie, exhausted from their journey and dispirited from his betrayal. And he looked terribly unhappy. None of them had meant this to happen.

She ached all over. *Must* she surrender her only chance at a secure future for the sake of a child's infatuation? In three years, when it was time for the Earl of Maldon's daughter to be presented during a glorious London Season, General Johnnie might be no more to her than a treasured memory.

"Why would you ask such a thing, Evie?" Johnnie stroked her blond hair. "You haven't the right to bind another person on . . . on speculation."

"You said that when you were seven years old, you knew that you were meant to be a soldier. Have you ever changed your mind?"

"You know I haven't."

"And I haven't changed mine about wanting to marry you. I know what love is, Johnnie. You don't love me, not yet. But you don't love her either. And if you marry her now, you will ruin everything for us all."

For Julia, another door—the last door—silently closed. Left only with herself, she dug inside, scraped up a few dregs of courage, and moved into the light of a torch so that Johnnie could see her face. "Lady Eve has the right of it, sir. I cannot say how your life, or hers, will turn out, but you cannot permit someone you have known for only a week to change everything, irrevocably, for you both. We should never have begun this, and under the circumstances, I find it necessary to jilt you."

That didn't sound quite right. But she was breaking apart inside. Within such a short time she had lurched from desperation to hope with news of the Sarnes' marriage scheme, and from there to excitement with Lord Whitley's proposal. Then came Lord Nicholas's explanation of why she could not accept Whitley, so off to Lord John, who dutifully and vaguely proposed. Now this. Any equilibrium she had brought with her to Scotland was entirely gone.

Along with everything else except, perhaps, her integrity.

With care, Johnnie set Lady Eve away from him and approached Julia. A glowering Nicholas moved aside to let him pass.

All the joy that had been in Johnnie's eyes had fled. Now there was only distress, and, she could tell, concern for her. "Are you certain?" he asked softly. "Evie is tired, and she's always been impulsive. She'll get over this."

"I don't think so, Johnnie. But you must not be prisoner to either of us. Your duty lies elsewhere, and you will require a clear mind for the difficulties ahead."

"But what will become of you, Julia? What about the toad?"

"Oh, I expect Sarne was using the same tactic Lady Eve employed on Lord Nicholas, making an empty threat to get his way. Frederick will never again lay his many fingers on my person."

"If he tries, I'll come back to England and shoot him."

Managing a laugh, she gazed up at his open, honest face. "Thank you, Lord John, for offering yourself as my champion. I will always remember your gallantry. Now bid farewell to your ensign and go to your ship."

"Yes, ma'am." A fist-to-chest salute, and soon he was

hunkered down in front of Lady Eve, speaking privately to her.

Julia saw that Nicholas had gone, probably to make arrangements at the stable. Mr. Branden had vanished as well. She went to stand beside Miss Crane, willing the tears in her eyes to evaporate. Nothing else must spoil Johnnie's leavetaking.

After a time, Mr. Branden emerged from the hotel with a satchel in one hand and leather saddlepacks slung over his shoulder. He was wearing greatcoat, hat, and gloves.

Johnnie rose. "Well, this is it, Ensign. Time to ride. Remember your promise. I will find out if you're not behaving yourself."

"I'll try," she said. "But I am not by nature obedient, you know. And you are to write to me. Every day. Even if it's hard. You'll be glad of it, because there will be a record of everything you did and thought and felt. It's the only way I can be in the army too, Johnnie. You have to let me be there with you."

"Very well. I'll start tonight, when we're on ship, and Robin will remind me if I get lazy. Ah, there's Nick."

Lord Nicholas had taken a shortcut across the grass. "Everything's ready. Take what you can carry from your portmanteau and buy whatever else you need in London. Or Edinburgh, if you get there too late for the sailing."

"We won't!" With a whoop, Johnnie sprinted across the lawn, waving a backward good-bye. Mr. Branden was close behind him, and Lady Eve brought up the rear.

"Go keep an eye on that hellion," Lord Nicholas told Miss Crane. "I don't want her following them across Scotland."

Julia turned, meaning to accompany her, and was brought up short by a harsh command.

"A word with you, Miss Flyte!"

Just what she required right now. Another lecture from the toplofty Lord Nick. Or maybe he meant to thank her for setting his brother free. If he did, she feared she'd start weeping like a disappointed child. *Just give me some time*, she begged silently. *Let me recover myself. Let me think what to do.*

Her turn became a slow circle, and then she was facing his stern face and forbidding expression. "I must warn you, sir, that if you rebuke me, I shall likely turn into a watering pot."

"I don't mean to. . . ." He removed his hat, looked at it, and put it back on his head. "This is difficult for you," he said meticulously, as if navigating a river full of poisonous snakes. "John will expect me to make certain you are cared for. I have no objection to that, although I suspect you will have many. You should know from the start that while I understand your reservations, they will not signify."

Cotton wool must have wrapped itself around her brain. "I beg your pardon, my lord, but I have no idea what you are talking about."

"Your reputation. It is compromised beyond redemption. You will have to marry me."

Shock rooted her to the ground. Paralyzed her tongue. She stared at him, unblinking.

"I know you dislike me," he said. "But you told me you were adaptable. That you learned to make do, whatever your circumstances. I am not so fine as Whitley or Johnnie, but over time, I expect you will grow accustomed to my failings."

"Are you . . . ?" She swallowed and tried again. "Are you *proposing* to me?"

"*Proposing* implies that you have the option to refuse, which you do not. To make of yourself a respectable woman, and for the honor of my family, you must throw yourself upon my sword." He frowned. "So to speak. I mean, of course, that you must accept."

"The devil I must!" At the oath, she slapped her hand over her mouth. And took it away again, because he could hardly think worse of her than he already did. "Even in Scotland, I have to give my consent to marry, and I don't. I *won't*!

"Why?" He looked genuinely confused. "You want admission to the family. I'm the only brother left. If you would have the others on two days' acquaintance, why not me?"

"I've known you almost a week," she said. "That should explain it."

Just when it seemed matters couldn't get any worse, a plump man wearing a floppy hat and smelling of ale came loping up the path. "Are you the ones what mean to wed yourselves? Come along, then. I haven't all night."

Lord Nicholas gave him a Lord Nicholas look. "You're Lang? Go inside and wait for us. All night, if that's what it takes. And no more drinking until we're done."

Julia thought Lang would protest. Thought about applying to him for rescue. But she stood there like a tree stump until he was gone. And inside that stump, green shoots were uncurling, gathering strength, forcing themselves through the hard, dead wood.

Could it be? Did she dare?

When Mr. Lang was gone, she straightened her spine and lifted her chin. "Just how, Lord Nicholas, do you expect to win my consent to this travesty?"

"I . . ." Off came the hat again. He tossed it onto the grass. "I am appealing to your common sense. To what I believe is your genuine affection for my brothers, who would be distraught to imagine you on your own, without resources, fending for yourself. And I'm appealing to your ambition. I will not be an easy man to live with, but I shall provide well for you. There will be opportunities, in future, for travel. For time spent in London. I have an extensive library."

"I should like those very well indeed. But you come along with them. And, of course, you're not exactly fond of me either. May I expect you to leave me fairly much to my own devices?"

"Is that what you wish?" His face darkened. "The answer is no. You may expect me to be demanding."

"That seems unfair. You wed me only from a false sense of obligation, and then insist I conform to your wishes. What exactly are those, Lord Nicholas? Do you intend to punish me for intruding in your brothers' lives? For ruining yours?"

"Good God. I may be impatient and abrupt and thick-headed, but I'm not a monster. About you I have been wrong. From the first I assumed you to be a scheming parvenu . . . well, you know what I thought. I told you often enough. But I have discovered you to be intelligent and generous. I watched you hand over a promising future not once, but twice, so that my brothers could pursue their own happiness. I owe you many, many apologies."

He appeared to brace himself. "I know you don't want me, or anything to do with me. But I am asking of you a third sacrifice. In this case, it is to accept me, which is the most difficult thing anyone could expect of you. And my reasons are entirely selfish."

"You told me. The honor of your family."

"Not that." He closed the short distance between them. His arms lashed around her. "This."

His lips were on hers, open and insistent. He drew her tightly against him, letting her feel his strength, his protectiveness. And yes, his passion.

She tasted him then, and desire surged through her, pulsing in every vein. The tingle of excitement she had always felt just to see Lord Nicholas, the anticipation of seeing him when he wasn't there, the thrill of jousting with him . . . She had wondered at it. Now she understood.

Like her mother, she had found a man to love. The one man for whom she would give up all the world, if need be. Her instincts had recognized him immediately, but her mind and heart had been slow to catch on. Now, after years of loneliness and near-despair, she let go her last, lingering uncertainties and opened her heart entirely. The hope she had kept alive for so many years, watering it with little drops of stolen happiness, sprang free.

"C-can you love me?" she murmured when they paused to steal a breath.

"How can I not?" he said, and lowered his head for another kiss.

"Tally-hoooooooo! Whoop! Whoop! Whoop!"

They broke apart, breathing heavily, and looked toward the stableyard. Johnnie and Mr. Branden, shrieking like banshees, stampeded toward the road, made the turn, and waved their hats in farewell.

"Godspeed," Nicholas said softly. "I hope we did the right thing."

"He would have found a way," she said. "The Branden men always do."

He laughed, sending new sparks dancing along her skin. "And don't you forget it. May I assume that when you returned my kiss, you were agreeing to marry me?"

"Just making certain I was altogether compromised, in case you had second thoughts."

"Since I saw you in the garden, flirting with the sunflowers, I've had only one thought. It concerns what we are going to do tonight, and every night. And sometimes in the daytime." He brushed his forefinger across her lips. "But first, the vows. Let us gather our two witnesses, shall we, and get on with it?"

"I see that I shall have to teach you how to be more romantic, sir."

"I think it is not in my nature." He took her hand in a warm, possessive grip and adjusted his stride to hers as they walked to the entrance of Gretna Hall. "Don't imagine you can wrap me around your little finger, the way you've done with every other man you've ever met."

She glanced up, her face tilted to show off her long lashes and the curve of her cheek. "You won't mind, though, if I try?"

"As a matter of fact, I'm rather looking forward to it."

A Match Made in Heaven—Or Hell

by
Barbara Metzger

1

Nicky and Pete were arguing over a broken soldier.
"He's mine."

"No, he's mine."

"I saw him first!"

"I've had my eye on him for ages."

"Have not."

"Have too."

But these were not two boys in the nursery; they were
two ancient adversaries overlooking the Spanish plains,
and the soldier was no cast-metal figurine. He wasn't
even a soldier, but a British lord. A battle had been
fought here, but now another battle was being waged,
this time for the soul of Hugh, Marquess of Hardesty.

Nicodemus, or Old Nick, as he was often called by
those who would not say his name out loud, sneered as
he looked down on the dusty field where the marquess
lay crumpled in a pool of blood, half under his fallen
horse. "Of course I have had this one in my sights. How
could you think otherwise? I've watched this Hugh
Hardesty for the last ten years, ever since he was tossed
out of university. I waited while he cut a swath through
London, drinking, whoring, gambling. Then I watched
while he seduced all those wives and widows. It was just
a matter of time before some jealous husband killed him,
if he did not break his neck in an absurd race, or lose
a brawl in a filthy tavern. Then he'd be mine. It just took
a little longer than I expected, but he is hellbound now."

Saint Peter wagged his chin. "No, he died a hero, saving all those other poor souls when he fought by their
side." He waved a gnarled hand at the ragged foot sol-

diers beginning to stir through the smoke and the stench of the battlefield. "He could have ridden off after delivering his message, but he stayed to help when he found the commanding officer wounded, rallying the troops, defending them with his sword. He was courageous and selfless, sacrificing himself and his horse for his king and his country. That makes him mine."

"What, so many years of profligacy forgiven in one instant? Not even you could be such a—"

"Now, now. You know how it works. He died with honor. That is enough for us."

"He died disobeying orders, as usual. The thirty-year-old heir to a duke would never be allowed in the thick of battle, not without ensuring the succession first. I believe there was something mentioned about honoring thy parents. Then there is the fact that they let him act as courier on the Peninsula simply because he was such an embarrassment in London. Not one but two undersecretaries' wives, at the same time." Nicky grinned, showing pointed teeth. "Absolutely a lad after my own heart. Let's see . . . adultery, coveting thy neighbor's wife, definitely blaspheming when he was accused, then bearing false witness when he swore he had been elsewhere."

"That last was nobly done, to protect the ladies' reputations."

"Stubble it, Peter. He's mine."

The brangling might have gone on for days—or decades—but the marquess moved an arm.

"Heaven be praised," Saint Peter said, predictably. "He lives."

"Not for long," the devil said. "If the scavengers don't kill him for his silver buttons, a little rain and a chill will finish him off, what with that head wound and the other injuries." He raised one hand, as if to call down the storm.

"You cannot," Saint Peter thundered. "His time has not come."

Never being one for formalities, Old Nick brushed that aside. "What's another hour or day? He'll be mine soon enough."

Saint Peter studied the wounded man, looking far deeper than the broken bones. "Perhaps not."

Nicodemus snorted. "Care to make a wager, old man? Not an actual bet, of course, knowing your attitude toward these things, but just a small bit of play between gentlemen, to liven up the job."

Saint Peter was tempted. "You're too sure of yourself, sir. There is always a chance he can reform, you know. A brush with death can do that, show a man the error of his ways."

"Or it can show him how fragile life is, so he should enjoy his few years to the fullest. He'll go back to hell-raking as soon as his wounds heal."

"Not necessarily. That is what redemption is all about. Even the worst libertine can change with enough encouragement. Why, the love of a good woman has been known to work wonders."

"Bosh. That is the stuff of fiction. Good women have been loving Hardesty for all of his thirty years, to no effect. He's never loved one enough to care to earn her respect, much less be faithful. I doubt the man has a heart."

"Oh, he has a heart, all right. And he'll love the woman I have in mind."

"Never. Good women do not interest him."

"This one will. I'll make sure she is beautiful enough to stir even his jaded senses."

"I'll make him blind so he can't see her."

Saint Peter was adamant. "She will be so good at heart that her inner beauty will show through."

The devil sneered. "I'll make him deaf so he cannot hear this paragon's sweetness."

"What? You'd make him deaf and blind, just to prove your point that he cannot be saved?"

Nick shrugged. "We all have our objectives."

"But he is not ours yet. No," Saint Peter declared, "I say we let Lord Hardesty's life take what course it will, without interference, then see who wins his soul."

Old Nick agreed. "No interference." He lied, of course. He was the devil.

As soon as Saint Peter left to gather those poor souls who'd perished here with a prayer on their lips, the devil snapped his fingers, calling forth a gremlin. Small, hairy, with big ears, a long tail, and sharp, snaggled teeth, the

creature drooled on its master's cloven feet. "You," Nicodemus ordered. "You will accompany Lord Hardesty
to keep all good women away from him."

The gremlin scratched its nether regions, then under
its armpit.

The devil realized that would not do, so he changed
the yellow-eyed demon into a monkey. No, that would
not work, either. Not even a decadent English lordling
was foolish enough to carry a simian into battle. A goat
would be eaten before nightfall, and a snake never could
be trusted. He snapped his fingers again. "A dog. Perfect. Do your job and you will be rewarded. Fail and
you will be roasted on a spit until hell freezes over."

Hugh awoke in pain and so weak he could barely open
his eyes. He could not feel his legs, and wished he could
not feel his head. They ought to let a fellow sleep off
his overindulgence in peace, he complained to himself,
although he could never recall feeling quite this
wretched after the worst debauchery. Then he recalled
the battle. This was no morning after; this was eternity.
He was dead, and right where his nanny, his tutors, the
gossip columns, and his father always said he'd end, in
hell.

The heat, the pain, the stench, the cries of agony all
around were overwhelming. Hugh sank back into whatever limbo he could find. When he returned to awareness the next time, the torture was as intense, but joined
with a din that threatened to shatter his skull. He tried
to separate the sounds: shouts, growls, and high-pitched,
frantic gibberish, although that might have been Spanish
spoken so fast he could not translate. Then one voice
rose above the others, assured, assertive, and in English,
thank whatever powers held sway in this purgatory.
"Sit," the unmistakably feminine voice said. "Sit, sir, or
I swear I shall shoot."

Hugh was already dead, so he wasn't afraid of the
threat, but he tried to sit up anyway. He saw no reason
to antagonize the authorities, not on his first day here,
at any rate. His legs would not move, his head was too
heavy to lift, and his muscles had turned to mush. He
sank back against what felt like a bed of nails.

"Oh, you are awake, my lord. Excellent. Please call off your dog so we might see to your wounds."

He was wounded, not dead? Someone was going to help him, take away his pain? Hugh almost cried in relief. In fact, he was weeping, to his embarrassment. He tried to brush the moisture away from his cheeks but his right arm appeared to be immobile, strapped to his chest. His left hand discovered a large bandage around his head and over one eye. He managed to open his other eye to look at his rescuer.

She was a tall woman, dressed head to toe in black, with a pinched face and a scowl that might have frightened small children. She wore a bloodstained apron, and had a pistol pointed right at his privates. Maybe he was in hell after all, Hugh thought. No, he could see a large cross on the wall behind the female. Surely the devil did not decorate with religious symbols. He had to be in some kind of Spanish convent, judging from the flock of other black-robed women clutching their Bibles and beads near a door. His aching brain tried to comprehend why one of the nuns was speaking such perfectly accented, educated English, but the more important question was why she was threatening to emasculate him. Hugh tried to ask, but his mouth appeared glued shut. Now that he was aware of it, he was parched and parboiled. "Water," he tried to beg, but managed only the sound of a fish gasping its last breath.

"Please, my lord, tell your dog to stand down."

"Don't . . . have a . . . dog," Hugh managed to croak.

"Tell that to the imp of Satan on your lap. The cur has already bitten two of the sisters. He will not let anyone but the surgeon come near you, and the poor man is run ragged as it is. You wound needs attention, and your next dose of laudanum is due, along with the fever powders the surgeon left."

Hugh raised his head an inch—all he could accomplish—and found himself staring into odd yellow eyes amid bristly brown fur. "Not mine."

"Well, he thinks he is, my lord, and no one has been able to convince him otherwise. He saved your life out on the battlefield, chasing away the looters and barking to draw the attention of the litter bearers who had left you for dead. Unfortunately, he insists on guarding you still."

The dog was a mangy-looking mongrel with big ears and a long, skinny tail. As ugly as the animal was, Hugh was doubly relieved to see him. The English abyss was not aiming for his apparatus, and his legs could move, once the creature shifted off them. He fumbled to pat the coarse-haired head, earning him a wag of that rat's tail, and a snaggletoothed dog grin. He'd seen uglier dogs, Hugh was sure, but he could not recall when or where. Then the beast snarled at the nun with the gun.

The woman was growing impatient. "We are too busy for this nonsense, my lord. Tell that ill-mannered menace to be quiet, for he has been disturbing all the other patients. And we really have to change your dressings now before you become infected, so make your watchdog behave or I will shoot him, I swear I will."

Hugh stroked the dog again. "We need help, old boy. I think the lady means to offer it."

The dog fixed his yellow-eyed stare on Hugh, then on the woman, as if he were trying to solve a conundrum. What kind of woman was this, he seemed to be asking himself, friend or foe? Sure as Hades, no good woman would shoot a dog. Satisfied, he circled Lord Hardesty's legs three times, tucked his nose between his paws, and went to sleep.

2

The sisters were still afraid of the dog, so nursing the grievously wounded gentleman fell to Marian. She believed that the nuns were more fearful of the marquess than of the mongrel. His lordship's valet might have remained behind in Lisbon, but Lord Hardesty's reputation had followed him to this tiny convent of Saint Esperanza in the desolate, devastated countryside.

Two days after the battle of Cifuente, Hardesty was a legend. The injured foot soldiers were full of his daring rescue, how he had ridden through the dust on a stallion as gray as English fog, delivering orders from headquarters. He had stayed, though, unlike any messenger they had ever seen, or any dandified civilian, for that matter. He had stayed in the fray, rallying the outnumbered, leaderless troop. He had been a madman, the soldiers declared, galloping here, there, sword flashing, a smile on his lips. He had performed more equestrian tricks than any bareback horseman at Astley's Amphitheatre, they swore, and Marian translated for the nuns. Dodging, bobbing, feinting, weaving in and out, Lord Hardesty had defended the small band of survivors until they could reload and re-form their ranks. He was a true hero, and a true berserker.

Battle rage was not what had the sisters of Saint Esperanza so wary of the English peer. His other, earlier reputation was the one no God-fearing female could accept or ignore. Hardesty was a womanizer by all accounts, an unprincipled, hedonistic rake, who was as successful at his chosen vocation as he was handsome. As far away from London as Hampshire, Marian had read about him often enough in the social gazettes, in association with some dashing widow or straying wife. His name was never linked to the younger, more innocent, marriage-minded ladies of the *ton*, which, Marian supposed, was to his credit. His eschewing wellborn virgins was about the only thing she had ever heard in his favor.

If she had gone to town for her own delayed presentation, as her parents had wished, they would not have traveled in the same social circles, despite her father's title. Still, Marian knew enough of the marquess to despise him and all he stood for. Men who used women for solely their own pleasure were lower than the hard-packed Spanish dirt beneath her feet. Marian would not be here on this blasted, blood-soaked Peninsula if not for another such lying, licentious, lizard-tongued blackguard.

So she had warned the mother superior, who had Lord Hardesty moved to a small cell far removed from the nuns' chambers, as if the wounded man were any threat in his condition. They all thought he would die, and if he did not, that his valet would arrive to tend him. Neither had happened yet, and Marian was left to care for the dastard and his dog while the sisters prayed for him. Considering his dire injuries, and her skill in the sickroom, prayers might not come amiss, Marian reflected.

The nights were the worst. During the day the true nursing sisters were in and out, or as far in as the marquess's mongrel would permit. The convent's manservant came to attend to the male patients' bodily needs, and the surgeon called. Marian could go rest in her own assigned guest room when the other wounded English soldiers did not need comforting, help translating, or letters written back to their wives and sweethearts at home. But at night, which started after evening prayers, nearly at sundown, all was quiet except for Lord Hardesty's labored breathing and the dog's snores. No prayers echoed through the stone walls, no conversations, no laughter from the wide-eyed village children who were always underfoot during the day, curious about the British troops.

The marquess could not be left alone through the

long, lonely hours of the dark, and Marian's bedchamber was too far away, so she dragged a palette into his sparse little room. She thought she could nap, but she feared sleeping through one of his lordship's prescribed medications. Then, too, her borrowed black gown was coarse and uncomfortable, but Sister Emanuella would be scandalized to find Marian in her nightclothes, no matter that the libertine lord was mainly unconscious. Her own frocks would have been just as outrageous in the good sister's eyes. Mostly Marian sat in the hard wooden chair at his beside until her back ached and her neck grew stiff, trying to read or do mending by the light of the one meager candle.

She had never mended anything in her life, although she had spent hours at fancy needlework, but no maidservant was going to repair her petticoats or stockings, and who knew how long before she could purchase new ones? Her best efforts would just have to be good enough, like her efforts to repair the battered peer.

While the nuns trusted in their prayers to heal Lord Hardesty, Marian relied on her own determination to keep the man alive. She had made mice feet of her own life; she was going to save his, even if it killed her. She might have wished for a worthier subject, one whose demise would not benefit all womankind, but the marquess's welfare rested on her shoulders, and she did not intend to drop this burden. She would not fail, not this time. He needed her, and she needed to be a success at something, anything, to prove her own worth, if even to herself.

So she bathed his fevered skin, dribbled broth down his throat, made sure he had both the surgeon's medications and Sister Conchita's herbal infusions, and laudanum when the pain was too fierce. And she commanded him to fight. "Live, damn you," she ordered when she was sure no one else could hear. "Live so some angry husband can put a sword through your black heart, or some scorned female can shoot you. Live so you can bedevil your poor family for ages more, and keep the scandal-sheet journalists in business. Live, you immoral maggot, live."

The dog wagged his skinny tail, and the marquess kept breathing.

While he slept, when her eyes grew too weary for sewing or reading, Marian studied this duke's profligate son who had become a hero of the Peninsula war. With nothing to occupy her thoughts but her own dismal past and more dismal future, Marian contemplated Lord Hardesty, trying to discover what made him so irresistible to women. The bandage around his head obscured most of his features, but Marian knew they were even, with high cheekbones, a straight nose, a wide brow. He had thick auburn hair, where the surgeon had not cut it away to dress the wound under the wrappings. One of his eyes was still swollen shut, all black and blue and purple, but the other was blue-green, with flecks of gold. Despite being glazed with pain and drugs and fever, that eye showed intelligence when he was awake, and awareness of his situation. He was no fool, this gazetted flirt. He knew he was inches away from shaking hands with the hereafter, and seemed to appreciate the efforts to widen the distance.

He had a strong jaw, and laugh lines around his mouth. Marian was sure that was what they were and wished she could see him smile. As handsome as he must be, a smile would make him devastatingly appealing—to a certain kind of woman, of course. That woman would not be disappointed when she unwrapped her gift, either. Marian knew from sponging his lordship's chest how well muscled he was, how fit, without an ounce of softness to him. There was nothing of the idle wastrel in his physique, so he must exercise regularly. Marian blushed to think of what form a rake's exertions might take. To maintain this form, he must practice a lot. Oh, my.

She dragged her eyes back to his face, where she saw pride and strength and something else she did not expect: sweetness. She knew he was courteous by how he tried to whisper his appreciation, and once his good hand reached for hers in thanks, but she thought she saw a gentleness, too, not just the boyish vulnerability suggested by his wounds and the bandage. She nodded. That was why so many women sacrificed their virtue to Lord Hardesty, then. Not merely for his good looks or his physical prowess, although those were great inducements, Marian supposed, but for that unspoken promise of being cherished. Females would indeed be attracted.

Marian was not, of course. Lord Hardesty was half-dead, for one thing, and she was never going to trust another man as long as she lived, for another. He could be an Adonis from Aylesbury, a Romeo from Rye, or the finest lover in the British Isles. No matter. She was finished with men.

She was different, the nurse they called Marian. Of course she was, Hugh told himself. That much would be obvious to a blind man. She spoke English, by George. More unusual, she spoke in educated, refined tones without a hint of an accent. She had been reared as a lady, unless he missed his guess, which was something Hugh seldom did when it came to females. A British Catholic gentlewoman was rare enough, but a nun? Even if his attendant had taken a page from Ophelia and gotten herself to a nunnery, what the devil was she doing in a poor Spanish convent in the middle of a war?

She was different from the other sisters in other conspicuous ways, too. She wore no cross, no wedding band, and no beads at her waist. Neither did she disappear for prayers when the bell rang. And she swore like a soldier. Perhaps she had not yet completed her vows, Hugh considered, since no one seemed to call her *hermana*. She was taller than most of the women he had seen here, and younger, from what he could tell beneath the shapeless black gowns and the shawl-like black head coverings, although she was no girl. He thought Marian had blond hair, knew she had clear blue eyes, and was positive her soft, competent hands had never toiled at the hard labor these dedicated churchwomen endured.

She was not nearly as timid as the rest of the nuns, either. He'd seen handfuls of them scurrying past his room, fearful of both him and the dog. Not his Marian. Why, she had even taken the cur for a bath, to rid his fur of that acrid smoky odor he carried from the battlefield. The dog had suffered quietly after her sharp commands, which told Hugh the woman was used to giving orders, with an air of authority that never came from humble stock.

All in all, her presence here was as much a mystery as the dog's. The mongrel could not answer his questions, and Marian would not. Every time he summoned enough energy to open his mouth to ask, she poured some noxious potion down his throat. For now he was content to have both of them nearby. The dog had saved his life, he understood, and so had the woman. He was comforted by the dog's warmth and steady heartbeat, and encouraged by his nurse's demands on heaven that he recover. Hugh's lips quirked up in amusement. What kind of nun gave the Almighty orders?

Soon he would insist on stopping the laudanum doses, before he grew too dependent on the drug. He'd seen other men succumb to the habit, and vowed not to take that pitiful path. Without the opiate his mind would clear, and then he could solve the intrigue of his English novitiate. Until that time he would rest and regain his strength, confident that he could charm the answers out of his Maid Marian. She might be a nun, but she was still a woman, wasn't she?

3

Hugh had not lost his wits with the cracked skull, and he had not lost his limbs despite breaks and bruises, but he sure as Hades had lost his touch with the ladies. Nurse Marian was as close as a clam when it came to her personal life. As his health improved, so that he was awake more, and more in his right mind, her temperament deteriorated. Soon she was meeting every friendly, flirtatious effort on his part with a scowl and a sharp word. Now he could well believe she had sworn a vow of chastity, not that many men would be tempted to wed—or bed—such a poker-backed, prune-faced, preachy female. He was not tempted in the least, but he was still curious as to why a well-bred young woman, even a homely spinster firmly on the shelf, would give up hope of a home and family of her own. Marian was no beauty, he decided, but neither was she an antidote. Some poor fool, a banker or a vicar, might find her stiff manner appropriate to his calling, even if he did not find her appealing to his senses. If she had a large enough dowry . . .

No, the sisters of Saint Esperanza would not use his gift of gratitude to bribe a bridegroom for one of their members. And, truly, it was none of his business that an Englishwoman had renounced English gentlemen, and Spanish ones, and Portuguese, it seemed. But he could still be curious. With little else to occupy his time and his thoughts, the conundrum of the nonreligious nun intrigued him. There was more to the situation than he'd first supposed. Why, the woman would not give him her last name, to see if he knew any of her family. She read to him, tended to him, spooned gruel into him, but she would not warm to him. He was wounded indeed.

"What, not even a little smile, Maid Marian mine?"

Maid Marian, my foot, Marian thought. As if he were Robin of Locksley, come to her rescue. More likely he was Robin Hood, come to steal her heart. His smile was as breathtaking as she had supposed, despite the empurpled eye and the bandage, and his charm was as devastating, as all-encompassing, as a blizzard. A woman could lose herself there—if she were a fool twice over. He was a rake, for heaven's sake. Of course he was charming. He meant nothing by it, and Marian took nothing from it but insult. She did not correct his presumptuous, provocative name for her, though. She was not about to tell him that she was Lady Marian Fortenham, daughter of Earl Fortrell of Hampshire. He would have heard of the scandal, of course, if not in England then here in Spain. Everyone on earth had heard of it, she was sure. Even Hottentots must be having a laugh at her humiliation. Marian was ashamed of her disgrace enough on her own, without seeing the condemnation on yet another face. His face. She frowned harder, and brushed a drip off his chin with a rough swipe of a towel.

"You do not like me, do you?" he asked, genuinely puzzled. She had struggled so hard to keep him alive, yet now she seemed to regret the happy results.

"I do not know you, my lord," she replied, then added, "I do not like your way of life, however."

"You must not believe everything you have heard, you know."

"If I believed half of what I hear about you, my lord, I would shoot you now, before someone else has the chance."

He winced, and not just from another heavy-handed dab at his skin. The prickly, prudish female would be harder to befriend than he thought, and that seemed the only way of learning her secrets. The army surgeon was too harried to chat, and Hugh's Spanish was too labored to converse with the convent's manservant. Even if he could have made himself understood by the other nuns, they were kept at bay by the dog, for some reason. Only

Marian was permitted to sit by Lord Hardesty's bedside without growls and snarling teeth. The more she frowned, cursed, or treated Hugh roughly, the more that bristly cur seemed to like her. The marquess decided to name the contrary beast Impy, since Marian kept referring to him as "that imp of Satan." The dog learned the name instantly, and wagged his tail. Now if Hugh could only get Marian to—

"I do not suppose I can convince you to find us a beefsteak, can I? That might sweeten Impy's temper, and I know my recovery would go that much faster if I had something besides gruel and broth."

The sooner he was well enough to be sent back to England, the better Marian would feel too, but nothing, not money or influence, could procure her patient a beefsteak. "The French killed every cow, pig, and sheep they found before their retreat."

"The officers had beef at headquarters."

"And they might have it still, but you are not in the army, my lord, which fact the surgeon keeps repeating in his complaints about coming out here to treat you. They do not want you at headquarters, it seems, for fear they will be blamed for your death if you do not recover."

He nodded. "My father must be apoplectic that I was wounded."

"And the general, the prince, and Parliament, from what I understand," she said with a curl of her lip. No one cared how many real soldiers were killed or wounded. One injured heir to a dukedom had them all in a quake. "But you are too weak to ship home, or to Lisbon."

Hugh rubbed the cut on his cheek where old Juan Marcos had nicked him. "Where my valet sits, doing nothing."

Marian supposed his valet would not spill as much soup down Lord Hardesty's chin as she was doing, but the lily-livered valet had refused to ride through enemy lines. He'd resigned his post and gone back to England, but Marian did not think the marquess was ready for that information, any more than he was ready for sirloin.

"You know the surgeon said you should have no

heavy fare for another week. If you stop trying to get out of bed—and falling on your face again, reopening the head wound—I might convince Sister Celestina to sacrifice one of her hens. The French did not get all of them, and they keep laying, thank goodness."

Chicken sounded like manna. Succulent chicken and a woman's smile—now that was Hugh's idea of bliss these days, which showed how low he had fallen. It appeared that he'd get the chicken sooner than the smile.

As bristly as the woman was, she was decent company. As long as they did not speak of personal matters, she was willing to talk with him for hours. She could converse more intelligently than many of his friends on topics as diverse as literature, politics, and the Corn Laws. She brought him news from the war, tidbits from the kitchen, and the aroma of lilacs. She had a pleasant voice when she read aloud, a neat script when she wrote letters for him, and a good head for cards. All of which brought him back to his constant question: What kind of nun gambled, used scented soap, and had nothing to do with her days and nights but entertain an invalid?

Hugh was no closer to winning her confidence than he was to dancing a jig. He considered her his friend; she thought of him, it seemed, as a penance for her sins. He'd give half his considerable fortune to know what moral crimes the blue-eyed female was atoning for . . . and if she were truly repentant. Not that he was thinking of his pious prude in any lascivious manner. Heaven forfend such a sacrilegious thought enter his battered brainbox. He liked women, though, and could not help thinking of the only likely one in his vicinity.

In London he would have a hundred entertainments to keep his mind and body occupied. Here he had Marian. Despite her efforts, he was often bored and lonely and concerned about the slowness of his recovery. She could not be with him every minute, of course, but she stayed in his mind. He'd rather think of her and the mystery she posed than think of facing the rest of his life as an incapacitate or, worse, think of facing his father. Hugh liked women, and they usually liked him. Hell, they always liked him, except for Marian.

He liked women. He did not like mysteries. So one day he moaned.

"What is it? Has your wound opened? Is your arm paining you? Your legs?" She was at his side before he finished the sound of suffering. He moaned once more anyway, for effect.

"Should I send for the surgeon?" She reached to feel his forehead for fever. The dog growled at her. "Oh, do be still, you silly creature. Not you, my lord. Tell me what hurts you."

He closed his eyes and held out his hand.

She put hers in it. "Yes, I am here. Tell me what I can do to help."

"The pain"—he gasped—"the pain . . ."

"Where, my lord? Where?"

"Here." And he lifted her hand to his lower region, properly covered with a nightshirt, a sheet, and a blanket, of course. He might have been naked the way she jumped back. Hell, he might have been on fire and her hand was burned. She waved it in the air, then brought it down on his cheek so hard his head snapped back on the pillows.

"How dare you?" she shouted. The idiot dog barked and wagged his tail, wanting to be friends again.

Hugh might need another week to recover from his concussion. Marian might need a month to recover from her anger. "I was right," she yelled from the doorway, where she was rubbing her stinging palm. "You are nothing but an unprincipled rake, an immoral cad, a . . . a *gusano*."

"What the deuce is a *gusano*?"

"It is a worm. A slimy, dirty, low worm. How could you take such liberties with a nun?"

"You are no more a nun than I am." Hugh put his hand on the dog this time, to stop the infernal yipping.

"I am a sister."

Impy sighed happily at the lie and went back to sleep at the foot of the bed.

"And I am a brother. That does not make me a monk."

"Very well, I am not actually a member of the sisters

of Saint Esperanza. But I am living here under their protection and I am grateful for their hospitality. I try to follow the rules of their order."

"No cursing? No gambling? No sops to vanity like scented soap?"

She blushed. "I have not quite managed to meet their high standards yet."

"No men?"

"Definitely no men. And let me tell you, you egotistical clunch who thinks women were put on this earth to satisfy your base impulses, and that every one of us is panting for your attentions, men are a lot easier to do without than a ladies' maid. They are easier to renounce than oil lamps and hip baths. Why, I miss my morning chocolate far more than I miss any male I have ever encountered. And I shall not miss your company, either," she finished with a dramatic sweep of her black skirts through his door. "Farewell, my lord libertine."

Well, at least he had the dog for company.

Besides, he had a far more serious problem than the loss of the man-hating Miss Marian. When he'd placed her hand on his groin, nothing had happened. He hadn't expected the little soldier to salute, not for the black-clad crone—but nothing? He put his good arm under the covers to test. Nothing. Lud, his father would kill him if he could not produce the next Hardesty heir. Lud, he'd kill himself.

He tried again.

The dog left the room.

4

Hugh spent a long, lonely night thinking of his sins and how he might never have the opportunity to commit more. Then he had a messy breakfast that he tried to feed himself with his left hand. That, at least, brought the dog back to his bed to lick up the scraps.

Nothing he could do, he feared, was going to bring Maid Marian back. The woman was right: He was lecherous and licentious and he should never have treated her like a wharfside doxy. Of course, she should never have struck him or shouted at him or left him to fend for himself when he was merely teasing. He was better off without the prickly female, he told himself, for a woman who would not smile was poor company for an injured man. He'd recover faster, too, he decided, without her to carp at him to rest, to stop trying to exercise his limbs before they all went limp. She was a nag and a shrew and he missed her more than he thought possible.

The afternoon, after a morning that lasted at least seven hours, it felt, brought Sergeant Kirby, thank goodness, and thank military headquarters. The grizzled old veteran was an orderly on the commander's own staff. He was delegated to be Hugh's batman until his lordship was fit to travel back to England, which could not be soon enough for either of them.

Kirby was offended that he was sent to wipe some swell's arse, no matter if the nob had shown courage in battle. Lord Hardesty was not army, and Kirby was no blasted baby-sitter.

He was rougher than Marian, smelled worse than the dog, and barbered Hugh as badly as Juan Marcos had.

He spoke of the war, but refused to gossip about the officers or any stray Englishwoman who might have some connection to the military. He could not read nor write, and would not have played cards with a gent even if he had the blunt to bet, which he did not.

He did, however, accept Lord Hardesty's coins to smuggle in a bottle of brandy from the officers' mess, and a steak and kidney pie from the general's own kitchen, so he was not entirely useless. Kirby was not permitted to stay under the convent roof at night, though, the mother superior declaring Hugh well enough recovered to do without constant attention while he slept.

Hugh did not sleep. He kept waiting for Marian to return, to read the next chapter of the book they had started, to resume the chess game they had begun. She did not. He damned her for being a moralistic prude and a coldhearted woman who would leave him with nothing but a rat-tailed dog for company. Impy nestled against his aching arm, so he damned the dog, too. Then he cursed at himself for landing in this situation.

By morning he was almost too despondent to care. The brandy was gone and so was his virility, still. He thought of speaking with the surgeon, to see if the man thought Hugh's condition could be temporary, caused by the trauma, but decided against that. The sawbones had to be more familiar with amputation than expansion. Kirby was an old man; he might know about such things. On the other hand, the sergeant already thought little of the noble class. To Kirby, Hugh and his ilk were nothing but a pack of effete, ornamental parasites on the backside of the British people, sending poor fools like him to fight their wars. How could Hugh admit to such an unmanly, embarrassing ailment?

He had to get home to consult a real physician. Hell, at home he could consult with Harriet Wilson and her sisters. If those birds of paradise could not make his eagle fly, his goose was cooked.

Determined, Hugh worked harder at his convalescence. With heartier fare than the convent provided, and Kirby not caring whether he overexerted himself or not, the marquess was regaining some of his strength. He could barely totter from one side of the tiny bedroom to the other without growing dizzy, but he was making progress. Kirby was obviously reporting back to headquarters, for, as soon as Hugh was free of fevers and likely to live, the general himself came to visit.

"Glad to see you looking in better twig than the last time I saw you, Hardesty."

"I did not know you had been here earlier," Hugh said after they were settled with cups of thick coffee flavored with a dash of cognac. Hugh had learned not to ask the source of Kirby's provisions, just to hand him more money.

The general leaned back in the hard chair beside Hugh's bed. "Of course I came. Had to judge your condition for myself, didn't I, before I sent those dispatches home? Told them I thought you'd survive. Glad to be proved right."

"I am certainly glad you were, too."

"Told them not to hack off the arm unless they had to."

Hugh had not known amputation was a possibility. He should have, for battle surgeons were too busy to set broken limbs, and the dirt and muck in the fracture usually festered anyway. His already pallid sickroom complexion turned gray. "I thank you for giving that order."

The general looked at him carefully through narrowed eyes. "No gangrene, is there?"

"No, thank God. It was a clean break."

"Thought so. That's why I had them bring you here. Better care, don't you know. You wouldn't have survived the wagon ride to Lisbon, and the field hospitals are rife with contagion. Fevers are killing more of my men than the French are, it seems."

"I am sorry to hear that," Hugh said, and meant it. He had more respect for the common soldiers now that he had seen how bravely they fought under dreadful conditions and incompetent officers. Not including the general, of course.

Hugh raised his cup in a toast to the loyal British troopers, and the general joined him. After a respectful silence, the army commander stared at his coffee, but addressed Hugh. "You've caused a bit of a pother, my boy."

"I can explain all that. The undersecretary simply misunderstood what he saw. His wife—"

The general brushed the sordid details away. "Don't care what tomfoolery you got up to in London. That's none of my affair, thank goodness. Shouldn't have been yours, by Harry, but that's water under the bridge."

"Yes, but that mess is what brought me here to volunteer for courier duty. I was definitely persona non grata in London. In fact, it was strongly suggested that I take myself elsewhere. I believe the Antipodes were mentioned."

"Don't suppose you thought of going to grass at one of your country properties until the contretemps was forgotten?"

"Where my father could find me?" Hugh took another sip of his fortified coffee.

The general knew Hugh's father. He had another swallow, too. "Can't say I was sorry to have you here. Fine job you did that day, although I'd have to bring you up on charges if you were under my command. I do believe your job was to deliver the orders and ride back to headquarters, not get yourself blown to flinders."

"I swear I did not intend to overstep my duties, sir."

"Humph. Well, I wrote that in the dispatches, too. Not your foolhardy rush into the thick of battle, but your valor under fire. Fine bit of riding, I understand. Wish I'd seen it. Saved lives, too. The country appreciates what you did, Hardesty. I'm sure the prince will show his gratitude. Might even throw a ball in your honor, or a parade. I appreciate your actions too, by Jupiter. Wish all my young officers had such bottom. Still, that's not the trouble I'm talking about."

Marian. Hugh put his cup down. "I swear I did not mean to offend the woman. I was merely—"

The general held up his hand. "Whatever it is, I don't want to hear it. But in a convent? Don't you have any limits?" He shook his head. "At any rate, it's not your coming here that's the issue. It's your leaving. The army will be moving on. You cannot stay here unprotected."

"I realize my presence is somewhat awkward, my being neither fish nor fowl, as it were. Not in the army, but under your command. I think I will be ready to depart for England in a week or so. I am as eager to see the last of this place as you are to see me leave."

"I have to admit you are taking too much time away from my own business, which is running this blasted war, but perhaps you won't be so eager to leave when you hear the terms."

"Terms?"

The officer did not meet Hugh's eyes. "The thing is, you nearly died. They'd have had my guts for garters if you'd stuck your spoon in the wall."

"They?"

"Whitehall, Parliament, Carlton House. Your father has a lot of friends, and a lot of influence. The heir to a dukedom is no bit player on that stage of power. Your father's only son, besides."

"I am well aware of my position, thank you."

"And you've been kicking at the traces for, what, the past ten years?"

"Fifteen or twenty at the least. But you were speaking of terms?"

"The problem is, they want you back, all right, but they don't want any more scandal. The prince especially sees your behavior as a poor reflection on his sovereignty."

"The prince is an ass. And a hypocrite. Why, his own behavior—"

The general cleared his throat. "That's treasonous sentiment. True, perhaps, but treasonous. The fact of the matter is, your father agrees with him. They both think you would do better settled down, with a wife."

"They think a wife will lead me to the straight and narrow? Ask the undersecretary about his loving spouse. Or Lord—"

"Damn, sir, I do not need a catalog of every married woman you've tupped. His Highness and His Grace are insistent. You are not to return to England unwed."

"Bosh. This is not the Middle Ages. No one can command me to marry."

"But your father can cut off your allowance."

"He has threatened me with penury for ages. No mat-

ter. I have property of my own, from my grandmother.
I can live on that income easily enough."

The general looked around for the flask of brandy and
poured more into his nearly empty cup. Then he looked
at Hugh and poured more into his cup, too. "You might
need it. You see, before you came to the Peninsula, you
did a wise thing. Surprised everyone, it seemed. But you
went to your man of business and put your affairs in his
hands, your estates and your accounts, with your father
as trustee."

"In case anything happened to me."

"Exactly. Well, something did happen to you. Seems
they can have you declared incompetent now. The head
wound, don't you know."

"Fustian. I am in my right mind, or I was until we
had this conversation. You can tell them so."

"The truth is, I need those votes in Parliament your
father controls. His Grace has enough power to affect
the funding for supplies and ammunition. We'll never be
rid of the Corsican otherwise."

"He wouldn't cost England the war just to see me
married! Not even my father is that pigheaded!"

"I'd say he is. The message was clear: If you don't go
home a married man, you go home a pauper."

"He can't do that! It's robbery! My own father, stealing my fortune. I'll stay here and join the army sooner
than let him get away with that."

"I'd be glad to have you, if you could ride."

Hugh could barely walk. Besides, his horse had been
killed in the battle. Without drawing on his London accounts, he could not afford another mount. The words
he used next had never been heard in the convent, that
was certain. The dog rolled over.

The general let Hugh curse until he started repeating
himself. "Fact is," he said, "I agree with him. Life's too
uncertain. You've seen that now. We all need to leave
more of a legacy than a mention in the *on dits* columns.
And you've sown enough wild oats for a regiment of
roisterers, so you can't complain."

Not complain? Hugh wanted to howl. He'd rather give
up his arm than his freedom. Why, he'd never met the
woman who could please him for two months—much

less a lifetime. Thunderation, a wife! Of course, he knew he'd have to do it eventually. He was not so lost to his responsibilities that he would let the dukedom go to some distant cousins. But he was not ready yet. Besides, getting a wife was not the same as begetting sons. What if he couldn't? Then he would have sacrificed his bachelorhood for nothing. He was not discussing that with the general.

Like a drowning victim clutching at straws, he said, "That's all very well and good, but proper English misses are not thick on the ground here on the Peninsula. I doubt my father would be happy with a dusky-skinned Spanish bride, or the daughter of a Portuguese noble."

"It so happens that I know of a young lady in the area of whom His Grace will approve. Lovely gal, daughter of an earl, don't you know. Make you the perfect bride."

"If she is so perfect, why is she not wed?"

"She had a spot of trouble herself. Nothing a ring on her finger won't cure."

"Good grief, is she breeding?" Wouldn't that be a joke on the duke, planting a cuckoo bird in his exalted family tree.

The general was offended. "I said she was a lady, didn't I? A fine, upright example of English womanhood. What we are fighting to protect, don't you know. She showed a mite of bad judgment, is all. Poor reflection on the army, too. In fact, you'd be doing me another service by wedding her. Gentle female like that does not belong in the war. Two birds with one stone, don't you know."

Hugh felt as if the stones were tied to his feet and he was going under for the third time. "The ideal woman, wellborn and virtuous, just happens to be waiting for me in Lisbon?"

"Fact is, she is somewhat closer than that."

How close? Hugh wanted to ask, but his throat was closing for lack of air. They said that dying men saw their lives pass in front of their eyes. That hadn't happened when Hugh had been shot, when he fell to the ground, his horse on top of him. It happened now.

"You won't regret it," the general was saying. "Lady

Marian Fortenham is a fine woman. She'll make you an excellent duchess someday.''

Marian. Who hated men in general and Hugh in particular. The poorhouse was looking better. Enlisting as a common foot soldier was looking better. Hell, hell was looking better.

5

Marian, Lady Marian, it seemed, was not looking better. If anything, her mouth was more pinched and her skin was more sallow. She still wore the black shawl over her hair and the sacklike black gown. She stepped into Hugh's room after the general left as slowly as if she were walking to a funeral. Hugh couldn't decide if it was his funeral or hers.

In a way he felt offended that she looked as upset as he felt. He was, after all, a premier catch on the marriage market: titled, wealthy—once he reclaimed his own property—and had all his teeth. An antidote like her ought to be happy such a choice plum had fallen into her lap.

Then he took pity on her. She could not like being constrained any more than he did. And she had been kind to him before he'd overstepped the bounds of propriety. He told himself she was intelligent, well-read, and born to his way of life. Everyone would think the match was ideal. He thought she might faint, so he poured her a glass of the cognac.

She sipped at it, silently staring at him over the brim of the glass as if he were an insect pinned to an entomologist's collection page. A rather noxious insect at that.

He swallowed. "It's a deuce of a coil, isn't it?" he asked, without wasting either of their time on pleasantries.

She nodded, not offering him any help with the conversation.

"I don't suppose they left you any choice, either?" Hugh was still hoping for divine—or the damsel's—intervention. If she refused to marry him, no one could place the blame on his plate. Unfortunately, she merely grimaced.

"Oh, they gave me a wealth of choices. I can stay here with the sisters as long as they will have me or the French come back to pillage the convent, or I can wed. The general was kind enough to let me select my own husband, too: you or the only man my father found who is willing to have me."

Hope bloomed in Hugh's breast until she gave the other fool's—the other possible fiancé's—name. "Simon, Lord Fredricks."

"Great gods, the man is sixty if he is a day. He is a perpetual drunk, and he has been through two wives already. The man lives for his horses and dogs and loose women."

"Precisely."

"Damnation, you cannot marry that dirty dish."

"Precisely."

"What kind of father would wed his daughter to such a loose screw?" he demanded.

"The same kind, I suppose, who would rather see his heir starve in the gutter than have him cause another scandal. What of your mother? Can she not sway your father?"

He shook his head. "She wants grandchildren. Yours?"

"Passed on ages ago. And Lord Fredricks's estate runs with ours."

"Surely there is some other gentleman. . . ." Hugh let his voice trail off when she set the glass down and took to studying her hands.

A wealthy earl's daughter alone on the Peninsula, with no horde of eager suitors to escort her back to Papa? The female must have blotted her copybook with a vengeance, Hugh decided, although he could not imagine the straitlaced Lady Marian letting down her hair enough to cause such a mare's nest. He might have liked her more if she did. "Perhaps you had better tell me how you landed here anyway," he said, when she volunteered no explanation. "I think it only fair that I know. Everyone seems to have all the details of my own fall from society's grace."

"The general did not tell you?"

"No, he felt it unnecessary, or your tale to tell."

"It is a simple enough story, and a common one. Never having a *tendre* for a suitor for all my twenty-five years, I fell in love with a soldier—an officer, to be exact. I met him at my aunt's house in Bath, where he was recovering from a wound and my father was taking the waters."

Hugh was surprised she was so young. He'd thought her older than that, but of course his father would never have approved a daughter-in-law past child-bearing age. Then he tried to visualize Lady Marian being swept off her feet by a handsome scarlet uniform. He could not. "And?"

"And my father disapproved, of course. The officer had no title, no lands, no vast income, no influence in government. In other words, Captain Sondebeck had no advantages to appeal to a narrow-minded, ambitious earl. We were well-off but not wealthy. My father saw my marriage as a way to repair that deficiency."

The captain's name was not familiar to Hugh, which was no wonder, if the fellow did not circulate among the quality. Which brought up another question. "How is it that I never met you in London?"

"Father hates the place. He says it makes him bilious. My aunt saw me presented at court at the proper time, but then he swept us all back home. Every year he had another excuse and another ailment for not letting me take part in the Season, where I might have found other gentlemen to my liking. I think he always intended me for Fredricks, when my brother was finished with university and could take over the running of our estate that I oversaw. Papa's health did not permit him to visit the tenants and survey the fields, you see."

"Forgive me, but I do not see. Your sire makes mine look like Father Christmas. Perhaps he never intended you to marry, but to stay on as his unpaid servant. But do go on. Captain Sondebeck returned your regard?"

"He said so. And I believed him, so I argued with my father to let us wed before he had to return to the army. Papa would not relent, telling me I would marry our neighbor or no one. So I told him Captain Sondebeck and I were . . . were lovers. We were not, of course."

Of course not. Hugh could tell by her blushes that such a happenstance, two mature adults in the throes of thwarted love expressing that passion, was beyond her ken.

She was going on, wanting him to understand, now that she had begun. "I thought my father would be happy to post the banns if he thought I was ruined for any other marriage. Instead, he threw me out."

"The coldhearted bastard. Forgive me. He is your father."

"You need not apologize. I have called him that and worse. At any rate, the captain had already embarked to rejoin his unit."

"So what did you do?"

"I followed him, of course. I was not entirely penniless, you see. I had my mother's jewelry, trunks full of pretty clothes, and the household money. I felt my father owed me that, for my years of keeping his accounts since my mother passed on."

"He owed you a great deal more, by Harry. He owed you his love and understanding. Tossing his own flesh and blood out on the street! If I had my hands on his neck he'd sing a different tune, I swear."

"At present your hands do not both work, but I thank you for the thought. Anyway, I had enough funds, and my maid along to satisfy the conventions, so I set sail for Portugal and true love."

Now he understood her black gowns and grim expression. Pity overcame him, so he reached out for her hand. "Poor puss. You came all this way, giving up everything you held dear, only to find that your soldier had died in battle."

"I wish," she spat out, slapping his hand away. "I found that the swine was already married, with a wife in Lisbon."

Now he understood her grim expression even better. "Gads."

" 'Gads'? That's all you can say when that man's lies ruined my life? Cost me my aunt's and my brother's regard, as well as my reputation and my dowry? Left me stranded at an army headquarters, where I was mortified at every turn, and an embarrassment to the commanders? 'Gads'? Surely you can find something more to say."

He could. He did. "Would you do me the honor, Lady Marian, of accepting my hand in marriage?"

Then his icy Maid Marian, indomitable, courageous, and more than a little stiff-rumped, melted. She started to weep. Hugh passed over a handkerchief, but that was like trying to dam a river with a pebble. She cried and cried, all the tears her pride would never let anyone see. Great racking sobs sent the dog under the bed and Hugh out of it, all of his protective instincts aroused. Lud knew nothing else was, for Lady Marian looked even worse than usual, her face all red and splotched, her nose running. Hugh tried to gather her close to comfort her, but with only one usable arm he found he could merely pat her back, noting how frail she seemed under the enveloping gown. "Hush, my dear. Don't cry. Things will get better, I swear. First thing I'll do is kill the dastard who lied to you. I can shoot with my left hand, you know."

"He's already dead," she murmured into the front of his now-damp dressing gown. "They sent him to the front to get rid of him. His wife blames me for that."

"She would have been a widow soon enough anyway. And better off without the muckworm."

Marian stepped back, out of his awkward embrace, to blow her nose. Hugh felt damp—and bereft, somehow. "But she told all of the other women," Marian said when she was through, "that I had thrown myself at her husband. No one would speak to me. And she wrote to her sister, who is married to Viscount Aldersham, so everyone in London knows of my disgrace and humiliation."

Hugh scratched his head. "I never shot a woman before. There is a first time for everything, I suppose."

She sniffled. "You cannot stop gossip with a pistol ball."

"No, but I can kill it with a ring. Do you think that anyone would snub a marchioness, a future duchess? The daughter-in-law of one of the proudest, most powerful noblemen in the empire? Not in this lifetime, they won't."

"Perhaps the political hostesses will overlook my history for your father's sake, but the high sticklers in the *ton* never will."

"Who? My godmother, my cousin, my sister's mother-in-law? They are all patronesses of Almack's, you know. That's the only reason I am still allowed into the wretched place. But you will be welcomed with open arms, I promise. You will have invitations to all the fetes and festivities your father denied you. Unless you prefer the country? I own a pretty cottage in Richmond, and another place in Somerset."

"I adored London the few short times I visited. The shops and the theater . . ."

Hugh was relieved, until he thought of the chaps whose wives were stashed in the shires so the husbands could continue their wenching. Perhaps marriage wouldn't be so bad if he had to spend only a few weeks a year with his wife. No, he did not want a polite, distant, occasional relation with the mother of his children. He'd never thought long enough about marriage to decide what he expected from it besides grandsons for the duke, but now the idea of leading separate lives did not sound appealing. It might be fun to introduce Marian to his friends and his pastimes in town, once she was dressed more presentably, of course. "Then London it is, except for visits now and again to the country. You'll have new clothes, new friends, a hundred new experiences every day."

"But I will be married."

"Aye, there's the rub. To me."

When she made a whimpering sound instead of chuckling as he expected, Hugh said, "It is not a fate worse than death, you know." He could not keep the bitterness from his voice that she was so appalled at the match. He was not getting any great bargain, either, but no one heard him complaining. Well, Kirby had, and the dog, but they did not count. Perhaps Lady Marian would do better in the country, after all. He wanted no unwilling wife to play the martyr.

"But you do not wish to marry me." Tears started to fill her eyes again. They were quite lovely eyes, he noted, despite the redness.

"No, I do not wish to marry anyone. It is nothing personal. But I do not believe either of us has a choice anymore, so what do you say? Shall we make a match of it?"

She started to rearrange the medicine bottles on the nightstand. Her face was averted, so he could not see her expression, but he could recognize misery even from the back. "I swear I will try to be a good husband," he said, "although I have no experience."

"You had no experience being a soldier and look where that got you."

Was that a joke? From the ice maiden? Hugh took it as a good sign that she was warming a little. "I seldom drink to excess, rarely lose my temper, never gamble away more than I can afford. If you are worried about the, ah, intimacies of marriage, we can delay that until we know each other better." And until he consulted with a London physician.

She stood straighter, as if a weight were lifted off her shoulders.

He went on. "But if we find we do not suit, we can conduct our lives as many other couples do, with courtesy, and discretion, and distance. So what do you say?"

"Yes."

" 'Yes'? Just that? After I have made my first and, hopefully, last ever proposal of marriage, all you can say is yes? What, do you want me to get down on my knees? We both know I'd never be able to get up, if I did not fall on my face at your feet."

She took a deep breath and said, "Yes, my lord, I shall accept your eloquent and gracious offer of marriage. I am struck speechless by the honor you are bestowing upon me. And if I had one other choice in all this world, by heaven, I would take it."

Hugh did not dare kiss her to seal their engagement. The woman was liable to box his ears. He did raise her hand to his lips though. "You'll see. It won't be so bad."

Not so bad? Hugh thought it would be hell to be married to a woman who never smiled.

Not so bad? Marian thought it would be torture to be married to a man who did not know the meaning of fidelity.

6

"You cheated!"
      "Did not."
"Did too."
"Well, you cheated first."
"Hah, then you admit you are not so holier-than-thou after all."

Nicky and Pete almost came to blows. The winds of their anger blew so strongly across the Spanish plains, in fact, that the war had to be postponed.

Nicodemus shook his fist. "You said no interference, and now you send in a general to order my sinner to reform. Speak of deus ex machina, that is Machiavellian."

"And how is the prince?"

"That is irrelevant. You cheated, so you forfeit the bet. Hardesty is mine. He can suffer a relapse and be rowing across the River Styx by morning."

"You speak of interference?" Saint Peter pointed at the gremlin dog and said, "Woof."

The devil had the grace to look embarrassed. "I didn't think you'd notice."

"How could I not, when the creature smells of brimstone, no matter how many baths they give it? Anyway, you should be happy the general stepped in. Your man was about to grovel to the woman for the sake of her company. Who knows how they might have gone on in their own time? They were already discovering a mutual respect that could have led to affection. But this way, your unrepentant rake will never be faithful to an unwanted wife, one foisted upon him by the authorities he's rebelled against his entire life. He'll go back to his licentious ways and you'll have his adulterous soul in your hands before you can say Genghis Rabbit."

"Hmm. You have a point. He'll take those sacred marriage vows because he must, but he'll never keep them, not if I know my man. He'd never fall in love with some featherbrained chit who ran off to wed a soldier, then got shoved his way when no one else would have her. So he'll forsake those holy promises and be back at the gaming hells and bordellos before the ink is dry on his wedding lines. Yes, that might work."

Saint Peter smiled. "But it won't work."

"What, you think he will stay true to that freakish, frumpish, frigid female, after he has known the pleasures of the flesh with the highest flyers in England?" Old Nick saw the opportunity for another wager, an easier win this time.

"I think he might not have a choice. It won't work."

"It? You mean *it* won't work?" the devil roared, and started two brushfires with the lightning. "You made him a eunuch just to win the bet?"

Saint Peter shook his snowy head. "I was not the one who had his mount fall dead on top of him."

Satan picked sulfur out of his teeth. "I simply wished to end the man's suffering more quickly."

"Angel feathers. You never had a charitable thought in your life. You just wanted to claim his soul that much sooner."

"I was busy. There was a war on, you know."

"Well, it might be a temporary condition."

"It had better be, or all bets are off. I mean, what's the point of putting your money on a horse that died last week?"

"He could still stray in his thoughts."

"If I collected the soul of every man whose imagination lusted for a woman not his wife, you would not have enough residents in heaven to hold a cricket match. Hardesty was—and would be, without your piss-pious interference—a true sinner, not just a dreamer. I want him."

Saint Peter smiled that all-knowing grin that Nick hated. "We'll just have to see what he wants, won't we?"

"He sure as Hades won't want to be singing soprano!"

As soon as the Guardian of the Gates left, the *Patrón* of Purgatory turned on the dog, who was cowering behind a bush, as if that could keep him from his master's wrath. "You! This is all your fault. If you weren't so busy licking your privates"—the new dog had learned an old trick—"this would never have happened. Well, he might get married, and he might be *hors de combat*, so to speak, but neither one will last, not with that lusty young buck. Your job will be to make sure that temptation lands at the sinner's doorstep."

So Impy dug up a bone and started to carry it to Lord Hardesty's room.

"Not something to tempt a dog, you flea-witted fool. Something to tempt a man into adultery! Find him a woman, I say, a sexy, seductive siren that no rake can resist. You know the kind. We have plenty of them below. Low necklines, wavy hair, painted faces. A female who will get his attention."

So Impy tore up Lady Marian's shapeless black gowns.

The wedding was held within the week. Somehow the general had produced a special license, an army chaplain, and a bouquet of flowers.

Marian clutched his arm in one hand and the bouquet in the other as he escorted her to the convent's tiny stone-walled chapel where the sisters of Saint Esperanza were joyfully gathered. If the nuns were happier that their two troublesome guests were leaving than that the wedding was taking place, their smiles did not reveal such sentiments.

Marian was wearing one of her own gowns, a lemony yellow silk with a white lace overskirt. It showed more of her bare flesh than she had seen since leaving England. She would have used lace from the ruffle at the hem to fill in the narrow bodice, considering she was going to a holy ritual, not a rout or reception, but Sister Marta took it to fashion a matching mantilla for her hair. Marian's long blond locks were loose beneath the head covering, trailing down her back in soft golden waves, like a bride from antiquity proclaiming her maidenly state. Marian would not have chosen such a hairstyle for her wedding day—she would not have chosen the gown, the guests, or the groom, either—but she had not been able to find her hairpins or ribbons, and hated to ask the sisters for anything so frivolous. They had been so kind to her, even producing a tiny pot of rouge from one of the village girls so she did not look as white as the chapel's plaster statues. Besides, the general was already waiting impatiently, a war to get back to, so Marian did the best she could with two ivory combs to keep the curls off her face.

Now if only she could keep from trembling. The general must have sensed her unease, for he patted her hand in comfort. "There now, my dear, do not fret. You have made the right decision."

They both knew she had had no choice, that all the decisions had been made for her. Marian could not keep on wishing it were otherwise, for that would be a waste of her time. Besides, if her wishes had come true, she would have been wedding a lying, cheating, conniving womanizer like Captain Sondebeck. What she had to wish for now was that the womanizing Lord Hardesty was not as unscrupulous.

At least he was not cozying up to her for her money, which her father had claimed was the officer's motive. Nor was he pressing her for intimacies she was not ready to share with a stranger, which she suspected might have been Sondebeck's purpose in pursuing her. No, Hardesty was wedding her because he had no choice, either. Why, she half suspected he did even like her. The other half suspected he would forget about her existence as soon as he returned to his own elite, immoral social circles. This was to be a marriage of convenience—his convenience. For Marian it was a chance to go home, but she did not think being the center of more gossip was convenient at all. She had suffered enough humiliation over a supposed betrothed. She could not imagine the mortification of reading of one's own husband's affairs in the newspapers every morning. Worse, she would be expected to ignore such fraying of the marriage bonds and lead a complacent, uncomplaining life. She could not do it. She would complain and kick and scream and shout and make Hardesty's life a misery, the same inconvenient misery that hers would be.

Marian pulled the general to a halt. She could not go through with this travesty, this sacrifice of two lives to satisfy someone's notion of propriety or dynasty building. Surely there had to be another way to get both of them back to England without being bound to each other for all eternity.

The general had handled hundreds of raw recruits on the eve of battle. He was not going to let one miss's megrims stymie his best maneuvers. "Wedding jitters, my dear. All brides suffer them, I am told. It will all be over in a trice, and then you need never do it again, eh? You'll have a handsome, wealthy husband of your own, and infants someday. What more could a girl ask?" He dragged her slowly, inexorably forward into the fray.

Hoping for a last-minute reprieve, Marian asked if it were legal, this English wedding in a Spanish chapel.

"All right and tight, I swear," he said, patting his pocket where the special license reposed. "Once you make your vows and sign your name, you are wed for all time. I suppose there are annulments and other havey-cavey legal goings-on that could dissolve the contract, but you'd have to prove Hardesty was insane or impotent, you know. Not likely, with half the females in London claiming otherwise, eh?"

Marian stumbled.

"Pardon, shouldn't have spoken of his prowess, what? Just an old army man, don't you know. Anyway, no one will be able to question the validity of the ceremony or the legitimacy of your sons. Important for the heir to a dukedom, don't you know. Else every fifth cousin would be crawling out of the woodwork to claim the title, should the marquess happen to die early. No, you and your future children are protected. Why, I even had my own man of business draw up settlement papers for you in case the young hothead you are wedding does something else rash. You'll be a wealthy widow, although I pray not soon, eh? So you'll never have to be selling off your mama's jewels or living in a convent again. That ought to please you, what?"

Nothing short of the earth opening up to swallow her was going to please Marian. "I . . . I . . ."

"No, my dear, you don't have to thank me. Just be happy. You will be, I know it. It's a fine man you are getting, brave and loyal. If Hardesty is a bit rough around the edges, why, that's nothing a good woman cannot smooth over. All will be well. You'll see."

What Marian saw was her groom. Hardesty had to be the handsomest man she had ever encountered, despite the raw scar that trailed down his temple to just above his eye. He was leaning on a cane and on Kirby, but he was dressed in formal attire, the first time she had seen him in anything but a nightshirt. He looked like a fashion plate, except for the scar and the sling and the unsteadiness of his balance. An elegantly tailored jacket was draped over one shoulder, but she well knew the muscles that were hidden there. His auburn hair was gleaming in the thin light through the tiny windows of the chapel, and his immaculate white neckcloth was tied in a knot that the Bath gentlemen would have envied. And he was smiling at something Kirby was saying.

Ah, that smile. Marian was half surprised none of the sisters of Saint Esperanza were swooning. She knew she felt her own senses go numb at the sight. He was always attractive; smiling, he was a god. Or a devil, come to seduce every woman in sight into indiscretion. He was a good-looking libertine, a handsome here-and-thereian, a man she could never, ever trust. And he was her bridegroom.

Heaven help her.

7

Hell, Hugh swore to himself, if the woman did not get here soon, he was going to miss his own wedding. His legs were watery, his head was light, his pulse was racing—and that was before he'd started out for the chapel. He was weaker than he'd thought, or a lot more lily-livered. He'd faced that entire French charge without a second thought. Now he was having second thoughts, and third and fourth ones too, every one of which involved fleeing, if his legs could carry him, and if he had somewhere to go. They couldn't, he didn't, so he might as well pass out instead.

Lud, he had never been a coward before. Of course, he'd never been married before either, but surely he could face a vicar and a dowdy female. So what if the vicar was issuing a life sentence, and the woman was to be his jailer? So what if his bride was bony, unbending, and unbiddable? He was a man, wasn't he? He could survive. Or he could collapse in a heap and beg for a quick death.

He could not turn craven. Lady Marian had suffered more than her share of ignominy, and another failed bridegroom meant yet another scandal. Hugh doubted even that pig Lord Fredricks would have her after that. Hugh would be consigning the unfortunate woman to the life of a pauper, an outcast, a social pariah. He could not do that, not when he owed her for saving his life.

Instead he would force her into a life of luxury among the quality, a life she deserved, but one she did not want, simply because he was sharing it.

And where the devil was she, anyway? If he could get

226

here, half crawling across the convent's courtyard, the least she could do was be on time.

He took out his watch again, and Kirby snickered. Now Hugh regretted asking the batman to stand up with him, although the sisters' handyman, Juan Marcos, had been his only other choice. Kirby was not precisely standing up with him anyway. The sergeant was more like propping Hugh up than acting as witness. From the iron grip Kirby had on Hugh's arm, he must be on orders to prevent desertions.

Still, Kirby did know how to tie a neckcloth, iron a suit of clothes, and put a shine on a pair of boots that the Beau himself would envy. The old soldier was also coming to appreciate the best attribute of the British aristocracy: its money. Hugh had been so generous with his blunt, and the lady so gracious, offering to teach him to read and write, that Kirby had decided to retire from the army and accompany them back to England. He was not about to let Lord Hardesty turn tail and cost them all that rosy future.

"She'll be here soon enough," he said when Hugh reached for the chain stretched across his white brocade waistcoat to check his fob watch yet again. "Unless she chose young Allenby instead."

Corporal Allenby was the youngest, least valuable member of the general's staff, so he had been used to carry messages and instructions from the command tent to the convent. Second son to a Berkshire baron, he was seventeen, skinny and spotted, and considered himself a poet. The lad was no more suited to army life than a three-legged kitten, but he adored Lady Marian. He reminded her of her younger brother, she said, and she treated the boy with kindness. She even listened to Allenby's dreadful verses, which more and more were dedicated to her eyebrow, her lip, her angelic voice.

"My arse," Hugh told Kirby, smiling at the thought of his black-clad bride wedding a green-as-grass youth. Then he turned forward—and she was there. Not his Nurse Marion, not the grim scarecrow he was expecting, but a true vision. This could not be his bride, could it? No, some fairy creature must have left her bower in the woods and wandered into this little chapel in error.

She was dressed in sunbeams, all yellow and bright, with hair like honey flowing down her shoulders—her nearly bare shoulders. Lud, the swell of her breasts above that scant neckline left little to the imagination. Hugh did not need Allenby's creative mind to supply a rhyme. His heart was beating in iambic pentameter on its own.

And her face . . . No mortal poet could do justice to that face. An artist could, perhaps, if he had magic in his fingers to capture the worry in her blue eyes, the determination in her pointed jaw, the pride in her graceful carriage—along with her astonishing beauty. No, he amended, his Maid Marian was not beautiful. She was too thin, too pale, too unsmiling. But, Zeus, she was stunning.

Perhaps he'd merely been away from pretty women for too long. The nuns did not merit a second look, although he did find the three hairs on Sister Paloma's chin to be intriguing. No, Marian would stand out in any crowd, he told himself, and not merely because she was taller than most women. The acknowledged belles of the *ton* had more perfect features, and a rounder, softer beauty, which was often marred by an artificial smile, a practiced, polite charm.

There was nothing false about Marian, except possibly the hint of color on her cheeks. She was lovely, and she was frightened, obviously as nervous as he was about this ordeal, and Hugh admired her the more for it. Feelings he did not know he possessed rose in him like an underground stream seeking the daylight. Protectiveness, possessiveness, pride, he was ready to burst with all three. Something else, recently gone missing from his life, rose slightly, lifting his spirits with it. *Hallelujah!* Dampened by the occasion and the environment and lack of exercise, that inappropriate twinge quickly dissipated, but it was a start. Hugh said a short prayer of thanksgiving.

He might have been forced into this marriage, but now he had hopes of making a success of it. Marian would fit into his world, into his arms, once the broken one healed, and into his life. She was beautiful and well-bred, everything his father wished for in the mother of

a future duke, and Hugh might just be able to beget
those necessary babes. She was beautiful and he was
attracted to her. A man would have to be dead not to
be, which proved how close to death's door he had been,
that he did not see the diamond under the coal. She was
beautiful and she was his bride.

Of course, he had said they would not consummate
the marriage yet, and she disliked him on principle.

Heaven help him.

So the wedding proceeded, with more prayers than
expected. The chaplain, more familiar with "dust to
dust" than "dearly beloved," fumbled a few times, but
the short service went on. The groom made his vows in
a firm voice full of conviction. If the bride sounded less
convinced, or convincing, she managed to repeat all
Lord Hardesty's names in the proper order. The duke's
son did not faint, and the earl's daughter did not fling
her bouquet at him, which was all that mattered to the
general. He cleared his throat a few times, signaling the
reverend gentleman to get on with the thing. War did
not wait on sermons and such.

The chaplain decided to forgo the words he'd prepared about the duties and the demands of marriage.
He went right on to the part about the ring.

Hugh had not forgotten the necessity of a wedding
band. He'd intended placing his signet ring on his bride's
finger until he could replace it with another of her choosing from the family vaults, or a London jeweler's if she
wanted something more modern. He started to take the
signet ring off the hand of his broken arm, but Kirby
nudged him. The sergeant had located a plain gold ring
somewhere, likely from the pocket of a fallen soldier. A
secondhand wedding band was better than Hugh's
heavy, masculine ring, so he started to reach for it, hoping the thing was not inscribed.

The general cleared his throat and held out a small
box that held two rings. They looked deuced familiar to
Hugh, who had last seen the Hardesty diamonds on his
mother's hand. The wedding band was a circle of perfectly matched diamonds, while the paired engagement
ring had a huge stone in the center, surrounded by sap-

phires. They must have been sent over to Spain with the government dispatches, or by carrier pigeon, Hugh thought. That or his father had sent the set to the general as soon as he received word that Hugh was injured. The two of them, along with his loving mother, must have planned this ambush, knowing a likely bride was already at hand. Damnation, he wanted to refuse the rings out of pique, but he supposed his marchioness was entitled to wear the family jewels. They had to be more satisfactory than a plain band from who-knew-where, certainly more fitting to a real lady.

Before he could lift the rings out of the box, Marian placed yet another one in his hand. This one was made of alternating pearls and emeralds. "My mother's," she said, a catch in her voice.

The general looked displeased. "The Hardesty set is more impressive."

Marian told him, "That is because this is not the official family heirloom ring. My brother will give that one to his bride when he is old enough. This is the one my mother wore every day of her life, though. It came to me when she died."

"Perhaps she is watching us today, then," Hugh said, taking a firmer grip on the ring and handing it to the chaplain to be blessed. "And perhaps she will give us her blessings, too."

Marian sent him a smile of appreciation, as if he'd brought her the moon. Hugh felt as if he'd climbed Mount Olympus. He'd made her smile, at last. He vowed, along with the other tripe the chaplain was nattering on about, to keep her smiling, to make Lady Marian Fortenham, momentarily to be Lady Hardesty, the happiest of brides. She'd never regret this day, he promised himself, not if he could help it.

Marian kept her eyes on the ring, her mother's gift to her and the man she would someday marry. She repeated her vows without hearing the words, swearing to herself instead that she would try to be a good wife to Lord Hardesty, as her mother had been to Papa, despite their differences. Mama had accepted her husband's foibles and found contentment in her children, her friends, and her community. Marian vowed to do no less. She would give the marquess no cause to regret this day, not if she could help it.

The vicar pronounced them man and wife, and Hugh leaned over to kiss his bride. After Kirby and the duke hauled him back up onto his unsteady feet, he glared at the giggling nuns, then made do with raising Marian's hand to his mouth. "Until later."

Marian took her hand back as if she'd been scalded. She might be married to a rake, but she was not going to fall prey to his charm. That way lay only heartbreak. She would give him her loyalty, her respect if he earned it, her maidenhood eventually, his heirs gladly—but she would not give him her love to shatter.

So they were wed, this groom who liked women too well, and this bride who liked men not at all.

Heaven help them both, for the devil was having a good laugh.

8

"**D**id you see that?" Old Nick asked the dog.
Of course the dog had seen the wedding. He'd
had another bath and had a bow around his neck. He
was hiding under one of the pews in embarrassment.

"They'll never make a go of this marriage." The devil
cackled. "He'll be committing adultery in a heartbeat,
until some irate husband finally shoots him. Unless his
new wife does the deed. Hmm. Then I'll have two souls
for the price of one." He rubbed his hands in anticipation. Then he kicked the dog. "And you'd better make
sure they never get any closer, or I'll reach down your
throat and pull your tail out from the inside. Understand?"

Impy understood. So he sat between Marian and
Hugh during the whole carriage ride to Lisbon. Anxious
to see them safely out of his domain, the general had
provided a luxurious travel coach and driver, plus a
wagon for Kirby and their baggage, and a detail of
mounted soldiers for protection. He also sent Corporal
Allenby to act as equerry, to carry messages to the Lisbon headquarters, and to get the versifying fool out of
the way of any French forces.

When they had to stop, Allenby made sure they had
the best quarters available at whatever inn or cottage or
casa grande belonging to the Spanish allies they found.
He made sure his goddess had a room of her own, even
if Lord Hardesty had to bed with the men and the horses
in the stable. The arrangements suited both of the newlyweds, and the dog. Impy slept on the bed with Marian,
just in case Hardesty decided to visit. The bed was

softer, and the lady did not take up as much room as his lordship, besides.

By nightfall Hugh was so exhausted from the jostling and the jolting over the rough roads, and in so much pain from his various wounds, that he did not care where he slept, or with whom. He could not have pleasured his wife if his life depended upon it. Nor could he protect her from marauders, so he was happy the mongrel had come along to act as watchdog.

Marian was happy with the dog's company, for she was tired of being alone with her thoughts. She was worried about what she would face in England, despite Hugh's assurances. What if her reputation traveled ahead of them, embarrassing Hugh until he grew to despise her? What if he sent her to live in the country by herself or, worse, with his father, who sounded thoroughly unpleasant, and as dictatorial and domineering as her own? Worst of all, what if he kept her with him in London, and kept his mistresses?

Hugh slept, Marian fretted, and the dog snored.

The days were easier. They never seemed to run out of things to talk about: their childhoods, their families, books they had read, politics, the war. Hugh told her about the people she would meet in London and his estate in the shires, as if, she thought, he really cared that she shared his life. In return, she helped perfect his Spanish, and started to organize his ledgers and account books, which were in a hopeless jumble in one of his trunks. They played cards and chess and charades and riddles, childish games that made the dusty roads less dreary. They tried to learn Portuguese from a textbook, and told each other about their favorite foods and colors and music, and lied about their worst nightmares.

His was purely physical; hers was purely mental. He feared not being a man to his wife; she dreaded falling in love with her husband. His infirmity seemed to be improving; hers was growing worse by the hour. The more Hugh looked at his beautiful, clever wife, the more he wanted her; the more Marian knew of her spouse, the more she liked him.

He did not have to be charming to her anymore, Marian considered. They were not courting, so he did not

have to impress her with his good humor despite his
pain, his care for her every comfort, his lively wit, and
his ability to make her feel as if she truly mattered to
him. Oh, how she wished that were true. A few days in
Hugh's company were enough to show her how happy
she could be if theirs were a real marriage, not one of
the general's war maneuvers. Hugh was not perfect, but
he was perfectly wonderful, and Marian feared she was
well and truly lost. This was no infatuation, as she'd felt
for Captain Sondebeck, where she could not see his
faults, would not hear of his failings until it was too late.
She knew Hugh at his worst, and still found him appealing. Her best efforts not to be smitten, like so many
other women, were lost on the road to Lisbon. Her intentions of staying heart-whole were blowing in the
Spanish dust.

For heaven's sake, how could she not be hopelessly
attracted to the handsome, auburn-haired devil? She was
only a woman, after all. He was good-looking and broad-
shouldered, with a smile that could melt glaciers, much
less one female's heart. He smiled and teased and listened and shared his thoughts. For the first time the idea
of sharing his bed was intriguing.

Why not? He was her husband, after all. She had no
hope of holding him to his wedding vows for a sennight
without the conjugal bliss that poets—although not Allenby, thank goodness—wrote about. She was already at
a disadvantage compared to Hugh's other women in that
she was inexperienced and nearly ignorant of the marriage act. Who was she supposed to ask, Sister Lupe?
But she did have one big advantage: her mother's ring
on her finger.

If the dog had not been lodged so firmly in the middle
of the cushions of the carriage, Marian might have been
tempted to expand her knowledge by narrowing the distance between Hugh and herself.

Instead she delayed until they reached Lisbon and the
elegant quarters Allenby found for them while they
waited for the next ship that could carry them to England. With the help of two maids, Marian had the most
luxuriously hot, long, perfumed and oiled bath she had
enjoyed since leaving England, a lifetime ago. The ser-

vants fixed her hair and pressed her clothes, filling her bedchamber with flowers and wine and their giggles.

After a meal fit for a king, or at least a marquess and his bride, Marian cleared her throat twice, then announced that she was ready.

"And you look exquisite, my dear, but I did not know we were going out this evening. I thought you would be so worn down from the journey that you'd want a quiet night. I promised to stop in at the officers' quarters to tell them what I know of the war's progress."

"Oh," was all she could say past the embarrassment she felt. At least he did not suspect that she had been planning their belated wedding night. "Have a good evening, then."

Hugh fled, not waiting to see the disappointment in his wife's eyes. Lud, he was liable to disappoint her a great deal worse if he stayed and accepted that invitation she had almost choked on. *He* was not ready, deuce take it.

The next day he made plans, bribing the captain of a private yacht to carry them home tomorrow. Now they would not have to wait for the army carrier, and now he would not have to be alone here with his tempting wife while he doubted his potential. There was nothing like doubts to dampen a fellow's desire.

For that night, he accepted an invitation to a reception for the departing officers and their wives at the ambassador's residence.

"I wish you had discussed it with me first," Marian said. "I thought we were to be partners."

"And so we are, but you would have said no."

"Of course I would have. I know these people, and they are cruel in their love of gossip. We will be their target."

"All the more reason to go. Put on your prettiest gown and your brightest smile and show them you have nothing to hide. Prove them wrong, whatever they think."

"Is that what you do when you are in the midst of a scandal?"

"Oh, no. They all think the worst of me anyway, so I prove them right by causing a bigger scandal."

"Then that is what I shall do, flirt with all the hus-

bands, drink too much, laugh too loudly. I'll see how
many improper offers I receive from those women's husbands—and then tell the wives."

Flirt? Laugh? Improper proposals? "Perhaps I am too
weak still to attend such an affair, after all." He coughed
once or twice to prove his febrile state. The idea of his
wife playing the seductress was appealing, but only if he
was the one being seduced.

"No, you are right. We have to face society sometime.
Better to know how they will accept our marriage, rather
than in London among your family and friends."

As soon as Hugh saw her dressed for the reception,
in a blue gown that matched her eyes, with a diamond
pendant between her breasts, he damned himself for his
doubts—and his plans for the evening. He was ready, all
right, ready to tear apart any other man who looked at
her, and ready to rip that pretty gown to shreds.

Marian had been lovely at their wedding. Now she
was magnificent. His heart swelled with pride, and something else swelled with want. Oh, he was more than
ready, ready to bring a smile of satisfaction and satiation
to his wife's face, if it killed him by morning. Unfortunately, they had to get through the ambassador's reception first.

Marian was everything proper, Hugh was relieved to
see, astonished that he wanted his bride to be better
behaved than the women he usually escorted. She was
a perfect lady, and they made the perfect pair, both
handsome, wealthy, titled. Heads nodded in approval,
and the ambassador beamed that he could make the first
toast to their marriage. Everyone laughed at Marian's
blushes, at Hugh's refusal to let her stroll the portrait
gallery with anyone but him, at the way they caught each
other's eyes in silent communication. Why, one could
get scorched by the sizzle between the pair. This marriage was no disastrous misalliance to reclaim reputations; this union was the envy of everyone there.

Except one guest. The recently widowed Mrs. Captain
Sondebeck was not envious. She was resentful and bitter
in her black crepe, angry at being forced to return to
England. Instead of being an officer's wife, she would
be nothing but an unwanted poor relation in her sister's

residence. And it was all that female's fault. She turned her back when she saw Marian approaching on Hugh's arm.

Hugh could feel Marian stiffen at his side. He was not about to let some harpy destroy her pleasure in the evening, her burgeoning confidence in her social acceptance. He stepped in front of Mrs. Sondebeck. "I do not believe I have had the pleasure of an introduction, but my wife and I wished to offer our sympathies."

"I will accept no condolences from the whore who caused my husband's death. He would be here with me now, if not for her."

A nearby matron gasped. Marian pulled on his arm, but Hugh was not leaving. "You are speaking of my wife, madam."

"Who is nothing but a highborn strumpet."

"My wife is a lady, Mrs. Sondebeck, a lady by birth, by marriage, and by nature, which is more than I can say for you and your wicked tongue. My lady"—he emphasized the *lady*—"was your husband's prey, not his pursuer. She came here to the Peninsula because of Sondebeck's professions of love for her and his promise to wed her, a promise he made without ever mentioning your existence. The traitor, the evildoer, was your husband, not his innocent victim. And my lady wife is no more responsible for his death than I am, except that I would have shot him if the French had not done the deed first. Consider yourself fortunate to be rid of such scum, for he would have gone on betraying you. And consider that if you had not been such a fishwife—perhaps, only perhaps, mind you—he might not have strayed in the first place."

Now Marian gasped.

Mrs. Sondebeck paled. "How dare you!"

"Oh, I dare a great deal. In fact, if you ever speak ill of Lady Hardesty, or show her any disrespect, you will see what I dare. All doors will be closed to you, all chances to make another, better marriage will be ended."

"Hugh," Marian whispered in his ear, "stop. She is a grieving widow. I feel sorry for her."

"I do not," he said, loudly enough to be heard by

those avid listeners nearby. "She is a spiteful shrew who made your life miserable here." Then he relented. "My wife and I are taking a private yacht home, so our cabin on the army transport ship is open. Please accept its use, instead of the women's quarters, with my compliments and condolences. Good evening, ma'am."

They left soon after, and as soon as they were in the carriage to return to their lodgings, Marian threw herself into Hugh's arms. "You were wonderful, my husband. You were brave and noble and defended me as no one ever had."

He was enjoying the feel of her in his embrace too much to notice the pain from his broken arm. "Of course I defended you. You are my wife. No one shall ever hurt you again, I swear."

"Not even you?"

"Especially not me."

And Marian believed him. For the first time in her life she felt truly safe, protected, cherished. If he did not outright love her, well, she might have to love enough for both of them. She was his, and he was hers, to have and to hold. So she held him, and kissed him, and let his good hand wander where it would, and let her own fingers go exploring. Soon they were both gasping. Then the carriage halted at their lodgings.

"Later, my love," he said, as he accepted a packet of mail from the majordomo. "I shall join you as soon as I read the post."

But the reading took longer than he thought, especially the letter from his solicitor. By the time Hugh went upstairs, undressed, shaved, and bathed again, to Kirby's aggravation, Marian was already in bed, waiting for him.

Except she was fast asleep. So was the dog, who nonetheless raised his head and snarled when Hugh would have joined his bride beneath the covers. Hugh knew how early they had to arise in the morning, and how exhausted Marian must be, so he let her sleep. He did tell the dog, "I will leave now, but you'd better remember who your master is in the future."

The dog remembered. He growled louder.

9

Hugh did not mind the wait. He would have his bride alone on the elegant yacht, in the luxurious stateroom, with the wind in the sails to serenade them and the gentle rocking of the sea to lull them when they rested afterward.

Unfortunately the rocking was not so gentle, and they had not even left the dock. The cabin smelled of stale cigar smoke and seaweed, and the oil lamp swayed in its gimbal. After five minutes Hugh bolted for the fresh air on deck, and the railing. Too late he recalled one of the reasons he had thrown himself so heartily into the battle against the French: He would never live through another water crossing anyway, so he might as well die in a good cause.

He did live, but barely. He had to be half carried off the yacht by Kirby and Allenby, who had been reassigned to London until someone at the war office found a use for the lovesick pup.

Hugh did not notice that no one met them at the dock. If he thought of it at all, he would have been happy that none of his friends or family saw how weak he was, how woefully debilitated, and not by his war wounds.

Marian noticed, and twisted the strings of her reticule. Her aunt could not have come from Bath in time, if her father had been willing to travel to the capital that he disliked, but surely someone in Hugh's family could have sent a carriage for them—if they wished to acknowledge the marriage. The strings on her purse were so tangled, she had to cut them when they reached the hotel.

Hugh's bachelor rooms at Albany House were not

suitable for a respectable woman, so he directed the hired hackney to take them to one of the new Mayfair hotels. With Allenby gone to report in to the war office, and Kirby left at the docks to see to the baggage, Hugh was able to make the arrangements he wished: one bedchamber, not two. And a cushion on the floor for the dog. Marian blushed, but made no demur. Hugh was feeling better by the moment.

He had a good meal in the dining parlor, his first in days. He was empty and starving, and the hotel's chef was trying to impress these important guests, to build his reputation. Hugh sampled everything, and declared it delicious. Marian picked at her food.

Old Nick picked on the dog.

"No! No! No!" he shouted, looking at the large bed in the room Hugh and Marian were to sleep. They would not sleep a wink, he estimated, and was furious. "Passion will ensnare him. He is already more than half in love with the woman. Sex would bind him to her side forever. Lawful fornication, faugh! What good is that to me?" He aimed a kick at Impy. "You keep them out of this bed, do you hear?"

Impy heard. He knocked over the candle and set the mattress on fire.

There was nothing for it but that they go to Hardesty House in Grosvenor Square. It was late, Marian was upset, Hugh was frustrated, and their clothes smelled of smoke. The dog needed salve for his burns, Marian needed a good night's rest, and Hugh needed . . .

Well, he was not going to find what he needed at Hardesty House, not anytime soon, at any rate. Chaos reigned there, with servants rushing in all directions and baggage in the hall, even before they arrived with theirs.

His mother shrieked when she saw him. Actually, she shrieked when she saw an unfamiliar dog lift his leg on one of her potted plants. Then she noticed her son.

"You? Hugh? But you are not due!" she wailed, hugging him tightly, then stepping back to survey her firstborn son for damage. "We expected you to arrive at the end of the week."

He handed her his handkerchief and said, "We chartered a yacht. What difference does it make?"

"Difference? My whole surprise is ruined, that's all. The ball is not for a few days."

"I did not know you were throwing a ball."

"Of course not, or it would not have been a surprise. And of course I am throwing a ball. How could I not when my son comes home a hero, and brings a bride with him, besides? It is to be the largest, grandest fete anyone can remember. His Grace says that it is already the most expensive ever. The prince is attending—more's the pity, since he'll be late as usual and the food will be cold, but no matter. He wants to give you a citation for bravery. Goodness, that was supposed to be another surprise. Oh, I am truly at sixes and sevens. Here you are, and I have not even greeted your bride!" She embraced Marian, not waiting for formal curtsies. "My beautiful new daughter-in-law!"

Marian had a lump in her throat at such a welcome. "You are throwing a ball for us?"

"Of course, my dear. How else are we to introduce you properly to the family and our friends?"

"Then you don't mind?"

"What, that I missed my son's wedding? Of course I do. I was going to plan another ceremony for you, this time at St. George's Cathedral, but His Grace said I should wait to see about your wishes."

Marian was overwhelmed. "I . . . I . . . The one in Spain was fine. But I meant, do you mind that I am your son's bride?"

"Mind? I am thrilled! You are everything I ever wanted for my son, for the mother of my grandchildren. I already adore you for saving Hugh's life, you know. And for writing to us about his condition. I am positive I shall come to love you too, for yourself and because you are going to make my son happy. I just know it. The general sent us a note in the army's dispatch bag saying so, besides."

There were tears in Marian's eyes as Hugh's mother led her off to the suite of rooms assigned to her, freshly painted in her favorite colors, with a wardrobe full of new half-finished gowns and with a maid to attend her.

"Well, you will have a day or so before the ball to get acclimated," Her Grace said. "Perhaps it is better this way, meeting the houseguests as they arrive rather than all at once at the ball. I expect you'll want to visit with your aunt and brother too. The young scamp left his university as soon as he heard of your return, and has been haunting the stables ever since. I expect your aunt is resting. She has been such a help, I don't know what I would have done without her. I'll send for them both, shall I, or do you wish to refresh yourself?"

"They are both here? That is the best surprise of all, for I have missed them sorely. Is my father going to attend the ball?"

"Oh, he is here too. His Grace insisted." The duchess's voice said she would have seen the curmudgeon rot in Bath instead.

Marian met up with her family as soon as her new maid tidied her hair. Her aunt blubbered with joy, and her brother kissed her cheek, thrilled to be in town, and with a top-of-the-trees brother-in-law who promised to introduce him to Gentleman Jackson himself and take him to Tattersall's.

Her father was . . . her father. The earl patted Marian's shoulder and noted that she had landed on her feet, after all.

"Are you happy for me, Papa?"

"I'd have been a deuced lot happier if you'd been a proper daughter and wed the man I picked. Now where is my cane? There is a new physician His Grace recommends. Quacks, all of them, but I might as well consult with the man while I am here."

Hugh's welcome-home took longer, and was more enthusiastic. His sister almost knocked him over, once his mother had stopped dampening his shirtfront with her tears, and his brother-in-law's slap on the back nearly brought him to his knees. All the aunts had to weep over his scars, and the cousins wanted to hear about his experience. But his father enfolded him in his arms—the first time since Hugh was in short pants—and said, "I am glad you came home, boy. I am proud of you."

They parted quickly, awkwardly, unfamiliar with such physical displays. They each turned aside to hide the evidence of tears in their eyes. Hugh would discuss extortion and blackmail and underhanded dealings with solicitors later. For now he was happy to be in the bosom of his family, happy to be in His Grace's good graces. He was happiest of all that what pleased his august parent pleased him, for once. His bride was being embraced by his family, and soon enough she would be embraced by him.

They had little time together, with the house so full of company and more arriving daily. Marian was swept off for fittings and morning calls and sight-seeing with her brother. Hugh was busy consulting with the war office, his man of affairs, and his tailor. He had to make time for that same brother, so the boy did not land in any of the London pitfalls he himself had blindly stumbled into. In the evenings the duchess kept them busy with the opera and the theater and plans for the ball. Hugh and Marian fell into bed at night, exhausted and alone, but content that they were growing closer in understanding, that their worlds were meshing, that their time would come.

The dog was exhausted too, but not alone. He had a bed in the kitchens, all the bones he could eat, and the cook's terrier bitch beside him. Impy was in love, and to Hades with his orders. He was a dog. He was staying a dog. He'd earned the choice and he was taking it. His might be a short life on earth instead of eternity in hell, but he'd die with his tail wagging. Saint Peter had rewarded him with a new life and freedom from Satan's shackles.

The day of the ball finally came, clear and temperate, just the way Her Grace had ordered. The music was superb, the refreshments sublime, and the decorations stunning. But it was the honored couple who starred that night. Hugh was at his most elegant, looking raffish with his scar and his sling, but Marian was magnificent. She wore a new gown of blue gauze, with the Hardesty diamonds around her neck, the Fortenham tiara on her head, and a new ring that Hugh had bought just for her, to start an heirloom collection of their own. Mostly she wore a smile, not a feigned social simper, but a genuine smile of happiness, all the brighter when she looked at him, which was often, if not always. And Hugh could not take his eyes off her, either. If anyone commented on the circumstances of the wedding, it was merely to mention that fate worked in mysterious ways, finding this perfect match in such an unlikely setting. If anyone commented on the fact that the bride and groom left their own ball hours before its end, they said it with a wink and a smile, happy that the newlyweds took such joy in each other.

Joy? Hugh had never experienced such passion, such completion. Marian had never known that such absolute, incredible ecstasy existed. What she lacked in experience, she made up for in enthusiasm. What he could not manage with his broken arm, he managed with his lips and his tongue and his words of love. And they truly were that, words of love.

"You do know how much I love you, don't you, Marian mine?" he asked when they were near to drowsing in each other's embrace.

"Hmm. But I think you'd better tell me again."

So he did, and showed her the evidence of his affection, so they were anything but sleepy. Later—a lot later—Marian stroked his face, feeling the coarse beard starting to form on his jaw. "We have to talk, my love."

Hugh could barely think, much less talk. "I am listening."

"Do you remember when you were hurt, and the dog would not let anyone tend you? I would have shot the stupid animal to save your life, you know."

"I recall the scene fondly. You were a Viking warrior priestess, calling thunderbolts down on the disobedient. Or else you were a shrew. I could not tell which at the time."

"Whichever it was, I truly would have fired at the animal to save you. Know this, my lord, my love, that if you are ever unfaithful to me, ever betray our vows, then I will shoot you to save our marriage and my sanity. I thought I could be a complacent, accepting wife, averting her eyes from her husband's indiscretions. I cannot, especially after we shared this." Her arm waved around the room to encompass the tousled sheets, the scent of lovemaking, their contented, floating-on-clouds conditions. "I could not face the idea of your making love to another woman this way."

"I have never made love to a woman this way," he swore truthfully. "For I have never been in love. But you still do not trust me, do you, Marian?"

"How can I, knowing your reputation? Why, half the women present tonight gave you such looks, I almost threw my champagne at them."

"Did they? I never noticed. No matter, for I shall prove to you that my reputation means nothing. Do you think thirty or forty years can convince you of my faithfulness?"

"Hmm. I suppose that ought to be enough for a proper, loyal husband. I was hoping for eternity, though."

"Then eternity it is. You see, I always intended to honor my marriage vows. That's why I never took a wife, because I never found a woman worth the effort of fidelity. Now I have, and I will never let her go. I love you, Lady Hardesty, only you."

"And I love you, Lord Hardesty, only you. Forever."

"Forever," he repeated, before falling asleep.

"You won."

"No, you won."

"But you were right."

"No, you were. I am honest enough to admit it. You said the love of a good woman would reform the man. He is as good as a saint now, blast it. You won."

"But you said her love would not be enough, that it was his love that mattered, and you spoke wisely, so you won. He had to love the woman in return before he put her happiness ahead of his own."

They both thought about such a love and what it could do. Then Saint Peter said, "You know, we were both wrong. It is neither the love *of* nor the love *for* a good woman that matters. It is the *right* woman for a man who can change his life, change the world."

The devil sighed, then brightened. "But that son she is carrying will be a real hellion. No doubt about it. He'll be one of mine, absolutely."

"It's a daughter she is carrying," the saint replied. "An angel as good as gold, as pure as new-fallen snow."

"A son, I say."

"A daughter."

"A boy, damn him."

"A girl, bless her."

Nine months later, to her husband's relief and delight, Marian, Lady Hardesty, was delivered of a beautiful blue-eyed baby girl. And a sturdy auburn-haired baby boy.

A Hasty Marriage

by
Carla Kelly

The marriage of Ann Utley, spinster, from an excellent Derbyshire family, to Capt. Hiram Titus, widower, of the *Hasty* sailing from Boston, came about because of an international abduction. Or so the matter was reported to Miss Utley's mother, who shrieked upon hearing the news, and prepared herself for a faint that never came, because the woman delivering the tidings seemed unappreciative of upper-class melancholia. In fact, Aggie Glossop, former governess to the said Miss Utley, appeared to be delighted by the whole turn of events. She even shook her finger at Mrs. Utley. "And don't say anything about marrying so fast. Ann has been waiting for this man all her life."

It came about this way. . . .

No matter how many times he made the Atlantic crossing, Hiram Titus, captain and owner of the *Hasty*, always felt a little easier when his merchant vessel had wallowed past the sleek men-o'-war in Portsmouth Harbor, and his papers were safely in the hands of the harbormaster. In this Year of Our Lord 1807, with American distress with England, he knew that the master would give his ship's lading a good scrutiny. He was ready; he was also prepared with a notarized crew roster, which listed all his boys as loyal sons of New England, conceived and born on American shores. Not for him the danger of an undercrewed warship hauling off his men because they were Britishers who had declared for American citizenship. God damn England anyway, a country that didn't recognize that a man could change

249

his allegiance. Because that was how matters stood, Captain Titus knew he had to dot every I and cross every T every time any of his merchant fleet left American waters. If Titus was anything, he was careful. He couldn't think of a time in his life when he had ever rushed into anything.

It helped to know the harbormaster, too. An exchange of pleasantries, an offer of Madeira, and then both men were comfortably seated in the office that overlooked the scruffy town.

"We haven't seen you in ages, Captain," the harbormaster said after his first appreciative sip. "You've not been shipping to France on the sly?"

"I would rather drink Boney's bathwater than do that," Titus replied promptly, because he knew it was what the master wanted to hear. He leaned forward in his chair, remembering how easy it was to take the man's mind off trade. No need for him to know that a ship or two of Titus Maritime occasionally wandered profitably into French Caribbean waters. "As a rule, I don't conn my own ships anymore." He was not the man to play a sympathy card, but the way things stood in the world, one never knew. "My dear wife died six years ago, and since then I have remained at home. Our oldest boy follows the sea, one twin is at Harvard, and the other works for Astor's fur company, but I still have a young daughter at home who needs me."

"Admirable of you," the master replied. He poured himself another drink, not even observing that Titus hadn't drunk more than the obligatory first sip. "You have relatives watching her now?"

"She came with me, sir. She is ten, and old enough. Besides, it is summer, and what is better than the ocean in summer?" *Even coming to Britain's cloudy, foggy shores,* he thought, but didn't add. Too bad that England was not blessed with American weather. "I lay the principal reason before you, sir: The captain of the *Hasty* came down with the shingles suddenly, so I took his place."

The harbormaster poured himself another glass. "I thought it must be something dramatic, Captain Titus.

You never were one to rush precipitately into a situation."

No, I never was, Captain Titus thought as he left the office, still quite sober, and full of information about the political situation that the master probably never would have divulged had he been more upwind of all that Madeira. So change was in the offing? He would be long on his way before that happened.

He stood outside the harbormaster's office, admiring the glint of the afternoon sun on the dark water of Portsmouth's excellent harbor. For one moment he felt a great longing to be sailing into Boston's own inimitable harbor. Despite all his years at sea, he was not a man to roam. Although he never would have wished sweet Tamsin's death, never in a million years, he was honest enough to admit that her untimely passing gave him every excuse to remain in port with their young children. He could hire others to sail his ships, and he did. So it went, and so it would go this time. Glossop's Nautical Emporium would have his return cargo in their warehouse already, of that he was certain: lace from Nottingham, knives and cutlery from Sheffield, woolens from Manchester's mills, straw-filled barrels of pottery, tea from India. In the morning, dockyard workers would be offloading pitch, rum, lumber, fur, and tallow from the *Hasty.* He would revictual promptly, and be gone in a week or so with a good tide. He would like to have taken Charity to London, but with the way events stood, it was probably best to stay close to Portsmouth. London would keep until more settled times. A week in port, another eight at sea, and he would be home in Boston.

It was a longish walk from the harbormaster's to the Nautical Emporium, but he relished every rolling step of it, secure in the knowledge that his sea legs would be gone by the time he crossed Ned Glossop's doorstep. Six years! He had been thirty-four on his last voyage. Now his sons were grown. Soon there would be wives and babies as another generation rolled around. The deuce of it: He was young yet, even though his shaving mirror told him middle age had approached, or was at least nigh. He smiled to himself; Tamsin would have laughed at his whining, and told him to get another mirror.

Well, no matter; here he was at Glossop's Nautical Emporium. He stood there in the wagon yard a moment, looking around. *Interesting,* he thought. He knew it had been six years, but things were tidier. There would always be a certain amount of clutter in a wagon yard, but the trash was stowed, the kegs lined up neat against the wall like good soldiers, and coiled rope obviously had a place to call its own. Titus could credit only one event with this unexpected order: Ned Glossop must have gotten leg-shackled, no easy feat when one limb was wooden. He smiled to himself, guessing that the old rogue probably couldn't run fast enough.

"As I live. It can't be! Captain Titus himself?"

The smile still on his face, Titus looked up to an open hatch on the second floor of the warehouse. "The very same, Ned! I can't believe the merchant marines haven't hanged you for one keg of squealing beef too many!" he called.

Glossop laughed. True to his naval roots, he wrapped his legs—one real, one not—around a rope and handed himself down to the ground. By the time he got there, Titus was across the yard to shake his hand.

"Didn't think we'd see you again, Captain," Glossop said, shaking his hand vigorously. "Captain Peabody told us of your wife's death, and we are sorry." He looked around. "But where's Peabody? The lading bill did say to expect the *Hasty*."

"And she is here. Peabody's laid up in Boston with shingles." Titus looked around the yard. "I've never seen this place so tidy. What's happened to you in the past six years?"

"A wife, sir, a wife," Glossop told him. He leaned closer, as though he expected her to leap out from some corner. "She was a governess to gentry, so I hop to when she barks."

The glint in the merchant's eyes assured Titus that Glossop suffered no ill-usage. So did the extra roll of flesh around the man's middle.

Glossop followed the captain's glance and nodded. "I haven't suffered overmuch." He patted Titus's flat stomach. "That and a wrinkled neck cloth tells me that you haven't fared as well, laddie." His voice was kind.

"I have been over seven weeks at sea," Titus reminded him. " 'Tis hard to get a laundress to come aboard. Did you ever try to put a flatiron on gimbals?"

The two men laughed over the nautical joke. Titus handed Glossop his stamped papers from the harbormaster. "What with the national climate, my friend, perhaps we'd better start swinging out my cargo tomorrow morning."

"Nothing simpler, Captain. Come on in now and meet Aggie Glossop." He tapped his wooden leg. "She keeps me on my toes! All five of 'em."

In less than a minute he was bowing to a dignified woman with impeccable posture on the downward slope of fifty. "Mrs. Glossop, I must commend you for the way you've cleaned up old Ned here. I never thought a warehouse could be tidy."

The look she flashed her husband was a fond one, even if her words were a trifle starchy. "Captain Titus, anyone can be neat if he puts his mind to it."

All of a sudden Hiram Titus wished he had found a way to smooth out his neck cloth, or at least brush seven weeks of stains from his coat. Time to change the subject, and fast. "Ned tells me that you were a governess for gentry."

It was a topic that must have suited her, because she seemed to relax. "Ah, yes, the Utleys of Derbyshire, for nearly twenty years," she said, and the starch was gone from her words. "An excellent family of quality, Captain. You won't find better-behaved young ladies anywhere."

Not until Ann Utley was sitting on her bum with her skirts up around her knees did it occur to her that perhaps she had just committed a rash act. She tugged down her skirts and looked around quickly for Papa's grip that he had taken with him on the Grand Tour years ago, when people could still visit France. It was lodged by Mama's roses, having missed the rain barrel by a few inches.

She stood up and wiped the dew off the back of her

dress, grateful that she had earlier thrown down her cloak. It was draped sedately over the lowest tree limb, quite within reach. With that subdued garment—sober enough for an old maid—around her against the morning chill, no one would see the grass stains on her kerseymere. She put on the cloak, and retrieved the grip, then waited, wondering if she wanted to be found, or wanted to escape.

Standing by the oak tree, she wavered. No one appeared to be about except the goose girl, who sat by the pond with her charges. Ann knew her mother never left her chamber before eleven o'clock, and the servants were still at breakfast. Her sister Clotilde—their brother in Spain called her Cloth Head—wasn't expected back from her fiancé's estate until later in the day. Ann looked at the timepiece in her reticule. She had at least until early afternoon, when Sir Barnaby Phillips would be toddling over for a serious conversation.

At least, so he had informed her with arch looks and a giggle over whist at Lord and Lady Stouffer's last night. "My dear Miss Utley, it is high time I spoke to your mother about a matter of the heart," he had whispered while Lord Stouffer was noisily shuffling the deck. She had almost burst into nervous giggles of her own when he thumped his ample chest and started to cough from the exertion. Lady Stouffer had only given him a squinty-eyed glance. "Raise your arms, you twerp," she commanded of her nephew, and he had meekly obeyed.

Ann had seen him ridiculous before, but there was something about watching a grown man with his arms in the air in the middle of a drawing room that made her decide that it was time to run away and avoid the proposal she knew was coming the next day. Never mind that she had promised her mother that she would accept whatever proposal she got, since it would be the fourth or fifth since her come-out years ago. Even if she had promised, no amount of cajoling would convince her that a man in subjection to his aunt was the husband for her.

She did not expect another proposal. True, she was a trifle tall, but never considered that a deficit, especially after her brother, in a sodden condition, had informed her that men liked women with long legs. She never had the nerve to ask why, but some innate delicacy told her that it was probably something ladies found out after the nuptials. She had a nice face, having been informed of such on several occasions by men who weren't even fortune hunters. Ann thought she was too bosomy; at least, Dame Fashion had decreed that bosoms were not à la mode this year. Even Clotilde, who understood almost no jokes, had to smile when Ann announced that she had no idea where to stash her bosoms until they became stylish again.

Her mother blamed her eldest daughter's lack of success on the independent income Papa had left her. "If you had a little less money, you'd be inclined to look harder," Mama had told her once in a rare burst of candor. "Young ladies with incomes can be notoriously picky."

As she continued to stand under the tree and stare up at the room she had quitted so impulsively, Ann did not doubt the truth of her mother's words. "Mama, I do not have to choose just anybody," she had announced several years ago, after Lord de la Ware—too old, too prosy, too *satisfied*—had slammed the door of their town house so hard that a Ming vase crashed to the parquet.

And so she had chosen nobody, not so difficult an enterprise when one was nineteen, or even twenty-one. In sad fact, it had become easier as the years passed. *Ah, well.* Ann brushed the dirt off her dress. While she had felt smug and wise at twenty-two, now that she was facing thirty-two, she admitted to some distress. No panic, though; Panic was only for the desperate.

She stared up at her window again. *Did I just crawl down the tree?* she asked herself with amazement. *Does the thought of Sir Barnaby terrify me that much?* When she realized that it did, she picked up her valise and started across the field to Stover Green and the Speckled Hound, where she knew the mail coach always stopped. She had left a detailed note on her pillow for her mother, telling her precisely where she was going, and assuring her that she would be home for Clotilde's August nuptials. *Don't be upset, Mama,* she had written. *I just cannot marry a man I see no hope of ever loving.*

Her long legs ate up the two miles to the village

quickly, but not so quickly that she did not have time
to admit that only a desperate woman would let herself
out of a second-story window and run away like a child.
She knew it was not a matter of disliking men; men were
fine and had their place in the world, same as she. Ann
Utley was just audacious enough to hope that somewhere in the world—certainly not in Derbyshire—there
must be a man who wouldn't incline her to flight.

The mail coach was a new experience. She hadn't even
been sure how one went about procuring a seat, but it
had been a simple matter to stand in the line at the
Speckled Hound and eavesdrop shamelessly on the comments of potential riders in front of her. By the time
she got to the agent selling tickets, she knew to state
Portsmouth as her destination and ask for an inside seat.

"Portsmouth, miss?"

"Yes, please." Thank goodness Papa had always ad-
vised her to keep money on hand. She had generally
used it to bail out Clotilde when she overspent her quarterly allowance and didn't wish Mama to know.

"You'll go as far as London, and purchase the rest of
your route there."

"London? Yes, certainly." In the city she would send
a letter by express to Mrs. Glossop, and visit her banker.
If she had lost her nerve by then, she could return to
Derbyshire and Sir Barnaby's sweaty, predictable embrace. What a pity that ladies could not purchase com-
missions in the army, or take Orders!

In his hurry to be away from England, Captain Titus
knew that he had miles to go before he could ever hope
to achieve his own father's legendary patience. What
should have taken only one long day, to swing his cargo
on deck and off-load it to a little fleet of lighters that
would ferry it to shore, had stretched into three days.
Ned Glossop had been apologetic; he had no more patience than Titus over the delays.

"I blame the French, Captain," the man had said two
nights later over dinner with Titus and Aggie. "What
with more and more warships sailing with each tide and
that blockade, the navy's sent out the press gangs until
hardly any blokes dare show their faces on the docks."

Although Titus knew that his daughter, Charity, didn't understand, she still pressed closer to him. She would have questions for him as they were rowed back to the *Hasty*, and he wasn't sure how to explain war to a ten-year-old. He could only reassure her that they would be on their way soon, and back on the open sea again, even as the days stretched longer in port.

"You can't get even a quorum of longshoremen?"

Ned shook his head. "Captain, I haven't managed that in over six months." He glanced at Mrs. Glossop. "Aw, Aggie, we've been through worse stretches, haven't we?"

"Indeed we have, Mr. Glossop," the woman said. She smiled at Charity. "In a few years things will look better, my dear Charity. You can come back here and your papa will take you to London." She leaned closer with an air of conspiracy that Titus figured had endeared her to many little girls. "I can tell him all the best shops when you come back again."

Charity nodded and relaxed against him. Titus tightened his grip on her shoulder. "Depend upon it, Chary," he told her. "I'll take you to emporiums and entertainments, and maybe even a play." He sighed. "But as for now . . ."

"I don't mind, Papa," she assured him. She looked at their hostess. "Papa says you were a governess. Do we have those in Boston, Papa?"

"You don't!" He took another sip of wine. "You have an aunt Mercy, who has consented to let you out of her sight for this voyage only."

Charity made a face. "Mrs. Glossop, does a governess make people mind, and keep their aprons clean, and insist upon clean stockings and soap behind the ears, even though it's only been two days since the last time?"

"That is *precisely* what governesses do, Charity," Aggie Glossop said as she rose to clear the table. "I also administered the rudiments of reading, spelling, arithmetical configurations, and provided heavy doses of good manners." She sat down again, and her eyes were kind. "Is that what your aunt Mercy does?"

"All the time." Charity sighed and glanced at her father. "She tells me I am her sole occupation."

Ned Glossop laughed, and handed her a bowl of nut

meats. "My dear, do you know that Mrs. Glossop received a letter yesterday from her last pupil? She told us she has run away from home."

"I tried that once," Charity said, "and Aunt Mercy helped me pack! She took all the fun out of leaving, so I decided to stay." The adults at the table laughed. "How old is she, Mrs. Glossop? Maybe she got tired of too much porridge, or . . . or brushing her hair one hundred strokes every morning and night."

"I rather think it was something else," the woman replied, and Captain Titus could not overlook the worry etched into her forehead. "Charity, she is thirty-two years old."

Charity gasped, then looked at her father with considerable alarm. "Papa, tell me that Aunt Mercy will not be looking out for me when I am so old! I could not endure that much porridge."

"I promise, Chary," he told her.

"I think it's a beau that won't step up to the mark," Glossop said. He popped a handful of nut meats into his mouth. "Right, Aggie?"

Titus tried not to smile, not with Mrs. Glossop looking so serious. Thirty-two and not married? Likely she was desperate because there was no beau in sight. For all the good breeding and manners that Mrs. Glossop insisted upon, this charge of hers must be a Gorgon.

The worry on Mrs. Glossop's face was genuine. "Maybe she just needs a change of scenery, Ned."

The merchant snorted. "Then she should be drinking the water at Bath, or taking a walking tour in the Lake District. Young ladies don't come running to their governesses in Portsmouth warehouses."

Thirty-two is hardly a young lady, Titus thought. *We call them antique virgins at home.* "Ned, perhaps you can put her to work in the warehouse," he said. "I notice you're shorthanded at the clerk's bench, too."

Ned slapped a meaty hand on the table and chortled as though the captain had told the funniest stretcher in years. "What will folks think of us, Aggie? Imagine asking quality to sit on a clerk's stool and copy bills of lading?"

"I think that might be an excellent proposition to put

forward to Miss Utley when she arrives," was Aggie Glossop's surprising answer. "If she is going to run away, she can at least be useful."

After Aggie Glossop had fussed sufficiently over Charity, advising her to bundle up against the dockside chill and vague disorders and diseases, Ned Glossop walked them down to the wharf. "Mind you, Captain Titus, I do not think that navy press gangs would waylay you"—he lowered his voice so not to alarm Charity—"but do warn your crew."

"I have, Ned, and thank you for your concern."

Ned saw them into the waterman's ferry. "Come back tomorrow or the day after, and perhaps you will see Miss Ann Utley sitting on that clerk's stool!"

Titus laughed and then nodded to the waterman to take them into the channel. "Not if your good wife fears that her former charge will blind us with her beauty!"

"Aye, she could do that," Ned replied as he waved them off. "She could."

I will believe that when pigs fly, Titus thought as he wrapped his own boat cloak around his daughter, who was shivering. Obviously the Glossops had blinkers on regarding the runaway Miss Utley. No thirty-two-year-old spinster of his acquaintance was easy on the eyes.

After two restless nights at the Claridge, and a lengthy, somewhat argumentative visit to her solicitor, Ann Utley was completely convinced that it was against man's nature to be anything but duplicitous. Even when she stood on the pavement again outside of the firm of Rindge and Rumble, her reticule heavy with coins and paper, it did not seem fair to her that it should be so *difficult* to accomplish what men of business did every day. She doubted that anyone ever argued with her brother when he came by for funds, and she was certainly his equal in prudence and sound management.

She sighed. By the time the young Mr. Rindge had shown her to the door, his lips were set in a firm, disapproving line. At least he had not tut-tutted like his father and assured her that her mother knew best. "Marriage will settle you down, my dear Miss Utley," the old man had said, as though she were a wild creature, and not a lady of mature years who was—until this regrettable incident—a non pareil of decorum. "Go home and marry Sir Barnaby," he had said, when she had poured out her distress to him, a family friend who also knew Sir Barnaby.

When she had asked him point blank if he would wish such a silly man on his own daughters, he had at least possessed the honesty to look away before he recovered with the argument that—little did he know—sealed his future career as her solicitor: "My dear, look at it in this light: He has his own family money, so he will never trouble you much, and you will eventually have children to occupy your time."

Her face went red as she stood there on the street. *And what happens when the children are grown and we are back staring at each other over the breakfast table?* she asked herself. *Is my next consolation the grave?*

She knew she was being overly dramatic, but her sense of misuse persisted all the way to Portsmouth. The only balm to her wounded heart was her dear Aggie standing there with arms wide open when Ned carried her band-box upstairs above the merchant office and stood back, carefully out of the way of two women with a long history between them. The tears came then. She let her old governess lead her to the settee, where she sobbed her misery onto the generous woman's shoulder.

"Aggie, *why* must I live my life to suit others? Have I truly become too discerning for my own good?"

From long acquaintance—although not recently—Ann knew that Aggie would answer neither question, but just hold her and let her sob; any homilies and advice would come later, when she was more of a mind to listen. Beef stew followed the tears, and then a comfortable bed with a warming pan followed the beef stew. The last thing she remembered was Aggie pulling the blanket up to her shoulders, touching a hand to her cheek, and saying something about "putting you to work to take your mind off your troubles."

Ann was in far better spirits when she woke. She put her hands behind her head and settled more comfortably into the mattress. *I really am too old to be so indecisive about Sir Barnaby,* she thought. *I have been completely*

*aware of his interest for these three years and more, so I
should not run away when he finally does what I had
thought he would do all long. Is he really too silly, or am
I too critical?*

No, he was too silly, she decided as she dressed and made
her bed. It was up to her now to weigh his faults against
the growing probability that no one else would ever offer
for her. What a shame that the world was so imperfect.

She had not misheard her old governess. Aggie
Glossop announced over tea and toast that she was putting her to work in the warehouse.

"Well, my dear, Mr. Glossop instructed me to ask you,
and I assured him that you would be delighted to be
of assistance."

Ann laughed and set down her teacup. "This is a
novel experience!" She leaned toward her former governess. "My solicitors will be relieved to know that I can
earn a living, considering my advanced years. That is, if
you intend to pay me!"

"Not a penny," Aggie replied, and both women
laughed. "This is for your room and board." She
frowned then. "I do not know how well insulated you
are against world currents, my dear, but we are nearly
at war with the Americans, France is a nuisance, our
navy is desperate for seamen, and dockworkers are in
short supply because the press gangs nab them. It has
become nigh impossible for us to hang on to our workers. Would you clerk for us?"

"I will, indeed," Ann said quietly, and then her merry
heart revived. "Obviously a spinster will be in no danger
from press gangs!"

And so she found herself in the warehouse in a sober
gown belonging to Mrs. Glossop (they were much the
same size), sitting on a high stool and copying lading
bills. Aggie herself walked the aisles of the warehouse,
reconciling the invoices to the merchandise, within easy
distance for help. So far Mrs. Glossop had patiently explained that *three cases of fried rod, exalted,* really meant
three cases of dried cod, salted.

"What dreadful handwriting," Ann murmured, as she
dipped the pen in the well.

Mrs. Glossop nodded to her when the door opened.

"There is the author of that wicked list, Ann. You can call him to account."

Titus was wrong. He was so wrong that he could only stand in the warehouse doorway and gawk like the greenest, most callow young man who ever shipped to a foreign port and ogled the local females. He resisted the urge to stuff his eyeballs back into his head.

The loveliest woman he had ever clapped eyes on sat at the clerk's desk, dangling one shoe off a foot that possessed—even at the distance of his perusal—a completely trim ankle. She looked at him in a quizzical way, then turned back to the document in front of her. He felt his heart almost thud to a halt in his chest.

She had taken little or no time with her hair, so he assumed that Aggie Glossop had snatched her directly from the breakfast table to the warehouse like the press gangs she abhorred. The lady—she could only be a lady—had wound her hair into a funny topknot, but most of the curls had already escaped. He didn't see many women in England with black hair, and none at home in New England, except among Indians. Her skin was radiant with health, her cheeks tinged with the delicate pink that a gentle, cool climate allowed. She frowned and pursed full lips as she stared at the paper in front of her. He wanted to sling her over his shoulder, row back to the *Hasty*, and have his way with her until they were both exhausted.

He brought himself up short then, embarrassed at his untoward flight of male fancy, and reminded himself that he was forty years old, sober, and the father of sons old enough to marry and make him a grandfather. Still, just gaping at that vision of loveliness in a Portsmouth warehouse was probably going to require a cold sea bath tomorrow morning. It had been years since he had, well, well, tingled.

And here was Mrs. Glossop now, talking to him, but it might have been Swahili or Urdu, for all that he was paying attention. He forced himself to listen to her.

". . . and she has consented to help me here in the warehouse."

"What? Who?" he asked, embarrassed when his voice

cracked like a fourteen-year-old's. Charity, standing beside him, giggled.

Mrs. Glossop began again, and he could not overlook the humor in her eyes. "Captain Titus, I want to introduce you to Miss Ann Utley of Derbyshire."

"Papa, you're supposed to move forward and bow, I think," Charity whispered.

That was all it took. Chary was but ten, and he couldn't have her thinking her father was a complete nincompoop. That would come later, when she was fourteen or so. "Oh. Right," he said, and crossed the warehouse, hoping that he would not trip over a dust mote, and wishing he were handsome and a wee bit younger.

It was gauche, but he held out his hand to her. Miss Utley's hand was cool and firm. "Delighted to meet you," she informed him, and weirdly, he hoped she meant it. "And this is your daughter?"

"Charity," he said. His heart lifted when his daughter made a pretty curtsy. "She is ten and making her first voyage to England."

Miss Utley smiled at his daughter. "You are probably wondering if the sun ever shines here, my dear."

"It *is* a little gloomy," Chary said.

Oh, my word, not to me, Titus thought. All the angels of social grace were urging him to stop staring, but he could not help himself. "We do get more sunshine in Boston," he informed her, then winced at the astringent Yankee-ness of his twangy voice. *You dolt, she does not need a weather report,* he told himself.

"And so do we get more sun in Derbyshire," she told him. Her eyes were the blue-green of the ocean in mid-Atlantic. She was looking at his daughter again. "But I am a runaway, Charity, and we must lump the good with the bad!"

Charity laughed, and he could not help smiling at the incongruity of Miss Utley's words. "Ladies who are your age do not run away," Charity said.

"They don't? Oh, dear me."

Charity looked at Miss Utley thoughtfully, and came closer. The lovely lady on the stool twitched at his daughter's collar, smoothing it flat in an unconscious gesture.

"Well, I did." She took a deep breath, and Titus could tell it was a touchy subject. "But enough of that. My dear, can you decipher your father's handwriting?"

Charity came even closer and leaned against Miss Utley. She had never taken so quickly to a stranger, but watching them both, Hiram Titus had to agree that there was something about Miss Utley that welcomed children. And him, too. Lord knew *he* wanted to lean against Miss Utley.

"I can read it mostly."

The lady looked at him again, the smile in her eyes unmistakable. "Then let us ask your father to find us another stool. You can sit by me and translate."

Surprisingly, Mrs. Glossop held out her hand to his daughter. "Come with me a moment, Charity. I can find a stool and you can carry it back." She clapped her hands and glared at Miss Utley. "And *you* can get back to work!"

Miss Utley only laughed and blew a kiss at her former governess. *My word.* He was alone now with her. If he hadn't already taken Mrs. Glossop's stern measure, he would have suspected her of doing that deliberately. Titus felt his collar growing tighter. It was as though he had never spoken to a woman in his life. He thought miserably that Tamsin must be sitting on some celestial cloud and chuckling over his dilemma. It was something she would do, bless her generous nature. And then, suddenly, he knew all was well.

"I can't have you getting crosswise with your employer," he joked.

"More like my slave master," she replied. "She's not paying me a penny for my labors. I must work for my room and board. Did you ever?"

Her easy wit pleased him. "At least she has not sent you to a workhouse, or to the law, wherever it is runaways go in England."

"Oh, no." She hesitated, and he thought she wanted to tell him why she had run away. She did not, but turned back to his infamous lading bill and frowned at it. "I know Aggie introduced you as Captain Titus, but I really cannot decipher your first name."

"Hiram."

She dipped the pen in the well and wrote it with a neat hand. "Hiram Titus it is." She blew gently on the page, and he wanted to sigh with the pleasure of it all. "That is a . . . a formidable name. Are all Yankees so very Biblical?"

"A good many."

"No one is tempted to call you Hi?"

It was his turn to relax then. "Not if your last name is Titus, Miss Utley. Wouldn't you agree that Hi Titus sounds like a disease?"

They laughed together, and Titus had never felt finer. As much as she had loved him, Tamsin had always seemed to stand a little in awe of him. Not so Miss Utley.

Charity emerged from one of the warehouse aisles, struggling under the awkward bulk of a stool. He hurried to help her, positioning it beside Miss Utley, then gave his daughter a hand up. He looked at his own bill of lading, almost but not quite leaning closer to Miss Utley, mainly because she smelled so delightfully of lavender, and that indefinable odor of the female that registered so pleasantly in his brain. He pointed at the next entry. "Mind that you record that as 'a hundred beaver pelts,' rather than 'a hundred feverish Celts,' " he teased. "I doubt we'd have survived an Atlantic crossing with raving Scots in the hold."

"Oh, Papa," Charity said. She glanced at the lady beside her. "He does that, and I don't know why."

Ann Utley twinkled her eyes at him over his daughter's head, and picked up her pen. "I cannot allow Captain Titus to be a distraction to my new assistant! Sir, you have our leave to go about your business." She put down the pen again. "Oh, have I nabbed her when you had something else planned? I wouldn't for the world disrupt your intentions."

If only she knew his intentions just then. His face reddened with the thought of them. "No, no, you're quite at liberty to snatch my youngest child and bend her to your will," he joked. "Mrs. Glossop had said something last night about helping her start a sampler this day, that is all. I am returning to the *Hasty* to swing some more cargo."

"Very well, then, sir, we will set *you* at liberty." She looked back at the lading bill, then at his daughter. "Charity, that cannot possibly be 'fifty cats.'"

"Fifty casks," he murmured, then bowed to them both, a gesture that made Charity's eyes widen in surprise.

In the yard, Ned was ready with the horses and wagon. Titus hauled himself aboard for a return to the harbor. He turned to Glossop, unable to restrain himself. "Ned, that is without question the most beautiful lady I have ever clapped my eyes on."

"She's a looker." Ned spoke to his horses and they crossed the yard. "I knew you were seeming a bit skeptical-like the other night, but now you know what I mean."

"Oh, do I! Why on earth did she run away from Derbyshire?"

Ned motioned for him to get down and open the gate. He drove the wagon through and Titus closed the gate and climbed up again.

"Captain, Aggie says she was afeared that some silly little prig was about to propose, and it put wings to her heels."

"That can't have been her only proposal."

Ned shook his head, then moved his wagon into Portsmouth traffic. "Aggie declares there have been many, but Miss Utley just hasn't found the right bloke yet to warm her cold feet on winter nights." Glossop looked sidewise at him. "How long'd it take you to decide?"

About ten seconds, maximum, he thought. "Oh! Tamsin?" He thought a moment, hoping that the warehouseman wouldn't notice that lapse. "I'd known her all my life, and it just seemed like the right thing to do." No quarrel there. It had been the right thing, but Tamsin had never poleaxed him as had one glance at Ann Utley.

"P'raps Miss Utley is pickier than most of us." Ned nudged him in the ribs. "It took me twenty-five years to convince Aggie that I was the man for her! Miss Utley's a late bloomer, too, I suppose."

To her personal amusement or chagrin (she wasn't sure which), it took Ann several moments to stop breathing at an elevated rate after Captain Titus had

closed the warehouse door behind him. Although she
could not recall when she had seen a more remarkable-
looking man, Ann was hard put to explain to herself just
what it was that attracted her. He was a tall man, which
never failed to arouse some level of interest. It may have
been the web of lines around his eyes that crinkled so
readily when he smiled. As she considered the matter,
she doubted that she had ever known a man with such
wrinkles around his eyes. The men she knew were
gentlemen, not sea captains who worked to earn their
bread by suffering exposure to raw wind and salt water.

And here was his delightful little daughter, eager to
help, and quite unaware that the lovely lady beside her
was deliberately plying her for information. By the time
noon came, Ann knew that Charity had three older
brothers. One twin was an agent for John Jacob Astor
and the American Fur Company; the other was at Harvard trying to decide on a course of law. The eldest
sailed regularly to the Orient with furs for emperors in
exchange for porcelain and spice. So much commerce
and activity seemed almost exotic to Ann, while to Charity, it was just the way the Titus family lived.

She also learned that Hiram Titus was forty years old,
a native of Boston, fond of squash pie (whatever that
was), and prone to snoring when he slept on his back.
Ann hadn't the slightest idea what to do with all this
refreshing knowledge, except enjoy the slightly clandes-
tine pleasure of eavesdropping on an interesting family.

The afternoon went much more slowly, because Aggie
had sat Charity down in her parlor to instruct her in the
fine art of samplers, and sent Ann back to her clerk's
desk to copy another lading bill, this one for a man-o'-
war bound for the blockade.

As the hours passed, she found herself looking at the
warehouse door, wishing for Captain Titus to material-
ize. She wondered at her interest, knowing herself fairly
well, and knowing that if he did appear, she would probably be speechless. After a moment's reflection, and four
more lines of hogsheads of salted beef, boxes of ships'
crackers, and eggs packed in salt, she decided that she
would have plenty to say to him, if he only asked the
right questions.

He came into the warehouse again when afternoon shadows were making her look about for a candle and her back was starting to ache from bending forward on the stool. With a smile, but no words, he took in the fact that his daughter was elsewhere, pulled out her unoccupied stool, and sat upon it. She watched him up close now. His eyes were emphatically brown, and his hair brown with flecks of light in it, obviously from much exposure to sunlight. When he spoke at last, what he said startled her.

"Miss Utley, what do you think of Americans?"

In her surprise, it did occur to her that only an American would ask such a question. Her knowledge was limited to so few of that species, but it seemed a logical surmise. And he seemed to actually expect an answer from her.

"They are brash, forward, opinionated, stubborn, and probably loyal," she said, her answer coming from nowhere she had ever been before. "I expect they are fun to know, but I should sincerely dislike to cross one."

She decided right then that his laughter was probably his best feature: no drawing room titter, but a full-throated delight, head back, eyes half-closed.

"You have just described my favorite hound!"

Ann put her hand on his arm, something she hadn't done with a man in recent memory. "Well, sir, you should not have asked, had you not wished to know!" She leaned toward him a little. "And you, Captain, are a wonderful father with a daughter who adores you." She leaned back, triumph in her eyes. "So this tells me that Americans are fine folk. Children are never wrong in such matters."

There was such a look in his eyes then. She knew she had touched the right chord in him, and it humbled her to realize how close he must be to his children. Her hand was still on his arm; she increased its pressure. "They mean the world to you, don't they?" she murmured.

"Aye," he replied, his voice equally soft.

Ann remembered herself then and removed her hand from his arm. Embarrassed now, and not looking at him, she capped the inkwell and wiped off the pen. All the while, she was thinking of Sir Barnaby Phillips and wondering if a man so enamored of his own company, and cowed around his relatives, would ever consider children more than a necessary nuisance. She thought not, and dismissed the man without another qualm, thankful all over again that at her advanced age, she was still agile enough to shinny down a tree and escape.

"I hope that Aggie Glossop will not summon the beadle from the workhouse if I announce to her that I have copied enough questionable handwriting for the day," she said to the captain.

"Quite the contrary. In fact, my duty here is to summon you upstairs to supper, provided that you remember your manners and do not eat more than your employers."

"Aggie said that?" Ann asked with a grin.

"I admit to some embellishment," he confessed. "Chary says that is one of my more regrettable failings."

"You have others?" she teased.

"According to my daughter, I possess the distinct character flaw of being far too predictable," he said promptly. "Let this be a warning, Miss Utley. Should you marry and have a family someday, please note that your children will always keep you well-informed of your more glaring deficiencies."

She thought he would get down from the stool, but he sat where he was, close enough to her so that she could smell ship's odors of tar and hemp. His presence emboldened her enough to ask, "In light of your question to me this morning, what do you think of the British, Captain?"

He didn't answer right away, but leaned closer momentarily to look at the bill of lading on the table in front of her. "So the HMS *Jasper* is headed out to sea soon. Will it be to the blockade, or will the *Jasper* search into American waters and meddle there?" He looked directly into her eyes, and she could see no apology. "Miss Utley, I do not trust your countrymen to do me no harm."

"But I would never," she said impulsively.

After a pause in which his eyes never wavered from her own, he said, "I do not doubt that, either. I have . . ." He paused again.

"A dilemma?" she prompted, amazed at her own temerity.

He got off the stool and held out his hand to help her down. "A burning urge to eat someone's cooking besides what comes from the *Hasty*'s galley. Do hurry, Miss Utley! How would it appear to my hostess if I were to leave you behind in my headlong rush to the Glossops' dining room?"

She had not anticipated a moment alone with Aggie before supper, but there was time for a word while Captain Titus was sitting with his daughter and admiring the rudimentary beginnings of a first sampler, as only a father could. She watched them a moment from the doorway, and was startled when Aggie Glossop put a hand on her shoulder.

"I hope you did not mind being herded into a clerk's work today," she began.

"I did not mind at all," Ann replied, as the other woman closed the door of the sitting room. They walked down the hall together, toward the dining room. "In fact . . ." She paused, uncertain of what she really wanted to say.

Aggie supplied the text with real aplomb. "He's a charming man, isn't he?"

"Oh, Aggie, I've never met anyone quite like him." The words tumbled out of her, and she felt like a schoolroom miss again. "But . . . but he's dreadfully common, isn't he?"

"I never noticed," was Aggie's quiet reply, her tone more tender than Ann could ever recall. This was not the starchy governess speaking to her charge, but woman to woman.

"I mean . . ." Ann stopped in confusion. She didn't know what to say, but to keep silent would be to deny the man's effect on her, and she had the strongest urge to share her feelings. "Aggie, I just wanted to look at him all afternoon, even as I kept telling myself that he isn't handsome at all." *What's the matter with me?* was her unvoiced plea. She trusted her governess, even after all these years, to hear that question. She also expected that proper and upright female to tell her to go home to Derbyshire and associate with those of her own sphere.

Aggie Glossop did neither thing. She opened the door to the kitchen, spoke to her cook, then looked at Ann. "You can direct the captain and Charity to the dining room, my dear."

"Aggie!" she whispered furiously. "What is happening to me?"

Aggie put her finger to her lips. "I knew Ned Glossop twenty-five years before I agreed to marry him. Do you know something? I always thought him extraordinarily handsome."

"Oh, but Aggie, he is . . ." She stopped, embarrassed.

"Not?" Aggie grinned at her with mischief in her eyes, something Ann never expected to see. "He is to me, my dear. Now go and be the perfect hostess, or Captain Titus will think I never taught you any manners."

She was quiet during dinner; indeed, she could not help herself. *You would think I have been living in a house with no doors and windows,* she thought. In her worry in recent months over her own puny state of affairs, she had paid little attention to any news beyond Derbyshire's borders. Listening to Captain Titus's sensible comments on recent Orders of Council, and Napoleon's latest Milan Decrees, she felt uncomfortable of her own ignorance. Somewhere between the soup and the sweets, she became aware that there was a wider world of working people trying to carry on in the face of war. She did not know why she had not realized this sooner, then comforted herself with the thought that many of her sphere never did experience such an epiphany.

She even began to suspect that these working people lived lives far more interesting than her own. She had only to look at how animated Captain Titus became when talking about a good wind, and the mew of seabirds that meant the coast was near, if not yet in sight. Ned Glossop shared his favorite moment, that time when all the stores in the warehouse were on hand, ample proof that no tar in the king's navy would be short-changed in his victuals. "It's a pledge I make every day, Aggie," he told his wife simply. "I was one of those tars some years ago; I know what it's like to go hungry." He leaned toward his wife and patted her hand. "Makes me proud to be called Honest Ned."

Aggie smiled at him and gazed with such pride and love on that unlovely man that Ann had to clench her jaw tight to keep from tears. It was absurdly simple chatter that someone like Sir Barnaby would ignore and avoid, but Ann found her throat constricting with the honor of it all. Before she had so uncharacteristically escaped from her bedroom window, the most serious decision of that week had been whether to choose bread and butter or cake at the tea table. These people knew more about the rich texture of life because they lived it.

The only one quieter at the table than Ann was Charity, seated on her left. She thought at first that the little girl was tired, but when she noticed red patches blooming in her cheeks, she gently put her hand against the child's face. Her hand came away warm. When Aggie got up to clear the table, Ann joined her, something she had never done before. She could see that Aggie was startled, but her former governess recovered quickly, nodding and asking Ann to remove the platter and bowls.

"Aggie, I think Charity is ill," she whispered in the kitchen.

"I did wonder," the woman said. "She sneezed a number of times this afternoon, and she has been so quiet. I fear our wonderful English climate is not agreeable to her."

Ann set down the platter for the scullery maid to scrape. "Should we ask Captain Titus if she can stay with us tonight? I have no doubt that he is an excellent father, but he might not know what to do for her."

She watched Aggie hesitate, but to her surprise, she shook her head. "I think not, Ann. We would be meddling."

"Oh, I hardly think this—"

"No, Ann," Aggie interrupted, her voice quiet. "They should both return to the *Hasty*."

She remembered that tone from the years when Aggie was her governess. "Very well. Let's at least suggest that she bundle up well against the night air."

"Certainly, my dear. Certainly."

By the time she returned to the dining room, the Tituses were preparing to depart. Charity carried the sampler she had begun that afternoon. Ann tied her bonnet on securely and stood back while the captain slung a cloak about his daughter's shoulders.

Aggie Glossop watched the proceedings a moment, then touched her husband's arm. "Ned, do go along with them and tell Charity about the time you were nearly shipwrecked on that cannibal island."

Titus laughed. "What, and give her nightmares?"

"Papa, you know it will not be any more fearful than the tales David tells about fur trading in Canada," Charity said, anticipation in her eyes.

He nodded. "And probably not any worse than Charles's adventures at Harvard, minus—hopefully—the cannibals! Do come, Ned, and enliven the walk."

"Ann, after a day in the warehouse, the bloom is quite gone from your face," Aggie said. "Go along and escort Ned back so a press gang does not apprehend him."

"Aggie, what would they want with a broken down old tar?" he asked affectionately, even as he held his arm out for Ann.

To Ann's delight, the captain held out his arm for Ann, too. "That's my office, Glossop," he told the man. "You're telling Charity a tale, and I can be the escort." He nodded to Ann. "Provided you approve, of course."

"Oh, I do," she said promptly, and felt her face go red. *Could I be more eager?* she asked herself. "Let me get my cloak."

By the time she returned with it, Ned and Charity were at the end of the road. Captain Titus waited for her. They started off together, but the captain was in no hurry to catch up to the old man and little girl ahead of them. She, who was renowned in some circles for her innocuous drawing room patter, could think of absolutely nothing to say. *Ask him about his sons,* she thought desperately. *Is there something about Boston you have been yearning to find out?* "Who is president of the United States?" she blurted out finally, when the silence was too great.

"Tom Jefferson," he said promptly. He stopped. "Miss Utley, what do you *really* want to ask me?"

She laughed out loud. "I can't for the life of me think of anything," she replied frankly. "I just feel a little shy, for no particular reason, and it seemed too quiet."

He resumed his stroll and she walked alongside again. "Miss Utley, what a pleasure it is to walk beside a female who can match me stride for stride." He tucked her arm through his. "Usually I try to be accommodating, but I forget, with the consequence that short females have to trot and turn red-faced."

That was humorous and harmless enough. "Consequently they avoid you?" she teased.

"Alas, no, Miss Utley. In American circles I am considered quite a catch."

I don't doubt that for a moment, she thought, at a loss again for any response.

But it was his turn. "Ned tells me that you fled Derbyshire to avoid a proposal, Miss Utley. Isn't that a bit extreme?"

"It was the basest sort of impulse," she replied. "One moment I was stalking around my room, ready to throw things, and the next thing I knew, I was headed down the oak tree."

He laughed that full-throated laugh that she found so charming. "One proposal too many, or not the one you wanted?"

She considered the matter. "Probably a bit of both. I had all but promised Mama that I would accept the next offer that came my way, but why did it have to be someone with pop eyes who is intimidated by his aunt?"

"Daunting, indeed," Titus murmured. "Was he too old, too?"

"Oh, not as old as you," she said without thinking, then clapped her hand over her mouth. "Do excuse that!"

"Nope," he said, but his tone was charitable. "I consider myself well seasoned."

"Well, Mama declares that I am too . . . too discerning." She got to her feet, and he rose, too. "Perhaps that is my frustration, sir. I would like to please my mother, and assure my brother that I will not be a spinster aunt to blight his sitting room in years to come. But . . ." She paused, not sure how to finish the thought.

"But the selection in Derbyshire is limited?" he suggested.

"Not to hear my mother tell it," she declared. "And so I ran away."

They were walking again. She couldn't see why Ned Glossop had not chosen a better road to the dock, considering how littered with rubble this one was. She made no objection when Captain Titus took her hand to help her around the broken cobblestones. She also made no objection when he continued to hold her hand, beyond the reflection that Aggie Glossop had told her years ago to beware of seafaring men. His hand was warm, and she wanted to hold it. What was even stranger, she felt that she should have been holding it for years.

But he does not trust the English, she reminded herself as they ambled along the dark street. *And we certainly do not dabble in the same social brook. My income is probably greater than his. This is folly, and so I shall remind Aggie. If only he were not so handsome.* She tightened her grip on his hand instead of turning him loose. "Captain, I'm thirty-two," she said, her voice soft. "I suppose that is what frightens me the most. I mean, I . . ."

She had no idea what she wanted to say, and no idea why she was trying to say it to someone she had met only that morning. But it didn't really matter, because he stopped walking, pulled her close, and kissed her.

She had been kissed before on several auspicious occasions by men who also knew what they were doing, but never before by someone who was precisely the right height and heft. Mama would probably have said he was holding her indecently close, but Mama wasn't there. Those other gentlemen—probably all of them long married by now—had smelled of eau de cologne or wood smoke, but she decided that tar and hemp were quite to her liking. His lips were warm, and she didn't want him to stop. For one moment she hoped she was not pulling in closer to him, and in the next, she didn't particularly care.

He stopped then, stepping back with a stunned look on his face, his eyes as wide as a child's. "My apologies, Miss Utley," he said, and he sounded far less confident than only a moment ago. "You . . . you . . . you have every right to haul off and slap me! I was only intending to give you a little kiss on the forehead to assure you that there was nothing wrong with being thirty-two . . . my Lord, I wish I were thirty-two again! And now I am babbling, which is something I do not ordinarily do. I—"

Amused now, Ann put her fingers to his lips to stop the stream of apology. She had no intention of slapping a man who had made an honest mistake. He startled her further by kissing her fingers. As amazed as she was, she could also tell that it was a natural reaction. When he started to apologize again, she stepped back and put her hands behind her back, but knew she could not disguise the twinkle she knew was in her eyes.

"Captain Titus, I simply will not have you apologizing! It is perfectly obvious to me that you are a man who has been away from the society of women too long."

He stopped and stared at her, then smiled and shook his head. In a more normal voice, he said, "I was going to babble something about being too long at sea, but you are right, Miss Utley. The voyage was only seven weeks, but Tamsin has been gone six years. I miss the ladies."

He said it so simply and with such frankness that her embarrassment died before it had a chance to raise the color in her cheeks. Plainly put, he was a man who liked women; not a rake, not a rascal, but a rudderless former husband with considerable goodwill toward the fair sex. She could no more understand why he had not been led away into marriage years ago than he could probably understand why she avoided proposals. She credited the whole matter to one of life's little mysteries, and decided to be flattered rather than offended. Not another man of her acquaintance would ever have said anything so honest.

"Captain Titus, you have quite cured me of my melancholy. Indeed, no one could have done it better!"

Ned Glossop had engaged a waterman before they arrived at the dock. With a smile and a bow, Captain Titus gave them both his good night, and helped Charity into the small boat. "Miss Utley, if you need help with more words tomorrow, I am sure Mrs. Glossop will let me take time out from my sampler," Charity called, and the waterman put his hands to the oars.

"Not the Aggie I remember!" she joked. "Keep Charity bundled up, Captain." Soon they were dark shapes on the darker water. Standing there watching the small craft, Ann knew that when the *Hasty* spread her sails and lifted anchor, she didn't want to be there to watch. Absurd tears tickled her eyes and she blinked them back, prepared to tell herself as often as she needed to that no one fell in love in less than twenty-four fours.

She never knew that a one-legged man could move so slowly. To her excruciating frustration, Ned Glossop was content, on that pleasant June evening, to amble slowly back to his Nautical Emporium. It was all she could do to walk quietly beside him, nodding where appropriate, and letting him continue a spate of sea stories that his conversation with Charity had begun. She wanted to grab up her skirts and hoof it back to the emporium, where she could pour her extreme distress onto Aggie's shoulder. To her dismay, she wasn't even sure if the first emotion was distress.

They arrived at last, and Ned offered some apology about having to go to the warehouse to make sure of a shipment for tomorrow. When he turned his back, she hoisted her skirts and took the stairs two at a time. She threw open the door to the sitting room and announced, "Aggie, he kissed me! What am I supposed to do now?"

To her credit, Aggie Glossop didn't even drop a stitch from the hose she was knitting. Beyond a slight start when the door banged open, that redoubtable female smiled and patted a spot on the sofa beside her. "Do sit down, my dear."

Shocked at her governess's calm demeanor, Ann did as she was told. She took a deep breath, and then another. "Aggie, men aren't supposed to do things like that."

"Perhaps not British men, my dear," Aggie suggested. "I have been around a few Americans in the twelve years I have been married to Mr. Glossop, and I have noticed a difference in them." She beamed at Ann. "Perhaps you have discovered what it is?"

"Aggie! He didn't ask my permission, or . . . or even stop to consider that I move in a vastly different sphere, or . . . or probably have pots more money than he does! What is the matter with him?"

Aggie put down her knitting and turned slightly to face Ann. "You aren't listening to me, my dear," she began calmly. "Let me say it more plainly. For all that they speak English, and heaven knows we share a common heritage, I do not believe that Americans think the way we do."

Ann gasped and put her hand to her mouth. "Do you mean . . . can you mean . . . that proprieties don't *matter*?"

"Not precisely, although his actions this evening may confirm that suspicion for some." Aggie patted Ann's hand. "It's something else. I'm not sure I can even define it."

Ann leaped to her feet and took a rapid turn about the room. "What on earth should I do?" She plopped down on the sofa, then got up quickly, as though the fabric burned her. "Aggie, he is so common!"

Her governess pursed her lips into a tight line that Ann recognized from years earlier. "You're still not listening, my dear. Americans don't care about formalities. If you told him he was common, I think he would only stare at you and laugh. Ann, they are *Americans*. If the thought of that frightens you, then by all means get on the mail coach tomorrow morning and go back to Derbyshire, where you are safe."

Ann sank onto the sofa again and leaned her head against her governess. "I am not looking at this in precisely the right way, am I?"

"I fear not."

"I think he is a lonely man."

Aggie laughed, and hugged her. "Perhaps not anymore, my dear."

She sat up, agitated again. "But Aggie, he's had time to find another American! Surely I am not the only woman on earth who has looked at him with admiration? He is so handsome, and kindness itself." She stopped. "Oh, dear, what am I saying?"

Aggie's voice was quiet. "And you have had years to

find an Englishman. I do not pretend to understand any of this, but I also do not disregard it." She looked at her charge, her expression puzzled. "There is something else. He appears to like the ladies, but it is so much more." She sighed and stood up. "I do not know. Go to bed, Ann, and try to sleep. If it's to be the mail coach tomorrow morning, Mr. Glossop will take you there."

Hiram never usually had trouble sleeping in a sheltered harbor, where his ship bobbed gently on the more mannerly swells than those found in the middle of the Atlantic, but tonight was an exception. He lay in his berth, hands behind his head, stared up at the compass, and tried to think of anything but Ann Utley. He succeeded for a while, thinking about the talk his first mate had overheard in a grogshop about the odds of England being at war with the United States within the month. He knew he could be at sea in less than a week, now that the *Hasty*'s hold was filling up with English goods bound for Boston. He resolved to prod Ned Glossop to revictual his ship at the same time he was loading the cargo.

"Damn and blast, he's shorthanded," Titus muttered out loud, turning over his pillow to find a cooler spot. Well, if he could get some sort of guarantee from the harbormaster, perhaps he could use his own crew to go into the emporium and help. He would ask in the morning. And if the man said no, Titus would break out his special store of Jamaican rum and bribe him.

Eventually, even these larger worries paled before the fact that he had made a complete idiot of himself tonight by kissing Ann Utley. He closed his eyes in the dark and felt the shame of it wash over him again. It was only going to be a harmless peck on the forehead, something he might do for Charity, instead of a kiss of breathtaking proportions. He groaned and rolled over. He was forty, but damned if his thoughts weren't awfully young.

And yet there he was, practically tingling at the thought of Ann Utley, like a man with nothing on his mind but bed. He was the kind of sailor he would warn Chary about when she was older and ripe for the Talk. Too bad there was not someone to sit *him* down for the

lecture on propriety, and how to treat females properly
and earn their respect. He would be lucky if the lady
said two words to him tomorrow when he returned to
the Nautical Emporium. *She will say precisely two words,
you chufflehead,* he thought sourly: *"Go away!"*

Sitting up, his head in his hands, he asked himself
why, out of all the ladies in Boston and contiguous
towns, none had kept him awake as Ann was keeping
him awake now. He had eaten many a meal in hopeful
widows' houses, and danced a jig with younger women
who made no attempt to hide their admiration. He had
even walked a few home from church, and sat on front
porches for afternoons of tea and biscuits. In every in-
stance he had paid his respects and gone about his business, content of a good night's sleep.

*Blast and damn, but this is a weird set of circumstances.
I walk into a warehouse in a seedy British port, and I
am in love,* he thought, more in awe than misery. *I
haven't seen a prettier face in years, and I think she is
even sensible. My sons will probably be bringing home
wives soon enough, and I am ready to clamber into the
marriage bed again myself. Good Lord, my children will
probably have uncles and aunts their own age!*

He chuckled at that, and felt the mantle of unease fall
away from his shoulders. He was making mountains out
of molehills; in a few more minutes he could sensibly
convince himself that he was just lonely and far from
home. His longing for a woman—no, damn it, for *that*
woman—would pass, and he would return to being the
sensible, sober Captain Titus, responsible man of business and the father of three grown sons and a daughter.
He lay down again and rolled onto his side.

He was startled awake an hour or two later. Someone
was standing right beside his berth. For one wild, irratio-
nal moment, he wanted it to be Ann Utley, even though
he knew that was utter folly. *We're at war,* was his next
thought, and then he heard the muffled sob of someone
crying into her sleeve.

"Chary?" he asked gently, reaching out to his daughter. "Are you not well?"

Her response was to sob out loud now. He sat up
quickly and pulled her onto his lap, holding her close.

She was warm, almost hot to the touch, and there was that smell of fever about her. He wouldn't have known that odor with his three boys, because it was always Tamsin who hurried out of bed to tend them in the middle of the night. But his wife had died when Charity was only four, so he knew many hours with a sick child. She sneezed several times. He found a handkerchief from somewhere and she dutifully blew her nose.

He gathered her close and lay down with her. With a thankful sigh, she burrowed in close to him. "I'm sorry, Papa," she murmured. "Maybe England does not agree with me."

He chuckled. "Go to sleep, honey. John Cook will make a poultice for your chest tomorrow."

"Miss Utley will help me," she said.

He smoothed the damp hair back from her face. "What makes you so confident of that?"

"I just know it," Charity replied with the logic of childhood. "Now go to sleep, Papa."

And he did.

After half a night's tossing and turning, thoroughly dissatisfied with herself, Ann resolved to petition Ned Glossop to take her to the mail coach stop in the morning. In the other half of the night, she changed her mind. After all, Aggie needed her help at the clerk's desk. If Captain Titus should come into the warehouse, she would look at him with equanimity, because hadn't he told her that the kiss was really a mistake? Surely she was enough of an adult to overlook a mere misdemeanor. Besides, she had no longing to return to Derbyshire, where nothing was resolved. She sighed and stared at the ceiling, knowing that she would eventually return to find Sir Barnaby Phillips as silly as ever.

Before she dozed off, Ann reminded herself that the captain had made some remark about hurrying to revictual the *Hasty* and be on his way before war was declared. "See there, Ann," she said out loud, her voice drowsy. "He will be gone in a matter of days and you will never see him again."

And why should that make her cry?

*   *   *

Knowing that she looked every one of her years, Ann avoided the mirror while she dressed, avoided her former governess's eyes over a hasty breakfast, and slunk off to the warehouse to complete the manifest for the HMS *Jasper*, interrupted last night when Captain Titus took her off to dinner. She hauled herself onto the stool, uncapped the inkwell, pushed a fresh steel tip onto her pen holder, and stared down at the manifest.

She sucked in her breath, wondering what had ever possessed her to write so plainly and carefully, *six barrels of Hiram Titus*. Aghast, she stared at the original, which read, *six barrels of salt beef*. Her face hot, her heart beating, she carefully scratched through her mistake, then looked back at what she had transcribed earlier. Oh, Lord, there it was again: *Hiram Titus packed in straw*, instead of *marmalades and jellies*. Scratch went her pen again. Panic in her heart now, she ruffled through the other pages, only to find *Hiram* where sticking plasters, ship's bread, and rice should have been. Perspiration beaded her forehead as she corrected her mistakes and prayed to the Almighty that Aggie Glossop had not checked her work that morning and found it seriously wanting. Surely not, she convinced herself, when her heartbeat slowed to its usual rhythm. Aggie would have made some comment over breakfast.

She had finished correcting the manifest when the warehouse door opened. Her small sigh of relief to see only Aggie quickly evaporated when Captain Titus came in right behind her. She looked down at the manifest, hoping that his name would not come popping through her careful corrections like a fishing bob.

It did not, and she glanced up again. The captain looked so serious this morning, almost, to her way of thinking, like someone who had slept as little as she.

Aggie spoke to her. "Ann, I . . . we . . . have a great favor to ask you."

"Ask away, my dear," she replied. "You know you can have anything up to half my kingdom." *That's right, Ann,* she told herself; *keep it a light touch.*

Captain Titus smiled at her feeble witticism, but his eyes were still full of concern. "Miss Utley, my daughter is ill and she needs someone besides a ham-handed father to look after her."

"I thought she felt warm last night," Ann replied, getting off the stool. "Of course I will tend her. Is she upstairs?"

"She's still on the *Hasty*. My cook has made a wondrously odorous poultice of sage and oil of eucalyptus, and Charity declares that no one will apply it but you." His eyes were both tired and full of apology. "She is only contrary when she is ill."

"And quite entitled, I imagine," Ann murmured. "Of course I will go, Captain."

"That's my girl," Aggie said. "I assured him that you would not shrink."

She felt her good humor returning. "Certainly not! Let me only get my cloak and—"

"Uh, there is a little more to it than that," the captain said, and it was Aggie's turn to smile. He held out a pair of trousers. "Getting onto the *Hasty* in a dress would prove a challenge, Miss Utley, as there is a rope ladder."

"But how does Charity do it?" she asked, trying not to stare like a wild woman at the trousers over his arm.

"She wraps her legs around my waist and I carry her up and down the ladder on my back," he said, his face quite red.

"Oh." Ann took the trousers and looked at them dubiously.

"I think we are much the same length in the legs, Miss Utley, if you will pardon the observation," he told her as he held out a thin rope. "I know your waist is not as wide around as mine, so this should keep 'em up." He looked at Aggie. "Mrs. Glossop says she can find a proper canvas shirt in the warehouse. Something for cabin boys."

"Very well," Ann replied, wishing that her voice were not so faint.

"I'll find that shirt right now," Aggie said. "Ann, go upstairs and pack your clothing in a bundle. I'm certain you will want to put your dress on again when you reach the *Hasty*."

"Indeed I will," Ann assured them both.

The captain managed a bow that struck Ann as quite elegant. "You're relieving this father's heart," he said to her, then nodded to Aggie. "I'm going to find Ned and urge him to revictual us as soon as possible." Again she saw the doubt in his face. "Aggie, I don't know. There's more talk on the wharf."

"You've heard nothing from an official source?" her governess asked.

His smile was wry. "If war is declared, Aggie, the only official source we will get is an officer of the Royal Navy climbing aboard to declare me a prisoner and the *Hasty* contraband!"

She stood there holding the trousers and rope as he loped off to the wagon yard again. "What on earth have I just agreed to, Aggie?" she asked.

"Something rather more exciting than transcribing manifests or boring yourself to death listening to prosy old Barnaby Phillips!" Aggie said tartly. "Hurry up now. I'm preparing a basket of lemons and lozenges you can take. I might even find one or two of those books I used to read to you when you were about that age, my dear." She squeezed her arm. "Oh, Ann! It will just be for a day or so."

They started for the stairs to the quarters above. "You should have listened to me last night when I suggested we keep Charity here," Ann reminded her.

"I know," Aggie replied, but to Ann's ears she sounded almost too contrite. It was on the tip of her tongue to accuse her governess of engineering this whole turn of events, but she reconsidered. Aggie Glossop was many things, but she was no manipulator.

In the privacy of her room, Ann removed her dress and pulled on the trousers. Captain Titus was right, which gave her another pause. To her knowledge, no man of her acquaintance had taken such a measure of her legs before. *Perhaps that is what Americans do*, she thought sourly. Aggie was right; they truly were a species apart.

Aggie brought her a canvas shirt that fit well enough without being oceans too long. She carefully tucked it into the waistband of the trousers and cinched the rope tight. "Well?" she asked.

"You'll do," Aggie said. She took Ann's bundle of clothing from the bed. "I've made another bundle of things for Charity. It will be an easy matter to tie a rope to them both and sling them up to the deck of the *Hasty*."

Captain Titus waited for her in the wagon yard. As silly as she felt, she was pleased a little to see the way the lines around his eyes crinkled up with good humor, lightening the soberness of his expression. "I was close," he said. "Just took one turn of the cuffs, eh?"

"Both my parents were tall, Captain," she replied, for want of anything better to say.

"Well, you look finer than frog's hair, Miss Utley."

"What?" she exclaimed, then laughed. "I pray *that* is an Americanism!"

"Probably." He winked at her. "Think of this as something to tell your friends next winter when conversation lags."

Ned insisted upon driving them to the dock, and even handed Ann up onto the wagon seat with all the grace of a coachman. The captain clambered into the back, content to sit upon a hogshead of salted beef, one long leg negligently propped up on the wagon side. He leaned down to take the basket meant for Charity from Aggie and listen to her last-minute advice. Ann watched him over her shoulder, and found herself admiring his easy grace all over again. She knew a few sea captains, even an admiral or two, and she could not fathom even one of them sitting so casually among ship's cargo.

And here I am in long pants, she thought, as Ned spoke to the horses and they rumbled slowly off. *At least my hair is not braided into a tarry queue and I do not brandish a cutlass in my teeth.* She smiled at the thought, and resolved to ask Captain Titus how on earth pirates managed it.

Before the gate closed behind them, she looked back at Aggie and waved. To her surprise, her old governess was dabbing at her eyes. Ann half rose in the seat and cupped her hand to her mouth. "Aggie, dearest," she called, "it is only for a day or two!"

That mild joke seemed to make Aggie cry harder. She was sobbing quite earnestly into her apron now. *This will never do,* Ann thought. "Aggie, I promise to write from America and send home my wages!" she teased, and sat down again.

She heard a mighty sniff beside her, and glanced in surprise at Ned, who was wiping his face with his sleeve. "Oh, for heaven's sake, what is the matter with you Glossops?" she scolded. "You would think I was bound for foreign lands, and not just Portsmouth harbor!"

For all that she could swear she saw tears in his eyes, Ned gave her a stern look. "I just got a cinder in me eye, you silly widgeon," he said with some dignity. "Now behave yourself, or I'll turn ye over to the press gang meself. They'd like a Long Meg who could climb a ratline."

Captain Titus laughed and reached over to prod Ned. "I'd fight you for her, Ned, 'cause I need a nursemaid now!" He stood up and propped his elbows on the back of the wagon seat. "This is what you get for climbing down a tree, Miss Utley."

His arm was pressing against her shoulder, but she leaned toward him anyway, simply unable to help herself. "You, sir, are a rascal. I am surprised that any American entrepreneur trusts you with a ship!"

To her further surprise, he and Ned exchanged glances, and both men started to laugh. Ned chirruped to his horses. "Sit down, Captain, before I bump you out. Miss Ann, I know you'll never believe this, but the captain here owns a whole fleet of ships." He made a face at the captain. " 'E's a regular Yankee-Doodle nabob!"

"I never would have reckoned," Ann said, unable to keep the surprise from her voice. "Captain Titus, are all uh . . . Yankee nabobs so casual?"

He made no pretense at dignity, but she watched the wrinkles around his eyes deepen. "Miss Utley, you would be amazed at me in my office, with my charts and graphs, and world map with colored pins."

"Maybe I would not," she said slowly. "I'm beginning to think that nothing would surprise me."

She considered the matter all the way to the docks, while Ned and Titus kept up a running commentary about the business of preparing the *Hasty* for sea. "How many ships do you own?" she asked as Ned stopped his team at the dock and waved his arms to summon a waterman.

"Ten merchant vessels, and I have half interest in four whaling ships out of Nantucket." He hopped down and held up his arms for her. "I like the ocean, Miss Utley, for all that I have not been to sea lately."

"Because of Charity?" she asked, and let him help her to the ground.

"Aye. She needed me at home." He looked toward the harbor. "And I wish we were there now."

She felt a little ripple down her spine. "You think war's coming any day now, don't you?"

He nodded, then ushered her forward to the dock as Ned hailed a waterman. "What will happen to Charity if I am incarcerated?"

"I would take care of her," she murmured.

He inclined his head toward hers. "I rather believe you would, Miss Utley. Mind your step now."

Her bundles around her, they sat close together in the stern of the boat as the waterman rowed toward the only tall-masted ship in the harbor flying American colors. The rain began when they were less than halfway across the choppy water. Titus pulled his boat cloak around both of them, tugging her close. "Your cloak's not waterproof," he offered for explanation.

Oddly enough, she wasn't sure she even needed an explanation. The rain pelted down, and she was comfortable and safe, pressed close to his chest. *I am far safer than he is,* she thought. *Why on earth should my government penalize this good man for trying to earn a living? Has the world gone mad?* Sitting there in a little boat, suddenly it mattered to her, and she knew why: She loved him. In fact, she would probably never love another. If she possessed any courage at all, or maybe just a little less dignity, she would have turned his face toward her own—they were so much the same height that scarcely any effort would be involved—and kiss him. He was even looking at her, and she almost didn't need to know what he was thinking. This could be the easiest thing she ever did.

"*Hasty*, Captain," the waterman said then, and backed

the boat with his oars until they bobbed alongside the tall ship. She stared at the dangling rope ladder.

Titus tossed him a coin and unlimbered himself from beside her. He stood up carefully and whistled. In another moment, a sailor was grinning down at them from the deck above that looked amazingly far away to Ann. "Send 'er up, sir," he hollered down in the same sharp, spare-toned twang as his captain. She forced herself to look at the ladder, and gulped.

"Stand up slowly, Ann, and grab hold of the rope," the captain said. "I'll give you a boost up on the next swell."

"I don't know," she said. The ladder looked so tiny as the boat rose and fell.

"Ah, now, any woman who can climb down a tree can shinny up a rope ladder," he assured her. He put his hand on her rump and grinned at her. "Didn't Aggie ever warn you about sailors? Now!"

Too terrified to do anything else, she did as he said as he boosted her to the ladder. She clutched it as the little boat dropped away and the *Hasty* rolled. She took a deep breath and started to climb. *You daren't look down,* she told herself as she climbed steadily. In a few moments she felt pressure below her that told her Titus was right behind. And then two hands from the deck above reached down, grabbed her under her armpits, and swung her quite handily onto the ship.

Titus came up quickly, and then the sailor sent down a line for the bundle and basket. Ann went to the rail and looked down—way down—at the small launch that was pulling away, and the still-dangling rope ladder. "I don't even want to contemplate climbing back down that thing," she murmured.

"Then don't," he told her. "Didn't Aggie ever make you embroider a sampler that said, 'Sufficient unto the day is the evil thereof'?"

She grinned at him, her equilibrium on even keel again. "I already told you what a mess I made of my first sampler." She stood still while the captain settled her cloak straight around her again. "Now where is my charge?"

"This way." He handed her the bundle, and took Aggie's basket on his arm. "Mind that you duck your head belowdeck. You have the same problem I have."

She was careful to avoid the overhead beam as she followed him down the companionway on the steep treads, and felt her hair just brushing the ceiling. "One would think that since you own this fleet, you could make the ceilings taller," she told him.

"Wasted space, Annie Utley," he said, and she smiled again at his free use of her first name. There was no denying that now he was back in his own domain, he seemed more cheerful. She would overlook his social blunder.

He led her down the narrow passageway to a chamber with many small-paned windows across the stern of the ship. "These are my quarters," he told her. "I put Chary in my berth and made up this cot for you, if you have to stay tonight." He glanced behind him. "I took her cabin out there."

Charity sat up when she saw Ann, her eyes wide. "Oh, Papa, you did get her," she said, and lay down again. "Miss Utley, thank goodness you have come."

"Such drama worthy of Siddons!" Ann exclaimed. She came close to the berth and touched the child's head. "Do call me Ann, my dear," she said, then glanced over her shoulder. "Everyone else seems to be doing that." She set down her bundle and turned around, quite firm in her resolution. "All right, Hiram, go fetch that poultice and close the door after you. I'll put on my dress again, so you had better knock."

He grinned and knuckled his forehead at her, but did as she said. She heard him whistling down the passageway in a moment. "Your father is considerably happier on his own ship," she told Charity. She let fall her cloak and undid the rope knotted about her waist. "Let me dress, and then I'll see what I can do for you."

By the time he returned bearing a small poultice, she had settled her cap about her head and was tying on her apron. "Just set it on the table," she told him as she hitched herself up into his berth. "I am going to comb Chary's hair first. Ladies always feel better when they look neat."

He stood there watching them both as she combed

the child's hair. Charity leaned against her with her eyes closed. "Excellent," he said quietly. "I am just not proficient at hair."

"Nor did I expect you to be." She lifted Chary's dark hair with the comb. "This is a beautiful color."

"Aye, like her mother's."

His voice was tender, and Ann felt the oddest moment of jealousy, which passed quickly, to her relief.

He came closer and touched Ann's shoulder. "I am supervising the last of the cargo this morning. This afternoon Ned's going to begin the revictualing. Water kegs come on board last, probably around noon tomorrow."

And then you will be under way, Ann thought, and felt that tickling sensation behind her eyes. *I should treasure this moment, I suppose.* She enjoyed the firm pressure of his hand much as Chary appeared to find pleasure in the combing of her hair. "We'll manage quite well, Captain."

"I like Hiram better."

"Actually, so do I," she said promptly, a little surprised at herself.

The pressure increased for a moment; then he went to the door. "Do take those lemons to your cook," she asked. "If he will make some hot lemonade for Charity and bring it here, along with some clear soup, I believe we will rub along pretty well . . . Hiram."

"Consider it done, Ann."

She wished he could have stayed, not that she needed help with the poultice—which was certainly odorous enough to be medicinal—but because she relished his company. She had known much wittier men, elegant fellows who could keep her in stitches for hours. She had danced many evenings with lords and officers who made her look far more graceful than she knew she was. But when all was said, they had not touched her heart. They had not even come close. But there was Hiram Titus, tall and genially commanding, with wrinkles around his eyes from too much sun and wind, and hands grown hard with work. He had that amusing Yankee twang that would have made him the laughingstock of many a refined salon. He was the kind of fellow that men of her social circle would have laughed about after dinner. If he ever came up in conversation, it would be with condescension.

She loved him, for all that their acquaintance was brief. If she had not taken momentary leave of her senses and climbed down that blessed tree, she never would have met him. How odd were the workings of fate! But swift on the heels of her joy was the reality that he was probably sailing in another day to prevent his capture in port if war broke out. There would never be an opportunity for courtship. Not that there ever was, she told herself bleakly, and a little ruthlessly. When would such a man ever be invited to her mother's estate? What circles could they possibly move in together? She sat quietly beside Charity's berth, nearly astounded at her rare good fortune, and her utter despair because of it.

The cook came with soup and lemonade; Charity dutifully ate, then promptly slumbered. Ann roamed around the small space allotted to the captain and his daughter. She could hear cargo being thumped deep into the hold. A glance out the small windows showed many boats plying to and from the shore laden with boxes and barrels. She turned away from that glaring evidence of a hasty departure.

Ann looked at what he read on the small table beside the berth, smiling to see a well-thumbed Bible, and a book on navigation, equally used. There was also a letter half-written, perhaps to one of his sons.

She picked up a miniature on the table and contemplated the lovely lady within it, a woman with dark hair and blue eyes and a smile most serene. She seemed to be looking beyond the painter as she smiled, and Ann wondered if the captain had been sitting there, and perhaps smiling back at her. She set down the miniature and looked away. Tamsin Titus was probably small and dainty, too, someone who would never climb a ship's ladder in men's trousers.

Oh, I am making mountains out of molehills, she thought, as she felt Charity's forehead, then resumed her traverse of the cabin. *He sails tomorrow probably, and I will never see him again. Life is not fair, Ann Utley, but you already knew that. Even if he does feel for you*

*even a fraction of what you feel for him, these things take
time, and the time of our few moments breathing the same
air is about to run out.*

"This will never do," she whispered. "You have to get
a grip on yourself, Ann." She sat very still then, knowing
from experience that she could will any tears away, if she
had the mind to. She did not, and cried quietly instead,
distressed to think that by tomorrow morning she would
be back at the Glossops'. Nothing would keep her there
for long; in fact, she doubted that she would ever visit
them again. The memories would be too great. Better
to stifle in Derbyshire than pine in Portsmouth.

Captain Titus was tired right down to his bones when
he rowed with his silent crew back to the *Hasty*. Night
was coming. He hoped Ann would not mind staying the
night aboard ship, but a press gang was already prowling
the docks, and he did not feel inclined to chance the
matter. He had rounded up all his crew that he could,
and left a message at their favorite public house for the
others to meet him on the dock at first light, without fail.

His last meeting with Ned Glossop had been disturbing. Looking around to make sure that no agents
lurked in his wagon yard, the old fellow had told him
that the skipper of the HMS *Corinthian*, waiting to be
revictualed, had let drop that he expected orders tomorrow to American waters. "I'll know something by two,
at least," he had said as he pressed his bill into Titus's
hand. "The tide'll be in your favor, too."

To his fear that they wouldn't have time for all the
water barrels, Ned only shrugged. "If you're first off the
block, laddie, you'll likely beat anything to the Azores.
Plenty of water there."

After finding his crew, and promising to pay Ned's bill
first thing in the morning, they rowed in three boats
back to the *Hasty*, no one talking, but everyone taking
a measure of the warships in the harbor. What they saw
relieved them somewhat: the *Jasper* was stepping a mast,
another ship had no sails, and a third was revictualing,
as he was. Only the *Corinthian* made him pause. Trust
the captain of such a renowned warship to leap for the
gate like a greyhound, food or not.

He felt a measure of relief on his own deck and quietly went to his cabin, where the door was ajar. The sight before him seemed to roll a weight off his shoulders, which, in itself, was a sensation he had not experienced since Tamsin's death. How many times, after fractious wranglings with victualers, or news of ill winds, had he come home to their house on Ousley Street, bearing the burdens of Sisyphus, only to be lifted by that welcome face? Tamsin could make him feel that the worst ailment was no heavier to bear than a sack of feathers.

Admiring Ann Utley, he felt that way again. She was not mindful that he stood in the doorway, and he relished the moment. She was leaning back negligently in his favorite chair, her long legs crossed at the knees in a distinctly unladylike way that suited her. As much as he wanted to admire the shape of her legs under that dark dress, he was more captured by the way her hand rested along Charity's arm. His daughter's eyes were closed, but Ann was reading out loud to her in a low voice. Everything about her showed how much Ann cared for his beloved daughter.

His father had told him years ago that it was the ladies who made life bearable. He had known this to be true with Tamsin, but until now it never occurred to him that he might be lucky twice. No, he should amend that; it would have been true, if he hadn't been in a pelter to be safely out of English waters, or maybe even if he had the tiniest notion how to court a woman. Tamsin had his heart from childhood, and had required no pursuit. Ann would require some time invested, and he had no time at all.

So he just stood there admiring her a moment longer, knowing that when he rowed her to shore tomorrow morning, he would be the unhappiest man in the universe.

He spent the next few hours with them. Charity was infinitely better, the feverish color of her cheeks fainter now. She ate a little, but cautiously, and kept everything in her stomach, which was another relief.

Ann was subdued, answering his questions in that serene manner of hers, but offering few observations of her own. Something told him that if he were not in the room, she would be pacing up and down. She sat still enough, but her energy appeared to be restrained on a tight leash. Perhaps she did not care much for the ocean.

As Charity talked to her, Titus tried to consider Ann Utley dispassionately. Certainly she was too tall for fashion, but he could find no fault with that, or with her womanly shape, quite unlike Tamsin's lifetime slimness. He itched to touch her. He decided that her creamy complexion was not something that could be duplicated in the United States. Maybe it was the result of life in a cool, misty climate. By the end of the evening, when he reluctantly bowed himself out and into his own chaste and narrow berth a door away, he dreaded his expected dreams.

He should not have troubled himself; nothing could have been farther from him than sleep that last night in Portsmouth Harbor. He worried about everything he could think of: Charity's health, the oncoming war, a chance that the *Hasty* might spring a leak midocean, that little bare but growing patch on his head where his part originated, the safety of his dear sons in their various locales, a certain but discernible weakness in his stomach muscles, the price of goods in Boston—anything to keep from thinking of the lady who slept so close to him in the next cabin, but so eternally far away.

He got up once; perhaps he shouldn't have. He heard her moving around in the cabin sometime between one and two o'clock, in response to what sounded like a question from Charity. Worried suddenly for his daughter, he wrapped a blanket around him and knocked softly on the door.

He had to smile. By the light of the full moon outside, he could see both Charity and Ann in the same berth now. He came close and touched Ann's shoulder. "All's well?" he asked.

"Aye," she said, and he laughed softly, because she was trying to imitate his own speech.

"Aye, is it? You're starting to sound like a Back Bay woman," he joked, "except that it's 'aye-yah,' not just 'aye.' "

He could see her smile, and also the way she held

Charity—asleep again—so close to her body. He rested the back of his hand against his daughter's forehead, relieved to find it cool. To his infinite pleasure, Ann wrapped her fingers around his wrist.

"You needn't worry, Hiram," she whispered. "I think I have an inkling what she means to you."

She released him too soon for his own satisfaction, and there was nothing he could do about it. In perfect misery, he leaned forward and kissed Charity's cheek. Then he couldn't help himself, because Ann lay so close. He kissed her forehead, then rested his cheek briefly against hers, which was the wrong thing to do, because it put him in amazing proximity to her. It was late and he was tired, but he couldn't be totally sure that he didn't plant another kiss on that stretch of warm skin where her neck became her shoulder.

She murmured something deep in her throat that he could feel with his lips. It took a supreme force of will to leave the room, but doomed him to stare at the overhead deck, wide-awake, for the rest of the night.

At first light he was on deck, dousing himself under the pump, letting the shock of cold seawater put him back into a businesslike state of mind. His congregational minister in Boston was never so right as when he spoke about the flesh being weak. Another pull from the pump sparked a small revolt. "And what the hell business is that of the Lord Almighty?" he growled under the water. His own Puritan guilt made him stop short and endure another unnecessary few minutes under the cold water as penance.

He stood on the deck, a towel around his middle, and watched the activity of the other ships in the harbor, the HMS *Corinthian* in particular. He could see no movement abovedecks yet, no signal flags, no small boats clustered about like iron filings to a magnet. He looked to the docks, where Ned Glossop's lighter was already setting out. Shivering now, he watched as the lighter came closer, and the cargo was water kegs. Now it was time for his own sigh of relief. By the end of the day he would have enough stored for a comfortable cruise, but by noon there would be enough to endure short rations to the Azores, if worse came to worst.

He dressed and knocked on his cabin door by seven o'clock. Ann answered it. He could tell by the blush on her cheek that he hadn't invented that early-morning kiss, but she kept her counsel—*drat her*—the lady that she was.

"The lighters are coming now with water," he told her.

He was sure he saw dismay on her face, followed by that cool, bland calmness that could mean anything. "I'm not ready to go yet," she told him. "Charity has eaten, but I want to help her with her bath."

"And you may," he replied. "I'm going on deck to watch them start down the water kegs, and then I'll go in to settle my account with Ned. Can you be ready by noon?"

"Most certainly," she said.

He wished mightily that he knew her better, that he could get some hint more of her feelings for him, beyond her fingers on his wrist this morning, or the way she had half turned her head to accommodate his lips on her neck. Or maybe it was all in his imagination. He didn't know what to think, and felt more like the most callow youth who ever flirted with the young ladies.

By the middle of the morning the lighters had gone ashore and returned with another cargo of water. He assigned two of his crew to row him to the dock, where he sent them in search of the few remaining crewmen, and took himself to Glossop's Nautical Emporium.

He thought he saw Ned at the window, but suddenly the door banged open and Aggie Glossop ran out. His nerves instantly on edge, he just stood there in the wagon yard, looking wildly around him for British marines with muskets held at port arms. To his surprise, Aggie grabbed him by the hand and pulled him toward the warehouse door, which Ned was even now holding open.

"My God, has it happened?" he asked.

Ned nodded, his eyes on Titus's face. "We just heard from the number one on the *Corinthian*, who is probably eyeing your ship, even now!"

Without a word, Titus slammed down the money he owed the Glossops and bolted for the door, his heart somewhere up around his ears. "I haven't a moment to waste," he shouted over his shoulder.

"One moment, Captain," Aggie said, and handed him an envelope. "This can wait until after you are at sea. Hurry now!"

He stuffed the letter into his shirt front, blew Aggie a kiss, and ran for the dock. Luckily, his crew had found their remaining comrades. When they saw him coming at a run, they hurried into the dinghy and sat ready with the oars. He loosed the rope from the hawser and stepped into the boat a split second before his sailors pushed away from the dock. "Fast as you can, lads," he urged, his eyes on the big warship riding at anchor too close to his vessel. "War's been declared and the hounds are loose."

No one said anything as they crossed the harbor. He stood up carefully to test the wind on his face, and knew that he had a chance. He was scrambling up the ladder to the *Hasty* before he remembered Ann Utley. *I hope she relishes an ocean voyage*, he thought grimly. *There's not time to send her back.*

Ann was pulling on her trousers when she heard kegs rolling across the deck above, then men running. She buttoned her pants and rolled the cuffs, listening. She glanced over at Charity, who was sitting up now, her face intent. "What are they doing?" she asked.

The little girl shrugged. "I don't know. This is my first voyage."

Ann hurried to button up her shirt and tuck it into the trousers. She was knotting the cord around her waist when the sails dropped with a whoosh that must have sounded all over the harbor. *My God,* she thought, *this ship can't be under way.*

But it was. She ran to the windows and stared out to see empty lighters pulling away quickly from the ship, the men rowing for all they were worth. The dinghy that she knew was to take her back to the dock was tied aft and bobbing just under the windows, quite empty. "We're moving. My goodness, Charity, do you suppose he forgot I was on board?"

Charity climbed out of the berth, tugging at her night-gown. "I don't think he's that absentminded."

Has war been declared? Ann asked herself as she smoothed back her hair with hands that trembled and tied it with a cord. Perhaps if she hurried she could convince him to at least summon a waterman to row her back to shore. She looked around the cabin quickly, and saw nothing of hers that she would take the time to bundle up. "I must hurry," she said, and opened the door.

Charity followed her into the narrow companionway. The ship was definitely picking up speed. Ann kissed Charity quickly, and gave her a hug, feeling all out of sorts with herself: unhappy to leave, and yet in a pelter to get away. Clotilde was getting married in August, and she had promised to serve punch on the lawn.

She ran for the ladder, intent upon gaining the deck. *Oh, you will get such a scold from me, Hiram Titus,* she thought as she picked up speed. *It doesn't do to kidnap Englishwomen, you dear, misguided man.*

It was her last thought. "Miss Utley, mind your head!" she heard Charity shriek, but it was too late. She slammed into the overhead beam and fell flat on her back without so much as a groan.

"Ann. Ann. Come now, Ann."

The voice sounded faraway and tinny, and someone was gently patting her cheeks. She opened her eyes, but everything was black. *Good Lord, I'm blind,* she thought in a panic, until she realized that there was a cool cloth on her forehead that covered her eyes, too. Her head definitely rested in a man's lap. She knew that etiquette dictated she should sit up immediately, but the matter seemed quite impossible. She couldn't even raise her hand to move the cloth, much less lift her head. *I will just stay here,* she thought. *It's improper, but I don't care.*

The deck gave a mighty heave, and then pitched forward. I *am* going to die, she thought, and didn't even try to stifle her groan. The hand stopped pummeling her face. He folded back the cloth, and she blinked in the half-light of the companionway, where she lay in Hiram's lap at the foot of the ladder.

"You hit just above the bridge of your nose," Hiram told her. "I think one of your eyes is going black."

She looked up at him. At first he looked like someone viewed from the bottom of a pond; then he quit shimmering as her brain stopped bobbing about inside her skull. She closed her eyes—or rather, her eye; the other one was already shut and swelling—and murmured, "I am supposed to serve punch on the lawn in August. Now what are you going to do about that?"

It seemed perfectly rational to her, and she couldn't imagine why his stomach began to shake. "It's not funny," she told him quite seriously.

He let out a sigh then, and carefully pulled her into his arms and close to his chest. "Ann, it's war, and I had to get across the bar before the tide turned."

If this was sailing, she wanted no part of it. She held her breath as the ship rose and rose, and then dropped into a trough. "I'm going to be sick," she said in a strangled voice.

He must have been prepared for that eventuality, because he pulled a bucket close and turned her face toward it. She obliged him by vomiting up everything she had eaten for the last three years. She didn't want to look in the bucket when she finished, because she knew her toenails were probably floating on top.

Hiram sat her up carefully, and wiped her mouth with his shirttail. She tensed when the ship rose again on a swell. He tightened his grip on her, pressing his hand firmly against her rib cage. She closed her eyes and moaned when the *Hasty* plummeted down the chute again.

"It's going to do this all the way to Boston?" she asked, her voice faint. Her gorge rose again, which surprised her, because she knew there was nothing left in her entire insides. "Six weeks?"

"Uh, more like eight on the return trip, Ann," he replied.

"That's Miss Utley to you," she snapped, but the effect was dulled by another humiliating perusal of the bucket. As angry as she was, she leaned back against him when she finished, exhausted. "If a man-'o-war finds us, I'll turn you over myself."

He only chuckled. "You and who else, Miss Utley? Come on, now, let me help you up."

She hadn't realized the extent of the appreciative audience until two crew members hurried to prop up her other side and help her to her feet. The bucket looked faraway, which alarmed her, because she felt a huge urge to hug it again. "If I die, will you bury me at sea?" she managed to gasp. "Tie a cord around my knees when you pitch me over, so I'm decent?"

Titus laughed. "You'll feel better in a few days. Everyone does."

He was right, of course, drat him. She didn't remember much of the next few days, except that he kindly unbuttoned her trousers, peeled off her shirt, and helped her into her nightdress without comment. As she gagged and retched, he bound her hair into pigtails—"To keep your hair out of the bucket, Miss Utley"—and kept a flannel-wrapped cask of hot water at her feet. ("I don't know why it helps, missy, but it does.")

She shook her head at his offer of broth, and prepared for death. It would have been an easy death, and much more pleasant than "kissing the wooden goddess," as Titus so aptly expressed it when she rolled from his berth and threw herself on her knees by the bucket. It was his continual good cheer that drove her to distraction until she wanted to throw a spike in his general direction.

The low point came toward the end of the interminable week, when she uttered a two-word sentence she had heard from her brother once when he had been unseated from a horse. Hiram looked at her, eyes wide, brows raised, and then that smile came again, even as she was preparing to cover her face with the sheet in embarrassment.

He had sat down beside her in the berth, and rested his elbow on her upraised knee as casually as though she had murmured something nonsensical and affectionate. He compounded her misery by smiling at her in that peculiarly disturbing way that must have been the reason she sprinkled his name so liberally through the *Jasper*'s lading bill. "I could be wrong, Miss Utley," he said, "but I think there is something special about a man who'll hold a lady's head steady over a bucket."

He patted her knee then in a most proprietary manner and left her to stew in her own juices. The door hadn't even shut before she realized that he was absolutely right. When he came back later that afternoon with broth, she was dressed—thanks to Charity's assistance—and sitting, if a trifle unsteadily, in the chair by the windows. She knew she should apologize to him, and opened her mouth to do so, but he was reaching for a hairbrush and telling her to lean forward.

When he finished unplaiting her hair and brushing out her snarls, she said simply, "I'm glad you do not hold grudges, Hiram."

"Wouldn't dream of it, Ann," he replied. He stood up and nodded to Charity. "Make sure she eats all that broth, dear. She's looking a little wan, and that won't do." He pointed upward. "My watch now. Maybe if you feel good enough tomorrow morning, you can join me on deck."

Humor seemed the best recourse. "That might put me too far from my bucket."

He laughed. "We have a lengthy railing to lean over and a whole ocean to puke in, Annie Utley." He came back to the berth then, and his face was serious as he put his hand gently on the bump on her forehead. "You'll be all right now. I know it."

And she was. Next morning when Ann came unsteadily up the ladder, practically hand over hand, Charity was already standing next to her father on the poop deck, her arm around his waist. Ann watched her, envying her casual stance, even as the *Hasty* continued its dip through the troughs of the waves. *The sea is in your blood, child,* she thought. She didn't think she could manage more steps, but he was there at her side to help.

Charity clapped her hands. "I knew you could, Miss Utley."

She let them lead her to a wooden spool and sit her down. Hiram handed her his own cup of coffee. "Hope you like it black."

"I prefer tea, sir."

"You're in the American merchant fleet now, m'dear," he told her. "Coffee it is."

She smiled and took a sip, glad to be in the open air

again, pleased that she had abandoned the idea of death.
Hiram handed his spyglass to Charity, who hurried with
it to the railing; he sat down beside Ann.

"I'm sorry it came to this," he told her. "You know
I didn't mean to kidnap you, but I had to beat the warships out of the harbor."

"Any sign of them?" she asked, handing back the cup.

He shook his head. "Can't figure it. The *Hasty* is small
potatoes, but we are a prize ship, if captured." He
touched her shoulder with his. "But I'm not one to borrow trouble from tomorrow." He took a sip and handed
back the cup.

She took another sip. "What are my chances of getting
some freshwater to wash my hair? I did my best to keep
it out of the bucket, but wasn't entirely successful."

He shook his head and accepted the cup. "Can't spare
it. We don't even have enough water to get us halfway
across the ocean." He looked at the cup. "Wonder if I
can mix half fresh and half salt water for coffee?"

"What will you do?"

He finished the coffee. "I'll gamble that no warship is
ahead of us to the Azores, and take on water there."
He hesitated, as though he didn't want to continue his
thought. He looked out at the ocean and was a long
time in speaking. "I can leave you in Terceira. There's
a British consulate who will see that you get home."

"Oh." She couldn't think of anything else to say.

There followed the strangest three weeks of Ann's
life. She settled into the ship's routine as surely as if she
had been born to it. She and Charity continued to share
her father's larger berth, the two of them staying awake
late to talk. It became sweet second nature to hold Charity close, enjoy her warmth, and hear about her brothers
and what little she remembered of her mother.

Even sweeter was her time with Hiram Titus. He
seemed to have included her into his life as though she
had always been there, even if he did say he was going
to leave her in the Azores. She wondered at first why
he continued to share his coffee with her every morning,
until it dawned on her that the homey habit must have
been something he did with Tamsin. She even wondered

if he was aware of it, or if his husbandly kindness—she couldn't think of a better thing to call it—was just an extension of his generous nature. It was as though something monumental had been decided in his mind, but nothing said.

She plucked up her courage one day, and asked the cook about the matter. She had developed a certain rapport with him during Charity's brief illness and his poultices for her own black eye—an interesting lime green now—and wounded forehead. Hiram had told her that John Cook had been with his fleet, in one capacity or another, since the days of the colonial revolt, when Titus was a pup of ten—Charity's age—and his own father's cabin boy. Cook seemed a logical vessel for the kind of information she sought.

She sat on an empty water keg in the galley, watching him stir up a barley soup that was more stew that soup because water was so scarce. "John, tell me," she asked. "Did Captain Titus and his wife marry young?"

The cook reached into the saltcellar. He raised his hand to sprinkle some salt in the pot, then must have thought better of it. "Best we don't have too much salt, Miss Utley," he told her. "Makes a body thirsty." He settled for a tiny pinch. "Aye, they were young. I think he was seventeen and just back from a voyage and she was the same."

"They couldn't have had much of a courtship," Ann suggested.

"Nay, none at all," he told her, and settled himself on a corner of the table. "His father told me once that he thinks Tamsin and his boy just happened to find themselves in the church one day when the minister was in a splicing mood." He leaned forward, as if relishing the little confidence. "Some wager he never even proposed."

"Surely he must have!" Ann said, unable to keep the surprise from her voice.

John Cook shrugged. "He has a way of just assuming things."

She couldn't deny that. "That's no way to court the ladies," she persisted. "No wonder he hasn't remarried."

"No wonder," he agreed, the soul of amiability. "I

reckon this, miss: The lady who wants him *this* time around will have to speak up. Ladies like Tamsin don't appear much."

Well, I *want him,* she decided, as John turned back to his stew. *But I wonder if I am any braver, particularly since he is another species altogether,* she thought, as she climbed to the quarterdeck. *I wish I knew, really knew, if he felt a tenth for me what I feel for him. I mean, is he just a man who loves women, or a man who loves* me? She knew her own nature well enough, she who had survived a number of proposals with her heart quite untouched but her mind wary. If he chose to let her remain in the Azores, then so be it. He would have to speak first; her character and pride required it.

It was a dismal consideration. She stood on the quarterdeck and looked at the sky. And looked again. Her heart thumped in her breast. Land birds wheeled and mewed overhead. She walked to the railing and looked out at the same time the man in the crow's nest called, "Land ho!" She heard the captain on the poop deck slam his spyglass inside itself. Seeing her there, he motioned to her.

He aims to show me the Azores, she thought, and shook her head at him. Charity called to her, too, but she quietly went belowdeck, crawled into her berth, and pulled a blanket over her head. She lay there until she began to sweat, then threw back the covers, angry with the lady who was too proud to march up the steps, declare that she loved him, and refuse to leave the ship, and sad for the lady who knew—really knew for the first time—what it felt like to love someone. There wasn't a thing she wouldn't do for Capt. Hiram Titus, and at the same time, she wanted to box his ears.

Trapped between indecision, despair, and a lurking humor over the absurdity of it all, she suddenly understood him. She stared at the compass overhead and then began to relax. He was forty, some fifteen years married and then widowed, with no idea how to court a lady. All he knew was how to be a husband. She had better swallow her pride and speak before the love of her life sailed away with the morning tide.

She got out of the berth, brushed her hair with his

brush, wished for the hundredth time that voyage that she had another dress, then went on the quarterdeck. She stood there watching the captain, who had trained his glass on the harbor. She looked up at the crow's nest, where a sailor was doing the same thing. She quietly climbed the steps to the poop deck and stood beside Charity. Already the water just inside the harbor was calmer, more serene. The air was redolent with what smelled like jasmine and orange blossom, and heavy with humidity. The buildings gleamed white, with red roofs, and smoke spiraled from chimneys.

As she watched the beauty before her, a bell began to toll. At home in England it would be evensong. She felt a sudden pang, a physical pain. *It may be that I never see my home again,* she thought. She closed her eyes, thought of everything lovely she would miss, and opened her eyes. *We make our choices,* she told herself. *I have made mine, even if the captain doesn't know it yet.*

Suddenly he was too faraway. She hurried to his side just as he put down the glass and nodded to his helmsman. "We're going in, laddie," he said. "Not a warship in sight."

If I just stand here, he will drape his arm around my waist and haul me up next to his hip, she thought. He did precisely that, and she took Charity's hand and pulled her in front of them both. Ann rested her hands gently on her shoulders, and enjoyed the feeling of the captain's long fingers on her waist. To her amusement, they strayed down to her hip, and he patted her in such a proprietary way that she knew she was right; this man was not one to court, but he was already the best husband she could ever hope for.

"It appears we beat the bad news, Annie," he told her. Only a deaf person would not have heard the relief in his voice.

"We can get water, Papa?"

"Most certainly."

"I have a favor then," Ann began, after directing his fingers back to her waist. "Since we are soon to have ample water, I would like to wash my hair."

"I'll have a water keg sent to the cabin right away. There are one or two left." He looked at Charity.

"Isn't there some Spanish soap in that cabinet by my berth?"

He seemed to recall everything he had to do then, now that they were sailing into a safe harbor, and turned away to bellow orders that sent sailors climbing nimbly up the ratlines to trim the sails. The water made a different sound against the ship as it slowed. He stood by the rail a minute more, a solitary figure, and her heart went out to him. *How difficult it must be to hold so many lives in your hands, my dear,* she thought. *You have my utmost admiration.* Impulsively, she went up behind him then at the rail, wrapped her arms around his waist, and kissed that spot just below his ear that she had been admiring for three weeks at least. How nice to be tall and able to reach it so easily, without jumping up and down, or standing on boxes.

"Annie, you're compromising me," he joked, his Yankee twang unmistakable.

She laughed and kissed him again, then left him there to stare out at the harbor and figure out what to do. The helmsman grinned at her as she walked by, and she smiled back. *I believe I will be a very good American,* she thought.

Charity didn't remain below deck except to take a long drink of water from the fresh cask. She looked at the glass and then drained the last of the water. "Ann, why is it that when I knew I couldn't have much water, it was all I wanted, all the time?"

"I don't know why that is, either, my dear." She paused, struck by the thought that she had felt the same way in the warehouse the afternoon she inadvertently wrote Hiram Titus's name all through the *Jasper*'s invoice. *I knew he would be leaving then, and all I wanted was for him to stay and stay,* she thought. "Maybe shortages are good for us, now and then. They remind us of what we have."

"They do."

When she heard Charity's feet on the deck overhead, she closed the door, sighed, and took off her dress that John Cook had so obligingly washed for her in salt water a couple of times while she had huddled in a sheet in the cabin. *I wonder if there is a ready-made dress in Terceira I could buy,* she thought, *or a generous woman of my height who would relinquish a dress of her own. I'm willing to wager that I'll be getting married tomorrow, and I'd rather not look like a penniless ragbag.*

With a sigh of satisfaction to be free of the dress, she dipped water from the keg into the washbowl and went in search of the Spanish soap. It was where he had said it would be, and there was also a letter wedged between the cabinet and the berth. She picked it up and recognized the handwriting. "Well, Aggie, what did you write to the captain about?" she asked out loud, and set it on the pillow.

She turned back to the basin and peeled down her chemise until she was bare from the waist up. It was only a moment's work to run a cloth with Spanish soap over her breasts and under her armpits, but oh, the pleasure of at least moderate cleanliness without salt. She dabbed the soap on her hair and began to work her fingers through the suds, humming to herself, enjoying the moment.

Then other hands were in her hair. She started in surprise, then couldn't help smiling underneath her mane of wet hair. "Captain, you have far trumped any possible compromise of mine," she told him, amazed at how matter-of-fact she could sound, when her heart was practically pounding through her rib cage.

"Oh, I don't care," he said mildly. His fingers massaged her scalp. "We'll take the dinghy into Terceira tomorrow morning."

"If you still think you're going to turn me over to the British consulate, you're mistaken."

"I thought we'd report to the harbormaster—I'm careful about these things, Annie—and then see if the consulate knows of a parson, or a minister, or whatever you call them."

She could hear him dipping clean water into a pitcher. He poured it carefully on her head, already the husband, or perhaps still the husband. She closed her eyes against the soap, and also against the thought that made her knees weak: *Thank God I climbed down that tree.*

"Is this a proposal?" she asked, knowing that her voice must be muffled under the weight of her hair and the water.

"Annie, I believe it is. Since the war is on, and I know none of my ships will be sailing from port until it ends, I need a rich wife."

She laughed, knowing that she could point out the obvious to him, that her money would be embargoed in its London bank as long as that same war lasted. "Then you should have found an . . . an . . . American nabobess with ready funds," she told him.

He squeezed the water from her hair and turned her around—wet and bare—to face him. "I wanted you," he said, and there was nothing of teasing in that tone. "I love you, Ann Utley. For the past three weeks I have been wondering how to tell you I'm crazy for you, and then how to ask you to marry me. Thank God for war."

She threw her arms around him and clung to him, even though the buttons on his jacket bit into her flesh, and she knew she was soaking him. He kissed her quite soundly, held her off and took a good look, rolled his eyes (which made her laugh), and kissed her again.

She just stood there, bare from the waist up, unembarrassed and calm. "I was resolved to wash my hair, go on deck again, and propose to *you*, my love," she told him simply. "You weren't going to leave me here in Terceira. I love you."

He just looked at her for the longest moment. "Dear Annie," was all he said.

She pulled up her soaked chemise—much good that did—and was drying her hair when he noticed the letter on the pillow. "It was on the floor . . ." she said, following his glance.

"Deck," he corrected automatically.

"On the deck by the berth. I'm certain that is Aggie Glossop's writing." Feeling a little shy, she wrapped the towel under her arms and sat by him "What can it be?"

He looked at it a moment, then tapped the letter on his forehead. "She practically threw it at me as I ran out of the warehouse, and told me to open it after we made open water. I completely forgot." He opened the letter with his thumbnail. "I recall stuffing it inside my shirt. I guess it fell out when I took off my shirt, and I didn't notice. Maybe I owe them more than the first bill."

He took off his shoes, then lay down on the berth. "Lie down, Annie," he said.

"What if Charity comes in?" she asked.

"She can lie down, too," he said affably, patting the spot beside him. "There's room." He pillowed her wet head on his arm and took out the sheets of close-printed paper with his free hand. She shut her eyes, content to lie there and bask in her good fortune.

"Well, I'll be damned," he said, and then burst out laughing.

Ann opened her eyes and sat up. His eyes merry, he handed her one of those infamous manifests from the HMS *Jasper*. "It says, 'Hiram Titus in oil,'" he pointed out, when he could speak. "And look there, 'Hiram Titus in cotton wadding.'"

She flopped down again beside him. "I thought I caught all those," she said in a faint voice.

But he was reading the letter now, and shaking his head. When he finished, he rose up on his elbow to look at her. "Ann, we've been diddled by champions."

"What can you mean?"

He lay down again, pulling her close, even though he was as wet now as she was. "There's no war, Annie! She and that rascal Ned said that just to get me out to sea with you on the *Hasty*."

She opened her mouth, too astounded to speak.

"Listen, my dear. 'Ann is far too proud and set in her ways to make a decision, so I am making it for her. Do take good care of her, Captain, and bring her back for a visit now and then.'"

Ann wasn't sure whether to laugh or to cry, so she did both. She took the soggy handkerchief that the captain gave her and wiped her wet face. She rose up to face him. "I was all prepared to take the mail coach back to Derbyshire when you rowed me ashore that noon, Hiram," she told him.

He kissed her. "And I probably would have let you go,

my love," he said softly. "I'm no expert at this love business. I couldn't woo a lady if my life depended on it."

"That is as bold a lie as I have ever heard," she replied as he kissed her eyelids, and then worked his way down to her throat.

"It's true, Annie," he said, his voice muffled by her breasts now. "But I am one hell of a husband."

There was no international incident over the kidnapping and subsequent marriage of Miss Ann Utley to Capt. Hiram Titus. The British consulate had grown lethargic and indolent from his years in the sultry climate of the Azores, and didn't want to face the paperwork involved in a major event. Better to let it slide, especially since the bride—dressed in a hideous gown, but quality nonetheless—clung to the Yankee like a barnacle. There was a vicar on Terceira who tended to the spiritual needs of the small British colony there, and he married them, even without banns or a special license.

Hiram had his own doubts that the marriage was strictly legal, but he knew he could make things right—or righter, anyway—when they fetched Boston and were able to make a binding civil arrangement. Besides, his legs were long and he wanted his own berth back. And truth to tell, the sight of Annie in a wet shimmy had taken a few years off his life. Waiting another five weeks for a parson to mumble over them seemed like a study in stupidity to someone who would be forty-one in November.

Charity was happy enough to return to her own cabin. Her father and new mother assured her that she could pop in every morning, but only after she knocked first, and waited for a reply.

Not too far into the voyage from Terceira, Ann Titus decided that making love on a seagoing vessel was quite to her liking. Thank goodness she had a well-seasoned husband. Someone else could pour punch for Clotilde's wedding.

Writer's note: That same summer of 1807 when the *Hasty* was returning from England, the HMS *Leopard* pounced upon the USS *Chesapeake* outside of Norfolk, killing three, wounding eighteen, and impressing four. President Jefferson's countermeasure, Embargo Act of December 1807, nearly destroyed New England shipping. War didn't come until 1812.

Allison Lane

"A FORMIDABLE TALENT...
MS. LANE NEVER FAILS TO
DELIVER THE GOODS."
—*ROMANTIC TIMES*

Emily's Beau
0-451-20992-3

Emily Hughes has her sights set on one man:
Jacob Winters, Earl of Hawthorne. But her
hopes are dashed when she discovers that Jacob
is already betrothed. She will have to forget
Jacob and marry another, which is just what
she plans to do—until one moonlit kiss changes
everything.

Also Available:

Birds of a Feather	0-451-19825-5
The Purloined Papers	0-451-20604-5
Kindred Spirits	0-451-20743-2

Available wherever books are sold, or
to order call: 1-800-788-6262

S908

"This is one romance that will not fail to enchant."
—*Booklist* (starred review)

"Romantic and funny—
I loved this book!"
—MARY BALOGH

Wedded Bliss

BARBARA METZGER

A Signet Paperback
0-451-20859-5

TWO WONDERFUL REGENCY ROMANCES IN ONE VOLUME!

EDITH LAYTON

IS "ONE OF THE ROMANCE GENRE'S
GREATEST STORYTELLERS."*

THE DISDAINFUL MARQUIS

AND

THE ABANDONED BRIDE

Don't miss this marvelous Regency 2-in-1
special—two stories by award-winning
author Edith Layton.

"LAYTON HAS A REAL GIFT...
[SHE] MESMERIZES THE READER."
—*ROMANTIC TIMES*

0-451-20628-2

AVAILABLE WHEREVER BOOKS ARE SOLD OR
TO ORDER CALL **1-800-788-6262**

S542